FLAMING MURDER

THE MARQUESS OF MORTIFORDE MYSTERIES
BOOK 3

SIMON WHALEY

THE MARQUESS OF
MORTIFORDE MYSTERIES

Blooming Murder

Foraging for Murder

CHAPTER ONE

"I knew you'd be a NIMBY, Lord Mortiforde." Abigail Mayedew's finger jabbed across the table as each word fired from her mouth.

Aldermaston pursed his lips as Borderlandshire District Council's Chief Executive continued her attack. At least she was sitting twelve feet away at the opposite end of the table in the Buttermarket's upstairs community meeting room. Otherwise, her jabbing finger could do some serious damage. Or rather, her fingernail. It was so heavily painted that it wasn't her nail at risk of breaking, but her finger.

"This Borderers Guild is your feeble attempt to dictate what goes on in this town. You're clinging on to some nostalgic, whimsical, outdated belief that because King George IV gifted the title of Marquess of Mortiforde to one of your ancestors in 1820, or whenever, that makes you Lord of the Manor."

Aldermaston's eyes closed. Not *this* again.

Stella Osgathorpe from the Historic Borders Agency interrupted. "That's how the British peerage system works, Ms Mayedew. When William the Conqueror invaded in 1066, he awarded his loyal supporters—"

"I'm not here for the history lesson!" Abigail snapped. "I'm here to drag this town into the twenty-first century with a project that could revolutionise Mortiforde's economic fortunes."

Cissy Warbouys' clattering size eight knitting needles paused. "What's a NIMBY?"

"N-I-M-B-Y," whispered Gerald Lockmount. "Not in my backyard."

Cissy tutted and resumed knitting. "Nobody could call Lord Mortiforde's three-thousand-acre estate a *backyard*."

Abigail ran her slender fingers through her stylishly tousled ash-blonde hair without somehow snagging her fingernails, and then slammed her flattened hand on the table. "Can we get back to the matter at hand, please?"

Aldermaston crossed his arms. "You want to drag us into the twenty-first century."

The Chief Executive opened a beige paper file on the table in front of her. "Page three of the document before you shows how the waste incinerator Rinde Industries plans to build on Mortiforde Meadows would not only burn waste material destined for landfill, but also generate enough electricity to power Mortiforde and several surrounding villages. It's a win-win for Mortiforde."

Stella Osgathorpe flicked through the document. "It'll desecrate the scenically outstanding meadows, the incinerator chimney will dominate the skyline for miles around, completely dwarfing St Julian's twelfth-century church tower, and it'll throw a poisonous cocktail of fumes across the Mortiforde Castle ruins. The Historic Borders Agency can't have tourists choking on incinerator smoke as they explore the medieval remains of one of Britain's iconic border castles."

Abigail sneered. "There is no smoke because the incinerator uses such high temperatures."

Aldermaston perused the document. An artist's impression

conveyed a modern-looking building with architectural curves and futuristic metal cladding, behind which a narrow, drainpipe-like, three-hundred-feet tall chimney punctured the sky. It looked so tall that NASA scientists were probably recalculating satellite orbits to avoid any collisions.

Dotted around the rest of the meadows, young families picnicked in the sunshine, swans slipped along the River Morte's sedate waters, and a buzzard soared in the pure blue sky. Yet inside the incinerator, its one-thousand-degree-centigrade inferno could nuke a dustcart within three milliseconds.

"Ms Mayedew," Aldermaston began. "You say Mortiforde needs dragging into the twenty-first century. Which century do you think we're in currently?"

Abigail snorted. "The early seventeenth century, judging by the way this Borderers Guild operates. Although looking at the styles of women's clothing in some of Mortiforde's stores, the 1950s may just be around the next corner. Then again, Mortiforde's decidedly dodgy mobile phone signal means we could be in the Dark Ages when it comes to communications. I'm surprised you don't all send messages via smoke signals."

Aldermaston's eyebrows rose. "A three-hundred-foot smokeless chimney will be of little use to us, then."

Abigail tutted. "Your Lordship. In the short time I've been in post, I've seen little evidence of Borderlandshire's industries adopting modern working practices."

"That's not true," Cissy interrupted. "Farmer Bell's got one of those robotic milking machines." She waved her knitting needle in a circular motion, tangling her wool into another knot. "The cows come in when they want to be milked, and the robot does everything. It even plays them classical music."

Stella shuffled in her chair. "Rachmaninoff would turn in his grave if he knew cows' udders were being stimulated to the rhythm of his semi-quavers."

Aldermaston checked his watch. Time to draw this evening's meeting to a close. "Isn't this rather academic, Ms Mayedew? This joint project between the local authority and Rinde Industries doesn't have Sir Hugo Rinde's support. And he owns Mortiforde Meadows."

"He didn't use to," Stella muttered.

Aldermaston looked at her quizzically, but she ignored him and continued scribbling notes. He returned to his point. "Sir Hugo's son Rupert might run the company, but Sir Hugo is against any development of *his* meadows."

He leaned forward, resting his elbows on the mahogany table. "And according to the latest audited figures, Borderlandshire District Council's ten million pound contribution is still half a million pounds short. I don't understand why you tabled this project on this evening's agenda. It's up in smoke before it's been lit." He closed the file.

Abigail shuffled her papers. "Your Lordship, the small funding shortfall is resolvable within months, not years. Rupert says he'll talk his father round. Sir Hugo only opposes the project because he's hoping to be selected tomorrow by the Socially Liberal Conservative Party as their next candidate for Westminster. Endorsing Rupert's waste incinerator project now would be political suicide."

She smirked. "Change is coming to Mortiforde. The sooner the community has a sensible, grown-up conversation about this project, the better."

"Let's put this to a vote," Aldermaston suggested. "Those in favour of the waste incinerator project raise their hands."

Abigail's hand shot up first, followed by those of Gerald Lockmount and four other Guild members.

Cissy prodded Gerald's rotund stomach with a knitting needle. "What are you doing?"

"It'll do wonders for house prices, Cissy. The waste incinerator will need a highly skilled workforce, who'll pay at least twice the price for the new executive units on the bypass estate."

Aldermaston counted the raised hands. "Six votes. And those against." He counted Cissy and Stella's hands, and three more. "That's five, and I, too, am against the development, which means six votes, too."

Abigail squealed. "A tie was better than I had hoped."

"Not so fast, Ms Mayedew," Aldermaston's hand slipped into his Radnor green Harris tweed jacket and pulled out a folded sheet of paper. He cleared his throat.

"I, Sir Hugo Rinde, instruct His Lordship to record my vote at this evening's Borderers Guild with those who are against this project. I am deeply opposed to any such development on Mortiforde Meadows."

Aldermaston looked around the room. "Sir Hugo's decision is clear. That's six votes in favour and seven against. I declare the Borderers Guild officially against the waste incinerator project development."

He refolded Sir Hugo's note and handed it to Lisa Duddon, sitting behind him, taking the minutes.

Abigail threw her hands in the air. "Do you think that stops the project? The council decides on planning issues, Lord Mortiforde, not this trumped-up community group."

Stella slipped her reading glasses into her bag. "You're correct, Ms Mayedew. The Borderers Guild has no jurisdiction over the council's planning process. But it is a respected community stakeholder, and the Borderers Guild carries tremendous influence. You would be wise to remember that."

She stood. "If you'll excuse me, Lord Mortiforde, I have another meeting to attend, but I'd like to chat with you soon on a related matter."

Aldermaston nodded.

The other Guild members, realising the meeting was over, collected their things.

Aldermaston opened the door for everyone. Their faces lit up when they realised the Marquess was holding open a door for *them* rather than the other way around. He stifled a smirk. His father had taught him this was the quickest way to clear a room when needed.

Abigail remained seated.

Lisa swept her jet-black hair behind her ear as she made to leave. "Need to talk about the Bonfire Night celebrations. Daniel texted during the meeting. Someone has stolen Mortiforde Millie."

Aldermaston frowned. "How do you steal a fifteen-foot-tall effigy?"

Lisa shrugged.

Aldermaston checked his watch. "I'll pop round to yours when I'm finished here. Ask Daniel to join us, too."

Lisa nodded and left.

Cissy Warbouys grabbed Aldermaston's arm. "We mustn't let this dreadful waste incinerator go ahead, Your Lordship. It's just not Mortiforde, is it?"

Aldermaston patted her hand. "I'll do whatever it takes."

Cissy smiled. "Your father would be proud."

"Thank you." He encouraged her out of the room and closed the door behind her.

Abigail stood, collected her paperwork, and then headed towards him.

"So, Your Lordship. You'll do whatever it takes, will you? Sounds like fighting talk to me."

Aldermaston leaned against the door. "Abigail, you've been here what - six weeks?"

"Five."

"I thought after the food festival's little kerfuffle that you understood we do things differently in Mortiforde. Perhaps a little more time getting to know us might help. You're right. I have no legal jurisdiction over the town whatsoever. After nearly two years, I'm still finding my feet as the Eighth Marquess. But my father always believed a community that works together stays together. We achieve more as a collective. That's what partnership working is all about, isn't it? It's why the council allows Lisa to be the Guild's administrative support, even though she's a council employee. It might only be a couple of hours a week, but we'd struggle without her."

Abigail pursed her thick, peach-pink lips momentarily, then looked along her elongated nose at him. "I might review Lisa's support of the Guild. Is it a good use of local taxpayers' money?" She sneered. "Mortiforde's yokels are so insular. You can't ignore the outside world because there are thirty miles to the nearest major town and forty to a motorway. Waste incinerators are the way forward. There's money to be made burning other people's rubbish. Several London boroughs send their household waste abroad for processing. Our waste incinerator could offer them a cheaper service, and provide us with a regular income."

She stepped closer, her nose barely inches from his. "Surprisingly, Your Lordship, we both share the same goals. We want to make Mortiforde a better place to live, work, and play. Think what Borderlandshire District Council could do with its share of that waste incinerator income. We could invest in decent community services."

Aldermaston's nose twitched. He smelt something, but it wasn't sincerity.

"By fighting the waste incinerator project," she sneered, "you're campaigning *against* more investment in Mortiforde. Is that what you want?"

"Of course not, but—"

Abigail pushed him aside and pulled the door wide. "I haven't spent thirty years in local government pandering to misplaced community opinion. It takes vision, determination, and guts to make changes for the community's benefit. And when a community doesn't have that vision, you build it so they can see it for themselves. I will get this project built, Your Lordship. And the sooner the bulldozers move onto Mortiforde Meadows, the better."

∼

Felicity handed a cup of coffee to their guest. He was admiring the display of swords, crossbows, and daggers neatly arranged in circles and criss-cross patterns on Tugford Hall's armoury wood-panelled walls.

"Sugar, Sir Hugo?"

He patted his dark yellow waistcoat, struggling to contain his fine-dining paunch. "Better not. Isabel worries that if I win the by-election, I'll put on more weight in Westminster's subsidised bars and restaurants."

He took the sugarless bone china cup and saucer and pointed to a gap in the wall's medieval dagger display. "So frustrating when you don't have a complete set, isn't it?"

Felicity scrutinised the medieval daggers arranged in a circular display, their points meeting neatly in the circle's centre while their metal cross-guards and hilts fanned out like a clock face. Except there was a gap at the six o'clock position.

"Cartwright's probably cleaning it. Or Basildon's using it as a letter opener. You know what His Lordship's half-brother is like." She gestured to the gathered crowd of seated guests. "Shall we?"

Sir Hugo nodded, and they took their positions.

Felicity tapped her teaspoon against her china cup. The rich, high-pitched tone bounced off the armoury's metal surfaces. The room held enough weaponry to equip an entire army, which it once did when the original Borderers Guild was the Lord of the Manor's private defence force. A hush descended.

"Ladies of the Legion," she began. "Welcome to this evening's meeting."

She paused briefly, taking in the women's expectant, beaming faces. She'd relished speaking in front of a large group of people in her previous life as a marketing consultant. But as the Eighth Marchioness of Mortiforde, and President of the Mortiforde Ladies' Legion, gatherings like this made her nervous. She'd never expected to become Marchioness with all of its community trappings. Would the ever-present knot in her stomach at these events ever untangle itself?

"Please welcome tonight's special guest, Sir Hugo Rinde."

A polite applause smattered through the thirty women seated in the three rows before them. Sir Hugo nodded his appreciation. As he did so, the light from the crystal chandelier above reflected off his forehead, just above the small red birthmark beside his left eyebrow, and highlighted a dour woman in a Gainsborough painting hanging on the wall.

Felicity picked up her bullet-pointed notes.

"I first learned of your marvellous project, *Verdant Endings*, when you kindly graced me with the position of president. Prior to that, I'd never considered how environmentally damaging our funeral services could be. Whether it's the energy required for cremation and the associated carbon dioxide emissions, or the precious wood resources we use to bury our loved ones in the ground, after we've pumped them full of contaminating embalming fluids. We can't continue in this way."

Her assembled audience nodded, apart from someone in the back row. A large-brimmed straw hat shielded the wearer's face. Despite Mortiforde being a small market town, there were still some faces in the Legion she didn't recognise.

"When I learned of your plans to create an environmentally friendly burial ground for Mortiforde, it made so much sense. Being able to offer the community a beautiful place where they can lay their loved ones to rest in coffins made from bamboo, wicker, wool, or even cardboard, means they still have somewhere to come and remember their family and friends, give them a wonderful service to celebrate their life, and do it in a way that doesn't kill the planet."

"Hear, hear," cried a woman in the second row.

Felicity smiled. She recognised Diya Parmer's petite circular face and cropped black hair.

Diya returned the smile.

"Our stumbling block," she continued, glancing at her notes, "has been finding a suitable location. The committee has visited several sites across the country for inspiration, because getting it right is so important."

Her audience nodded.

"We want somewhere families can go for remembrance, but still enjoy the environment and the surroundings. It shouldn't be a place of sadness, but somewhere to enjoy, too."

"Exactly," cheered Margaret Hillbrow in the front row. "A burial ground should be a place to celebrate that we're still alive, not just remember those who've passed on."

A wave of approval washed across the room.

"This evening, ladies," Felicity continued, "our wonderful guest, Sir Hugo, would like to say a few words on the subject."

Another smattering of applause welcomed Sir Hugo as he stood. Felicity returned to her seat.

Sir Hugo placed his cup and saucer on the table, shoved one hand into his brown corduroy trousers pocket, and cleared his throat. His jowls wobbled. "Your Ladyship, and wonderful women of the Ladies' Legion," he began. "This," he gestured around the large room with his free hand, "is far more enjoyable than sitting in one of those boring Borderers Guild meetings."

He turned to Felicity. "Not that your husband is boring, Your Ladyship!"

Her nose wrinkled. "Try living with him."

The assembled women giggled.

Sir Hugo continued. "Ladies, I wish to support your project. An environmentally friendly burial ground is exactly what this community needs."

He picked up his brown leather briefcase, placing it on the table beside him. With a couple of resonating clicks, he opened it and extracted a framed document.

"If I may, My Lady?" He offered her the document.

Felicity stood and took hold of the frame.

Sir Hugo turned to the audience. "I hereby grant Mortiforde Ladies' Legion the legal right to use Mortiforde Meadows as the town's first environmentally friendly burial site."

An enormous cheer erupted from the audience. Margaret Hillbrow dabbed the corner of her eye with a lace handkerchief, then gave Felicity a double thumbs up.

Sir Hugo leaned closer to Felicity. "There are a couple of minor clauses you need to abide by, but nothing onerous." He tapped the framed document. "It's all on here."

Felicity nodded. A flash startled her as Tugford Hall's butler, Cartwright, captured a photo of her and Sir Hugo gripping the framed document.

As a prospective candidate for the town's next member of parliament, Sir Hugo's sixth sense for spotting a photo opportunity contorted his facial muscles into a gurning grin milliseconds before the flash had rebounded off his bald spot. For a second time, the dour woman in the Gainsborough painting was dazzled. She wasn't impressed.

A high-pitched, ear-splitting shriek shattered the celebratory atmosphere, along with Sir Hugo's bone china coffee cup, and two crystals in the chandelier. Margaret Hillbrow collapsed into her chair, desperately trying to assess her hearing aid damage, while those around her clasped their ears tight.

"This is a smokescreen!" yelled a voice that sounded two octaves higher than it was used to speaking. "Sir Hugo doesn't care about your project. Tomorrow, the Socially Liberal Conservative Party might choose him as their candidate for Westminster. This is just a vote-buying publicity stunt, isn't it, Sir Hugo?"

Felicity peered around the chaotic ladies, still recovering from the auditory assault, to see the large-brimmed straw hat owner now standing and holding aloft a personal alarm.

"Nonsense!" Sir Hugo waved the framed document emphatically in the protester's direction. "The waste incinerator will NEVER happen. My son has two problems. First, he's working in partnership with the local council, which doesn't have all its money in place. Second, I own Mortiforde Meadows, not him. So the council will need a compulsory purchase order first. A waste incinerator on Mortiforde Meadows? Over my dead body, ladies!"

The protester stepped into Felicity's view, but was concealed by an oversized beige macintosh and an enormous straw hat.

"Be careful what you wish for, Sir Hugo," sang the falsetto voice. The protester spun round and dashed to the door, their white trainers squeaking against the parquet flooring.

They slammed the door shut with such force that the bang echoed like gunfire, exciting the displayed weaponry lining the walls, and sending the Gainsborough crashing to the floor.

~

Aldermaston cut through the deserted traders' stalls in Mortiforde's Market Square. A place so often bustling, even on a cold, foggy November day, yet at seven-thirty on a crisp, foggy November evening, it was eerily quiet. The local youths preferred the warmer confines of the local pizza outlet, whose windows glistened with the condensation of teenage troubles.

He recoiled when a piercing firework squeal shattered the still air as it shrieked high into the night sky. Bonfire Night was still a couple of nights away yet.

He quickened his pace. He passed the cordoned-off wooden platform by the castle's main entrance, where the town would burn Mortiforde Millie at the stake during their Bonfire Night celebrations, and entered Castle Avenue, a meandering road following the castle's imposing Norman perimeter wall. He pressed the doorbell at Lisa and Mark's bed-and-breakfast establishment.

"We're in the snug," greeted Lisa. She led him through to their establishment's rear private quarters, then smacked the sofa's arm. "Come on, you. Off!"

Aldermaston ruffled the top of Esme's head as the golden retriever's tail beat an excited rhythm against the cushion. "You're fine, Esme. Just budge up." He forced himself between Esme and the sofa arm.

A mug of coffee appeared. "There you go." Mark threw a tea towel over his shoulder. "You'll have to excuse me. We've a couple of guests dining with us tonight."

Aldermaston watched Mark in his black-and-white chequered chef's trousers and white, short-sleeved jacket disappear through the door.

Lisa slipped into the green-winged armchair opposite, clasping a mug in her hands.

"Got many guests?" Aldermaston sipped his coffee.

"We have two occupied rooms. They're here for Friday's Bonfire Night celebrations and Mortiforde Millie's parade through town."

The snug door swung wide as Aldermaston's personal

assistant, Daniel, dressed in jeans and a navy marl funnel neck overcoat, entered. "Got here as quickly as I could."

"Okay, what's going on?" Aldermaston watched Lisa pour Daniel a mug of tea.

Daniel removed his thigh-length coat and threw it over the sofa arm. "Has Lisa not said?" He took the offered mug and sat, crossed-legged, on the floor beside the snug wood burner.

Lisa returned to the armchair. "I was waiting for you, as you have the note."

"Note?" Dread cartwheeled through Aldermaston's stomach.

Daniel rummaged in a coat pocket. "Here." He handed Aldermaston a folded sheet.

"Where did this come from?" Aldermaston unfurled it.

"No idea." Daniel cradled his mug. "I nipped out of the office for five minutes, and it was on my chair when I returned."

Aldermaston held it aloft. "This was hand-delivered to our office inside Tugford Hall?"

Daniel nodded. "Cartwright knew nothing about it. Too busy setting up the armoury for Felicity's meeting."

Aldermaston panicked. Who was wandering around Tugford Hall unchecked, hand-delivering notes? "When did it arrive?"

"Just before I left at seven. That's when I messaged Lisa."

Aldermaston read the note.

To the Marquess of Mortiforde, Defender of the Establishment,

We've stolen Mortiforde Millie. We've saved her from the heat.
History likes the reminder: make her, burn her, repeat.
But Millie was a hero. She helped Guy's fellow plotters.
You should be the ones to burn, you landed-gentry squatters.

*There's a revolution coming, Lord Mortiforde. Come Bonfire
Night, the truth will out. It's time for the Establishment to burn.*

BANG!

Daniel shuffled closer to the wood burner. "I've seen a few
crank emails in the short time I've been your assistant. But this
seems different." He shuddered. "Finding it on my office chair
spooked me."

Aldermaston reread the note. "It's typical BANG. And if
Mortiforde Millie is missing, then stealing a fifteen-foot-tall
puppet is exactly what BANG would do." He paused. "That
last statement." He sucked in air between his teeth. "That's
different."

"BANG is a group?" Daniel placed his mug on the table.

"Borderlandshire Against Nefarious Government," Lisa
clarified. She turned to Aldermaston. "I thought they were
more about daft publicity stunts than anything serious."

"Usually," Aldermaston confirmed. "They launched five
years ago and declared Borderlandshire an independent state
on a May bank holiday. Caused chaos on the bypass,
demanding to see caravaners' passports. They've turned away
holidaymakers from their holiday homes, too. Infuriating
publicity stunts, but I always thought their heart was in the
right place."

"What do you mean?" Lisa took the note from
Aldermaston.

"They've always highlighted rural inequalities. Second
homes price local families out of the housing market. We don't
get the same public transport investment that cities do. Then
there are lower wages, the disproportionate cost of fuel, that
sort of thing."

Lisa held the note in the air. "But this is not just about a

Bonfire Night effigy being stolen. This is a direct threat. This says the Establishment is going to burn. That's you."

Aldermaston pondered. *Defender of the Establishment.* He'd never been called that before. Nor had he ever considered himself a landed-gentry squatter. But as the Eighth Marquess of Mortiforde, he was now part of the Establishment. Whether he liked it or not.

Peredur swigged some beer from a bottle and collapsed into his living room's threadbare armchair, exhausted from his evening run. The bottom hem of his combat trousers rose above the cuffs of his black combat boots, which he'd changed into from his trainers. He caught a bead of sweat running down his forehead with the back of his hand, smudging his camouflage face paint.

He surveyed his room's furnishings in his small, two-up, two-down terrace. A wooden drop-leaf table, once rescued from a skip, sat in front of the window opposite, with one semicircle leaf balancing precariously on a wooden strut. An arc cut through what little carpet was left, where the table leg had scored its travels. A single wooden chair sat at one end. Two laptops dominated the tabletop.

In a corner, a forty-inch television screen crowned a salvaged, four-foot-tall, one-hundred-and-twenty-gallon wooden whisky barrel. Between that and Peredur was an open fireplace housing a portable fan heater. Behind him, an energy-saving eleven-watt bulb, perched naked on a tall wooden standard lamp base, was dribbling barely enough light across the room's corner. It was enough to read the dog-eared letter, though.

Peredur took another swig of beer. The Lockmount Estate Agency logo dominated the letter's top right corner.

Mr PG Jones
42 Brominster Way
Mortiforde
Borderlandshire
MF1 3TF

Dear Mr Jones,

*Notice requiring possession of a property in England, let on an
Assured Shorthold Tenancy.*
Housing Act 1988 section 21(1) and (4) (as amended)

*Further to our earlier letter of 1st September, and your subsequent
written correspondence of 8th October, I'm writing to inform you
that, having discussed your tenancy with my client, the Section 21
Notice seeking possession of 42 Brominster Way remains
effective.*

*As per the attached Form 6A, your tenancy agreement will end,
and you must vacate the premises by 9 o'clock on 5th November to
allow the property owner to take full possession.*

*Should you be interested in viewing any of our other available
properties, please call into our office at your earliest convenience.*

Yours sincerely,
Gerald Lockmount
Lockmount Estate Agency

"Pompous, self-centred, free-market-loving prat. You've no idea, have you?" Peredur screwed the letter into a ball and hurled it across the room. "All I want to view, Mr Lockmount, is the look on your face when you realise what's coming to you."

~

Rupert Rinde sat by the roaring fire in Knowton Manor's drawing room, drinking brandy. The mantelpiece clock chimed nine. Only the flickering flames illuminated his thinning blonde hair, angular face, and familial small red birthmark above his left eyebrow. His upturned hand drew gentle circles in the air, swirling the brandy around the glass. His other hand clasped a phone to his ear.

"As you say, Abigail," his baritone voice carrying far into the room's shadows, "seven to six against is better than I ever imagined."

He sipped some brandy. "Business is all about upsetting people."

A door creaked. "Hang on." Rupert glanced into the darkness and clutched his phone to his chest. "Farringdon?"

A woman in her late seventies stepped into the fire's ambient glow. She tucked her flaxen hair behind her ears, allowing her ruby earrings to glow in the firelight.

"Mother, I'm busy." He waved his phone in the air.

Isabel steadied herself against a sideboard. "Have you heard from your father?"

Rupert scoffed. "Why would he talk to me? I'm ruining his business, apparently."

"He's not contacted you?"

Rupert stared at her. "Was there anything else?"

Isabel shuddered. "He's an hour late, and he's not answering his phone."

Rupert waved a dismissive hand at her. "Probably at The Nooseman's Knot canvassing for votes for his new political career, if he's selected tomorrow. Now, go. I'm trying to run a business here."

Isabel turned and disappeared into the darkness.

"Hang on," Rupert called. "Did Farringdon let you in?"

Isabel stepped back into the light. "He saw I was worried about your father."

Rupert threw the brandy glass into the fireplace. A mini fireball exploded up the chimney as glass fragments shattered across the logs. "I categorically told him not to let you in. He can pack his bags in the morning. Go back to The Lodge, Mother. Close the door on the way out."

He stared into the darkness until he heard the door latch click. He relaxed again as he stood. "Sorry, Abigail. Where were we? Oh, yes. I must say how refreshing it is to have someone with vision leading the local authority. Borderlandshire's previous Chief Execs have been somewhat myopic when it comes to long-term planning."

Rupert leaned against the pink marble mantelpiece, the flickering flames adding a warm glow to his grey eyes. "But when Rosemary told me all about you, I knew you were different. Yes, Rosemary Sedgewicke. Your Director of Finance. We go way back. Nearly thirty years." He paused. "We were close. Once."

He glanced at the mantelpiece clock. "I mustn't keep you. Delighted with what you've achieved already, Abigail. I'm confident life in Mortiforde is about to become extremely interesting."

He cut the call and stared into the fire's flaming heart as a broad grin cut across his strong jawline.

CHAPTER TWO

Diya Parmer's Wednesday morning began like every other weekday morning. Her pale blue Morris Minor Traveller screamed into Borderlandshire District Council's staff car park and braced for impact. Directly ahead was her designated parking bay. Her job title, Head of Planning Finance, clung desperately to its metal post, which leaned backwards at forty-five degrees. Diya stomped both feet on the brakes. The front tyres screeched, the rear tyres rose two inches off the ground, and the front bonnet nudged the post, knocking it back another degree. The engine died, and the Morris Minor shuddered.

Diya grabbed the rear-view mirror, titivated her black, cropped hair, and then grabbed her beige handbag. She stepped out of the car and threw the handbag over her shoulder, but missed and retraced her steps to retrieve it.

"Morning, Sheila," she sang, swiping her security badge as she strolled past the receptionist.

"I love your skirt." Sheila pointed to Diya's pleated, beige A-line piece. "Is it new?"

Diya grabbed it below her knee and fanned it outwards.

"One of Mother's. Found it at the back of a wardrobe last night."

"It's so you," Sheila cooed, "but then, I always thought your late mother looked more like your sister." Horror contorted Sheila's face. "Not that you look old. We fifty-somethings are in the prime of our lives, aren't we?" She giggled nervously, then pointed to her telephone switchboard. "Your phone's ringing again. That's the third time this morning, and it's not even eight o'clock." She gestured to her handset. "Want to take it here?"

Diya shook her head. "Catch you later." Her black court shoes clattered along the highly polished floor as she hurtled down the corridor towards her office. She burst in through the door, threw her handbag onto her chair, and grabbed the handset.

"Diya Parmer, Head of Planning Finance. Sorry to have kept you waiting. How may I help you?" she blustered.

"Diya, it's Abigail. I've just read your email."

Email? What email?

"Wondrous news!" Abigail continued.

Diya powered on her computer.

"It's about time we dragged this town out of the seventeenth century, and the waste incinerator project is just the ticket."

She froze. "But—" She wiggled her mouse frantically, hoping to speed up her computer's startup. Her heart pounded. The waste incinerator project was half a million pounds short. "But, Ms Mayedew," Diya countered, "the shortfall is—"

"No longer a problem, as per your email," Abigail interrupted. "I don't know where you found the money, but this is why you are Head of Planning Finance. I've issued a press statement, so I don't doubt things will get lively once this godforsaken town wakes up."

"Abigail, I'm afraid—"

"I understand that, Diya. There's always public opposition to these large-scale projects. It's your job to find the money. You've done that. Leave the public relations to me. We'll celebrate later. Bye."

The line went dead. Diya stared at the handset.

Her computer chimed its start-up confirmation. She collapsed into her office chair, jumped up to retrieve her handbag, and then sat down again. She double-clicked her email programme icon and wiggled her mouse again frantically. Why were council computers so slow?

She selected her *Sent* folder and then— There!

To: Abigail Mayedew.
Subject: Mortiforde Meadows Waste Incinerator Project.
Sent: Today, 7.40 a.m.

7.40 a.m.? That was ten minutes before she'd arrived. She double-clicked the message, then clasped both hands to her mouth.

Dear Abigail,

I'm delighted to announce that, thanks to some prudent financial planning and savings secured on some of the authority's other capital projects, I've identified £500,000 of funding we can allocate to the waste incinerator project. This means we can now proceed with the fully funded project.

Yours sincerely,
Diya Parmer
Head of Planning Finance.

A stomach-clenching nausea enveloped her. Diya dialled Abigail's extension. It barely rang before it was answered.

"Oh, Abigail, I'm terribly sorry," Diya blurted, "but—"

"IT Helpdesk, how can I help you?" The male operator stifled a yawn.

"Sorry, wrong number!" Diya's finger bounced frenetically on the telephone hook, then dialled Abigail's four-digit extension again.

"IT Helpdesk. How can I help you?"

"What?" Diya grabbed the internal phone directory from her top drawer and fumbled through the pages. "I need to speak to the Chief Executive urgently. Although I need to chat with you because I think someone hacked my work email. But I must speak with Abigail Mayedew immediately." She thrust the handset back onto its cradle.

Her finger traced the Chief Executive Division in the phone directory and located Abigail's extension. This time, she picked up the handset and precisely punched in the four-digit extension.

"I.T. Helpdesk. How can I help you, Diya?"

She was about to scream, but a thought occurred. "How do you know it's me?"

The IT technician chuckled. "We're the IT department, Diya. We know *everything*. You swiped your pass to gain entry to the council building ten minutes ago. You logged onto your machine two minutes ago, and now I've got a call from your extension number. It doesn't take a rocket scientist to work out who's calling."

Diya's olive-skinned hand clenched. "Fine, but I must speak with the Chief Executive immediately. Every time I dial her extension, you answer."

He chuckled again. "Yeah, I've programmed your phone to do that."

Diya rubbed her brow. "Why?"

The IT operative's voice dropped an octave. "The Chief Executive is delighted with your email about the waste incinerator project. Do you really want to spoil her mood?"

Diya stood and paced behind her desk. "But I didn't send it. That's why I need to talk to Abigail."

Another soft chuckle filled her earpiece. "I know. This is the IT Helpdesk, Diya. I sent that email on your behalf."

Diya glanced at her office door. "I'm going to see her."

"You can't!" The IT operative sniggered. "I've altered your security clearance. You can't get within shouting distance of the Chief Executive's office. And don't think about using another phone line to reach Abigail. Because what would Nani Nagma in Mumbai say when she heard the terrible news?"

Her eyes widened. "How do you know about my Nani?"

The IT operative sighed. "Diya, when I say IT knows everything, I mean we know *everything*." His voice slipped into a sinister whisper. "Nani Nagma loves Diya, doesn't she? Even fonder of you since your mother passed away five years ago, heh? Especially as you send so much of your monthly wages home to her and the rest of the family."

Diya's eyes moistened.

"Think of the family shame and embarrassment if darling Diya was sacked from her respected local authority job because of some … Oh, I don't know … inappropriate images found on her computer."

Diya stared at her computer's desktop image of her silver tabby cat. "It's only Daisy. Nani Nagma has seen loads of photos of Daisy."

"I'm not talking about Daisy," the IT operative hissed. "I could put a selection of illegal images on your work machine without you knowing. Images that would make everyone gossip about the quiet, reserved, conscientious, and fastidious Diya they thought they knew."

Diya collapsed into her office chair.

"So, if anyone asks about the waste incinerator project, what are you going to tell them?"

"Er—"

"No, Diya. Sound convincing. Is the waste incinerator project fully funded?"

Diya's hand shook so much, she was bruising her ear with her phone handset.

"Y…y…yes," she whispered.

"Sorry, Diya. Didn't quite catch that."

"Yes," she blurted.

"See? That wasn't difficult, was it? Keep that up, and I'll have no need to message Nani Nagma. And I know Nani Nagma's email address, because you send so many personal emails to her from your work computer. Technically, that breaks the council's Personal Use of Council Technology policy, but I won't tell anyone if you don't."

Diya shook her head. "N…No."

"There's a good girl. And to show you how nice we in the IT department are, you're now on annual leave for the next two weeks."

"No, I'm not on leave until Christmas."

Another deep sigh travelled down the line. "Diya, I've updated the council's electronic annual leave calendar. I've even said you're visiting Nani Nagma in Mumbai. That way, nobody will bother you at home, either. Is there anything else I can help you with today?"

"No," she whispered.

"Thank you for calling the IT Helpdesk. On a scale of one to ten, how would you rank our service today?"

"T…ten?" Diya proffered.

A guffaw echoed in her earpiece. The line went dead.

Diya stared at the email on her screen. Now what? He was right. Nani Nagma would literally die of shame if the IT technician carried out his threat.

She returned the telephone to its cradle. There was only one thing she could do. If the Chief Executive had an email from Diya saying the waste incinerator project was fully funded, then Nani Nagma would insist Diya was true to her word. Which left Diya with just one minor problem. Where the heck was she going to find half a million pounds?

Aldermaston walked into their private kitchen at Tugford Hall to find Felicity and Harry sitting at the table, eating breakfast. Harry shovelled cereal that turned the milk a muddy colour into his mouth quicker than he could chew it. Thankfully, the milk's cereal-softening ability meant minimal chewing was required.

"Harry! You'll give yourself indigestion." Aldermaston stared at the seven-year-old's bulging cheeks.

"Finished now," he muttered, without spilling any cereal. He jumped down from the table. "Dad, can we go swimming today?"

"Sorry. I'm busy today. Perhaps tomorrow."

Harry turned away from him and huffed. "That's what you always say."

"Where are you going?" Felicity barked.

Harry stalled, then swallowed. "Brush my teeth. Then I've got ten minutes to capture Theo and steal his gold and weaponry before school." He dashed out of the room.

Aldermaston looked at Felicity. "Please tell me that's a computer game he's talking about."

"We need some ground rules for that games console." She peeled a banana. "You could distract him from it by taking him swimming. How many times has he asked you?"

Aldermaston popped some white bread into the toaster.

"I'll work something out." He lowered the slices. "What are your plans today?"

Felicity leaned back in the chair. "A *Verdant Endings* committee meeting. After yesterday's announcement from Sir Hugo, we can push forward with our green burial idea."

The toaster popped. Two white slices stared back at Aldermaston. He dropped them again. These days, manufacturers seemingly coat their bread with some sort of flame retardant. Then he switched on the radio.

"Goooooooooooooooood morning, Borderlandshire," screamed Breakfast Benny from the loudspeaker.

Aldermaston dialled down the volume.

"It's eight o'clock and we have some breaking news." He rustled his script dramatically. "Borderlandshire District Council has announced they have all the money in place for their contribution towards the Rinde Industries Waste Incinerator Project. Chief Executive Abigail Mayedew says work will start soon to move this project forward."

Felicity choked. "The meadows! *Verdant Endings*! I need to talk to Sir Hugo."

"Don't panic," Aldermaston suggested. "Just because the council's funding is in place doesn't mean the meadows are at risk. Sir Hugo won't sell to Rupert or the council."

The toaster popped. Aldermaston's slices were the colour a paint manufacturer might call *Fresh Flour* or *Almost Oyster*.

"Apologies for the intrusion, Your Lordship, My Lady." Their butler hovered in the kitchen doorway.

"What is it, Cartwright?" Aldermaston dropped the slices for round three.

The butler clasped his white-gloved hands. "There appears to be a dagger missing from one of the armoury's wall displays. I noted it when clearing up after last night's meeting."

Felicity nodded. "Sir Hugo spotted that last night. You're not cleaning it, then?"

Cartwright tilted his head. "Alas, no, My Lady. Perhaps I'll have a word with His Lordship's brother."

Aldermaston tutted. "Where is my half-brother? I've not seen him for days. I worry when Basildon drops off the radar."

Felicity poured some more tea. "Perhaps MI5 has finally recruited him, and he's undercover somewhere in Outer Mongolia."

Aldermaston turned the dial on the toaster up another three notches. "If only."

Felicity's phone erupted into a musical crescendo on the kitchen table. She glanced at the screen. "Strange. Isabel's calling early." She answered it. "Isabel, how lovely to hear from you."

Her smile disappeared. "No, dear. He left about eight-fifteen last night... I'm sure you must be... If we hear anything, we'll let you know. Bye."

"Problem?" Aldermaston grabbed a knife and a plate.

"Isabel says Sir Hugo didn't come home last night."

In his living room, Peredur focused on his reflection in the camouflage paint tin lid as he reapplied a mixture of Earth Brown and Woodland Light Green to his face.

There was a loud thud from next door. The partition wall shook, and the reverberations knocked the camouflage tin lid shut. Through the window, Peredur saw his neighbour slip into the passenger seat of a waiting red Land Rover Defender.

A smile creased his warpaint-covered cheeks. He'd only spoken to his neighbour once, a couple of months ago, on the day they had moved in. Peredur was wearing his camouflage trousers, jacket, and war paint, and mentioned to Daniel that he was on leave for a couple of days. He knew Daniel, like everyone else, would assume a man in his mid-twenties, dressed in such gear, was a member of His Majesty's Armed Forces.

Peredur chuckled. He was in an army. Just not His Majesty's.

∽

Daniel slipped into the passenger seat of Lisa's waiting Land Rover Defender. The fan heater was on full blast.

"Kind of you to offer me a lift to work." He slipped on his seat belt. "Especially when it's out of your way."

Lisa released the handbrake and set off towards the bypass. "We need to check something first."

Daniel's hands hovered near the warm air vent. "What?"

"The Highways Depot. It's where the Guild keeps Mortiforde Millie."

"The note could be fake."

Lisa pulled out onto the main road. "Only one way to find out."

He wiped the condensation from the side window. "Who was Mortiforde Millie?"

Lisa turned down the roaring heater a couple of notches. "You know Guy Fawkes tried blowing up the House of Lords at Westminster during the State Opening of Parliament on 5th November 1605?"

Daniel stretched his fingers in the warm air. "Isn't every preschool kid taught that's why we burn effigies of him every fifth of November?"

Lisa pulled up behind a queue of cars waiting at the bypass roundabout. "Although Guy Fawkes was captured at the Houses of Parliament, many of his co-conspirators fled. Several sheltered at Holbeche House, near Wall Heath, which is only thirty-five miles away. The house was owned by Stephen Littleton. Although not a key conspirator, he helped them flee.

Some conspirators continued to Boningdale, barely thirty miles away, but Littleton and another Gunpowder Plot conspirator, Robert Wintour, disappeared."

She paused, watching for a gap in the traffic, then pulled out onto the bypass.

"Between 8th November 1605 and 9th January 1606," she continued, "Littleton and Wintour roamed the countryside. For two months, they hid in barns and isolated houses, evading the authorities."

Daniel twisted in his seat. "I never realised the conspirators got this far from London."

"Millie had a smallholding on the edge of Mortiforde Meadows. Just before Christmas 1605, the rector of St Julian's was collecting for the local poor people, and went to knock on Millie's door when he heard voices coming from her wooden cowshed. Through a knothole, he witnessed Millie handing bread and water to two men."

Daniel smirked. "Keeping men in the cowshed. That's definitely suspicious."

"The vicar suspected who they were immediately," she continued, "and marched in, accusing Millie of harbouring traitors. The two men knocked him to the floor and fled. Millie claimed they were homeless labourers, but two weeks later, soldiers captured Littleton and Wintour at Hagley Hall in neighbouring Worcestershire. During their interrogation, the Anglican rector positively identified them as the homeless labourers to whom Millie was providing food and shelter."

"Ah," Daniel exclaimed. "So locals saw Millie as a co-conspirator, too."

"Exactly. The authorities executed Guy Fawkes and some of the main conspirators for treason. Millie was sentenced to death nearly a year later." Lisa braked as they approached the slip road of the next junction.

"How did she die?"

Lisa checked the junction before pulling clear. "In the seventeenth century, women accused of treason were burned at the stake."

Daniel rubbed his hands together. "I can think of better ways of keeping warm."

"The King's soldiers paraded Millie through the town. Some locals threw rotten fruit and vegetables at her. They thought she deserved it. The soldiers burned her at the stake outside the castle entrance." Lisa checked her rear-view mirror. "Others felt sorry for her, believing she was being punished to set an example. So they tried to make her execution as painless as possible." She changed gear. "They threw a bag of gunpowder around her neck at the last minute and draped the fuse into the fire below. The explosion killed her before she suffered severe burns."

"With friends like that—"

Lisa braked as she approached a junction. "Which is why, here in Mortiforde, we don't burn a guy on top of a bonfire like the rest of Britain. Instead, we have a Mortiforde Millie puppet parade through town, so locals can throw rotten fruit and tomatoes at her until she reaches the stake just outside the castle entrance. Then, we tie her up, set fire to the stake, and watch her burn. We place fireworks inside her head and chest to reconstruct the moment the gunpowder bag exploded."

"And that happens on Friday?"

Lisa glanced at him quickly. "Only if we can find where Mortiforde Millie is."

The toaster ejected two charcoal slices high into the air. A smokescreen trailed behind them. Aldermaston caught them and then dropped them onto an awaiting plate. "Ouch!" He sucked his fingertips.

Felicity tutted. "Just ask Cartwright to make you some breakfast."

"I am more than capable of making a couple of slices of toast." Aldermaston spread some jam on the first slice. It shattered into tiny shards.

Felicity raised an eyebrow.

Cartwright appeared in the kitchen doorway and cleared his throat.

Aldermaston waved dismissively. "Cartwright, please don't trouble yourself."

"I wasn't going to, Your Lordship." The butler approached his employer's ear and whispered. "There's an unexpected item in the compostable waste bin."

Aldermaston's shoulders dropped. "Basildon's always contaminating it with unknown substances."

Cartwright leaned closer. "It's a little more delicate than that, My Lord."

"Can't you move it to the right receptacle?" Aldermaston suggested.

Cartwright gestured to the kitchen door. "Your Lordship?"

Aldermaston admired Cartwright's Butler Academy training. That simple gesture meant that, at this moment, Cartwright had the upper hand. Literally.

Aldermaston sighed. "Lead the way, Cartwright."

Daniel grabbed the door handle as Lisa turned sharply into the council's Highways Depot and parked up beside a gritting lorry and jumped out. A series of reversing beeps echoed around the salt chamber as a wheeled loader refilled a gritting truck.

Daniel's nose twitched at the excessive diesel fumes hanging in the air. There was little else to see within the cavernous salt store apart from the wheeled loader, the gritting vehicle, and several tons of pink rock salt.

"If Mortiforde Millie is in here," he said, "she can only be under all that." He pointed to the mountain of red-tinged road de-icer.

Lisa checked behind them. "She's usually kept just inside the door there. It's enough to protect her from the elements." She tugged Daniel's arm. "Follow me."

They headed to a small office unit tucked inside the main entrance. No larger than a garden shed, it had a small window and a door. Lisa knocked and then stepped inside.

"Hi, Sandy," she sang.

Daniel squeezed into the cramped office space and closed the door behind him. The beeping noise abated.

"Sandy, this is Daniel, Lord Mortiforde's PA."

Daniel smiled at the fluorescent-jacketed man sitting at the small desk with a single computer monitor.

Sandy checked the calendar above his desk. "You're a bit early for the next Highways Drainage (Seepage and Sewerage) committee meeting."

Lisa pointed through the office window. "Where's Mortiforde Millie?"

"Some bloke collected her yesterday afternoon," said Sandy. "Something about making some adjustments before Friday night."

"Who collected her?" asked Daniel.

Sandy shrugged. "Said he was from the Borderers Guild."

Daniel looked at Lisa. The BANG note was genuine.

Lisa tapped Sandy's computer monitor. "This got CCTV?"

He nodded.

"Any chance we could review the footage to see who collected her?"

Sandy interrogated his keyboard. "It was yesterday, between two and three. Quiet then, you see. These guys," he motioned outside his window, "were taking a break before loading up for last night's spreading."

He double-clicked on the timed entry and opened a view of the scene outside the window. On the other side of the barn's entrance sat Mortiforde Millie, her body propped up against the side of the barn, her head leaning forward slightly, mimicking the inward curve of the barn's dome-shaped walls. Her legs were bent at her knees, practically touching her chest.

Daniel whistled. "*That's* what this town burns at the stake every year?"

Mortiforde Millie was a huge puppet. Long brown hair flowed down her back, and two huge brown eyes stared intently at the rock salt in front of her. She wore a multicoloured woolly cardigan over her barrel-shaped chest, a plain brown skirt, and long black wool stockings on her legs. Leather boots covered her feet.

Lisa tapped the screen. "Can we fast forward?"

The playback flickered until a low-loader suddenly reversed in through the barn's entrance.

"There!" cried Lisa.

Sandy resumed playback at normal speed. A crane arm came into view. Moments later, it swung towards Mortiforde Millie. A man slipped around the back of the low-loader, carrying two strips of webbing. He looped one behind Millie's back and under her arms and another under her knees.

"Freeze!" Lisa screamed, just as the man walked towards the camera.

Sandy hit pause. "Want me to zoom in?"

"If you can," said Lisa.

They all leaned closer to the monitor. The screen pixilation settled, and suddenly the face became clearer.

"No way!" cried Daniel.

There, on the screen, was Aldermaston's half-brother, Basildon.

~

Felicity tapped Aldermaston's shoulder as Cartwright led them out of their private kitchen. "What's going on?"

"Compostable waste bin inspection, apparently."

"What?" Felicity hissed. "You're the Eighth Marquess of Mortiforde. Tell him you have better things to do."

Aldermaston stopped abruptly, and Felicity collided with him. "How many times has Cartwright asked us to do anything unnecessary?"

Felicity's face twisted as she pondered.

"Exactly. So let's see what the problem is, and then I'll decide whether to issue him a verbal warning for wasting my time."

Cartwright led them downstairs, past the main hall's kitchens, and out through the Tradesman's Entrance into a wide courtyard area. Opposite were three large industrial waste bins, each the size of a compact car, lined up against a retaining wall. The middle bin's lid was propped up against the brick wall behind.

Cartwright paused a few feet from the bin. "I'm sorry, Your Lordship, but I didn't see what was inside until *after* I'd thrown in the kitchen scraps."

Cautiously, Aldermaston stepped forward, placed both hands on the top rim of the metal waste bin, and rose on tiptoes. Nervously, he peered over the top.

A pair of lifeless, startled brown eyes gazed up at him. Chubby jowls pulled the chin downwards, exacerbating the occupant's surprised, open-mouthed look.

The middle button on the dark yellow waistcoat had lost its battle to contain the paunch, while the two remaining buttons struggled valiantly to continue the fight. The brown corduroy trousers now looked a little on the short side, revealing a pair of white-socked ankles above the black, highly polished shoes.

Felicity grabbed the top of the waste bin with both hands and pulled herself up to peer in. "Whatever's all the fuss ab—"

Her scream reverberated around them.

Aldermaston gulped. Cartwright was right. As usual. This was most definitely an unexpected item in the compostable waste bin. It was a body. And not just any body. For there, above the left eyebrow, was a small red birthmark.

Sir Hugo Rinde was dead.

CHAPTER THREE

Diya's Morris Minor squelched to a halt on the grass verge outside her three-bedroomed, semi-detached house in Clee Way. She hurried along her short garden path, thrust her key into her front door lock, and let herself in.

Her heart raced as she collapsed against the door. A silver tabby cat poked its head round the living room doorway, then mewed.

"Daisy, come to Mummy!" She crouched and opened her arms. Daisy turned and disappeared back into the living room.

Despite being the family home she and her parents moved into over forty years ago, a sense of unease surrounded her as she entered the living room. A red light flashed on the telephone answering machine, perched on a nest of tables beside the television. Diya pressed play.

"Hello, Diya!" boomed the IT Helpdesk operative's voice.

She grabbed the sofa's corner to steady herself.

"Don't think about calling Abigail from home. We have ways to check up on you there, too, thanks to when we set up your working-from-home system." The caller burst into a cackle before the line went dead.

Diya clutched her chest. It wasn't safe here. She tickled Daisy's chin. "Mummy's got to go away for a few days. Just while I sort this mess out. I'll ask John next door to feed you."

Oh! Was there enough cat food? She hurried to the cupboard under the stairs and found only three tins.

"Better order some more now," she muttered, whipping out her phone and ordering online.

She ordered a carton of twenty-four tins and was about to confirm the order when she saw the box to leave instructions for the delivery driver. *Leave package by back door*, she typed. John always came round the back to feed her, so he'd miss a delivery on the front doorstep.

Then she hurried upstairs to pack.

Aldermaston paced up and down in their private kitchen. "Sir Hugo must have been in the compostable waste bin all night."

Felicity cradled a mug of strong coffee. "The meadows! I bet Rupert inherits. And now the council has all the money it needs." She threw her hands in the air. "It's game over for *Verdant Endings*."

The kitchen door swung open, and Cartwright stepped in. Aldermaston knew from his expressionless face that it was more bad news.

"Apologies for the intrusion, My Lord, My Lady. The undertakers from Earth, Wind, and Fire are currently collecting Sir Hugo." He paused. "And PC Norten would like a word." Cartwright stepped aside.

As Mortiforde's only police presence stepped into the kitchen, his eye-line level with their ceiling-hung kitchen spotlights, Aldermaston wondered if the waste incinerator's chimney had been modelled on the officer. Although both were tall and slender, there was one stark difference. The waste incinerator chimney would have a far greater intelligence.

"Lord Mortiforde. Lady Mortiforde." PC Norten bowed his head.

Aldermaston never knew whether the constable was officially bowing, not that he needed to, or simply looking down on them.

"I'm returning some property." From behind his back, he produced a short-handled medieval dagger and thrust his long arm of the law towards Aldermaston. "I've washed the blood off."

Gingerly, Aldermaston took the weapon. "Cartwright, is this the missing item from the armoury display you mentioned earlier?"

The butler leaned closer and squinted. "Yes, Your Lordship."

PC Norten stooped towards Aldermaston's ear, yet nodded at Cartwright. "You need to watch him, Your Lordship. Putting a metal implement in a compostable waste bin is not exactly … you know…" PC Norten tapped his forehead. "…common sense. Had Cartwright disposed of that properly, Sir Hugo wouldn't have impaled himself when he accidentally fell back on it, would he?"

PC Norten stood upright. "I can't impress upon Your Lordship the life-saving practice of placing the correct materials in the correct recycling receptacle."

The police officer placed his hands on his hips and looked at Cartwright, Felicity, and then Aldermaston in turn. "Strictly speaking, I should report this health and safety incident. But, as we're only talking about one item of contamination, I'm prepared to look the other way."

Aldermaston's eyebrows rose. The blasted copper hadn't looked the right way, let alone the other way. A waste incinerator chimney could deduce that Sir Hugo had been murdered.

"On that note, I'll leave you, Your Lordship. You won't believe the paperwork even a minor recycling transgression generates. But first, I need to break the news to Sir Hugo's wife." He nodded at them each again before turning, dropping to his knees, and exiting through the kitchen door.

Cartwright stepped forward. "Your Lordship, I can assure you, there's no way—"

Aldermaston held up his free hand. "Cartwright, the only logical explanation is that someone stole this from the armoury last night and stabbed Sir Hugo in the back with it."

Peredur sat at his dining table and woke his personal laptop. He entered his thirty-four-character password, and a dashboard of CCTV camera feeds appeared on the screen.

He selected one and surveyed the interior of a vast stone barn containing a wall of hay bales at one end and several others littering the floor. Light from a half-hearted November morning dribbled in from the huge floor-to-ceiling doorway where two vast double-doors once offered the interior some protection.

Peredur flinched as a barn owl flew from behind the camera and swooped low through the barn's interior space, pouncing on something on the straw-lined stone floor. Moments later, it took to the air again, a dead mouse between its talons. He jumped back and screamed. He had hated mice ever since one shot up his combat trouser leg while on manoeuvres and bit him somewhere painful. He'd never gone commando on manoeuvres again.

Then he saw her. Propped up in the far corner, sitting on a hay bale. Mortiforde Millie's bulbous eyes stared at her leather boots, her long brown hair trailed across her multicoloured cardigan, and her hands rested on the plain brown skirt.

Peredur whistled. She looked tiny inside the vast barn. He'd been told Millie would be stored safely on the Marquess of Mortiforde's estate, in a building the Marquess didn't know existed. Peredur shook his head. How could anyone own so much land that they didn't know where all the buildings were?

He slammed shut the laptop screen and pounded his desk with a clenched fist. A fifteen-foot-tall effigy was currently being housed in a building five times the size of the rented accommodation from which he was being evicted. Where was the justice?

"Why do *I* have to see Isabel? She's *your* friend, too." Aldermaston found a clear plastic food bag in the cupboard under the sink, dropped the dagger into it, and then tied a knot in the end.

Felicity headed towards the door. "She was *your* mother's closest friend. The family's condolences should come from you as Marquess." She pointed to the bagged dagger. "What are you doing with that?"

"Preserving evidence, for what it's worth. I'll call Chief Constable Stoyle. We know Sir Hugo was murdered, even if PC Norten doesn't. Where are you going?"

Felicity hovered in the kitchen doorway. "To organise an emergency Ladies' Legion meeting."

"Perhaps gather in the main drawing room rather than the armoury." He held aloft the dagger.

"Are you accusing a member of the Ladies' Legion of murdering Sir Hugo?"

Aldermaston considered his options, then shook his head.

Felicity went to turn, but stopped. "There was something

unusual at last night's meeting. Someone set off a personal alarm and declared Sir Hugo's offer was a publicity stunt to stop the waste incinerator. Sir Hugo disagreed naturally, but the accuser then dashed out of the room."

"Who was it?"

Felicity shrugged. "Not one of our regulars. Anyway, must dash. Give my love to Isabel."

With that, she disappeared out the door.

Aldermaston grabbed his second charred slice of now-cold toast and bit into it. It, too, shattered, sending burnt shards in every direction. The council didn't need a waste incinerator. They could borrow his toaster instead.

Rosemary Sedgewicke stood at her kitchen's Belfast sink, staring through the kitchen window, deep into the garden. Water gushed from the hot tap but missed the mug she held mid-air to rinse.

Breakfast Benny had just interrupted Psychic Simone's horoscope section with more breaking news, which was even a shock to Psychic Simone. Sir Hugo was dead.

"Ouch!" The sink's scolding water level rose and stung her hands. She grabbed a towel from the green Aga handrail, dried her hands, then turned off the radio and tap. She sat at her kitchen table. This changed everything.

Rosemary grabbed her phone and selected Rupert's number. Her fingers drummed the top of an opened letter while she waited for him to answer.

"Morning," he puffed. "Do you mind if we walk and talk? I'm behind with my daily run."

His normality made her uneasy. Had she misheard Breakfast Benny? "The radio said something about your father. Is it true?"

"Yes."

Rosemary gasped. "Rupert. I'm so sorry. They said something about an accident."

Rupert tutted. "PC Norten found my father dead in a compostable waste bin on the Tugford Estate."

"What?" Rosemary picked up the opened letter. "What was he doing there?"

Rupert stopped running. "No idea. He's dead. This changes nothing about our plan."

Rosemary slipped the letter out of the envelope. "It must do, surely? They'll have to postpone this morning's selection interview."

"On the contrary," Rupert replied. "Tom Burthson, Chair of the Socially Liberal Conservative Party, called earlier. He offered to postpone, but I told him not to."

"Why?"

Rupert caught his breath. "This is perfect. Mortiforde urgently needs a new Member of Parliament. Grenville Gastrell's sudden death set a ticking clock. There must be a by-election within five weeks. The Socially Liberal Conservative Party needs a replacement candidate. I told Tom to proceed. They can pay their respects at the funeral." He paused briefly. "You're the only candidate left."

"But—" Rosemary ran her free hand through her hair. "It's disrespectful."

"My father's dead. He doesn't care, and neither do I!"

Rosemary bit her bottom lip. There he was. The single-minded, heartless businessman she knew of old. A horrifying thought crossed her mind. "Rupert, you didn't—?"

"Didn't what?"

She shook her head. No. Even Rupert wouldn't stoop *that* low. Although, this was the man who tried sabotaging her European Parliament career over twenty-five years ago. He was capable of far worse. "Nothing," she whispered. "It's shock. I'm not thinking straight."

"Anyway," he continued, "the council's waste incinerator funding news has broken. The ball's already rolling. We've got to roll with it. I bet the Mortiforde morons are already setting up their opposition campaigns."

Rosemary leaned back in the chair. "Rupert, I know you and your father fell out, but townsfolk will expect you to mourn. The optics won't look good if we push through our plan now."

Rupert sighed. "I'll shed a tear in public when necessary. The Socially Liberal Conservative Party needs a candidate who will win the next by-election. You're their only candidate now. And, what better person than the council's Director of Finance, who knows the council does not have all the money for the waste incinerator project, despite what the new Chief Executive said this morning? These are good optics. Prove it and you'll be the saviour of Mortiforde Meadows. The other party candidates won't get a look-in. Tom Burthson and his cronies need you."

Rosemary stared at the interview invitation letter. Sir Hugo had always been kind to her, especially in those early days, when she'd first met Rupert. His death wasn't part of their plan. A thought occurred to her. "How does Abigail think the council's funding is all in place now?"

"I know a chap in the IT department," said Rupert. "He's clearly made his move."

"How? I'll have to fight Abigail on this. I don't want any nasty surprises."

Rupert chuckled. "You worry too much. Stick to the plan. Get selected as the SLC candidate, then you can campaign against my awful waste incinerator project. With those optics, nobody will know what we're really up to. And when you win the by-election and become the town's Member of

Parliament, then we can make some serious money around here."

~

Aldermaston held up the bagged dagger and squinted at it while clutching the phone to his ear. "There must still be some forensic evidence on it, surely?"

The Chief Constable's exasperated sigh echoed down the line. "Who knows what other contaminants that dipstick transferred onto it during his so-called cleaning?"

Aldermaston dropped the bag onto the worktop. "Which proves the point we've been making for years now. We need a better police presence in Mortiforde. One intellectually challenged officer isn't enough." Aldermaston paused. "Not that two intellectually challenged officers would be better. I mean—"

"Your Lordship, I don't have the resources. Most crime in our region happens in Shrewsbury, Worcester, and Hereford. That's where I focus my limited officer numbers."

Aldermaston gazed across Tugford Hall's formal gardens and out towards the rolling hills of Borderlandshire. Even on a grey, overcast day, autumn's russet colours were still visible from the few hardy leaves clinging desperately to twigs, awaiting the first real winter storm.

"We might be the rural hinterland, Chief Constable, but we pay for a police presence. Someone murdered Sir Hugo. If you're interested, I have the murder weapon in a bag here at Tugford Hall. We'll stop using the armoury and the compostable waste bin for the foreseeable future. If you want to send an intelligent officer round to carry out their own investigation, you're more than welcome to. I'm sure Sir Hugo's wife will be grateful."

"If our man has trashed the crime scene and contaminated

the evidence—" Stoyle sighed. "I'll advise the coroner that Sir Hugo's death is potentially unnatural."

Aldermaston stared at the dagger. *Potentially unnatural?* Sir Hugo had been stabbed in the back!

Stoyle continued, "I'll see if I can spare someone to make some further inquiries. Should anything else happen, you know where to find me."

Yeah, thought Aldermaston. *In the neighbouring county.*

~

Felicity slipped into Tugford Hall's armoury to find the top table and chairs from last night's meeting still *in situ*. Cartwright had propped the fallen Gainsborough against the wall, albeit upside down. The dour woman's disdain was palpable.

Her shoes clattered across the parquet flooring as she weaved between the abandoned chairs to the top table where they'd left Sir Hugo's framed document.

She scrutinised its contents. The document declared the *Verdant Endings* project free use of the meadows, followed by Sir Hugo's florid signature. Underneath, in a smaller font, was a series of sub-clauses.

Felicity moved under the chandelier for better light.

1. Verdant Endings may only use Mortiforde Meadows for environmental burials and the scattering of ashes.
2. No traditional stone headstones are permitted. Burial spots can be marked by the planting of an appropriate tree.
3. This agreement shall continue in perpetuity, whosoever becomes the legal landowner, subject to clause 4.
4. In the event of my death, this land shall pass to the beneficiary identified in my will. If no burials or scatterings occur before my body's interment in the Rinde Family vault, this agreement is void.

Felicity shuddered. Clause four could be the final nail in the coffin for the *Verdant Endings'* dream.

~

Aldermaston pulled onto Knowton Manor's beech-lined drive, then immediately turned left and parked beside The Lodge. The cosy but substantial idyllic property had a yellow limestone-walled ground floor and a black-and-white timber-framed upper floor containing two enormous bay windows. Crowned with a red-tiled roof, punctured by an ornate, red brick chimney, it was reminiscent of the home he, Felicity, and Harry once lived in on the Tugford Estate before his parents' unexpected death.

Aldermaston stepped up to the large white wooden door and grabbed the heavy lion-head door knocker. He rapped three times. Few birds sang on this grey November morning. The clouds smothered the surrounding hilltops, muting the landscape in deference to Sir Hugo's death. The heavy noise of releasing interior bolts broke his thoughts. Isabel's tearful eyes peered around the door.

"Isabel, we're so sorry for your loss."

She opened the door wide, revealing her black trousers and a long-sleeved, dark grey round-neck jumper. "Come in, Aldermaston. Excuse the mess."

He stepped into a wide hallway with a flagstone floor and wooden-panel-lined walls, and hugged her.

"Tea?" Isabel gestured to the kitchen.

"Don't go to any trouble."

She smiled. "Gives me something to do." She slipped into a modern kitchen and switched on the kettle.

Aldermaston pondered how to begin, but Isabel cut straight to the point.

"He was murdered, wasn't he?" Her hand gripped the dark grey marble worktop.

The kettle's raucous bubbling subsided, and Aldermaston watched Isabel warm the china teapot. "PC Norten's analysis—"

Isabel waved a teaspoon in Aldermaston's face. "That man is as useless as a rural village bus stop."

Aldermaston placed a comforting arm around her. "Yes. I believe he was murdered."

Her moist eyes thanked his candour. She poured some tea into a mug. "I'm drinking gallons of the stuff. Using the fine china cups and saucers is a waste of time. Milk?"

"Let me." Aldermaston headed for the upright fridge freezer. "What did PC Norten tell you?"

"That my husband was found in your compostable waste bin, having tripped and fallen backwards, impaling himself on a—" Her hand clasped her mouth briefly. Another tear ran down her cheek.

"I've demanded that Chief Constable Stoyle arrange a proper investigation. He says he'll notify the coroner, so you won't be able to make any funeral arrangements yet."

"Hugo never wanted a funeral."

"No?" Aldermaston handed her the milk.

"He doesn't … didn't … mind a service of remembrance," she explained. "He never understood why the body had to be part of the service. We'll inter him in the family vault whenever the authorities release his body."

Aldermaston took his tea.

Isabel placed a hand on Aldermaston's forearm. "It might be useful if the police weren't all over this to begin with. Can you do something for me?"

"Anything."

She scrutinised the sincerity on his face. "Find out who did this."

Aldermaston's forehead furrowed.

Isabel's grip tightened. "In recent years, Rupert and Hugo, they …" She sipped some tea as she considered her words. "… Disagreed over the business. Hugo couldn't stop himself from meddling, even after he'd handed over the running of the company to Rupert." She shook her head. "Biggest mistake Hugo ever made. It was the start of the downward spiral."

Isabel inhaled deeply. "Rupert threw us out of Knowton Manor."

"What?" Aldermaston placed his mug down on the kitchen worktop.

"Everyone thinks we retired here. Don't get me wrong, it's lovely here. But Knowton Manor has two dozen bedrooms. There's ample room."

She released her grip on Aldermaston. "The business arguments became more heated. Then, about a year ago, Rupert flipped and threw us out."

"Is that legal?"

Isabel shrugged. "The atmosphere was so toxic, I was happy to leave. Knowton Manor is a business asset. A tax thing Hugo sorted years ago. At least he had the sense to put The Lodge in my name." She waved her hand around the kitchen.

"Isabel, I'm so sorry. I knew nothing of this."

She smiled. "Why would you? Families like ours don't wash their dirty laundry on magazine covers, do they? Even Rupert wanted it kept quiet. Wouldn't be good for business, he said."

She paused, then peered over his shoulder. A solitary finger touched her lips briefly, then she walked past him and closed the kitchen door. "Farringdon's here. Rupert fired him last night. And as much as I trust Farringdon, far more than I trust my own son, families like ours only survive because we're careful with whom we share our secrets."

Aldermaston stepped closer.

"My son never gets his hands dirty," Isabel continued. "He

delegates. Just because he was here at the Manor last night doesn't mean he wasn't involved."

Aldermaston shifted his weight.

Isabel smiled ruefully. "What sort of mother considers her son might be her husband's murderer?" She paused. "And why tell you?" She grabbed his shoulder and leaned into his ear. "You owe me."

Pulling back, her blue eyes scrutinised his puzzled expression. Her smile broadened.

"Your mother was a dear friend. If she were alive, I'd be sharing these thoughts with her, not you. We shared all our secrets." She patted his arm. "*All* our secrets."

Aldermaston's eyes narrowed further. "You knew about Mother's affair?"

Isabel squeezed his arm. "I knew Basildon was not your father's before he was born."

Aldermaston's heart raced. He'd always assumed his half-brother's history had only become known to the wider world after his parents' fatal road accident, when everyone had expected Basildon to inherit the estate and title.

"Your mother's written confession left with your family solicitor to be opened on your father's death was my suggestion. She didn't like it, but deep down, she knew I was right."

Isabel chuckled. "She feared facing the world after your father's death. I said she could always hide here."

She released her grip. "That's why I need *you* to find out who's behind Hugo's death. If it is Rupert, I need to know. A mother should be prepared for that sort of thing."

She tapped the kitchen workshop. "I kept your mother's secret. It's time you repaid that loyalty."

Aldermaston nodded. It was the right thing to do.

She hugged him. "Thank you. Your mother always said

you were your father's son. He was a good man. Taken far too soon, just like my Hugo." A tear fell to her chin.

Aldermaston bit his bottom lip. "When my mother shared her secret with you, did she?"

"Basildon's father?" She nodded and tapped the side of her nose.

~

"Bye, Daisy," Diya waved. "Be good for Mummy." She slammed the front door, pushed against it, then grabbed her overnight holdall and headed to her car.

"Glad I caught you," a voice called behind her.

Diya spun around to see her local postwoman, Pippa, standing there with a small brown package and a handheld device.

"Need a signature. Anywhere on the screen will do." She spotted the overnight bag. "Going away? Want me to hold on to your post?"

Diya tucked the small brown package under her arm and scribbled her indecipherable signature. The last thing she needed was Postie Pippa gossiping to everyone about her disappearance.

"It's no trouble," Pippa continued. "Doing it for the Smythes at number sixty-two. Marriage on the rocks, apparently. They're in the Seychelles rekindling things." She sniggered. "I'd let my husband play away if I could get a Seychelles trip out of it!"

Diya pondered. She planned on finding a hotel somewhere, but it could be useful if gossiping Pippa peddled the visiting-Nani-Nagma-in-India story. "That would be most helpful," she smiled.

"Going anywhere nice?"

"Mumbai," she said. "Two weeks with family."

Pippa nodded at Diya's overnight bag. "You travel light!"

Diya closed the Traveller's rear door. "I keep a wardrobe of clothes over there. Saves lugging them across continents."

Pippa pressed a few buttons on her device. "Good thinking. See you in a couple of weeks, then." She waved and continued her round.

Diya slipped into the driver's seat and tore at the parcel. A fluffy, grey, long-tailed toy mouse dropped onto her lap. "Oh, Daisy will love you!"

She held it aloft by the tail. The online auction site price was a third of that in the town's pet store. Really, it hadn't cost her anything, because she'd sold Daisy's toy spider via the auction site for a similar price. Everything had a value, and online auction sites allowed her to extract that value from many of Daisy's unwanted toys and—

Online auctions! That's how she'd raise the shortfall. All she needed was something to sell. Where did the council put things it no longer needed? She grinned. The Basement of Despair.

Buoyed by her newfound enthusiasm, Diya slipped the toy mouse into her handbag and started the engine. She was going back to the office, but not through the IT-monitored front door.

She floored the accelerator. The engine squealed and, as she released the clutch, the car lurched into the road, just as Pippa stepped out between two parked cars.

The postal worker back-flipped over the nearest car bonnet, but the Traveller's bulbous nose smashed into Pippa's postbag, sending it high into the air.

Diya hurtled towards the end of Clee Way and indicated right. In her rear-view mirror, she was puzzled to see a shower of marketing leaflets, brown envelopes, and mobility-aid catalogues fluttering to the ground.

～

Aldermaston's mind was a whirlwind as he steered his Jaguar through town. *Isabel knows who Basildon's father is!* Would she share this information if Aldermaston discovered who killed Sir Hugo?

The Jaguar's screen displayed an incoming call. Abigail Mayedew. He accepted it.

"Congratulations, Abigail, on what must be one of the fastest council fundraising efforts in history. Half a million pounds in barely fifteen hours is some achievement."

"I told you it was only a matter of time," she replied. "I was surprised, too, but that's why I have staff to deal with these finer details. My goal is the bigger picture, and I would be foolish to let this one smoulder any longer."

Aldermaston shuffled in his driving seat. "May I remind you that the Guild voted against the project last night?"

Abigail chuckled. "I didn't *have* to bring the project to the Guild's attention. I consulted you. You gave me your verdict."

His grip on the black leather steering wheel tightened. "You can't ride roughshod over this community. You must give them a chance to share their views."

"I will, Your Lordship. I'm offering a public consultation. It helps with the grieving process."

"Grieving process?"

"Yes," Abigail continued. "Communities move on quicker if they *feel* they were involved in the decision-making process, even if they don't achieve the outcome they wanted. So I'm organising a NAF."

He frowned. "Sorry, Abigail. I'm driving. Lost the signal briefly. You're organising a naff what?"

Abigail tutted. "Neighbourhood Area Forum. A public meeting where people can raise questions. Many communities find NAFs a cathartic process. I'm arranging a NAF in the council chamber this Friday evening at seven o'clock."

"But that's just after the parade and firework display."

"Well, there's your answer, Lord Mortiforde. If the town finds a few sorrowful sparklers and contemptible Catherine wheels of more importance than a public meeting, their lack of attendance would be clear evidence of support for the waste incinerator project."

Aldermaston was about to interject, but Abigail beat him to it.

"And in the spirit of balance and fairness, I'd like to invite you to the NAF Selection Panel at eleven o'clock this morning."

Aldermaston checked that the next junction was clear. "A naff what?"

"Selection panel," she clarified. "A meeting's direction can be greatly influenced by its chair, so I'm interviewing a couple of candidates. Come and help me choose. Think of it as partnership working."

Aldermaston could almost hear the smug smile on her face. Take part, and he could be accused of endorsing Abigail's consultation process. Turn it down, and she'd claim he was dismissing the wider democratic process to the detriment of the town.

"Okay, you win. I'll be there."

"I've not won yet, Your Lordship. But I will."

CHAPTER FOUR

Felicity banged the table in Tugford Hall's main drawing room, calling the urgent Ladies' Legion meeting to order. A hush descended.

"Ladies of the Legion," she began. "Thank you for coming at such short notice. Little did we know when Sir Hugo was here last night that events would take such a dramatic turn. Please join me in a minute's silence in memory of our dear friend."

She and the assembled women stood, although Margaret Hillbrow needed some help standing without her Zimmer. As they silently reflected, heads bowed, Felicity surveyed the shoes before her.

Margaret Hillbrow's cushioned slip-on black leather shoes looked sensibly comfortable, boasting a small side zip for easier removal. Heidi Yail's pink running shoelaces were double-knotted to save having to stop and retie them during her morning runs. Arabella Bebbington's bright red three-inch heels were already marking the parquet flooring, as were Cordelia Prichton's kitten-heel black suede shoes. The ball of pale blue wool Cissy Warbouys was knitting with partially hid her black court shoes, and Kitty Catchpole had come straight from milking the cows, such was the splatter of cow faeces across her wellington boots.

"Thank you, ladies." Felicity returned to her seat, and the two dozen women before her followed suit.

She held up Sir Hugo's document. "Sir Hugo's generous offer for *Verdant Endings* to use the meadows still stands, although there is one concerning clause on this agreement." She tapped the bottom of the frame. "We may only use the meadows after Sir Hugo's death, provided a burial or scattering of ashes precedes his interment in the family vault."

A collective gasp washed around the room.

Margaret Hillbrow raised an unsteady hand. "Who inherits the meadows?"

"Bound to be Rupert," Kitty called out. "Did you hear Breakfast Benny earlier? The council has its money for the waste incinerator project. It's over, isn't it? The meadows will be decimated."

A cacophony of disgusted condemnation echoed around the room.

Cordelia stood, tugging at a few strands of her short-cut, merlot-red hair near the nape. Her soft Welsh accent wafted across the room. "Is Diya Parmer here? She works for the council, doesn't she? She'll know what is going on."

Felicity scanned the gathering as other members twisted in their seats, searching.

Arabella stood waving her arm about. "It must be true if Diya's too scared to show her face here. So much for solidarity with the cause! I vote we expel her from the Legion."

The discordance of members' opinions crescendoed around the vast room.

"Ladies, please!" Felicity's sternness surprised even her. "I understand the anger, but let's be sensible. I called this meeting at short notice. Diya probably couldn't get time off work."

She scribbled a note to call Diya later. "We need a plan of action now. Does anyone have any ideas?"

Arabella jumped up again. "Protests! Let's blockade the streets and raise a petition to save the meadows."

A chorus of "Hear, hear!" swamped the room.

Felicity made further notes. "And what about *Verdant Endings*? Should we look for alternative sites?"

"We have no choice, do we?" said Margaret.

Arabella pointed at Sir Hugo's document. "What does the contract say, Your Ladyship?"

Felicity read it out, then emphasized the final clause. "*In the event of my death, this land shall pass to the beneficiary identified in my will. If no burials or scatterings occur before my body's interment in the Rinde Family vault, this agreement is void.*"

Arabella clapped her hands with excitement. "There you go, then! We need a dead body in the ground as soon as possible!"

"Starting with Rupert Rinde's," called another woman at the back. A series of cheers and foot-stomping pulsed around them.

Felicity shuffled in her chair. "It could take us weeks to get something organised."

Arabella placed her hands on her hips. "Are we not women? If Sir Hugo's agreement says whoever inherits the meadows must abide by the agreement, then we need a dead body in the ground quickly."

"Protests would work better," said Margaret. "We've no experience of holding a green burial or scattering. It's a lot of work."

Heidi Yail looked over the top of her half-moon glasses. "Why not do both? Protest and find someone to bury in the meadows?"

Felicity saw a sea of female faces staring at her, waiting for direction. She shuffled uncomfortably. "Hands up, all those in favour of peaceful protests."

A forest of hands shot up.

"And those in favour of…" She considered her words. "… Encouraging a quick uptake in our green burial offer?"

Another plantation of upright arms appeared before her.

"Motion carried," screamed Arabella, punching the air. "Come on, ladies! There's work to be done!"

They rose en masse and stampeded out of the room.

Briefly, Felicity sat alone at the table, pen in hand.

There was a knock on the door, and a vision of red stepped back in.

"Your Ladyship," Arabella began. "Could you have a word with Sir Hugo's wife? Might she consider a green burial for Sir Hugo? I mean, what better way to show his support than to be our first customer?"

Felicity tapped the framed document. "Sir Hugo's document stipulates he'll be interred in the family vault. Giving him a green burial could risk this very agreement, too."

Arabella nodded. "It was just a thought. Cissy says she'll go down the obituaries in *The Mortiforde Chronicle* today, and Kitty's going to the hospital to talk to any recently bereaved relatives. It would mean a lot to the Legion if you joined her."

She nodded. "I'm happy to help Cissy."

"I meant Kitty," Arabella clarified. "Accident and Emergency can be extremely busy. It's a two-person job."

"Er—"

"Excellent!" Arabella beamed. "I'll tell Kitty you'll be with her shortly." She hurried out the door.

Felicity froze. Helping Kitty at A&E was bordering on ambulance-chasing, wasn't it?

~

Aldermaston immediately recognised his half-brother's gangly frame and cropped hair in the CCTV image on Daniel's computer screen. "What's Basildon playing at?"

"If he's working for BANG," Daniel continued, "he could have left the note on my chair. He has full access to this building."

Aldermaston collapsed into his leather captain's chair. "But that doesn't make sense. Consider the last line. *You should be the ones to burn, you landed-gentry squatters*. I live in the East Wing, and his apartment is in the West Wing. That makes him a landed-gentry squatter, too."

"Perhaps Basildon killed Sir Hugo?" Daniel considered. "He could have grabbed the dagger from the armoury and stabbed Sir Hugo in the back. And he knows where the recycling bins are."

Aldermaston dismissed the supposition. "Basildon might be obsessed with joining MI5 or MI6, but he wouldn't kill Sir Hugo. He's eccentric, not deluded." At least, he hoped that was the case. "The theft of Mortiforde Millie and Sir Hugo's death are not connected." Aldermaston selected a pen and jotted a note in his notebook. "Isabel thinks Rupert could be behind her husband's death. And he has more to gain from that than Basildon."

Daniel leaned on his desk. "Isabel Rinde thinks her son murdered his father?"

"*Thinks*. She has no evidence." Aldermaston dropped the BANG note onto his desk. "We need to talk to Lisa."

Daniel hit his phone's loudspeaker button and pressed the quick dial button. A series of tones and beeps echoed around the office, followed by a ringing tone.

"Lisa Duddon, how can I help you?"

"Lisa, it's Daniel," he answered. "You're on speakerphone. Aldermaston wants a word."

"I take it Daniel's shown you the CCTV image," she said.

"Yes, but we'll deal with that later. Millie's disappearance is a classic BANG publicity stunt. Why Basildon is involved, I don't know. Our priority is Sir Hugo's murder and saving the meadows. Isabel asked me to investigate Sir Hugo's murder. She thinks Rupert could be involved."

The speaker amplified Lisa's gasp.

"Rupert was home all last night," Aldermaston continued, "but Isabel confided that his relationship with Sir Hugo had deteriorated since Rupert took over Rinde Industries. We know Sir Hugo was against the waste incinerator project, and his demise removes one obstacle from the project."

"And the council's funding shortfall magically disappearing overnight resolves another," Lisa concluded.

"Exactly. Impeccable timing. I wonder where the missing money came from."

Lisa rattled a pen between her teeth. "My access to the authority's accounts system is limited to transactions relating to our work in the Democracy Support Team."

"Don't," Aldermaston warned. "You'll leave a digital trail. Find someone to talk to discreetly."

"Diya Parmer is Head of Planning Finance," Lisa suggested.

"Try her. I'll see you shortly, anyway. Abigail has invited me to a selection panel in half an—"

"Selection panel?" Lisa interrupted. "We've no selection panels in the diary today."

"Abigail thinks otherwise."

Lisa's keyboard clacked. "What's a Waste Incinerator NAF?"

Aldermaston chuckled. "Not the same as a naff waste incinerator."

"Oh, heck!" cried Lisa. "Do you know who you're interviewing?"

Aldermaston's eyes closed. "Hit me."

"Councillors Prendeghast and Taplinski. Sorry, Aldermaston. Gotta go. I need to prepare the council chamber for this."

"Catch you later."

"One more thing," Lisa snapped. "Stella rang. She's desperate to talk to you."

"About?"

"Didn't say." The line went dead.

Daniel silenced the phone. "Who are Prendeghast and Taplinski?"

Aldermaston fell back in his chair. "Prendeghast is as effective as a one-legged sheepdog."

"And Taplinski?"

Aldermaston tutted. "A relentless businessman who'll be on Abigail's side. The best outcome is if I can persuade Abigail to appoint Prendeghast as the NAF chair. The trouble is, he really will be a naff chair."

"What do you want me to do?" Daniel asked.

Aldermaston stared at the CCTV image on Daniel's computer monitor. "I bet if we find my half-brother, we'll find Millie."

"How?"

Aldermaston retrieved a bunch of keys from his trouser pocket. He jingled them in his hand, searching. "Take this." He selected a silver key and handed it to Daniel. "It's the master."

"Master?"

"It'll get you into Basildon's flat," Aldermaston clarified.

Daniel gulped. "You want me to break into Basildon's apartment?"

"You're not breaking in. You have a key. I own Tugford Hall, so I can ask you to go anywhere in the building."

Daniel tentatively took the key. "What am I looking for?"

"Anything that might explain where he is." He pointed at Daniel's monitor. "That proves he was in Mortiforde yesterday.

But he's not been here at Tugford Hall for days. So where's he staying?"

∾

"Thank you for calling." Peredur ended the call, removed his headset, and placed it between his work and personal laptops on his living room table.

There was a rap at his back door: three knocks, a pause, two knocks, another pause, followed by a single knock. Peredur grinned. He headed through to his kitchen and opened the back door.

"Enter Agent 117." He gestured to the gangly visitor with short salt and pepper hair, standing there in black trousers and a black polo neck jumper.

Agent 117 pointed to Peredur's face paint. "I say, old chap. Didn't expect to find you fully kitted out at home."

"Agent 117, you're to address me as Commander." Peredur stifled a smirk.

"Yes, Commander, old bean." Agent 117 saluted. "I brought you these. Mother said one should never arrive at someone's house empty-handed." He handed Peredur a purple box of Cadbury Milk Tray chocolates.

Peredur was momentarily dumbfounded. Nobody had given him a present before. He placed them on the kitchen worktop. "Oh, thanks. Come through."

They stepped into the sparse living room. Peredur lifted his personal laptop screen to display the CCTV image of Mortiforde Millie hiding in the barn. He grinned at his visitor. "You have done well, Agent 117."

"Thank you, Commander." He waved a finger at the laptop. "That surveillance camera was a doddle to set up." He peered closer. "Resolution's excellent. Where did you get it?"

"Know an army surplus chap in Wales." He lowered the laptop screen.

Peredur paced the room, scrutinising Agent 117. His brown eyes, snub nose, and thin lips didn't convey the image of a mercenary. Nor did the black polo neck jumper clinging to the slight five-foot-eight frame. Yet somehow he'd shifted a fifteen-foot effigy into this amazing hiding place.

"Your initiation is complete." Peredur extended a hand. "Welcome to the team, Agent 117."

Agent 117 gripped it firmly and shook.

"Did you deliver the note, too?"

Agent 117 nodded. "Right into His Lordship's office, Commander."

Peredur's eyes widened. He needed Agent 117 to think he was impressed. "You actually broke into Tugford Hall?"

Agent 117 winked. "By Jove, it's as if I had a key to the front door."

"Time for phase two, then."

"Yes, Commander?"

"We must show The Establishment we mean business. They've ridden roughshod over the little guys, like you and me, for too long. Where are the homes for local people? And what about all those four-and five-bedroom executive houses being built near the bypass? Incomers buy them. Where's the smaller housing for single people like me?"

Agent 117 glanced around the room.

"Your place has … character."

Peredur paused by the mantelpiece, his hand hovering over his eviction notice. "Appearances can be deceptive," he muttered. "So BANG has planned a two-pronged attack." He stepped closer, his mouth inches from Agent 117's ear. "We shall stop incomers buying our houses, and show The Establishment what it's like to be bullied."

Agent 117 shuffled from side to side. "Bullied, Commander?"

"Yes, Agent 117. Bullied. That's what they do to us. How big is the Tugford Hall Estate?"

Agent 117's bottom lip protruded as he glanced at the ceiling. "Over a thousand acres?"

"Try three thousand!" snapped Peredur. "With Lord Mortiforde owning all that, there's less land for us to live on. The council grants permission to build four-or five-bedroom executive houses that only Londoners can afford. And yet, they reject applications for smaller developments. That's a conspiracy!"

Peredur grabbed his twice-folded notice-to-quit letter from the mantelpiece and held it six inches from Agent 117's face. "Do you know this man?" Peredur pointed to the Lockmount Estate Agency logo on the letter.

"Gerald? Oh yes, Commander. Lovely chap. Got himself a nice little business, being the only estate agent in town. His grandfather established—"

"I'm not interested in that!" Peredur snapped. "All I'm interested in is disrupting his business. No estate agent. No house sales." He crouched down under the table and pulled out some chains and a padlock.

He handed them to Agent 117. "Estate agents like chains. Let's see how much he likes these." Peredur winked. "I think Mortiforde Millie could do with some company, don't you?"

Agent 117 saluted. "Message understood, Commander."

Peredur nodded. "I sent Mr Lockmount an email earlier. He'll arrive at the stone barn of his own accord at two-thirty this afternoon. Got that?"

Agent 117 nodded, saluted, turned on the spot, and marched out of the room. Moments later, Peredur's back door slammed shut.

Peredur grinned. This was going much better than he'd

imagined. It was as if Agent 117 thought he was undercover. Which merely highlighted how stupid he was, because everyone in Mortiforde knew Basildon was the Marquess of Mortiforde's half-witted half-brother.

~

Alone in his office, Aldermaston returned to the BANG note. Was his half-brother part of BANG?

Basildon's unfettered access to Tugford Hall meant he could have easily placed the note on Daniel's chair. His obsession with working for MI5 or MI6 made him do some stupid things, but why join an organisation campaigning against all governments? Unless—

Was Basildon having second thoughts? When their parents' sudden death revealed the shocking news that Basildon was not the Seventh Marquess's firstborn, Basildon seemed relieved. Having the title's heavy responsibility lifted from his shoulders allowed him to pursue his dream of working for the Secret Service. But did he now feel cheated at losing the Marquess title he'd grown up believing was his?

Aldermaston pondered further. Basildon lost part of his identity the day their parents died. Isabel knew who his father was. Perhaps she'd consider sharing that knowledge with Basildon? Helping Isabel might ultimately help his brother. He dialled Knowton Manor's number and an officious secretary answered.

"Rinde Industries."

"Good morning. It's Lord Mortiforde. I wondered if Rupert was available sometime today."

"He has just lost his father, Your Lordship. I'm sure you'll understand the family is grieving and doesn't wish to be disturbed."

"As our parents were close friends, I wanted to pay my

respects in person." He paused. When a response wasn't forthcoming, he continued, "And it would be useful to chat about the waste incinerator project. The Borderers Guild is against it, but perhaps we don't fully appreciate the project's true benefits."

"One moment, Your Lordship."

The line crackled before clearing suddenly.

"There's a ten-minute gap in Mr Rinde's schedule at three-twenty this afternoon."

"Wonderful."

The line dropped. Aldermaston checked his watch. He had just enough time to see Stella before Abigail's NAF chair-selection process. He sighed. Why did that sound like a half-hearted furniture-buying spree rather than a democratic procedure?

In Mortiforde A&E, Kitty Catchpole stepped out of the curtained cubicle and bumped into Felicity hovering outside. "No good." She pulled a pen from her blue farming overall chest pocket and crossed off a name from the list. "Heart attack. Wife says he'll make a full recovery."

Kitty checked the row of hospital bays, then pointed with her pen. "I'll take bay five and you take bay two."

The knot in Felicity's stomach twisted. This was not becoming of a marchioness. Then again, as the Ladies' Legion president, they expected her to play her part in the endeavour. She nodded to Kitty's list. "Where did you get those names from?"

Kitty indicated a whiteboard on the wall. "Names and cause of admission. No point in talking to bays three and four. One's a broken leg, the other has a deep laceration to their arm." She chewed her pen briefly. "Once had a calf with a lacerated hind leg. Died of septicaemia. I'll question mark bay four."

Felicity swallowed. "Who's in bay two?"

Kitty checked her list. "Mr Podmore. One hundred and two. Kidney failure, heart failure, and liver failure. Erratic breathing." She shook her head. "Wouldn't let one of my animals suffer like that. Bay five won't be of any use, but it's too good an opportunity to miss."

"Pardon?"

Kitty grinned. "It's a lad from the Young Farmers' Club. Seems the gear stick of his Massey Ferguson broke off and somehow ended up where the sun doesn't shine. I'll offer to bury his reputation in the meadows for him." She winked. "Good luck with Mr Podmore. Remember, we need him in the ground as soon as possible."

Felicity took a deep breath and stepped across to the second bay. Her hand hesitated, then pulled the curtain aside. "Mrs Podmore, I wonder if I might have a word."

Daniel squashed his ear against Basildon's apartment door. Three times he'd knocked loudly, and there was no sound of movement inside. It still felt like snooping, even though he had Aldermaston's permission. The key slid into the lock. He twisted the handle and stepped inside.

"Basildon?"

Silence.

Oil paintings lined both walls of Basildon's apartment hallway, including a Stubbs and a couple of Turners. Daniel's shoes squeaked against the tiled floor. The first door on the right was ajar. He glimpsed Basildon's four-poster bed.

A separate bathroom was opposite. A single toothbrush stood in a glass jar on a shelf above the sink, alongside a half-squeezed tube of toothpaste. Fresh white Egyptian cotton towels were neatly stacked on a shelf above the radiator, and the bath mat was slung over the heated towel rail.

In Basildon's kitchen, the breakfast bar was spotless, with two metal stools slipped neatly underneath. The oven gleamed, and the sink was empty.

Basildon's study was an airy room with sash windows overlooking Tugford Hall's front drive. A twin-pedestal, green leather-topped desk, strewn with paperwork, a green-shaded banker's lamp, and an Apple iMac computer dominated the room. Knowing Basildon, the iMac would be biometrically protected.

He flicked through some of the desk's paperwork. Bank statements, the insurance renewal for his car, and reams and reams of website article printouts for spy gadgets.

Daniel rubbed the back of his neck. Not knowing what he was looking for was frustrating.

He returned to Basildon's bedroom. The four-poster bed commanded the room, while two yellow armchairs and a wooden coffee table occupied the large bay window. Built-in wooden wardrobes with sliding doors lined the wall opposite the bed.

Daniel opened each in turn, revealing shelving units housing hanging space for Savile Row trousers, shirts, and jackets. One held two Samsonite wheeled suitcases and two Barbour leather holdalls. If Basildon was away, he was travelling light.

Daniel scanned the room again. He spotted a pile of stacked paperbacks on Basildon's bedside table and traced the titles with his finger: *My Silent War* by Kim Philby, *Code Name: Lise* by Larry Loftis, and John le Carré's *The Spy Who Came in from the Cold*.

His finger stopped. Sandwiched between *Casino Royale* and *The Ipcress File* was Leo Tolstoy's *War and Peace*. Daniel vaguely remembered studying it at school. Wasn't that the one where Pierre Bezukhov is the illegitimate son of a count?

Daniel slid the paperback from the pile and flicked through it. A folded sheet of paper dropped to the floor. He unfurled the document: a newspaper cutting from *The Powys Gazette*, dated over two decades ago. A photo illustrated a baby in the arms of a nurse, beneath a large headline: *Baby Found at Household Waste Site*.

He scanned the article. Why had Basildon hidden this? His eyes widened. He spotted Basildon's handwriting in the margin. *The birth of BANG?* He'd also circled the baby's head.

Daniel flattened the sheet as best he could, took a photo with his phone, and then returned it to the book.

His heart pounded. Was this abandoned baby Basildon's love child?

CHAPTER FIVE

"Take a seat, Lord Mortiforde." Stella Osgathorpe pointed to a chair.

Aldermaston's hands fell naturally onto the wooden, hand-turned curves of each arm, worn from decades of clasping. Stella's mahogany pedestal desk groaned under piles of historic documents, each weighed down with a cannonball or medieval axe head.

Her computer monitor displayed the Historic Borders Agency logo: the letter H in the shape of two circular towers separated by a drawbridge. Through the window behind her, Aldermaston spied the grounds of Mortiforde Castle's impressive outer bailey, with its stone, thirty-foot-tall curtain wall in the background.

Stella finished scribbling some notes. "Thank you for coming at such short notice, Your Lordship. Considering this morning's waste incinerator news, I thought your family's involvement needed putting into a little more historical perspective."

Aldermaston's mouth went dry.

Stella leaned forward. "The council's announcement this morning is deeply disturbing."

"I agree."

"It's further exacerbated by Sir Hugo's death. There's a significant risk Rupert Rinde will inherit the meadows, and with the council funding in place, it seems noxious fumes will soon billow from a chimney just over there, within months." She pointed towards the window.

Aldermaston shifted in the chair. "We don't know Rupert will inherit."

"We don't know he *won't*, either," Stella continued. "The risk to Mortiforde Meadows is catastrophic. And your father is partly responsible."

Aldermaston frowned. "My father?"

Stella unfurled a Land Registry map, with Mortiforde Meadows outlined in red, on the desk between them. She pointed at the meadows with her fountain pen. "The Seventh Marquess once owned this land."

Aldermaston's forehead furrowed further. "I wasn't aware—"

"It was thirty-five years ago." Stella slipped another piece of paper on top of the map. "He needed to raise some cash to re-roof Tugford Hall."

Aldermaston slumped back in the chair. He vaguely remembered scaffolding shrouding Tugford Hall for several months while they carried out the work. He was about ten years old and at boarding school then.

"I never realised the meadows were part of the estate." He pointed to the surrounding land. "We've never owned any of this, so I can see why my father would sell off an isolated pocket of land." He stared at Stella. "Are you accusing my father of stitching us up now, based upon a piece of land he sold over three decades ago?"

Stella stared back. "Selling to Sir Hugo wasn't the original deal." She slipped another piece of paper onto the desk and tapped it.

Aldermaston scanned the document. *Proposal to make Mortiforde Meadows inalienable.* Inalienable? *Proposed sale of Mortiforde Meadows to the Historic Borders Agency.* He peered over the top of the paper. "Why do you have this when Sir Hugo is … was the legal owner?" He scrutinised the document again. "What does inalienable mean?"

"Greed, Your Lordship. That's what it amounts to."

Aldermaston slipped a finger between his shirt collar and his neck. "What exactly are you accusing my father of, Stella?"

She took the document from Aldermaston's hands. "Your father needed to sell the meadows to raise some cash to re-roof Tugford Hall. He approached us because he appreciated that, under the Historic Borders Agency's ownership, the meadows would further protect the castle's surrounding environment. And we agreed to pay his price."

Aldermaston chewed his bottom lip.

"But then, Sir Hugo came along and offered your father more money, making this document useless."

Aldermaston stood. "Look, Stella, I understand why you're upset about the current threat to the meadows. I am too, and we'll do everything we can to stop this from going ahead. But you can't blame my father for taking up a higher offer. That's business."

"What about this document, Your Lordship?" Stella waved it in the air. "Your father agreed to sell the meadows to us because he understood the power of *this*." She stared at him. "This would have designated the meadows inalienable. His greed snatched that away from us and has, ultimately, left Mortiforde in the situation we are now."

Aldermaston sighed. "What's an inalienable designation?"

Stella fell back into her chair and twiddled her thumbs. "It prevents land from being sold, mortgaged, or even compulsorily purchased. The Historic Borders Agency is one of the few organisations in the country that can declare our land inalienable. Your father understood that. Selling the meadows to us would have protected them *forever*. Nobody could even think about putting a waste incinerator on inalienable land, let alone go into partnership with the council to put one there."

She folded the map and handed it to him. "*That's* why your father is responsible for this mess. Greed. Plain and simple. He didn't need to sell to Sir Hugo. The agency's deal was enough to cover Tugford Hall's re-roofing costs. So I'm afraid, Your Lordship, you owe the people of Mortiforde."

He shuffled on his feet. "Owe them?"

"For your father's mistake. You need to right your father's wrong. Otherwise—"

Otherwise? Aldermaston stepped closer to her desk. "Stella, we've been friends for years. Is this some sort of threat?"

She shook her head. "What with?" She pointed to the map in Aldermaston's hand. "It's all in the public domain. Anyone could find these documents if they knew what they were looking for." She gazed at the meadows out of the window behind her. "But not everyone knows where to look. I wonder if Rochelle Rimmerroad at *The Chronicle* knows. I'm sure, given the meadows' current topicality, a headline about how the Seventh Marquess's greed shafted the town would make fascinating reading, don't you think?"

Aldermaston gripped the map tightly and offered a feeble smile. "Leave it with me, Stella. I'll see what I can do."

~

"Rosemary Sedgewicke, pleased to meet you." She offered her hand to each of the three Socially Liberal Conservative Party's selection panel members, then sat on the single chair opposite them. She gazed around the Buttermarket's first-floor community meeting room. The table between them swallowed most of the space, and the nineteenth-century single-glazed, diamond-leaded windows did little to stop November's drafts.

"Thank you for coming, Mrs Sedgewicke," Tom Burthson, the panel's chairman, began. "We intended to postpone this interview out of respect for Sir Hugo, but Rupert Rinde reminded us of our urgent need for a successor."

"Actually, it's Ms, but please, call me Rosemary." She smiled at the white-haired chair, whose beard still contained the detritus of this morning's breakfast cereal.

The woman on Tom's right burst into tears. She grabbed a handkerchief from her magnolia cardigan sleeve cuff and covered her face with it as she sobbed. Tom placed a comforting hand on her back.

"Our secretary, Jessica, remains quite traumatised. I'll be honest with you, Rosemary. Sir Hugo was our preferred candidate." He turned to the black-and-grey pin-striped suited gentleman to his left, whose hair matched that of his suit and whose vintage glasses magnified his eyes so much the bloodshot veins appeared to replicate the London Underground map. "And this is Cyril Clinken, our Deputy Chairman."

Rosemary nodded in acknowledgment.

Tom Burthson pulled a dog-eared sheet of paper from his thick brown corduroy jacket and flattened it on the table with the palm of his hand. "We have a set list of questions, but my co-panel members may ask supplementary questions depending on your answers. Is that okay?"

Rosemary nodded. Was that one of the set questions?

"Excellent. First, a bit of housekeeping," Tom began. "Running for Parliament takes financial resources. We will assist with campaign costs. However, elected candidates must secure most of their campaign funds and sufficient resources to cover the first three months of administrative office costs should they win the seat. You must initially cover these costs, although you can claim reimbursement later. We recommend a cushion of at least one hundred thousand pounds. Will that be a problem?"

Rosemary shook her head. "I'm currently selling a second property, but I have a guarantor bankrolling me until that sale has gone through."

Tom nodded as he scribbled down a note. "Perfect. Which brings us to our most important question. Why are you the right person to be the Socially Liberal Conservative Party's next Westminster candidate?"

Rosemary interlocked her fingers. A tingle of excitement coursed through her. This was it. Her Westminster dream was within reach. "Because I can win the Mortiforde seat for this party at the next election."

Jessica Wallows wiped her nose with her handkerchief. "We're hardly going to appoint someone who claims they'll lose, are we? *How* will you win this seat?"

"I can get this ridiculous waste incinerator project stopped, just like that." She snapped her fingers.

All three panel members looked at each other and then leaned forward.

"Go on." Cyril's eyes doubled in size again.

"The council is half a million pounds short."

Tom scratched his beard. Two cornflakes and some breadcrumbs dropped onto the table. "But this morning's radio announcement confirmed the council *has* the money."

Rosemary beamed. "I'm the Director of Finance at Borderlandshire District Council, and I can tell you categorically, when I left work yesterday evening, the waste incinerator project was still half a million pounds short. I can prove it. Select me as the next Socially Liberal Conservative Party candidate, and I will stop the waste incinerator project and save the meadows."

Jessica dabbed the tears from her face again. "Grenville's tragic death means we must have a by-election within five weeks. Can you stop it before then?"

Rosemary leaned back in her chair. "I can get this matter resolved by Bonfire Night."

Cyril's eyes widened beyond his glasses frames. "That's Friday!"

Rosemary smiled. "Select me as your candidate, and I'll print off the figures from the council's financial system that prove the shortfall. I can even instruct the council's Financial Scrutiny Committee to double-check the data. They'll soon confirm the Chief Executive's announcement is premature."

Jessica scowled. "So *your* actions to save the meadows depend upon *our* decision to appoint you as the Socially Liberal Conservative Party's candidate? Seems self-centred to me." Her chest swelled as she fought back another wave of emotion. "Grenville Gastrell would never put himself before the community like that. Nor would Sir Hugo!" Another surge of tearful sobs washed her face as her now-sodden handkerchief attempted to mop them up.

Tom Burthson whispered in Cyril's ear, then turned and whispered in Jessica's. Moments later, he stood.

"Ms Sedgewicke. We're not used to self-centred motives in the Socially Liberal Conservative Party."

Rosemary's stomach writhed, spasmed, and knotted. Her Westminster dreams were being fed into the waste incinerator and disappearing up a smokeless chimney. She'd blown it.

She was about to apologise profusely when Tom Burthson extended a hand across the table.

"But if that delivers the greater good, then we'd be mad to turn you down. Congratulations! You are officially the Socially Liberal Conservative Party candidate in the upcoming Mortiforde by-election. Get the waste incinerator stopped by

Bonfire Night, and the people of Mortiforde are bound to vote for you as our next Member of Parliament."

She grabbed Tom Burthson's hand and shook it so hard two more cornflakes fell from his beard. "You won't regret your decision."

~

In the council chamber, Abigail peered down at the councillor sitting on a lonely red-cushioned chair. "Tell me, Councillor Taplinski, why would you be the best person to chair the Mortiforde Waste Incinerator Neighbourhood Area Forum?"

The dais on which Abigail and Aldermaston sat was three feet higher than the rest of the oak-panelled council chamber. Her preferred God-like position from here overruled Aldermaston's suggested less formal approach of sitting in chairs opposite the candidates.

"Because I'm fair, firm, and fun," Councillor Taplinski replied, winking at the *fun*.

His blue eyes sparkled. Or was it the way the fluorescent lighting caught his thin-framed metal glasses? Taplinski crossed his arms. His pearly-white teeth joined in the sparkle-fest. Even his receding white hair, beard, and moustache glistened.

Aldermaston cleared his throat. "That's good to hear, Councillor. Speaking of fairness, what steps would you take to ensure both sides of the argument received an equal hearing at the forum?"

Councillor Taplinski's focus remained on Abigail. "Timing. Both sides must have comparable time to air their views. But I'd silence idiots with spurious views. A forum is not a place for time-wasters."

Abigail scribbled some notes. "And what are your personal views of the waste incinerator project?"

The sixty-two-year-old councillor nodded. "Well-paid jobs,

a reliable income stream for Rinde Industries and the local authority, a huge economic boost to the town—" He threw his arms in the air. "What's to lose?"

Aldermaston thumbed toward the meadows. "What about the historic and scenically outstanding Mortiforde Meadows?"

Councillor Taplinski waved a dismissive hand. "This is Borderlandshire. We've plenty of beautiful English countryside around here. There are Mortiforde Woods, the Morte Valley, the Clee Hills, the Long Mynd, and the list goes on. We can afford to lose a couple of meadows."

Councillor Taplinski faced Aldermaston. "The local landfill site has five more years' capacity. Then what do we do? Destroy another bit of countryside to bury our next twenty years of rubbish under? Thinking long-term, Your Lordship, the waste incinerator actually saves the countryside."

Abigail scribbled more notes. "Fascinating perspective, Councillor." She turned to Aldermaston. "It's so refreshing having someone thinking long-term about the town's future, rather than harking back to the past. Any more questions, Your Lordship?"

Aldermaston smiled, hoping it didn't look like a sneer. "I've heard all I need to hear."

Abigail put her pen down. "Thank you, Councillor Taplinski. We've another candidate to interview, but I'll be in touch later today with our decision."

Councillor Taplinski rose, buttoned his light beige linen jacket across his navy blue shirt, then approached the dais. He slid a small business card across the table towards Abigail. "Please call me Stefan. And you can call me … anytime you like." He tapped the card and winked. "My personal mobile number. The waste incinerator isn't even built yet, and I am already. . ." His eyes narrowed. "Smouldering."

He strode towards the exit, then waved behind his head without turning. "Bye, Your Lordship."

Abigail slipped the business card into her trouser pocket. "That went exceedingly well. Ready for the next candidate?"

"Let's hope Councillor Prendeghast is having one of his more lucid days." Aldermaston crossed his fingers under the table.

Abigail grabbed a phone and dialled a four-digit extension. "Lisa, send Councillor Prendeghast in, please. What? It can't be *that* bad. Send him in anyway."

A foul aroma assaulted their nostrils as soon as the council chamber door swung open. A pink-haired nurse, young enough to be his great-great-granddaughter, wheeled in ninety-three-year-old Councillor Prendeghast. A saline drip hung from a pole attached to the back of the wheelchair. On the adjacent side, hanging beside the wheel, was a colostomy bag. The young nurse trundled Councillor Prendeghast towards the dais and applied the brakes. Then she patted the councillor's hand.

"Come along, Mr Prendeghast, wake up. Time for your meeting. Let's not keep these lovely people waiting."

Aldermaston's eyes watered. The overpowering stench devoured the room's fresh air. Abigail discreetly pinched her nose with her fingers and thumb.

"Mr Prendeghast, wake up," the young nurse continued. "It's your eleven-fifteen meeting. Wakey, wakey," she sang. "If you're a good boy, I'll give you a nice warm bed bath when we get back."

"Take him away!" snapped Abigail, desperately trying not to breathe in through her nose. "Councillor Prendeghast is clearly in no fit state to work."

"He'll be fine when he wakes," the nurse countered. "Don't let this equipment fool you. He's alert when he's awake." She stood upright and took two steps back, then swung her arm wide behind her back. Her hand whizzed through the air and slapped the councillor's face so hard his head flew ninety degrees right and his false teeth shot across the chamber floor.

Abigail stood. "What are you doing?"

The nurse placed her hands on her hips. "He came round much quicker last week."

Aldermaston approached the slouching councillor and placed two fingers against Prendeghast's neck. "You won't wake him," he said. "He's dead."

The nurse grabbed her head, her fingers disappearing into her pink hair. "No! This job's paying for my Greek holiday next summer."

Aldermaston threw open some windows and drew in a huge chestful of clean, sweet-smelling air.

Abigail grabbed the phone. "Lisa, call an ambulance. Councillor Prendeghast is dead. Tell them to hurry. The sooner we get him out of the building, the sooner we can fumigate the council chamber."

Aldermaston placed a comforting arm around the weeping young nurse.

She sniffed. "At least he died in the council chamber. He always felt at home here, even if he was asleep most of the time," she reminisced.

Aldermaston winced. "He's cold."

"Elderly people are always cold. He's been sleeping a lot, too."

"When was the last time he was awake?"

She counted some fingers on her left hand. "Saturday."

"Four days ago?"

The nurse nodded tearfully, then broke into a full flood. "It was difficult bending him into his wheelchair this morning." She paused, her face horrified. "He's been dead since Saturday, hasn't he?"

Abigail waved Stefan Taplinski's business card in the air. "I'll call Stefan."

For a split second, Aldermaston considered whether a dead

Councillor Prendeghast would make a better NAF chair than a live one.

A tremendous boom echoed from underneath the council chamber. The floor shuddered, and the oil paintings of previous town mayors shivered on the walls. Abigail grabbed a chair for support.

"What the blazes was that?"

Aldermaston feared the bowels of hell were opening, ready to accept Councillor Prendeghast. Instead, the colostomy bag fell from the councillor's wheelchair, hit the council chamber floor with a splat, and regurgitated its putrid contents all over the carpet.

Diya panicked. All she'd done was give it a little tug.

Rummaging around the council's barely above-freezing basement, she'd found the ornate Persian rug that once adorned the Chief Exec's office. It commemorated Queen Elizabeth II's coronation. No one knew its origin, but they deemed it the perfect size to cover an unidentifiable stain on the Chief Exec's office floor. When workers installed new flooring in the 1990s, they discarded the rug into the basement with the authority's other unwanted items.

It was the first thing Diya thought might raise a few pounds on an online auction site while driving back to the council offices. When she'd eventually found it, one corner was trapped underneath a filing cabinet. No matter how hard she'd tried, she couldn't release it from underneath the four-drawer unit.

Diya dropped to her knees and opened the bottom drawer. A cloud of dust broke free, invoking a frenzied sneezing fit. When that settled, she'd grabbed the thick paper files and heaved them out. That's when the perishing elastic bands snapped, releasing a tsunami of paper across the basement floor.

She repeated the exercise with the second drawer's contents. Their elastic bands were just as exhausted. A sea of faded documents surrounded her feet.

The filing cabinet now wobbled when Diya pushed against the top. She picked up the far end of the rug and pulled. Nothing. A few sheets of thin carbon paper slid off the rug. She caught a bead of sweat running down her temple with the back of her hand. What if she pushed against the top of the cabinet at the same time as pulling on the rug?

Diya turned around, stood astride the rug, and picked up the far corner. Then she leaned back against the cabinet's top two drawers. Her feet crumpled the paper on the floor as she sought a grip. Slowly, she rocked back and forth, gradually building momentum, magnifying the filing cabinet's wobble. When she sensed the cabinet rise a few millimetres off the floor, she tugged the rug.

It was only a little tug, but the tired sheets of paper underneath Diya's shoes lost their friction. Her feet flew up into the air, throwing her entire body weight against the filing cabinet. Despite her slight frame, momentum exaggerated its power. The filing cabinet lurched backwards. Diya slid to the floor, her fall cushioned by late twentieth-century paperwork.

The only cushion for the filing cabinet's fall was another cabinet a few feet behind. The metallic clang as the first hit the second echoed around the basement. Seconds later, a second clang resonated, then a third, a fourth, a fifth—

Diya watched a line of filing cabinets toppling like dominoes as the momentum gathered pace. Fourteen cabinets later, the final cabinet overbalanced. With nothing to catch its fall except the heavily worn municipal blue carpet, it crashed to the floor with a wall-shuddering boom that echoed around Diya's ears.

She froze. The final cabinet blocked the basement's only interior exit. Somebody was bound to investigate the noise. With the internal door now blocked, the only other way in was via the external loading doors through which Diya had discreetly entered.

There was no time to escape undetected. How would she explain what she was doing down here when, according to the council's centralised annual leave system, she was supposedly in India?

"Oh, Nani Nagma," she whispered. "What have I done?"

"Ambulance is on its way." Lisa dashed into the council chamber, covering her nose. "What's going on in the basement?"

Aldermaston spotted Abigail hanging out of a window for fresh air as she gave Stefan Taplinski his NAF news.

Lisa headed for a heavy curtain hanging in a dark corner of the room.

"Where are you going?" Aldermaston's fingers pinched his nose.

"The basement. Somebody could be hurt down there." Lisa pulled back the curtain, revealing a wooden door.

"I'm coming with you." The air had to be cleaner down there.

The door clanked shut behind them, trapping their echoing footsteps in the concrete stairwell.

"While we're alone," Lisa's hushed voice bounced off the breeze block walls. "I need to tell you something."

Aldermaston braced himself. "Go on."

"Diya Parmer." Lisa paused when they reached the half landing. "Head of Planning Finance, remember?"

He nodded.

"She's on annual leave this week and next. System says she's in India, visiting family."

"Can you talk to someone else?"

Lisa continued down the stairs. "That's not the problem. Sheila on reception spoke to Diya this morning, just before eight, and Diya said nothing about going to India today."

"Perhaps she just nipped in to turn on her email Out-of-Office message."

Lisa dismissed that notion. "The last time Diya went to see family in India, she told everyone for weeks beforehand. She's not mentioned this trip at all. When I checked her office, I found everything switched off and the blinds drawn. It *looks* like she's on annual leave."

Aldermaston shrugged. "So she is in India."

Lisa reached the basement door. "I'm not sure. The woman who knows exactly what's going on with the waste incinerator project funding suddenly disappears on the morning the news breaks that the council's funding is all in place. And why not tell Sheila she was flying off to another continent later this morning? Something's not right."

She swiped her pass on the security pad and twisted the door handle. It released and moved half an inch, then hit something. She pulled it closed, then tried again.

"Let me." Aldermaston shouldered the door. It didn't budge. "Ow!"

Lisa leaned closer to the small gap in the door. "Hello? Is there anybody there?"

Aldermaston was about to speak, but Lisa raised her finger to her lips.

"I heard something."

Aldermaston rubbed his shoulder. "Any other way in?"

"Rear entrance via the car park. The ground slopes at the back, so there's an external loading bay door."

~

An arriving email pinged on Peredur's work laptop. It could wait. More importantly, he needed someone he could trust for his planned four o'clock fun at Tugford Hall. He checked the time. Agent 62's lunchtime. He dialled the direct line.

"Neil Vallets, Planning Assistant, how can I help you?"

"Agent 62, this is your Commander."

A muffled rustling echoed in the earpiece. Peredur pictured Neil hiding behind his computer monitor for some privacy in the council's open-plan office.

"Go ahead, Commander," he whispered.

"Just checking the team will be at Tugford Hall at four o'clock, yes?"

"Yes, Commander. There'll be thirty of us."

"Perfect. I may be otherwise engaged. Could you deputise?"

"I finish at three. It will be an honour to stand in for you, Commander."

"Excellent!" said Peredur. "Speak later." He ended the call. One down. One more to make. But before that, there was the small matter of creating an irresistible offer the Marquess of Mortiforde couldn't refuse.

CHAPTER SIX

Aldermaston followed Lisa down a long tarmac slope at the council office's rear to the basement's huge metal external doors.

Lisa stopped mid-step. "Why's Diya's car parked there?" She hurried across to the blue bulbous bonnet partially visible from behind three vast circular waste bins.

"You said Diya was in India," Aldermaston called.

Lisa hurried back. "Exactly! Who leaves their car at work when they're on annual leave?"

Aldermaston pulled the basement door handle, grimacing as his shoulder twinged. Slowly, the door clanked open enough for them to slip through.

"Lights are on," Lisa commented. "Somebody's definitely been down here."

They saw the toppled filing cabinets, all balancing precariously on the final cabinet wedged up against the interior staircase door. "That explains the bang and why the door wouldn't budge." Aldermaston rubbed his shoulder.

Lisa wandered over to the first cabinet. "Hello? Is there anybody here?"

Aldermaston checked the narrow gaps between the toppled cabinets. "It could be a coincidence," he began. "Perhaps someone was down here recently, moved something and not put it back properly, then—" He moved back to the previous cabinet gap in time to see a face disappear behind the other side of the cabinet.

"I know there's someone there," he said. "Come out."

Lisa hurried over.

Aldermaston extended a hand through the cabinet gap.

Lisa bent down and peered through. "Diya?"

"Who else is with you?" called Diya.

"Lord Mortiforde." Lisa beckoned her out.

Nervously, Diya edged forward on her hands and knees and grabbed Aldermaston's hand to hoist herself upright. She looked around furtively, dusting herself down.

Aldermaston gestured to the doors. "Let's get you upstairs and make you a strong cup of tea."

"No!" Her head shook frantically. "Not upstairs."

Lisa's hand rested on Diya's shoulder. "What's wrong?"

Diya began convulsing. "I can't say."

Aldermaston slipped his phone back into his tweed jacket pocket. "Is this about the waste incinerator project?"

Horror washed across Diya's face. She wiped her eyes with a trembling hand.

Lisa took Diya's other hand. "The annual leave system says you're in India."

Diya's gaze flitted between them both.

Aldermaston checked over his shoulder. "Is someone here threatening you? Is that why you won't go upstairs?"

Diya glanced towards the open doorway, then back at them. Fear consumed her.

Lisa held up her security pass hanging on a lanyard around her neck. "I didn't need to swipe this to get in through those doors." She pointed to the rear entrance. "But you do to use that one over there." She turned to Diya. "You came in the back way." Her eyes narrowed. "Nobody knows you're here, do they?"

Diya shook her head.

Aldermaston stepped forward. "You know I'm not a council employee. We're the only people who know you're here. And Lisa won't say anything."

"You have my word, Diya. If someone from this authority is frightening a fellow female colleague, then I'll do anything to keep you safe."

Aldermaston gestured towards the doors again. "Tugford Hall. You'll be safe there."

Diya's eyes flitted between them again. Her breathing quickened. She clutched her chest as she fought to inhale huge, deep breaths. Suddenly, her eyes rolled backwards, and she collapsed to the floor.

"Diya!" Lisa checked for a pulse. "She's fainted."

Aldermaston grabbed an office chair with two missing wheels and dragged it closer. "Elevate her legs. You stay here with her. I'll bring my car round. The sooner we get her out of here, the better."

Peredur admired his handiwork on the laptop screen. *Borderlandshire Defence* screamed the advertising flyer along with a photo of two armed guards struggling to control a couple of snarling Alsatians. *Battle-tested security with mission-driven solutions. Call 07700 900461 NOW!*

He'd print it later and hand-deliver it to Tugford Hall after meeting Agent 117 at the stone barn this afternoon. Now, for the second call. Peredur dialled a number and listened for the heavy Welsh accent.

"Welsh Military Surplus Supplies, 'ow can I help?"

"Dewi, how are you?"

"Perry, mate! Three calls in two weeks. Yer must be up ta nah good. Wot d'ya need now?"

Peredur grinned. Dewi knew him well. "Have you still got that MBT used by the Welsh World War Two re-enactment group?"

"How long d'ya need it for? They got it booked again in a fortnight, y'see."

Peredur beamed. "You'll have it back after the weekend."

"Looks like we 'ave a deal." Dewi huffed and puffed a bit. "I'm assuming you want mates' rates again? Lucky you were born on the right side of the border. My English mates' rates are pricier than my Welsh mates' rates."

Peredur's grin drooped. Memories of his Welsh foster-care childhood flooded back. The world assumed he was Welsh. Only he knew better. And his mother.

"Actually, mate, I'm not paying."

There was a sharp intake of breath. "I canna do a freebie, Perry. Not an MBT. I knows ya hired the four Bedford QLT personnel carriers, the machine-gun-mounted jeep, and a platoon's worth of battle rifles and gunpowder, but ... an MBT? That's big, that's—"

"Dewi," Peredur interrupted. "You can charge whatever. *I'm* not paying. Someone else is. You'll get a phone call from Tugford Hall this evening."

"Lord Mortiforde's place?"

"Yes, I'll get someone to drop off a burner phone to you. When it rings, answer as *Borderlandshire Defence*. They'll need some security for their front gates."

Dewi whistled. "Oh, I gets ya. And ya want me to deliver the MBT to their front gates?"

"Got it in one. Recommend the MBT, but don't tell them what an MBT is. They'll love the surprise."

"Yeah, but they'll see it when I turn up with—" Dewi sighed. "Oh. Your preferred two-hour delivery time slot is under the cover of darkness, isn't it?"

Peredur beamed. "Dewi, this is why we're mates. You know how I operate. How about between four and six tomorrow morning?"

"One condition."

"Name it."

"A full Welsh cooked breakfast at ya place after."

"Dewi, I'm out the door now to get the ingredients."

Peredur cut the call. Now he needed to send Radio Borderlandshire a Tugford Hall tip-off.

Rosemary skipped down the Buttermarket stairs into the narrow alleyway lined with small independent shops. The cheese shop's aroma of dairy delights assaulted her nostrils, followed by a saltiness from the neighbouring fishmongers as she dashed towards the Market Square.

The market was in full swing on this gloomy November morning. Rosemary ignored the regimented rows of blue-and-white striped awninged stalls and turned into the Market Square car park. Frequently touted as having the best view in Borderlandshire, even on a grey day like today, its elevated position overlooking the gently rolling hills and undeveloped Morte Valley gave it another perk: a semi-reliable mobile phone signal. She called Rupert.

"You get it?"

"As you said, they had no other option."

His fingers tapped away at a computer keyboard. "What questions did they ask?"

Rosemary stuck a finger in her other ear to cut out the

wind. "The personal money one. Told them I was selling a property but had a guarantor. Didn't mention that was you."

"Excellent. Now all you have to do is win the by-election," he chuckled. "Won't be long before the Palace of Westminster cottons on to your European Parliament experience. They'd be idiots not to put you on some committee looking at boosting European trade. Could make some useful business contacts then."

"Well, thank heavens I salvaged my European Parliament career after you tried sabotaging it!" She grimaced. "Rupert, I'm sorry, I—"

"No, you're right." His joviality disappeared. "I often wonder what might have been. Marriage? Family?" He sighed. "I lost several business deals by not having you by my side. You always were good for my business."

Rosemary clamped her phone tighter against her ear. Trust him to remember the lost business deals.

"You still there?" the business voice clipped.

"Lost you briefly," she lied. "You know what the signal's like round here."

"Have dinner with me tonight. Let's celebrate our little plan."

"That would be lovely," she said, her gaze stretching far into Borderlandshire's rolling hills as her mind still reeled from his use of the word *family*.

He chuckled.

Rosemary frowned. "What's funny?"

"I'd love to see Abigail's face when you tell her you're resigning to fight a by-election that will campaign against her flagship incinerator policy. Good luck with that." He hung up.

~

Aldermaston eased the Jaguar onto the A492 Mortiforde bypass. He watched Lisa driving Diya's Morris Minor in his rear-view mirror.

Diya stared out of the Jaguar's passenger window. "I've never had a panic attack before."

"Stress," Aldermaston suggested. "The waste incinerator is big news."

"I *didn't* send that email to Abigail!" Diya snapped. "You must believe me."

He saw fear in her eyes. "Sir Hugo's sudden death suggests this may be orchestrated."

"You mean he was—"

He nodded. Hiding it from her would be counterproductive. He needed her to trust him. "It happened after last night's Ladies' Legion meeting."

Diya gasped. "I was there! The killer could have been there, too!" She grabbed Aldermaston's arm. "Am I in danger?"

He paused, realising she needed reassurance. He shook his head. "There's nothing to be gained from harming you. But Sir Hugo's death definitely kick-started this whole mess."

"I shall die of shame if that man places any inappropriate images on my computer." She glanced out the window again. "The shame will kill Nani Nagma, too." A tear trickled down her cheek. "She's all I have left."

Aldermaston indicated left and pulled off the bypass. "It won't come to that."

"No, you don't understand!" Diya clutched her chest. "It would kill my Nani. I have *no* choice."

Aldermaston sensed her staring at him while he focused on the winding road. "No choice about what?"

"Finding the shortfall. That's why I was in the basement. I was looking for things to sell. Abigail has an email from me saying the project is fully funded, and it isn't. My name is on that email. I'm responsible."

Aldermaston wagged a finger. "This isn't your fault. We'll sort this."

"When?"

He shrugged. "Abigail is holding a public meeting on Friday evening."

"I have until Friday evening, then," she concluded.

Aldermaston turned to her. "What?"

A pulsating beep warned him he'd crossed the road's central white line.

"Look out!" screamed Diya.

Aldermaston swerved to avoid an oncoming tractor. "Sorry." He regained his composure. "You have until Friday evening to do what?"

"Raise half a million pounds," she said calmly.

"That's two and a half days."

Diya's face softened. "You'll help me, won't you, Lord Mortiforde? My family honour is at stake. You, of all people, must understand that."

Yes, he knew all about *that*. His mother's affair, the bombshell that Basildon was his half-brother. She'd brought disgrace upon the family name, causing a sensation among the local community and the wider aristocracy at the time of his parents' death. So he'd stepped up, because that's what the British aristocracy and society expected. Family honour had driven his actions so far. But was he trying too hard to be the Eighth Marquess? Then there was Stella's news. Not only had his mother let down the town, but so, too, had his father, it seemed. Why had his father sold the meadows to Sir Hugo?

"Lord Mortiforde?" Diya interrupted. "Will you help me?"

Aldermaston turned in through Tugford Hall's main gates and proceeded along the gravel drive towards his ancestral home. The three-storey sandstone building with the porticoed entrance and curved steps to the front door dominated the windscreen. This was home because of family honour and duty.

He nodded. "Yes, Diya. I'll help you."

"Enter!" Abigail looked up from her computer to see Rosemary Sedgewicke enter her office.

Her Director of Finance smiled nervously. "Thank you for seeing me at such short notice, Abigail."

Abigail pointed to the chrome-framed chair opposite. "I'm just sorting out Friday evening's Neighbourhood Area Forum. There'll be plenty of opposition, but now we have the funding sorted, it's time we got started."

Rosemary sat down in the chair. "Announcing this on the radio before informing staff is a little unconventional."

"At the London Borough of Thameside, I found that taking swift, decisive action gets things done." Abigail leaned back, rested her elbows on the chair arms, and formed a steeple with her hands. "The project has councillor approval. We were just waiting on the money."

Rosemary picked her fingernails. "Who told you about the changed funding position? As Director of Finance, I expected to tell you."

Abigail rested her chin on her hands. "We have a diligent Head of Planning Finance who notified me first thing this morning."

Rosemary shuffled in her chair. "Diya told you?"

"Something about prudent savings from other projects."

"News to me. I'll go through the numbers with her later."

"You'll have to wait until she's back."

"Back?"

Abigail tapped at her keyboard and rotated her screen. "Annual leave. She's in India for the next two weeks."

Rosemary scrutinised the screen. "I've not authorised any annual leave."

Abigail stared at Rosemary. "Diya seems a conscientious member of staff who gets things up straight before going away. We could do with more like her. And. . ." She paused. "Why are you here if it isn't about the waste incinerator project?"

Rosemary slipped her hand into her mustard corduroy jacket, retrieved a folded sheet of paper, and handed it to the Chief Executive. "My resignation." Rosemary beamed. "The Socially Liberal Conservative Party has selected me as its candidate in the upcoming by-election."

Abigail dropped the letter onto her desk. "Wasn't Sir Hugo a potential candidate? I'm surprised they interviewed you, considering his death."

"They liked my pitch."

"Which was?"

Rosemary crimsoned. "I don't need to go into my policies right now—"

"I'd love to hear what the Socially Liberal Conservative Party is desperate for you to do," Abigail interrupted.

Rosemary pulled her jacket sleeve hems taut. "I'm campaigning *against* the waste incinerator."

The Chief Exec crossed her arms. "On what grounds?"

"I don't think Diya's figures are correct. I'll get the authority's scrutiny committee to check, but where she's found half a million pounds within the last twenty-four hours, I really don't know."

Abigail scowled, then grabbed her phone and dialled an extension. "Stacey, could you pop into my office, please?" She returned the phone to its cradle.

Rosemary shuffled awkwardly. "Abigail, this is politics. It's not personal—"

Abigail's office door swung open. Stacey stepped inside, closed the door, and leaned against it. Her black, short-sleeved shirt revealed heavily tattooed lower arms. She'd tied her long brown hair into a ponytail, and hanging from her black trouser belt were a mobile phone, a walkie-talkie, and what appeared to be a taser.

Abigail gestured to Rosemary. "Stacey, could you escort Ms Sedgewicke off the premises, please?"

"What?" Rosemary stood. "You can't! I'm contracted to work my notice and—"

Abigail stood, placing her hands on her hips. "I'm putting you on gardening leave with immediate effect. Allowing you to return to your desk could compromise council data." She held out her hand. "Security pass, now!"

"But I promised the party I had evidence of the shortfall—"

"Not my problem," Abigail snapped. "Pass. Now!" She clicked her fingers.

Rosemary slipped the lanyard over her neck.

Abigail snatched it from her. "Stacey, she's all yours."

Stacey grabbed Rosemary's upper arm. "This way, please, Ms Sedgewicke. Please don't speak to anyone until you're off the premises."

Rosemary checked over her shoulder. "Abigail, is this really necessary?"

"It was extremely naïve of you to think you could campaign against this authority while remaining in post with full access to council systems."

The security guard dragged Rosemary out of the office and slammed the door behind her.

Abigail threw Rosemary's pass into a desk drawer. Why was everything such bloody hard work out here in the rural hinterland?

~

Aldermaston opened his office door and pointed along the Hall's long corridor. "Turn left at the end, and it's the first on the right."

Diya smiled. "Thank you, Your Lordship." She closed the office door behind her.

"While Diya's powdering her nose," he said, returning to his captain's chair, "I want to clarify that nobody must know she's here."

Daniel glanced towards the office door. "*Is* she in danger?"

Lisa shrugged. "She's the one who knows the true financial situation. If somebody wanted her dead, they'd have done it by now, wouldn't they?"

"Putting her on two weeks' leave," Aldermaston surmised, "means if her life is at risk, nobody will miss her until she's due back at work. It's safer if nobody knows Diya is here. *Nobody.*"

Daniel chuckled. "I'm sure you've got a spare room here."

Aldermaston's nose wrinkled. "I trust Cartwright implicitly, but he knows everything that goes on in this building. The more people who know, the bigger the risk. I'll find her somewhere on the estate."

Diya slipped back into the office and took a seat between Lisa and Daniel.

Aldermaston locked the office door. "From now on, this remains locked at all times, got that?"

Three heads nodded in unison.

He returned to his chair. "Diya, does anyone else have access to your computer? Could anyone else have sent that email to Abigail?"

"I thought someone had hacked my computer," she began. "Every time I called Abigail, someone from IT answered."

"Easily done," Lisa interjected. "Everything is

computerised. We moved offices a couple of months ago, and IT redirected our phone extensions electronically."

"And," Diya continued, "the email to Abigail appeared in my Sent box ten minutes before I arrived at the office this morning."

Aldermaston jotted down some notes. "Lisa, can you chat to someone in IT? Find out how easy it is for anyone to hack into a council email account."

Lisa nodded, then turned to Diya. "Why were you in the basement earlier?"

"Looking for things to sell via an online auction."

Lisa chuckled. "Have you seen the rubbish kept in the basement? It's only there because nobody has the guts to throw it away."

Daniel bashed at his keyboard. "People sell anything on these auction sites. Look." He twisted his computer monitor. "They even sell bits of old rope on there."

Aldermaston tutted. "It'll take a lot of rope to raise half a million." He turned to Diya. "Is this legal?"

"Oh, yes!" Diya became more animated. "Several authorities use online auctions. They've sold bus shelters, rubbish bins, street furniture and—" She gasped. "We left the rug behind!"

"Rug?"

"It was caught under a filing cabinet, which I pulled and—"

"That's why we found the mess," Aldermaston finished. He turned to Lisa. "Any chance you could get it?"

"Might as well rummage around for anything else while I'm down there," she suggested.

"Good idea." Aldermaston turned to Daniel. "Get anywhere in Basildon's apartment?"

"Doesn't look like he's been in his apartment for days." Daniel passed his smartphone across to Aldermaston.

"What's this?" Aldermaston zoomed in.

"I found it inside a book beside his bed. Is that Basildon's handwriting near the bottom?"

Aldermaston swiped downwards. "The birth of BANG, question mark," he read out. "Looks like his handwriting."

Daniel pointed to the image. "That newspaper cutting is a couple of decades old. It's about a baby abandoned at Knighton's Household Waste Site, whatever that is."

"It's what we used to call Household Waste and Recycling centres," Aldermaston explained, "before recycling was a thing." Aldermaston handed the phone back to Daniel. "Send me a copy, can you?"

Considering what was now happening, Basildon's escapades weren't the priority. He opened a metal wall cabinet behind his desk and perused the collection of neatly labelled, colour-coded keys.

"What are you looking for?" asked Lisa.

Aldermaston grabbed a set of keys. "Shepherd Cottage." He held the keys aloft. "Diya, it's only two rooms. But it's in the woods and only accessible by a stone track on the estate. It's a holiday let, but it's empty at this time of year. Nobody goes up there. You'll be perfectly safe."

"There's no internet or mobile phone signal at Shepherd Cottage," Daniel reminded him. "Diya can't run any online auctions there."

Aldermaston returned to his chair. "She can work in here during the day," he suggested. "Lisa, I'd better run you back to work." He pointed to Diya and Daniel. "You two set up the online auction account so we can start selling stuff as soon as possible."

He watched Diya slip into Daniel's chair and interrogate the computer. Her tenacity was admirable. She had two and a half days to raise half a million pounds. It just showed how desperate she was to protect her family name.

∼

Gerald Lockmount grabbed his car keys and the emailed route directions. His secretary, Maureen, was pointing at some thatched properties in the Lockmount Estate Agency window to a newly retired couple from London.

"Just off for my two-thirty appointment. Won't be long, Maureen."

She acknowledged him as her hand guided her prospective clients towards a property with so many zeros in its guide price that it literally "Oooed" at them.

Gerald stepped out onto the pavement and grabbed the parking ticket wedged under his black BMW's wiper blades. He threw it onto the passenger seat, heaved himself into the driving seat, and checked the email instructions.

Use Tugford Hall's rear entrance, turn left onto the farm track, and follow for two miles. The property stands at the end of this track.

Gerald set off down Watling Street, lined with its elegant three-storey Georgian properties. As he turned a corner, his BMW's automatic crash detection system spotted Margaret Hillbrow lying in the road. It applied the brakes so hard that it nearly gave him whiplash. Behind her, a row of Ladies' Legion members stood holding placards demanding *Save the Meadows*, *Waste Not, Want Not,* and *Ban the Incinerator*.

"What the—?" Gerald lowered his window. "Out of my way! Some of us have business to attend to!"

Heidi Yail stepped forward, clutching her *Fresh Air, Not Hot Air* placard, and thrust a pen and clipboard through his driver's window. "We're campaigning to save the meadows. Will you sign our petition?"

"Certainly not!" Gerald gestured to the placards surrounding his BMW's bonnet. "This is real economics, not home economics. Out of my way!"

As his BMW edged forward, the dashboard screen

displayed Margaret Hillbrow lying on her side, cushioned by three strategically placed hot water bottles, blocking the road. Audible beeps and flashing obstruction warnings echoed around Gerald's car interior as frantic Ladies' Legion protesters fervently banged his bonnet, demanding he stop moving.

Gerald placed both hands on the steering wheel and looked straight ahead. His tyres edged closer to the horizontal Margaret Hillbrow, whose hair was turning whiter by the second.

Suddenly, the placards fell to the floor. Gerald watched a frightened Margaret sway back and forth, as the Ladies' Legion tug-of-warred with her, conflicted on which way to pull her out of harm's way.

Heidi Yail bellowed some instructions. The ladies on Gerald's left dropped Margaret's feet. Their action caught the group on the right by surprise, sending them toppling backwards. Margaret zipped out of the way in one swift movement, as a shock of white hair whizzed across Gerald's dashboard display.

The BMW's warning klaxons silenced themselves. Gerald floored his accelerator and sped towards the bypass, bursting two hot water bottles and leaving several disgruntled Ladies' Legion protesters mouthing obscenities at him.

Joining the bypass, his mind returned to the job at hand. This was the first time the Eighth Marquess had approached him to sell some property. He grinned. This could be the start of a profitable relationship.

His smile drooped as his BMW nipped along the single-track lane towards Tugford Hall's rear entrance. The wing mirrors smacked through the overgrowing foliage, collecting autumn's remaining berries and dead insect fragments. He'd have to factor an extra car wash into His Lordship's fee.

Gerald eased between the stone pillars marking the

Tugford Estate's rear boundary and crossed the cattle grid. Ahead, Tugford Hall's chimneys poked above the treeline. He turned left as instructed, onto a substantial stone track. This he followed for several minutes, his speed dropping as the track's surface deteriorated. This would need resurfacing if the Marquess was serious about making a sale.

The stone track became a compacted grassy route as he weaved deeper into the estate. It ended in a field bounded by a stone wall and, in the corner, what looked like a vast dilapidated stone barn.

Gerald clambered out of his car. Lord Mortiforde hadn't arrived yet. From his grey suit jacket pocket, he pulled out his smartphone and recorded a voice memo.

"A charming opportunity to purchase an airy, idyllically located, spacious, historic property with developmental potential."

He stared at the vast open hole in the barn's stone wall where wooden doors once hung. Several roof slates had slipped, ultimately plummeting to the ground below and smashing into shards.

"This well-ventilated. . ." he paused and slipped a compass from another suit pocket. The red needle settled within its housing. "East-facing property benefits from. . ." he checked over his shoulder. "A sheltering large wooded area and. . ."

A crack from deep within the dark forest caused him to stop.

"Lord Mortiforde?"

Gerald scanned his surroundings but saw nobody. He dismissed the interruption and stepped into the barn, marvelling at its sheer size.

"The vaulted ceiling offers huge potential for creating a spacious living area within the first floor level."

His eyes took in the hay bales piled high against the stone

walls and, as he panned round, he spotted Mortiforde Millie propped up against the stone wall in the opposite corner.

"Fancy seeing you here." Just as he stepped closer, another crack echoed behind him. He spun round, but before he could acknowledge his visitor, a huge black cloth swallowed his head.

Gerald gasped for breath as two leather-gloved hands wrapped themselves around his throat, squeezing tighter and tighter, until he blacked out.

CHAPTER SEVEN

Felicity's Range Rover crunched along Tugford Hall's drive and pulled alongside Aldermaston's Jaguar. She killed the engine and took a deep, calming breath. She was never going to do *that* again.

In A&E, Kitty's comments about Mr Podmore's failing organs were the failure, not his organs. Mr Podmore's only failure was his sense of humour. Someone had stepped on his ingrown toenail, and he'd lost all feeling in his foot. When Felicity had raised the topic of a green funeral, Mrs Podmore's comments were distinctly blue.

She grabbed her handbag and phone and remembered her promise to call Diya. The line rang briefly before an answering machine cut in. Of course. Diya's home number. She must be at work, which is why she hadn't attended this morning's meeting.

"Diya, it's Lady Mortiforde. Sorry you couldn't make this morning's urgent Legion meeting. I don't doubt you're busy at work, what with all this news about the waste incinerator. Obviously, the Legion is worried about our *Verdant Endings* project, so we'd be grateful for any light you can throw on the matter. Can you call when you get this? Thank you."

She jumped out of the car and strode towards the Hall's main entrance, but stopped mid-step. Was that Diya's blue Morris Minor beside Aldermaston's Jaguar?

"There you are, dear!"

Aldermaston and Lisa strode towards her. She pointed to the Morris Minor. "Is that Diya Parmer's car?"

Aldermaston's face flushed briefly as he looked at Lisa.

"It *looks* like Diya's car," Lisa began.

"It's not," Aldermaston snapped. "No, it's um—"

"Daniel has a visitor," Lisa interjected. "It's their car."

Felicity stared at it. There weren't many Morris Minor Travellers about these days. To have two in Mortiforde of the same colour was quite a coincidence.

Aldermaston slipped his arm through hers and encouraged her towards the Hall. "So, how's your morning been?"

Mrs Podmore's expression flashed through her memory again. "Awful. I've been trying to encourage people to consider green burials. What we really need is a dead body we can shove into the ground quickly. If we could show people what a green burial looks like, more people are bound to be interested."

Aldermaston stopped. "Haven't you heard? Councillor Prendeghast died this morning." He wrinkled his nose. "Actually, he probably died over the weekend, but we only found out today."

Felicity shrieked. "That's wonderful!" Guilt prodded her conscience. "I mean, how awful for his family."

Lisa chipped in. "He has no relatives. Said the council was his family."

Felicity clapped her hands excitedly. No family meant no one to organise his funeral. This was it! She marched back to her Range Rover. "I take it Earth, Wind, and Fire are looking after him?"

"Who else is there?" Aldermaston quipped.

A sense of excitement overwhelmed her. Had she found *Verdant Ending*'s first customer?

"Everything all right, dear?" Aldermaston called.

Felicity blipped the key fob as she turned towards him. "Couldn't be better," she beamed. "Councillor Prendeghast will go down in history." *He'll go down in the ground, too, if this pans out.*

~

Rosemary brushed her corduroy jacket sleeve where Stacey's fierce grip had flattened the material and most of Rosemary's bicep. She watched Stacey disappear effortlessly through the council's main revolving doors that many struggled to set in motion.

"Nnnngggggg!" she screamed, debating whether or not to use a rude hand gesture. She stopped herself in time, fearing someone hiding behind a hedge might capture it on their smartphone and share it on social media. Her eyes scanned the surrounding car park for any signs of Mortiforde's hoi polloi filming her undignified expulsion. Thankfully, all seemed quiet.

This wasn't part of the plan. She called Rupert.

"Problem?" he enquired.

Rosemary stormed across the car park. "Abigail has put me on gardening leave for the rest of my notice."

Rupert chuckled. "More time for campaigning, then."

"I won't have a campaign if I can't print off the evidence from the council's computer system showing the waste incinerator project shortfall."

"Ah."

Rosemary waved her free hand in the air. "Exactly! The entire campaign is dead and buried before—" She froze.

"Rupert, I'm so sorry. You're still mourning the loss of your father and—"

He tutted. "You should have printed off the figures before seeing Abigail. Can't you ring someone on the Financial Scrutiny Committee?"

"Abigail will have warned them. I'm persona non grata now."

"There must be other ways you can prove the shortfall."

Rosemary shook her head. "The printouts are the hard evidence."

"What about an external organisation, a third party completely unconnected with the council, to show the Mortiforde muppets there's a discrepancy?"

Rosemary froze. He was right. And she knew exactly who to call. "Rupert, you're a star!"

She hung up and searched online for the number she needed, then made a second call. Rosemary paced up and down the council car park, waiting for it to connect.

"National Audit Office. How may I help you?"

"I'd like to report a fraud at Borderlandshire District Council."

"That was close." Aldermaston watched Felicity's Range Rover kick up a tsunami of gravel as she sped towards Mortiforde's undertakers. He pointed to Diya's car. "We need to move this."

"Where?" Lisa slipped the keys from her jacket pocket.

Aldermaston rubbed his chin. "Diya can drive it to Shepherd Cottage later. Nobody will see it there."

"You'd better take these." Lisa handed him Diya's car keys as they slipped into the Jaguar's seats. "While it's just us, can I ask a question?" She put on her seat belt.

"Go on."

"Why *are* we helping Diya raise the missing cash?"

Aldermaston started the engine. "She made me promise. She fears the family consequences, which I understand. I doubt she'll raise the cash in time, but if nothing else, it'll keep her occupied."

"Even so," Lisa continued. "By helping Diya raise the shortfall, we're working to make the waste incinerator a viable project. The Borderers Guild voted against it at last night's meeting, remember?" She wagged a finger at him. "You're trying to keep everyone happy again, aren't you?"

Aldermaston reversed the car. "Sometimes I wish I were Basildon and could disappear off the face of the Earth."

Lisa smiled. "And what if Felicity finds out you're helping to raise the cash that could lead to the destruction of the meadows?"

Aldermaston selected first gear. "In that case, we'd better make sure she doesn't."

Peredur released his grip of Basildon's waist and climbed off the quad bike. A November breeze swirled through the surrounding trees, their branches seemingly swaying in deference to his arrival. He marvelled at the surroundings. Behind the barn was open countryside. The rolling hills stretched far into Wales, although at nearly three o'clock, the day's light was fading. Behind him, a thick deciduous forest sheltered the barn from chilly easterly winds. Enormous trunks, thicker than Tugford Hall's porticoed column entrance, supported branches for over a century in the growing.

Peering into the forest's darkness, he glimpsed a smaller stone building among the trees, barcoded by tree trunks. He tapped Basildon's shoulder. "What's that, Agent 117?"

"Shepherd Cottage, old bean. Tourist accommodation. Empty at this time of year. This way, Commander."

Peredur's fist clenched. Seasonal tourist accommodation only exacerbated housing shortages for locals. And knowing many were empty for several months of the year made him even angrier.

"Commander?" Basildon stood in the vast open doorway of the stone barn and extended an inviting arm.

Peredur's thick-soled assault boots crushed the woodland debris littering the ground as he marched towards the barn's entrance. Mortiforde Millie sat motionless on the hay bales to his right, but their other visitor was nowhere to be seen.

"Where's our guest, Agent 117?"

Basildon clambered onto a platform of rectangular hay bales, grabbed one, and heaved it to one side. Then he bent down into the exposed cavity and dragged out the bound estate agent. Gerald's ankles were trussed in chains, his wrists bound behind his back, and a black hood covered his face. Basildon positioned him on the edge of a bale with his feet dangling over the side, facing the Commander. He whipped off the hood. Rope gagged Gerald's mouth.

The estate agent's eyes blinked as they accustomed themselves to the remaining daylight. He tried twisting to see who was behind him.

Peredur saluted. "Agent 117, you are now dismissed."

Basildon adjusted his black balaclava and saluted. "Yes, sir!" He turned and marched towards the barn entrance when—

Peredur screamed. "Something's run up my leg!" He pranced on the spot, lifting his knees high, while brushing his combat trousers aggressively. "Get it off me, Agent 117!"

Basildon strode towards him, knelt, and pulled off his gloves. He huffed on his hands while focusing on the haphazard movements inside Peredur's trousers, near his groin.

Hands poised, Basildon yanked Peredur's combat trousers down to his knees, then thrust his bare hands into the now-saggy trouser crotch and grabbed the wriggling creature.

"Have you got it?" Sweat oozed through Peredur's camouflage-painted face.

Basildon stood and gently eased apart his hands. A whiskered mouse nose ventured forth. "I have the little insurgent, Commander. *Apodemus sylvaticus*, to give it its scientific name."

Peredur hoisted his trousers back up, tightening the belt an extra notch. "Is it dangerous?"

Basildon kissed the twitching nose. "A wood mouse? Harmless little fella. Probably thought you looked warm and cosy." He held out his hands. "See? Friendly chap."

Peredur stepped back and waved his hands at him. "Get rid of it. And if you breathe a word of this to the lads, Agent 117, I'll—"

Basildon brought a finger to his lips. "I saw nothing. No mouse phobias round here." He winked, then walked to the stone barn entrance and released the wood mouse into the open.

"Before you go," Peredur called. He rummaged in his pocket and pulled out his security leaflet. "Take this." He waved it in the air. "Leave it where His Lordship can't miss it. Understood?"

Basildon took the leaflet. "Security, heh?"

Peredur crossed his arms. "Just deliver it."

"Sir!" Basildon saluted again, jumped onto the quad bike, and sped off into the fading light.

As the quad's throaty engine disappeared deep into the estate, Peredur settled his breathing and returned his gaze towards his captive. "Mr Lockmount, do you know who I am?"

The sniffling estate agent shook his head.

"Peredur Jones."

Gerald shrugged.

Peredur's leather gloves creaked as his fists clenched and unclenched. "You *must* know who I am. You've written to me many times recently."

Gerald's face contorted as he thought harder.

Peredur lunged, his right fist pulled back, ready to punch. "You smarmy—" He smacked his hand flat on the adjacent bale. "You don't give a toss about local people. All you're interested in is selling houses to the highest bidders and pocketing the commission, you capitalist coward. You're turning Mortiforde into a town of retired Londoners. They're the only ones who can afford to buy here."

He turned and walked away, then spun back and placed his hands on his hips. "I am Peredur Jones, Commander of BANG, Borderlandshire Against Nefarious Government."

Gerald continued sniffling.

Peredur crossed his arms. "But you probably know me better as 42 Brominster Way."

Gerald's eyes widened. He nodded frantically, noises of acknowledgement squealing from his rope-filled mouth.

Peredur sneered. "And that, Mr Lockmount, is why I detest you. Selling and letting properties should be about building communities. But you don't know me as a person. You only know me as an address."

Gerald wriggled frantically and squealed. Peredur moved to within an inch of his face.

"SHUT UP, you idiot! I hate people like you." He sneered at the estate agent. "You're practically socially cleansing the town."

Gerald shook his head vigorously. Globules of snot flew from his nose.

Peredur smacked a hay bale again.

Gerald flinched.

"Don't deny it! You don't want people like me in this town. You'll do anything to make sure I'm priced out of the market."

Gerald shook his head.

"Liar!" Peredur scanned Gerald's terror-stricken face. "Mortside Park Homes mean anything?"

Gerald's eyes widened further.

Peredur nodded. "Yeah, I know all about Farmer Bell's plan to build a park home site on his fields near the meadows. Not ideal, but affordable on my local wages. Something I could call home."

He sneaked closer to the sniffling estate agent. "Not much commission on park homes, is there? Attracts low-income households, doesn't it? What did you write on the Borderlandshire District Council Planning Portal?"

Peredur stroked his chin, recalling Gerald's comments. "Such a development would create a detrimental impact on the neighbouring amenity. Forty-five densely packed park homes and their inhabitants would be an eyesore next to the scenically outstanding Mortiforde Meadows, and the associated increased traffic accessing the site would damage the historic late eighteenth-century Morte Bridge."

He pointed at Gerald. "You called park home inhabitants an *eyesore*!"

Gerald's agitation became frenetic. He screamed through his rope gag. Sweat poured from his temples as his nostrils flared.

"This is how you and the Establishment control who lives in Mortiforde. And you say this isn't social cleansing? I can't afford to live in Mortiforde, and you're part of the system that's evicting me on Friday!"

Peredur's foot lashed out at a metal bucket sitting inside the barn's vast opening, sending it flying deep into the darkest corner, where it crashed with a clatter.

He stepped over to Mortiforde Millie. "Well, that's going to change, Mr Lockmount. Estate agents can't keep cleansing the town of true locals."

Peredur clambered onto some bales beside Millie and unbuttoned her multicoloured woolly cardigan, revealing a large, wooden barrel-shaped torso.

"So, BANG is doing a little social cleansing ourselves." His hand rose to Millie's face. Carefully, he placed a finger against her nose and pushed. It clicked, releasing a catch. Peredur's hands pulled open two doors in her barrel-chest. He turned to Gerald and smiled.

"Look! There's space inside Mortiforde Millie's chest to hide. . ." His finger tapped his chin, then pointed at Gerald. "An estate agent."

From the back pocket of his camouflage trousers, Peredur pulled a box of matches, slipped it open, and selected a match. With a deft swipe of the red phosphorus tip against the powdered-glass strip, the match-head exploded into a fizzling flame.

Gerald's eyes widened so far that Peredur could see the flickering flame reflected in the estate agent's pupils.

"And then Mortiforde Millie's Friday night burning will be flaming wonderful, won't it, Gerald?"

Felicity stepped into Earth, Wind, and Fire's sombre offices in Southgate Street, triggering the musical notes of Chopin's 'Funeral March' to fill the silence. It signalled to the staff that life had entered the building.

A display of wooden samples along the far wall caught her attention. Coffin colour choices far exceeded those of kitchen cupboard options in most home improvement stores. Underneath was an overwhelming array of handle options. Some even resembled kitchen cupboard handles.

"Can I be of assistance, madam?"

Felicity turned to find Mr Earth standing before her in a dark suit and black tie. His broken-veined cheeks, wispy white hair, and bloodshot eyes looked up at her. He looked like he'd entered his second century several decades ago.

"Your Ladyship?" He staggered back. "Not His Lordship! So soon after his parents, too." He bowed. "Please let me be the first to offer our condolences at such a tragic time. Your husband was—"

"No!" Felicity interrupted. "His Lordship is in fine fettle. I'm here about someone else."

Mr Earth eased himself upright from his bow. Slowly. "That is good news." He paused. "About His Lordship." He gestured to the armchairs in the corner. "How can we help you?"

Felicity perched on a cushion and watched Mr Earth ease himself into a chair opposite. "I understand Councillor Prendeghast has no family."

Mr Earth shook his head. "Sadly, no."

"So what happens regarding his funeral?"

Mr Earth took a deep breath. "A pauper's funeral. The local authority is legally bound to deal with the final disposition."

Felicity frowned. "Disposition?"

"Disposal of the body, Your Ladyship."

She clapped her hands. "Excellent!"

Mr Earth's confusion reminded her she had some explaining to do.

"This is Councillor Prendeghast's lucky day," she continued, before realising the Councillor probably wouldn't see it like that. "The Ladies' Legion will gladly handle Councillor Prendeghast's funeral."

A smile invaded Mr Earth's broken-veined cheeks. "I'm sure Earth, Wind, and Fire can meet the Ladies' Legion wishes." His arm extended to the coffin sample display opposite. "We have some fine materials with which to lay the Councillor at rest and—"

"Oh, we don't need any of that." Felicity waved a dismissive hand in the air. "We'll sort the coffin. It needs to be something far more appropriate."

Mr Earth glowered. "Do you have a date in mind?"

Felicity bit her bottom lip. They had to act quickly, but there was still so much to sort out. "Tomorrow afternoon," she smiled. "About three o'clock?"

Mr Earth baulked at the suggestion and considered questioning it when he caught Felicity's no-nonsense gaze. He nodded. "Will you require a family car and the hearse?"

"Why would a man with no family require a family car?" Her look of contempt told him it was a rhetorical question. "Nor shall we need a hearse. This will be an environmentally friendly burial on Mortiforde Meadows. Councillor Prendeghast will arrive by horse-drawn carriage."

"I'm not sure we can arrange a horse at such short notice," Mr Earth began.

"We'll sort that," Felicity continued. "Which reminds me, I'd better have words with the Reverend Makepiece."

Mr Earth coughed. "You've booked a funeral for three o'clock tomorrow, and you haven't spoken to Reverend Makepiece? My Lady, one cannot rush the organising of a funeral."

Felicity stood. Judging by the speed with which Mr Earth operated, he rushed nothing. Life. Or death.

"Mr Earth, *Verdant Endings* will prove to the Mortiforde townsfolk that we can handle funerals quickly, efficiently, and in an environmentally friendly manner. Seeing as we don't require any of your services, I would be most grateful if you could ensure Councillor Prendeghast's body is ready for collection by two-thirty tomorrow. Good day to you."

~

"Thank you, Crystal. On the end will be fine." Rupert turned to Aldermaston, sat opposite. "Tea, Your Lordship?"

Aldermaston smiled. "Thank you."

Crystal eased the tea tray onto the edge of Rupert's desk, pushing against a vast pile of paperwork on the corner. She picked up the milk jug.

"Careful!" Aldermaston yelled. The pile of paperwork teetered momentarily before plummeting to the floor. He lunged, hands outstretched to break its fall, but was too slow.

"Cretin!" Rupert snapped. "I told you yesterday to file that lot!"

Crystal scrambled to the floor, frantically grabbing all the loose papers and files.

Aldermaston collected the papers closest to him and handed them to Crystal. Her eyes moistened. He offered a consolatory smile.

"Completely avoidable if she had done her job properly." Rupert's baritone voice resonated around them.

Some architectural drawings caught Aldermaston's eye. *Castle Ridge*. It was the front elevation of a grand two-storey property with vast bi-fold windows and—

"I'll take that." Rupert snatched the document from him and handed it to Crystal, whose arms now cradled most of the other paperwork. "Take this and file it away properly, like I instructed yesterday."

"Yes, Mr Rinde." She backed away, then hurried through the office door, closing it behind her with her foot.

Rupert poured some tea. "Decent staff are so scarce these days." He passed a cup to Aldermaston.

"I'm sure no harm has been done," Aldermaston suggested. "Looks like an extensive building project you have there." He sipped some tea.

Rupert scowled.

He pointed to the door. "The architectural drawings—"

Rupert dismissed the suggestion. "Consultation exercise. Adjacent landowner's development. If only the council emailed such documents instead of posting physical copies." He stared at Aldermaston as he brought his cup to his mouth. "So, why am I honoured with this personal visit?"

Aldermaston returned his cup to the saucer. "To offer our condolences. Your father was a close friend of my father."

Rupert placed his teacup on his desk. "Whatever. It's common knowledge my father and I didn't get on, so I'm hardly going into six months of mourning." He pointed briefly. "I understand you discovered my father in your waste bin. Is that how you treat all your guests?"

Aldermaston crimsoned. "PC Norten's assessment of the situation appears a little misguided."

"What do *you* think happened?" Rupert's stare fixed on Aldermaston.

Aldermaston took another mouthful of tea. "He was at Tugford Hall at the invitation of the Marchioness, but we know nothing of his plans after he'd left. Do you have any thoughts?"

Rupert leaned back in his chair. "No. I was here all evening. You can ask my mother. She even popped in here to see me at one point. She was worried he hadn't returned home."

"Were you worried?"

Rupert glanced up at the ceiling. "What he did was none of my business."

"Really?" Aldermaston wiped a speck of dirt from his trousers. "Sir Hugo gave the Ladies' Legion permission to use Mortiforde Meadows for their green burial service. Right where you want to build your waste incinerator."

Rupert chuckled. "Ah! So you think I killed my father to inherit the meadows."

Aldermaston shuffled in the chair. "No, of course not."

"LIAR!" Rupert pointed to the door. "This meeting is over, Your Lordship. GET OUT!"

Aldermaston rose sheepishly. "Rupert, I'm sorry—"

"Lord Mortiforde!" Rupert reclined in his office chair with his highly polished black brogues resting on the desk. "My father's last will and testament leaves the meadows to my mother. Not me. The viability of the waste incinerator project has never pivoted on the meadows' ownership. The local council can always buy the meadows through a compulsory purchase order." Rupert smiled. "Shut the door on your way out, Your Lordship."

~

Diya leaned over Daniel's shoulder and pointed to the screen. "Select micro-payments."

"Not direct debit?"

Diya scratched her head. Selling council assets online meant the money had to go somewhere. Ideally, somewhere nobody would look, at least not for a few days. But setting up the online auction account meant verifying the council's bank details.

"We can't use a council account that accepts direct debit mandates. The accounts team checks those daily. It's too risky." She paced the room. "It has to be the micro-payments option. But we need a bank account that nobody checks frequently."

Daniel twisted around in his chair. "What are micro-payments?"

"To verify the account, the auction site pays in two small payments. It's only pence, but once they've been deposited, we can check the account and confirm how much—" Diya clasped her head. "I'm so stupid!"

"Why?"

"I can only check the council bank accounts from the office. As soon as I log in, they'll know I'm in the building."

Daniel hit Lisa's speed dial number on his mobile and put it on speaker. "Could Lisa check?"

Lisa answered quickly. "What's up? Can't talk long. I'm in the basement."

"We need a council bank account to pay any auction sale proceeds into," Daniel explained, "but preferably one that isn't checked daily. Diya can't log onto the council's system. Can you access any council accounts?"

Diya stared at the phone, her fingers crossed.

"I can access the Local Democracy bank accounts. They're used for by-election expenditure and—"

"No," Diya interrupted. "There's a by-election in five weeks. Finance will check that daily for the foreseeable future."

Lisa sighed. "I'm not sure about any of the others."

Diya grabbed Daniel's arm. "Lisa, do you have access to *all* Democracy Support bank accounts?"

"Yes, I think so."

Diya smiled. "GMISC!"

Daniel frowned. "G what?"

"GMISC," she repeated. "Every department has a General Miscellaneous Irreconcilable Sundry Credit account. It's a dumping ground for any unknown credits. People only look there when they've checked every other account."

"If you say so," said Lisa. "But I don't know the account number."

"You don't need to." Excitement spread across Diya's face. "Each department's bank accounts begin with the same four digits. The final four digits denote the account type. All GMISC accounts end in zero, six, one, three. What numbers do all Democracy Support accounts begin with?"

"Two, zero, seven, nine," Lisa replied.

"Yes!" Diya clapped. "We're on! Thanks, Lisa!" She tapped

the council's sorting code and Democracy Support's GMISC account number into the website and clicked *Submit.*

A confirmation screen advised that the payments would arrive within the next two hours. Diya sighed. This might just work.

~

Lisa slipped her phone into her pocket and made a mental note to check the GMISC bank account when she got back to her desk.

She'd been browsing the council's basement for potential online auction items and, apart from the rug Diya had mentioned, she'd not yet found anything worth a pound in her opinion, let alone half a million.

She tucked her hair behind her ear as she resumed checking what the council staff called the Basement of Despair. The first item was a bucket with three holes in the bottom. She put it back.

Rummaging in boxes, she found a silver platter and two trophies. These had potential. The eighteen-inch silver platter had weight to it and bore an inscription. *For forty years' service to the local community.* The recipient clearly thought they were worthy of more, having discarded it down here. She turned it over. Were those hallmarks?

The trophies were from an old school display cabinet. One was for the boys' team who'd beaten their opponents from a neighbouring county at British Bulldog in 1934, while the other was for the girls' team who'd successfully cooked their way to home economic stardom two years before war rationing was first served up.

Lisa tucked them under her arm, turned, caught her foot in something, and fell. The silverware clattered against the floor, and the rug landed with a whoompf. Her foot had caught in a dust sheet covering something large behind a taller unit. She yanked it, setting free a decades-in-the-making dust storm.

Once her sneezing fit subsided, Lisa's watery eyes saw the huge wooden box. Cautiously, she lifted the lid. There were stacks of school library books, including copies of Michael Morpurgo's *War Horse*, Roald Dahl's *Charlie and the Chocolate Factory*, and Cressida Cowell's *How To Train Your Dragon*.

Underneath, she saw J. K. Rowling's first children's book, *Harry Potter and the Philosopher's Stone*. She picked it up and read the back-cover blurb. Typical. A spelling mistake. The second O was missing in *Philosopher*. At least the American edition, *Harry Potter and the Sorcerer's Stone* didn't have that issue.

Her heart pounded. Hang on. This misprint was well known, wasn't it? She grabbed her mobile phone and searched online. Yes! The misprint was infamous, found only on the initial five hundred copies printed in the UK.

Lisa gulped. In the box, next to where this book once sat, were another four copies. Diya was right. There were treasures to be found in the Basement of Despair, after all.

CHAPTER EIGHT

Aldermaston's Jaguar whooshed through the winding, high-hedged country lanes towards Tugford Hall in the fading twilight. The back roads were quieter and gave him time to think. Was Rupert telling the truth about Isabel inheriting the meadows?

He negotiated a long bend, then hit the brakes when he came face to face with a bleating, woolly blockage. Farmer Bell's two-thousand-strong flock of Kerry Hill sheep hurtled towards his car before squeezing between it and the hedges a few inches away. His parking sensors erupted into a beeping frenzy thanks to the passing fleeces busy buffing his silver paintwork.

An incoming call lit up the dashboard display. Radio Borderlandshire. Aldermaston sighed. What did Drivetime Benny want?

"Goooooooooooood evening, Your Lordship!" screamed the radio presenter. "You're live on the Drivetime Benny show this Tuesday evening. Are you safe to chat?"

Aldermaston peered into the failing late-afternoon light and saw a bobbing fleece sea stretching deep into the darkness.

"I'm in the car, Benny, but I'm currently parked. How can I help you?" Aldermaston wedged his elbow on the driver's window ledge and cradled his head.

"It seems your father's partly responsible for this mess with the town's meadows. How do you respond to that?"

Aldermaston scratched his forehead. Had Stella carried out her threat? "I'm sorry, Benny. What do you mean?"

Benny chuckled. "Some thirty years ago, your father sold Mortiforde Meadows to Sir Hugo for an extortionate amount of money, instead of to the Historic Borders Agency, as promised. Had he not reneged on the Historic Borders Agency agreement, we wouldn't have this mess with the meadows today, would we, Your Lordship?"

Aldermaston squirmed. "Who told you that?"

"I'm sorry, Your Lordship. Drivetime Benny never reveals his sources. But this note from BANG claims the Seventh Marquess flogged the meadows to Sir Hugo for more than the cost of Tugford Hall's new roof."

A cacophony of bleating surrounded his vehicle as the sheep jostled past. Were they agreeing with Benny?

"I've only recently learned of that historical note myself," Aldermaston waffled, "but what I can tell you is that I and the rest of the Borderers Guild is doing everything we can to save the meadows. And I also know that the Ladies' Legion are campaigning hard to save the meadows for their first environmentally friendly burial—"

"Is that where Mortiforde Millie is hiding?" Benny interrupted. "Did someone bury her? Only, rumour has it, Mortiforde Millie is missing."

Aldermaston ran his finger around his shirt collar. BANG was busy briefing this afternoon. "Mortiforde Millie will be ready for Friday's annual parade through town," he blustered.

His dashboard displayed another incoming call. *Gerald Lockmount Estate Agents.*

"Sorry, Benny, I have another incoming call that I must take. Lovely chatting with you. Bye!"

Relieved, he selected the incoming call. "Gerald, what can I do for you?"

"It's Maureen, Your Lordship. Gerald's secretary. Is Gerald still with you? Only I was expecting him back earlier."

"With me? No, I've not seen Gerald since last night's Borderers Guild meeting."

A burst of keyboard clatter echoed down the line. "You had a two-thirty meeting. I'm looking at your email now."

"Email? From me?"

Maureen read out his personal email address. Aldermaston gulped. "I didn't send that. What were we meeting about?"

"A stone barn on the estate. You wish to liquidate some assets."

Aldermaston's fingers massaged his forehead. What stone barn?

The roar of an approaching quad bike broke his thoughts as the last of the sheep trundled past. Farmer Bell pulled into a field gateway, allowing Aldermaston to pass.

"Sorry, Maureen. Must dash. I'll check with my office and be in touch."

He ended the call, released the handbrake, acknowledged Farmer Bell and his two Border collies perched precariously on the back of the quad bike, and continued home.

Only Felicity and Daniel could access his personal emails, and neither would liquidate any assets without telling him.

Confusion swirled through his many thoughts. The last mile back to Tugford Hall barely registered until he turned the last corner and his foot crushed the brakes again. A large group of jeering, chanting protesters blocked Tugford Hall's main entrance. Some were lying across the tarmac, some sat cross-legged, while others stood, all waving placards and chanting in unison.

"What do we want? Affordable housing. When do we want it? NOW!"

Aldermaston read the placards. *Homes for All, not Tugford Hall. Born and bred here, can't afford to live here.* And *Local Homes, Not Second Homes.*

The protesters surged towards him, thumping the car's windows and bonnet, while shouting and jeering at him.

Aldermaston activated the door lock. He checked over his shoulder for an escape route but was surrounded. A protester with blonde hair and a red bandana shielding his nose, mouth, and chin held a phone to his ear. He smacked the driver's window with his free hand and motioned Aldermaston to lower it.

Aldermaston blipped the switch. The window dropped half an inch, and the protesters' shouts and jeers filled the cabin.

"What's going on?" Aldermaston asked Bandana Man.

Bandana Man nodded toward Tugford Hall. "Going home to your little thirty-bedroomed house, are you?"

Aldermaston flinched when a bald protester in shin-high, black leather boots jumped onto the bonnet and pounded the windscreen with his bare hands.

"What do you want?" Aldermaston's breath misted the driver's window.

"The Establishment is over, Lord Mortiforde," Bandana Man bellowed. "When your father sold Mortiforde Meadows to re-roof that monstrosity," he pointed at Tugford Hall, "it showed a disregard for the real people of Mortiforde. The Establishment thinks nothing of spending vast sums of money on a stately pile for one family to live in. *One* family, Your Lordship! Tugford Hall is big enough for all of us to live in."

Bandana Man leaned against the car door, the phone still clamped tightly to his ear. "So, Lord Mortiforde. What are you going to do?"

The surrounding protesters continued shouting, jeering,

and taunting him. He was trapped. His hands gripped the steering wheel, whitening his knuckles. Had his father ever faced such hostility? This uprising seemed so unexpectedly sudden, so—

BOOM!

A deafening, pulsating shockwave sent protesters scurrying in all directions.

Bandana Man dropped to the ground, crouching beside Aldermaston's car. "What the hell was that?"

Ahead lay a clear route to the main gates of Tugford Hall. Aldermaston squinted. Was that a puff of smoke rising just above the parapet of Tugford Hall's porticoed entrance?

A muffled thud caused Aldermaston and Bandana Man to recoil. Aldermaston's eyes widened. Lying barely two metres away was a nine-pound, four-inch diameter cast iron cannonball.

Bandana Man jumped to his feet. "Holy moly, Peredur!" he shouted into his mobile phone. "Someone just fired a cannonball at us! A cannonball! Sorry, Commander, but we're out of here!"

He turned to Aldermaston. "Firing on the proletariat, Lord Mortiforde? You're gonna regret that." Bandana Man and his compatriots fled up the lane.

Peredur clamped the phone to his ear as he walked home, straining to hear through the kerfuffle. "Agent 62? What's happening?"

"Holy moly, Peredur! Someone just fired a cannonball at us! A cannonball! Sorry, Commander, I'm out of here!"

"What?" Peredur rubbed his forehead, smearing some of his camouflage paint. Agent 62 had used his first name. Loose talk costs lives. But … a cannonball? Peredur smirked. Only desperate dictators used cannonballs against the masses. He heard Agent 62 mumble to Lord Mortiforde before running away.

Eventually, Agent 62's breathing settled as his pace slowed. "No idea who fired at us. Lord Mortiforde was in his car on the road beside us. The cannonball could have hit him! Who fires a cannonball at a group of unarmed protesters?"

Peredur skipped as he turned onto Brominster Way. This was better than he'd planned. Now, all he had to do was to gather together his troops tonight in Mortimer Forest for the next stage of his master plot.

Aldermaston abandoned his car on the drive, looked up at the balustraded rooftop, and then hurtled up Tugford Hall's main entrance steps two at a time. He was relieved when he stepped inside the main hallway without being crushed by a falling cannonball.

"Daddy!" Harry dropped his school bag at the bottom of the stairs, ran across the hallway, and threw his arms around Aldermaston's legs. "Have you come to take me swimming? You promised you'd take me swimming. Can we go now? Please?"

Aldermaston brushed the blonde fringe from his son's eyes. "Sorry. I'm busy. Perhaps tomorrow?"

"Aww, you're always busy!" Dejected, Harry released his grip and hurried back to pick up his rucksack.

Cartwright appeared at the top of the main staircase. "Master Harry, I asked you to—"

"Have you just come from the roof?" Aldermaston interrupted.

Cartwright descended the staircase. "Yes, My Lord," he whispered. "I thought someone had fired a rooftop cannon."

"Someone has! The damn thing nearly hit me and could have killed one of those demonstrators out there." He thumbed over his shoulder.

"I asked them to move earlier, My Lord, then Her Ladyship instructed me to collect Master Harry from school. We'd just parked by the Tradesman's Entrance when I heard the shot." Cartwright slipped a white-gloved hand into his jacket pocket and retrieved a spent match. "This was beside the cannon nearest the rooftop door."

Aldermaston sniffed it. "Fresh. Was the roof door locked?"

Cartwright shook his head. "No, My Lord. The fire brigade recommended leaving it unlocked in case of emergencies. I left the Main Hall unlocked when I went to collect Master Harry because I assumed Daniel and Lisa were in your office. Their cars are parked in the rear courtyard."

"We need to review security." Aldermaston returned the spent match to Cartwright. "BANG may have more tricks up their sleeve." He headed towards a door set back in a corner alcove. "Can you take Harry up to our private quarters and give him something to eat?"

Cartwright nodded.

Aldermaston paused mid-step. "Where is Felicity?"

"Urgent meeting with the Reverend Makepiece."

He nodded, then slipped through a door to the back stairs and hurried down to the basement floor and along the main corridor to his office.

He was about to knock on his office door when he saw a leaflet taped to it at head height. *Borderlandshire Defence*, it declared. *Battle-tested security with mission-driven solutions.*

He ripped it off. That sealed it. They needed to up their security.

❧

In the vicarage drawing room, Felicity waited for the Reverend Makepiece to emerge from his kitchen. She'd not seen him since he'd offered to make tea fifteen minutes ago. At least she couldn't hear snoring.

Eventually, the clattering of trembling china on a tray announced the Reverend Makepiece's shuffling arrival. He placed it on the table between them. Behind them, a log fire was dying a slow death.

"Sorry for the delay." The vicar's liver-spotted hands arranged the cups on the saucers. "Sometimes I go to do something, and then my mind wanders. The next thing I know, ten minutes have disappeared."

Felicity smiled. If only the Reverend's Sunday morning sermons disappeared in the same way. "Shall I be Mother?"

The Reverend collapsed into his chair. "Thank you."

"Are you free tomorrow afternoon to help us with something we're doing at the meadows? About three o'clock?" Felicity poured tea into each teacup, added milk, and handed one cup to the Reverend.

"Three o'clock, you say?" He picked up a television listings magazine. "How long for? Only there's a quiz show I like at four-thirty and—"

Felicity waved a dismissive hand. "You'll be home in plenty of time." She giggled. "How long does it take to say 'Earth to earth, ashes to ashes' and lower a body in the ground?"

Reverend Makepiece's eyes widened. "A committal? Whose?"

Such was her excitement, she realised she'd not explained anything to the Reverend. His eyes glazed over several times while she brought him up to speed. "All we need," she continued, "is a short blessing for Councillor Prendeghast's life, and then the relevant burial rites as we lower his body into the ground. We'll have him all tucked up in Mortiforde history before you can say, 'Councillor Prendeghast is a trailblazer'."

The Reverend slurped his tea. "The meadows, you say?"

Felicity nodded.

"I thought Prendeghast always wanted his ashes interred in the council chamber."

"Sadly, Councillor Prendeghast's non-existent finances mean he has little choice in the matter, which is why the Ladies' Legion is conducting this groundbreaking committal."

The Reverend opened a sideboard drawer beside him and selected a sheet of paper. He passed it to Felicity. "My fees. I'll knock off ten per cent as there's no church service."

Felicity balked at the price. "What about a twenty per cent discount?"

The Reverend Makepiece clasped his hands together and closed his eyes.

Felicity bit her bottom lip. Was he seeking higher authorisation?

His eyes popped open. "Where was I?"

"Offering a twenty per cent discount," Felicity blurted hopefully.

"One cannot negotiate with the Lord," the Reverend suggested. The clock on the mantelpiece chimed five. "Especially with less than twenty-four hours' notice."

Ultimately, Felicity was prepared to pay anything to get Councillor Prendeghast in the ground tomorrow at three. She perused the Reverend Makepiece's price list again. Who knew death was so lucrative? Her heart lurched when she reached the bottom of the list.

"Do you have Damien's contact number?"

"Damien's? I do, but there's no point in giving it to you. He's visiting family in Australia." He chuckled. "Australia," he wheezed. "The gravedigger's down under." He sipped more tea, oblivious to the horror now shrouding Felicity's face.

She'd got a body and a vicar. What she didn't have was a hole in the ground to put Councillor Prendeghast in.

~

Aldermaston hammered on his office door. "It's me."

The clank of releasing locks echoed along the corridor. The door swung open, and Aldermaston practically fell in. Daniel re-bolted the door immediately.

"What was that bang?" Lisa twisted around in her chair beside Diya. "Sounded like the army was on manoeuvres."

"How long have you been here?" Aldermaston thrust the leaflet at Daniel.

Lisa checked her watch. "About an hour. Why?"

"Any problems getting in through the front gates?"

"No."

Aldermaston pointed to Diya. "We need to move her now! There were protesters at the main gates when I arrived. That explosion frightened them off, but who knows when they'll be back?"

Diya trembled.

"What's this?" Daniel checked both sides of the leaflet.

"Someone taped that security leaflet to the other side of that door!" Aldermaston pointed to his office door.

"Who?" asked Daniel.

"Exactly!" Aldermaston snapped. "We need to improve our security." He pointed to the leaflet. "Find out what they charge and get some other quotes. We need something for the next few days."

Daniel nodded. "What's the budget?"

Aldermaston shrugged. "Check with me if it's over ten thousand."

"Why are there protesters here?" Lisa rose from her chair, clutching one of the first edition books.

Aldermaston grabbed the Shepherd Cottage keys from the cabinet and threw them at Daniel. "Local homes for local people. Local homes, not second homes. How I have all this space." He waved his arm around. "They called me the Establishment again. It's BANG." He ran his fingers through his hair. "I'd feel happier if we moved Diya now."

"Ten more minutes?" Lisa held up the book. "I found five first-edition books in the basement and a few other items. We've nearly finished listing them on the online auction site. Which reminds me——" She pulled a scrap of paper from her skirt pocket and handed it to Diya. "I checked the GMISC account. Two micro-payments have gone in. One for six pence and another for nine pence."

Aldermaston shook his head. "No time. Let's move Diya. Daniel can continue with the online auction stuff when he gets back."

Daniel held aloft the leaflet. "I'll give these a call first." He motioned to the door. "I'll nip outside. Better signal."

Aldermaston nodded, let Daniel out, and then bolted the door behind him.

Lisa returned to her chair. "What was that bang earlier?"

"Cannonball."

"What? Who fires a cannonball?"

As soon as she'd uttered those words, Aldermaston knew. "Basildon!"

Daniel dashed out through the Tradesman's Entrance, triggering the security lighting. His phone's signal strength improved to three bars. He dialled the number on the leaflet and leaned against his car, waiting for it to connect.

A strong Welsh accent answered. "Borderlandshire Defence, 'ow can I help?"

Daniel turned his back to the breeze. "I'm calling on behalf of the Marquess of Mortiforde."

"Tugford Hall, yeah?"

"That's it," Daniel grinned. Mentioning his employer often caught people's attention. "We need some temporary security for the next few days. How much for some security guards and dog patrols?"

The sound of air being sucked between teeth echoed down the line. "How high is Tugford Hall's perimeter wall?"

"About ten feet all the way around."

"How big is the estate?"

"Three thousand acres."

More air was sucked between teeth. "That's a lotta wall. Thirty grand at least for two or three days."

"That's way over my budget," Daniel disclosed.

"Well," the operative continued, "a wall that high will keep out all but the most determined of invaders. What ya got at the main entrance?"

"Nothing really," Daniel explained. "There are gates, but they haven't been closed in decades," Daniel explained. "Difficult to keep opening and closing them as they're in constant use."

"You need an MBT. It's movable."

"A what?" Daniel pushed his phone harder against his ear.

"MBT. It guards entrances. Acts as a deterrent, you see."

This sounded hopeful. "How much to hire that for a few days?"

More air rushed between teeth. "Let's check ma records. This be your first time using us, is it?"

"Yes. His Lordship has never needed security before."

"That's tidy then. Three days would normally be twelve grand, but I'll do it for nine."

Daniel balked at the price. But nine grand was better than twelve, and within Aldermaston's budget. He checked the time. Nearly five-thirty. The chances of finding another local security firm open now were slim.

"When can you get it here for us?" he enquired.

"Would first thing tomorrow help?"

"I'll take it."

"That's crackin'. I take it His Lordship has a company credit card. I just need the long number from the middle."

Daniel slipped the Tugford Hall business card from his wallet and read out the details.

"Perfect, boyo. See you first thing tomorrow. Cheers."

The line went dead. Daniel stared at his phone screen. So what was an MBT?

Aldermaston, Lisa, and Diya stepped out into the security-lit rear courtyard just as Daniel ended his call.

"Daniel, you go with Diya round the front and get her Morris Minor. Lisa and I will take the utility vehicle." Aldermaston pointed to a green and yellow John Deere two-seater utility vehicle tucked beside an outbuilding. He turned to Diya. "Bring your car around here and then follow us, okay?"

Diya nodded, threw her handbag over her shoulder, and missed.

Daniel picked it. "How far is Shepherd Cottage?"

"Couple of miles up that track," Aldermaston pointed.

Daniel and Diya disappeared around the side of Tugford Hall.

Aldermaston jumped into the utility vehicle driver's seat and started the engine. Lisa slipped in beside him. They headed past the industrial waste bins and out to where the rear drive met the stone track. Aldermaston stared in his wing mirror, waiting for Diya's Morris Minor headlights to appear.

"I spoke with Ronni Rickers earlier," said Lisa. "She confirmed that any IT technician could email from any staff member's email account, and intercept phone calls, if they wanted to."

The security lighting went out.

Aldermaston's eyes remained fixed on the darkness in the wing mirror. "Can't the IT manager run a security check on their technicians' machines? There must be an audit trail tracking every keystroke."

Lisa sighed. "Only for IT staff based in the council offices."

Aldermaston glanced at her briefly. "Don't tell me the council outsourced its IT department to India."

"Put it this way," Lisa sneered. "When my computer's Windows operating system was last upgraded, English wasn't the default language. Anyway, Ronni explained that there are a handful of staff based in the council offices to deal with physical issues. However, the council outsources some IT Helpdesk support to an agency with workers based globally. Some locally based agency staff have security passes to the building."

Aldermaston continued staring at the wing mirror. "So Diya's IT technician could be anywhere in the country?"

"World," Lisa corrected.

Aldermaston shook his head. "Whoever spoke to Diya is local. The waste incinerator project is a local issue."

Two full-beam headlamps urgently swept round the corner, temporarily blinding Aldermaston. He grabbed the steering wheel. "They're coming fast!" Aldermaston floored the accelerator. Lisa grabbed the safety bar beside her seat.

The utility vehicle lunged forward, its rear end slip-sliding as it struggled to gain purchase. Aldermaston flicked a switch on the dashboard, and two floodlights on the roof illuminated the tree-lined stone track ahead. He slowed, but Diya's headlights grew bigger in the wing mirror. He gripped the steering wheel as the rough track bounced them out of their seats. His wing mirrors dazzled in Diya's headlights, and the frenzied screeching of her engine sounded millimetres behind them.

"Why's she going so fast?" Aldermaston motioned with an arm, encouraging them to slow down. Seconds later, the utility vehicle hit a pothole and bounced so hard the vehicle's frame almost buckled.

Lisa grabbed her phone and dictated a text message to Daniel. "Tell Diya to slow down!"

Aldermaston scanned the road ahead for potholes. Their speed barely gave him time to avoid them when the floodlights illuminated them.

"How much further?" Lisa bellowed at him.

"Nearly there." He swerved left, then right, avoiding another deep hole. Diya's headlamps pitched downwards, then soared upwards as her car ploughed through the uneven surface.

Lisa twisted her phone towards Aldermaston. "Daniel's reply contains several swearing emojis. He's not enjoying his ride."

Ahead, Aldermaston spotted a faint gap in the trees where a grassier track veered right towards Shepherd Cottage. He turned, leaving the main track. Seconds later, Diya's Morris Minor shot past them.

"Where's she going?" Aldermaston screeched to a halt. The utility vehicle's spotlights illuminated Shepherd Cottage ahead.

Both he and Lisa watched the Morris Minor's headlamps disappear into the forest's darkness. Suddenly, there was a loud screech, a bang, and the tinkling of glass. Darkness fell as Diya's headlamps died.

Aldermaston wrenched the steering wheel hard right and floored the accelerator again as he headed towards them. "Please let them be okay."

∼

Mark Heathson eyed the kitchen clock. Where was Lisa? Probably running some errands for Aldermaston, which was becoming increasingly common. He huffed as he moved some pans off the gas burners in Castle View Bed and Breakfast's kitchen and headed to reception, where someone had rung the bell. The whole point of Lisa covering the front of house in the evening was so that he could cook guests' evening meals.

A short, elderly, bald chap wearing a navy suit, a light blue shirt, and a bright red tie was waiting at their reception desk.

"Good evening, sir." Mark smiled. "How can I help?"

"The sign says you have vacancies." A wrinkled hand motioned towards the front door.

"We do. How long are you looking to stay?"

The potential customer shrugged. "My line of work requires a flexible approach."

Mark punched at the reception computer keyboard. "And what line of work is that?"

"Truth seeker."

Mark's heart sank. Great. One of *those* guests. "What's the name?"

"Offermans. Norris Offermans." His hand slipped into his breast pocket and removed a leather wallet. "My credit card. I'll require a fully itemised bill at my departure."

"Thank you." Mark placed a slip of paper and a pen on the reception counter. "Please complete your details here. We serve breakfast between seven and nine. Evening meals are available on request. Here's the key to room four."

Norris Offermans completed the registration slip, then held it at arm's length and scrutinised it. His nose twitched.

"Everything all right?"

Norris's green eyes stared intensely at Mark. "Thinking of charging an extra night?"

Mark frowned. "Sorry?"

Norris pointed to the slip's arrival date. "You've dated it the second. Today's the third."

Mark changed the date. "I'm terribly sorry—"

Norris touched his right temple twice, then pointed at Mark. "I'm watching you."

~

"There they are!" Relief washed over Aldermaston as the utility vehicle's spotlights picked out Diya's Morris Minor, embedded in what looked like a stone barn wall.

Daniel stumbled out of the passenger door, dazed, then staggered around the car to help Diya.

Aldermaston pulled up alongside and jumped out. Together, they helped a shocked and shaking Diya out of the driver's seat.

Lisa inspected the damage. "One headlamp is broken and the bonnet's a bit crumpled, but we should be able to move it over to the cottage."

"Can't we leave it?" Daniel questioned.

Aldermaston struggled to get his bearings. "I don't recognise this barn. I doubt anyone comes up here."

"Somebody does," said Lisa.

Aldermaston turned to see Lisa standing in the barn's giant open doorway. "What makes you say that?"

She pointed inside.

Stone barn, Aldermaston remembered. Is this what Gerald's secretary was referring to? He wandered to the doorway and scoured the darkness. "What am I supposed to be looking at?"

"There." Lisa pointed.

Aldermaston looked up and—

In the darkness was an even darker shadow.

Mortiforde Millie.

CHAPTER NINE

Rosemary's fingers toyed with the silver fork beside her as she looked around Knowton Manor's dining room. How different might her life have been had Rupert not tried to sabotage her European Parliament career? He'd proposed afterwards as an apology, but she could never have trusted him as a life partner. Fifteen years later, when she moved back to the UK, she tied the knot with him as a business partner. Business contracts were easier to nullify than marriages.

The dining-room door swung open. Rupert swaggered in with a white tea towel draped over one arm and carrying two plates, each containing a perfectly cooked lamb shank resting on a pillow of smooth mashed potato, surrounded by a rich dark gravy and sprinkled with finely chopped coriander leaves.

"Couldn't find the bloody coriander." He placed one plate in front of her, rotated it so the shank bone pointed right, and then placed the other on his placemat. He grabbed a bottle of red Châteauneuf-du-Pape and filled Rosemary's glass. The single candle flame illuminated his smile.

It was that enigmatic grin that first attracted her. Mysteriously, it only appeared in candlelight. Anything harsher illuminated Rupert's business facade: brusk, unemotional, and remote. Just like the birthmark above his left eyebrow.

He sat down opposite, poured himself a glass, then raised it. Rosemary collected hers and followed suit.

"To Westminster," Rupert declared.

"To Westminster," she repeated. Her gaze remained fixed on his grey irises. This was what he excelled at. Moments like this made her want to tell him everything. Yet. . .

Rupert picked at his lamb shank. "Everything's going to plan."

She snorted. "Being forcibly escorted off the council's premises was *not* part of the plan."

Rupert pushed some mashed potato onto his fork. "All projects have curveballs. You've batted it away, haven't you?"

She nodded. "I made the call earlier." She sipped more wine, her gaze fixed on him as he tucked into his lamb shank.

He glanced up and caught her staring. That smile appeared again. He placed his knife on the side of his plate and let his fingertips slide across the table towards hers.

She snatched her hand back. "Rupert," she clipped, waving her fork in the air. "We're business partners. Nothing else. That's all in the past."

Rupert's free hand reclaimed his knife. His smile disappeared. A buzzing noise escaped from his shirt pocket. He pulled out his phone and checked the number. The candlelight couldn't hide his need to take the call.

She nodded.

Rupert left the room as he answered. "Speak, but make it quick."

Guilt washed over her. Briefly. If he ever found out … He was a businessman, not a family man.

Her phone pinged with a text message. The National Audit Office.

An associate will make their presence known at
Borderlandshire District Council's offices
tomorrow.

Abigail will be apoplectic. She picked up her glass and
swallowed half its contents as the dining-room door swung
open.

"I'm not contactable tomorrow. Business meeting in Paris.
No, I am leaving later tonight. Helicopter to Heathrow, then
private jet. I'll be back tomorrow. Late afternoon. Good work."
Rupert returned his phone to his shirt pocket, then topped up
Rosemary's half-empty glass.

"Work?" Rosemary resumed eating.

"You know me." The candlelight glistened in his eyes.

"Unusual time for a work colleague to call."

Rupert speared some lamb with his fork. "You know
business. There's the glamorous front office stuff, and then
there's the back office work that nobody sees, but without
which none of the front office miracles happen." His enigmatic
smile appeared once more.

"Abigail told me Diya Parmer notified her of the revised
waste incinerator funding. There's no way Diya sent that email.
How did you manage that?"

He winked. "I have the right IT contacts."

"Someone in the council?"

Rupert's hand wavered in mid-air. "Sort of. Freelance." He
sniggered. "They'll do anything for money."

"Where did you find them?" She savoured the coriander
mash. "On the dark web?"

He stared into the darkness behind her briefly. "Crystal had
a computer virus. Clicked an email link she shouldn't have.
Bloody useless sometimes. Anyway, we needed a specialist,
which she found. We got chatting while they checked my
computer and—"

"The rest is history." Rosemary relaxed. Not a council employee then.

Rupert sipped some wine. "A relatively long history," he continued. "Had to give them a few minor jobs first. Needed to know they were trustworthy." He smirked. "One job turned out to be quite fortuitous."

Rosemary's eyes narrowed.

"Grenville Gastrell." Rupert rested his wine glass against his bottom lip and stared at her.

Rosemary's jaw dropped. "You didn't—" She'd cursed herself this morning thinking Rupert might have been involved in his father's death, and yet now . . .?

Rupert guffawed. "No! Our last MP died of a heart attack." He finished his glass of wine. "Probably brought on by the shock of discovering some inappropriate images on his computer that my new accomplice had put there."

"What?"

Rupert shrugged. "Someone capable of planting indecent images on a Member of Parliament's computer would have no problems infiltrating your Head of Planning Finance's email account."

Rosemary felt the colour drain from her face. Rupert hadn't killed Grenville Gastrell. But he was complicit in the man's death.

Peredur returned his mobile phone to his camouflage jacket chest pocket and wandered back to his troops assembled in Mortiforde Forest. His head-torch illuminated the ground before him. A brief break in the clouds shone moonlight across his gathered troops with a flare-like clarity.

The valley clearing in Mortiforde Forest's deer park created a natural amphitheatre, surrounded by regiments of dominating Douglas fir and larch trees. His soldiers, all BANG members, sat in four semicircular rows, twenty-five in each, dressed in full combat gear, awaiting further instructions. Peredur jumped onto a bottled-beer-crate podium.

"Apologies for that interruption, fellow BANG members. As our rebellion draws close, it's imperative I keep in close contact with everyone involved."

He checked the faces before him. Agent 117 wasn't here. Good. He must still be guarding Mortiforde Millie. The moon slipped behind another cloud. Darkness swallowed them.

"Tonight is dress rehearsal night," he bellowed. "Tomorrow we storm one of Mortiforde's grandest properties."

A series of whoops and cheers echoed around the valley.

"I will send the exact location coordinates electronically at 0600 hours tomorrow. I've mocked up the outline of the property in question, five hundred yards to my left. We have about sixty minutes to practise."

He was about to jump down from his temporary platform when he remembered something. "One more thing."

A hush descended again.

"Friday night, after you've paraded Mortiforde Millie through town, we'll march to the council offices, where I'll dismiss you. I've put money behind the bar at The Nooseman's Knot for two rounds."

His troops cheered and punched the air. A voice called through the darkness. "Agent 62. Permission to speak, Commander."

"Go ahead, Neil."

"Why can't you join us at The Nooseman's Knot?"

Peredur kicked his boots against the plastic crate's surface. "I have a few fireworks of my own to set off in the council offices."

～

Aldermaston depressed the accelerator, and the utility vehicle took the strain. Diya's Morris Minor screeched painfully as the wall released its grip.

"Keep going," Daniel bellowed.

Slowly, Aldermaston towed Diya's bruised car towards Shepherd Cottage. Daniel, Lisa, and Diya followed on foot behind.

As they approached the cottage, Aldermaston pulled Diya's Morris Minor behind the single-story building and unhooked it from the utility vehicle.

He handed the cottage keys to Lisa. "Take Diya inside and help her get settled." He shone his phone's torchlight at Daniel. "Get anywhere with that security firm?" Aldermaston kicked the front tyres.

"They recommended an MBT for the front gates," Daniel replied.

"A what?"

"MBT. Sends a clear signal to any would-be attackers, apparently," said Daniel.

"No patrols and dogs, then?"

"The chap I spoke with suggested the weak spot is the front gates. The MBT deals with that."

Aldermaston returned his phone to his jacket pocket. "What is an MBT exactly?"

"Find out tomorrow morning when it's delivered, I suppose."

A sense of unease toyed with Aldermaston's stomach. "And what about the back gates——"

A high-pitched scream from inside the cottage penetrated the forest.

Aldermaston stared at Daniel. "Diya!"

They charged into the cottage. To the left was the living room area, with an open fire, a green two-seater settee set against the back wall, and a small table and two chairs placed underneath the window opposite. Directly in front of them, an open wooden staircase ran up to a mezzanine bedroom in the eaves on the right.

Aldermaston turned to the small kitchen area on his right and saw Diya clutching her chest.

Lisa's hands were on her hips. "I thought you said this place was empty."

"It is!" Aldermaston checked the living area.

"Apparently not." Lisa pounded on the closed bathroom door. "You can come out now!"

The bathroom door clicked open, and a half-naked man with a white towel wrapped around his waist stepped out.

Basildon grinned. "Hello, Old Bean. Fancy seeing you here."

A tremendous cheer erupted in Tugford Hall's main drawing room as Felicity entered. The entire Ladies' Legion stood and applauded. The cacophony of clapping, foot stamping, and cheering from the two dozen assembled ladies drowned the clock's eight-thirty chime.

A red-faced Felicity motioned for everyone to return to their seats. She beamed broadly and held her clipboard high in the air. "We have our first client!"

Another enormous cheer erupted.

She allowed them their moment of celebration, then motioned for order again. "Ladies, we can't be complacent. There's still much to do. Councillor Prendeghast's passing is our opportunity to show this town just what an environmentally friendly burial can look like. I have booked the Reverend Makepiece to conduct the burial at three o'clock tomorrow."

There was a huge intake of breath.

Cissy Warbouys raised her size eight knitting needle. "That doesn't leave us much time to publicise the event."

Felicity tapped her clipboard. "Sir Hugo's agreement only stands if our first burial takes place before he's interred in the family vault. We can't waste time."

She glanced down at her list on the clipboard. "How are we getting on with the anti-waste-incinerator protests?"

Heidi Yail stood and slid her half-moon glasses down her nose an inch as she read from her notebook. "We had protests in Watling Street, Weir Street, and outside the Castle, and have, so far, collected over five hundred signatures supporting our campaign."

There was a ripple of applause.

She continued. "The Watling Street protesters suffered minor injuries when one motorist drove straight at us and, had we not moved when we did, Margaret here would now be in hospital … or worse."

A chorus of boos and hisses filled the air.

Felicity shook her head. "Ladies, never put yourselves at risk. We must be more strategic with our protests."

Cordelia stood. "If we're having our first burial tomorrow at three o'clock," she said, her soft Welsh accent floating across the room, "why don't we block Watling Street above Curtain Wall Road, and Southgate Street above the old town gate?"

Heidi scribbled in her notebook and gasped. "That forces everyone past the meadows!"

"Exactly," beamed Cordelia.

"We'll need more than some cardboard placards to stop mad motorists charging at us," Heidi commented. "Margaret doesn't enjoy being a BMW target practice."

Cordelia snapped her fingers. "My husband has bought several metres of metal intruder deterrent spikes for the top of our brick walls."

Felicity frowned. "How does that help?"

"He hasn't used them yet," Cordelia continued. "They come in one-metre strips. A couple of those across the road will puncture any tyre driving over them."

"We'll take them," Heidi snapped.

Felicity jotted this information down and ticked off another item on her list. "There are several other formalities we still need to sort out."

A hush descended around the room.

"We need a grave in which to bury Councillor Prendeghast. Does anyone have a spare husband who can dig one for us tomorrow morning?"

Kitty Catchpole raised her hand. "My Otis can do it. Assuming I can wake him. You know what teenagers are like at half-term. But it won't take him ten minutes with the farm's mini-digger."

"Kitty, you're a star." Felicity wasn't sure a diesel-powered mini-digger was particularly environmentally friendly, but time was of the essence. That was something to consider for the future.

Arabella Bebbington raised a hand. "What are we burying Councillor Prendeghast in? Do we have a coffin to use?"

"What about a shroud?" called one member. "It's what they used centuries ago."

Cissy raised a knitting needle. "People will expect a casket of some kind."

Felicity sucked on her pen. "Earth, Wind, and Fire had nothing suitable. We'll have to source it ourselves."

"How are we getting Councillor Prendeghast from Earth, Wind, and Fire to the meadows?" asked Arabella.

Felicity tapped the pen against her chin. "I enquired about a horse and carriage, but the funeral directors couldn't help."

"My Wilfred could," called a voice from the back row. A woman with strawberry blonde hair, wearing a two-tone grey jumper, stood.

"No way, Nancy!" Arabella exclaimed. "We can't have a rag and bone man bring a dead body to a burial on the same cart he uses to collect other people's junk. It would be like throwing him out with the rubbish."

"He has a horse and a flat cart. Isn't that what we need?" Nancy defended. "We can drape the cart in black cloth."

Felicity smiled. "That's perfect. What is a rag and bone man if he isn't the epitome of an environmentally friendly business? Thank you, Nancy."

She tucked her clipboard under her arm and clasped her hands together. "I'm speaking on Breakfast Benny's radio show tomorrow morning, just after eight o'clock, to publicise this momentous occasion. If the protests divert traffic towards the meadows tomorrow afternoon, we stand a good chance of making our first interment an enormous success. Ladies, what we have achieved in such a limited time is truly remarkable. Let's give Councillor Prendeghast the send-off he deserves. Tomorrow will be a momentous day for the Ladies' Legion and for Mortiforde."

Aldermaston collapsed onto the green two-seater settee next to a still-quivering Diya and stared at Basildon. "Why did you take Mortiforde Millie from the Highway Depot and hide her in that stone barn?"

"Ah!" Basildon walked wet footprints across the kitchen floor towards the living room area. "I have some explaining to do." He pulled one of the two dining chairs out and sat down, knees apart.

Diya shrieked and covered her eyes.

"Legs, Basildon," Aldermaston instructed.

Basildon swiftly crossed them. "Terribly sorry, old gal." He looked at Aldermaston. "Are you going to introduce us?"

"This is Diya." Aldermaston pondered how much information he should share with Basildon. "Lisa's colleague. Diya, this is my half-brother, Basildon."

Diya nodded, but didn't smile.

Basildon's right hand twisted the signet ring on his left hand's little finger. "Bet you're glad I fired the cannon at those troublesome protesters earlier, heh?" He smirked. "They could have held you out there for hours."

"It *was* you." Aldermaston wagged his finger at Basildon. "You could have killed somebody!"

Basildon dismissed him. "Poppycock! It was a blank. A puff of smoke and a loud bang."

Aldermaston's eyes widened. "The sodding cannonball landed barely three feet from my car!"

Basildon's bushy black eyebrows bowed to one another. "Could have sworn the barrel was empty." He beamed. "No harm done, heh?"

Daniel clattered about in the kitchen.

Basildon called across to him. "Milk, no sugar, if you're making one for everyone." He shuffled in the chair. "So, why are you here? Felicity finally chucked you out?"

Aldermaston jabbed Basildon's bare knee. "I asked first. What's going on? You dropped that BANG note into my office, didn't you? And you stole Mortiforde Millie, for which BANG has claimed responsibility. You're helping BANG, aren't you?"

Basildon brought his finger to his lips. "Shhh. Walls have ears, you know."

"And these are two-feet thick." Aldermaston knocked his knuckles against the whitewashed stone wall beside him.

Basildon pursed his lips.

"Fine." Aldermaston grabbed his half-brother's bare arm. "Outside. Now!"

Aldermaston dragged Basildon out of the cottage as fast as his half-brother's tight towel-skirt would allow.

"Good grief," Basildon shivered. "It's cold enough to freeze the—"

"So start talking." Aldermaston pulled the cottage door to.

"I'm undercover," Basildon hissed.

"Hardly." Aldermaston watched the rivulets of water running down Basildon's bare chest and legs.

"I've infiltrated the enemy."

"Pardon?"

Basildon checked over his shoulder. "I thought it might help me to … you know … get into MI5."

Aldermaston couldn't understand how MI5 might benefit from Basildon's infiltration of a parochial publicity stunt group designed to embarrass, at least, and confuse at best.

"If I can bring about BANG's downfall, MI5 might take my applications to join them seriously."

"You seem to be doing most of BANG's dirty work. How are you bringing about its downfall?"

Basildon leaned closer. "Early days, old bean. Give a chap a chance."

"Did you know about the protesters turning up outside the front gates this evening?"

Basildon rubbed his chin. "I heard them arrive, and when I saw the placards, I knew Peredur was behind this."

"Peredur?"

Basildon shot a glance through the cottage window before locking eyes again with Aldermaston. "The Commander. Nice chap once you get to know him."

Aldermaston thought back to the earlier protest. Wasn't Bandana Man talking to a Peredur on the phone?

"I say nice chap," Basildon continued, "but, come to think about it, I've never seen him without his warpaint."

"Sorry?"

Basildon drew a circle in front of Aldermaston's face. "His

face is always camouflage-painted. Probably sleeps like that, too."

Aldermaston shivered. "So what's BANG's big plan?"

Basildon's voice dropped to a whisper. "Not sure yet."

"Why not?" Aldermaston hissed.

"Gaining trust is a slow game."

"Well, hurry up!" He pointed towards the stone barn. "Because tomorrow morning, the Borderers Guild will collect Mortiforde Millie and prepare her for Friday night's parade and firework display."

"No!" Basildon hissed. "You can't! The Commander thinks I've hidden her somewhere safe. You could blow my cover!"

"Not my problem," Aldermaston snarled.

Peredur collapsed into his dining table chair. The dress rehearsals in Mortiforde Forest had gone well. After all these years of planning, everything was coming together.

He lifted his laptop screen and checked the stone barn's CCTV images. Something caught his eye. Was that smoke wafting through the barn's entrance?

A woman appeared in the doorway and stared at Millie. Peredur zoomed in. Night vision wasn't as high quality as day vision, but whoever it was, she'd definitely seen Mortiforde Millie.

Peredur shuffled to the edge of his seat and watched her point to the oversized effigy. Someone else entered the barn. A man. The Eighth Marquess of Mortiforde.

He slammed the dining table hard. "No!" he bellowed as he watched Aldermaston step closer to Mortiforde Millie.

Peredur paced his living room. So much for Basildon claiming the Marquess knew nothing of the barn's existence.

He screamed, then turned and punched a hole through the nearest wall. Plaster fragments fell to the floor.

Peredur wagged a finger at the screen. He'd hoped to get more use out of the Marquess's half-brother. But now it was time for Plan B. He grabbed his camouflage jacket off the back of the chair and slipped it on. "Agent 117. You'll regret crossing me."

Basildon bid Diya goodnight and closed the door to Shepherd Cottage behind him. He threw his rucksack on his back, switched on his head-torch, and pondered his next move. Not Tugford Hall. Perhaps Gerald would be grateful for some company.

Silently, he made his way through the trees, with only an occasional far-off fox screech to accompany him. All seemed still as he stood in the stone barn's entrance. His head-torch illuminated Mortiforde Millie's bowed head. Then he turned to the hay bales where he'd hidden Gerald. The top bale was off to one side.

He dashed across and peered inside. By Jove, it was empty. Had Gerald escaped?

"Lost someone?"

Basildon spun around to see his head-torch spotlighting the Commander's camouflaged face. "Where's Gerald, Commander?"

Peredur lunged, grabbed Basildon's hand, then twisted his arm around his neck and spun him round with such force, something clattered to the floor.

"My ring!" Basildon screamed.

Peredur clamped his free gloved hand tightly over Basildon's mouth and nose. "Don't worry about Gerald. He's got nothing to worry about now. You have, though."

Basildon fought and writhed against Peredur's powerful grip until the lack of oxygen caused him to pass out.

157

CHAPTER TEN

"ALDERMASTON!"

A blinding light accompanied the sharp swish of wrenched-open curtains. Aldermaston sought darkness under the duvet.

"No, you don't!" Felicity's voice penetrated the goose-feathered, ten-tog duvet before she ripped it back, leaving Aldermaston with only some baggy Y-fronts keeping him warm.

He grabbed Felicity's pillow and smothered his face with it. "Ten more minutes," he whined.

Felicity ripped the pillow from his face. "There's something you need to see." She grabbed his wrist and pulled him out of bed.

"Ow!" His shoulder still twinged from yesterday. "Where are we going?"

She hauled him along their apartment corridor. "You'll have to sort this out. I'm live on Breakfast Benny's radio show in seven minutes."

Aldermaston rubbed the sleep from his eyes as his bare feet stumbled to keep up. They blustered down the stairs, through the false bookcase door, and into Tugford Hall's main hallway. Cold pains shot up his calves as his bare feet smacked against the freezing marble floor.

Felicity unlatched the Hall's main wooden doors and pulled them wide open. She pushed Aldermaston onto the porticoed entrance.

His toes curled up to avoid the stone floor. "What should I be looking at?" He stifled a yawn.

Felicity grabbed his shoulders and twisted him towards the driveway. "How can you miss that?"

Aldermaston blinked and shivered as the frosty November air swirled around him. He squinted towards the gates. There, parked tightly between the main gateposts, blocking the entrance completely, was an MBT. To everyone else, it looked like a post-Second World War Chieftain tank with its eleven-metre gun pointing directly at anyone approaching Tugford Hall.

Daniel was right. It definitely sent a message.

Abigail stepped out of the lift and headed towards her office. Ahead, through the glass partition, she saw Pamela's dark auburn hair above the top of her computer monitor. Finally, her secretary realised she was supposed to be at her desk *before* Abigail arrived. How else could a chief executive hit the ground running first thing?

Abigail swiped her security pass and entered her inner sanctum. "Morning, Pamela. Bring your notebook when you've made my coffee. We've plenty to sort today regarding tomorrow's Neighbourhood Area Forum."

Pamela half-stood, pointing to Abigail's office. "There's already—"

"You've made it already? Perfect!" Abigail smiled. "Give me five minutes to get settled, then come and join me."

"No, what I mean is—"

Abigail stepped into her office and closed the door. She slipped her handbag onto a metal coat stand hook and then hung her white jacket on an adjacent hook. She smoothed her light khaki sleeveless, boat-necked dress, then stepped towards her desk. Only then did she see someone waiting.

"Sorry, have you been here long?" She cursed Pamela under her breath and strode towards the waiting bald-headed suited gentleman.

He offered his hand. "Norris Offermans."

Abigail shook hands. "Is this a scheduled meeting, only I —" She switched on her computer and gestured to the chair. "Please take a seat."

Mr Offermans remained standing. "I won't, Ms Mayedew. It's imperative I start immediately."

She froze. Her bottom hovered just above her chair seat. "Start what?"

"Our investigation." He released the catches of his briefcase and withdrew a sheet of paper. "This explains everything."

Abigail took the document. She skim read as she spoke. "We're being investigated? For what?"

Norris Offermans grasped his briefcase. "Irregularities."

"What irregularities?"

"The waste incinerator project. It's come to our attention—"

Abigail slammed the paper down on her desk and pointed at Mr Offermans. "This is Rosemary Sedgewicke's doing!"

Norris didn't flinch. "We don't reveal our sources. If you can point me to your Head of Planning Finance's office, I can get on with my task and be out of your hair as quickly as possible."

Abigail seethed. She'd show him what it was like to have someone in his hair … Light glistened on his bald head. She exhaled. Slowly. "Our Head of Planning Finance is on annual leave at present."

Norris smiled. "We won't be fighting over who sits in the chair, then, shall we?"

Abigail stood. "Could this not wait until she returns in a fortnight?"

He stepped forward. "The NAO waits for no one."

"Wouldn't it make sense for the woman who confirmed the waste incinerator project's funding status to be here and show you that?"

Norris nodded.

"Well, you'll have to wait until she returns."

"Or you could ask your member of staff to take their annual leave at some other time."

"She's in Mumbai!"

Norris pulled back his heavily starched pale blue shirt cuff and checked his watch. "Mumbai to Birmingham International is about twelve hours. I see no reason why your staff member couldn't be back here first thing tomorrow morning."

"What?"

"How quickly do you want me gone?"

Abigail snatched the phone from the desk handset. "Pamela, get me Diya Parmer on the phone immediately."

Peredur placed a large cooked breakfast in front of his guest sitting at his dining table.

Dewi inhaled deeply. "That's banging, boyo!"

Peredur set down his fry-up opposite Dewi and placed another smaller plate beside it. "An army marches on its stomach. Breakfast is the most important meal of the day."

Dewi pointed at the smaller dish with his fork. "That's why you're having two servings?"

Peredur tutted. "Got a guest upstairs. They can have it later."

Dewi waved his knife in the air. "Always cook with your face painted?" He frowned. "Thinking 'bout it, I don't think I've ever seen you without your war paint on."

"A soldier must always be ready for battle. You can't put a war on hold for twenty minutes while we put on our make-up."

Dewi slipped the burner phone from his pocket and passed it across the table. "You can have this back."

"Cheers, mate." Peredur extracted the phone's SIM and snapped it in half. Then he pulled a sheet of paper from his back pocket and slipped it across the tabletop to Dewi. "Another order. We're going to add some spice to Mortiforde Millie's parade on Friday night."

Dewi unfolded the paper. His eyebrows rose. "Two hundred kilos of gunpowder?"

"Can you do it?"

"Of course, boyo. Them battle re-enactment groups use gunpowder all the time." He looked around the room. "Not keeping it here, are ya?"

"I know somewhere at work that's safe. I'll text you the details later when I send you the money. Need it delivered Thursday night."

Dewi nodded.

Peredur picked up his knife and fork and then set them down again. "Almost forgot. We need to listen to this morning's entertainment. Sent Benny another press release late last night." He switched on the radio, perched on the mantelpiece, and caught the end of the weather forecast.

"Goooooooooooood morning Borderlandshire," screamed Breakfast Benny across the airwaves. "It's ten past eight on the fourth of November, and we're joined by Lady Mortiforde, who has some exciting news for anyone waking up dead this morning. Isn't that right, My Lady?"

"Morning, Benny. Yes, the Ladies' Legion has news of a first for Mortiforde."

"I think today will have many firsts," Benny muttered a little too loudly. "So what have the Ladies' Legion been up to?"

Felicity took a settling breath. "We want to change the way we say goodbye to our loved ones and do it in a more environmentally friendly manner."

Benny burst out laughing. "What should we do instead? Put our dead relatives in the fortnightly green recycling bins? Should they go feet first, or head first?"

Dewi sniggered.

"No, Benny, the Ladies' Legion received permission to use Mortiforde Meadows to lay our loved ones to rest. But we won't use embalming fluids that destroy the environment when they leach into the soil, nor will we use MDF coffins that use synthetic glues, some of which emit toxic gases and don't biodegrade."

"You're not using those starch-based supermarket carrier bags that hold nothing more than a lettuce, are you?" Benny suggested.

A nervous chuckle echoed down Felicity's microphone. "The best way to find out is to come along to the first green burial this afternoon at three o'clock at Mortiforde Meadows, where we shall lay Councillor Prendeghast to rest in a dignified but planet-friendly manner."

"Talking of the meadows," Benny interrupted, "how does this fit in with the council's waste-incinerator proposal? Will you be going into partnership with them? Perhaps the waste incinerator could double as a crematorium?"

Peredur giggled and wiped some baked bean sauce from his plate with a piece of fried bread. "Burning dead people to produce electricity is pioneering. It'll be the most useful thing

Councillor Prendeghast has ever done for the local community!"

Felicity's tone changed. "No, Benny. The Ladies' Legion opposes the council's waste incinerator project, and we'll invite Councillor Prendeghast's funeral attendees to sign our petition to save the meadows. We're taking direct action because we cannot see the meadows destroyed like that."

There was a rustling noise as Benny shifted some paper about on his desk. "Talking of direct action, BANG has tipped me off that Lord Mortiforde is also taking direct action."

"Er—" Felicity's nerves silenced her.

Peredur winked at Dewi. "Here we go."

Breakfast Benny cleared his throat. "It seems Lord Mortiforde fired a cannonball at peaceful protesters outside his gates yesterday evening," he proclaimed. "How far will you go to keep the riff-raff out?"

Felicity floundered. "I'm sure it was a simple misunderstanding."

"Misunderstanding?" Benny interjected. "Is that why there's a World War Two tank blocking Tugford Hall's driveway this morning? What are you frightened of, Your Ladyship?"

"I —"

"Are you worried the townsfolk will storm Tugford Hall and rip the tiles from your roof? Tiles that were paid for thirty years ago when the Seventh Marquess sold Mortiforde Meadows to Sir Hugo instead of the Historic Borders Agency, like he'd promised," Breakfast Benny continued.

"No—"

Peredur and Dewi giggled in their seats.

"Had he stuck to that original plan," Benny continued, "the meadows would be safe and the town wouldn't be in this waste incinerator mess. No wonder His Lordship is bringing out the big guns. How do you answer that, Your Ladyship?"

Silence.

"Your Ladyship? Are you still there?"

Silence.

"It appears we've lost the line to Tugford Hall. Perhaps Lord Mortiforde has blown it up. Stay tuned for more explosive developments—"

Peredur switched off the radio, still laughing. "The Marquess has no idea what I have planned."

Dewi leaned back in his dining chair and patted his contented belly. "Is that why you asked me to leave a couple of live shells in the tank?"

Peredur winked. "Possibly."

~

Now dressed, Aldermaston stared at the Chieftain tank blocking Tugford Hall's driveway. The muddy green hunk of metal had been reversed in through the driveway, far enough to ensure it was off the road, but that still maximised its imposing eleven-metre gun barrel threat. It was enough to stop an army in its tracks.

Army. Realisation dawned. BANG taped the security leaflet to his office door. Probably Basildon again. Perhaps he should have closed Tugford Hall's gates. But they'd never been closed in his lifetime. He wasn't even sure if they moved. His father always said gates were a barrier.

Aldermaston squeezed through the narrow gap between its caterpillar tracks and the ornate gatepost and slipped out onto the road.

Behind him, Cartwright cleared his throat. "Chief Constable Stoyle is asking for you, My Lord." He held up a phone handset.

Aldermaston grabbed it. "If it's about the tank, it only arrived this morning."

"Tank?"

Aldermaston paused mid-pace. "You've not had a complaint, then?"

"No. Why do you have a tank?"

Aldermaston ran his fingers through his hair. "I had a little trouble with some BANG protesters yesterday—"

"And you've bought a tank?"

"I ordered some security. This isn't what I had in mind, though. I'm not breaking any laws, am I?"

Stoyle deliberated. "Is it on the public highway?"

Aldermaston double-checked. The caterpillar tracks sat neatly on his land. "No."

"Is it blocking a public highway or a public right of way?"

"Just my driveway."

Stoyle sounded more relaxed. "If it's on private land, then it's a private matter and nothing to do with the police. Anyway," he continued, "I've arranged some support for PC Norten."

"At last!" Aldermaston punched the air.

"I'm sending PCSO Ceri Marker to Mortiforde."

"PCSO? Somebody murdered Sir Hugo, and all you can send is a Police Community Support Officer?"

"PCSOs play a vital role in today's modern policing practices. They have the power to issue fixed penalty notices, demand a name and address, and—"

"That'll come in handy when they come face to face with a murderer. Can they actually arrest anyone?"

"Marchlands Constabulary PCSOs have the power to detain someone for up to thirty minutes until a police officer arrives—"

"Thirty minutes?" Aldermaston's voice rose an octave. "You lot take an hour to get here on blue lights from Worcester."

Aldermaston hung up and passed the handset back to

Cartwright. "If Stoyle calls back, tell him I'm too busy driving a tank around the county to take his call."

Cartwright nodded, pressed another button on the handset, and said, "Are you still there? I'll pass you across to His Lordship now." He offered the handset back to Aldermaston. "There's another call on line two."

Aldermaston took it. "Lord Mortiforde speaking."

"It's Maureen from the Lockmount Estate Agency." She struggled to catch her breath. "I've had to unlock the agency this morning." She grabbed another breath. "Gerald's definitely missing."

Abigail wrenched open her office door. Pamela jumped, spilling coffee all over her computer keyboard.

"Why isn't Diya on the phone, like I asked twenty minutes ago?"

Pamela upturned her keyboard and patted her desk with a clump of tissues. "There's no answer from her home phone—"

"SHE'S IN MUMBAI! Try her mobile!"

"It goes straight through to voicemail."

Abigail seethed. "Any next of kin contact details?"

Pamela grabbed a reporter's notebook and turned a page. "Diya's only relatives are in Mumbai, so it's a contact number for her grandmother."

Abigail snapped her fingers. "Call it and put it through to me."

"I can't," Pamela cowered.

"Why not?"

"It's a Mumbai number."

Abigail hit her forehead on the doorframe. "Well, if that's where her grandmother lives—"

"Council regulations." Pamela dabbed her keyboard with

more tissues. "The system blocks international calls after Councillor Uxterby's long-distance relationship with a Greek waiter she fell in love with on holiday—"

Abigail raised a hand. "Spare me the details! What's the number? I'll use my mobile."

Pamela scribbled it down and handed it to her. "I spoke with Sheila on Reception earlier. She's not convinced Diya is in India."

Abigail grabbed her mobile phone and entered the number. "Tell Sheila I'm on my way down." She brought the phone to her ear.

There was a series of clicks and tones as she barged through the glass doors. Her heels clipped authoritatively along the vinyl corridor flooring. Office doors opened and staff half-stepped out, then disappeared back inside as she approached.

"The number dialled is not valid," declared an automated message.

Abigail cursed and cancelled the call. She pressed the lift call button, waited a few seconds, then took the adjacent door and the stairs.

Sheila stood as soon as Abigail entered the reception area. Her hands fidgeted with a handkerchief, and she struggled to maintain her nervous smile.

Abigail leaned against the counter. "Pamela says you don't think Diya is in Mumbai."

Sheila looked at her fidgeting hands. "She never mentioned it yesterday morning."

"Is it something she'd usually mention?"

"Oh yes! She'd be counting down the days for weeks. 'Only four more days,' she'd sing when she arrived each morning. And then the following day, she'd sing, 'Only three more—'"

"Yes, I get the point," Abigail interrupted. "And she's not mentioned this trip at all?"

Sheila shook her head vigorously.

"Who told you Diya had gone to Mumbai?"

Sheila's brown eyes searched the ceiling. "Lisa Duddon was looking for her yesterday, and she checked the staff annual leave system on my computer. That's where we saw Mumbai."

Abigail frowned. "Why was Lisa looking for Diya?"

Sheila's bottom lip protruded. "Not sure."

"Sheila, you've been most helpful." Abigail spun round, dialled another number on her phone, and heaved against the external revolving doors, encouraging them to let her out of the building.

"Abigail, I'm about to go into a national Chief Constable meeting with the Home Secretary."

"Colin, I need you to find out if a member of my staff by the name of Diya Parmer appears on any passenger manifest for flights between Birmingham International and Mumbai yesterday."

The Chief Constable chuckled. "Abigail, that's not possible unless you wish to report a crime."

"I have the National Audit Office investigating the waste incinerator project, and the woman who says it's financially viable has mysteriously disappeared. If I can establish whether she got on a plane to Mumbai yesterday, then I may find out what is—"

Stoyle interrupted. "No, Abigail. I can't."

She paced outside the council office entrance. "Fine. I'll call the Home Secretary and tell him how obstructive you're being."

Stoyle gulped. "You know the Home Secretary?"

Abigail savoured the moment. "Yes, David and I go way back. We met regularly when I was Chief Exec at the London Borough of Thameside."

There was a deep sigh. "Leave it with me."

The call went dead.

Abigail tapped her phone against her chin. Now, why was

Lisa looking for Diya? Of course! Partnership working. It wasn't Lisa looking for Diya. It was Lord Mortiforde.

Aldermaston hurried across Tugford Hall's rear courtyard towards Daniel's approaching twelve-year-old silver Toyota. He motioned to Daniel to keep the engine running.

Felicity thrust open the kitchen window high above them. "Aldermaston! Move that tank! I want this evening's *Mortiforde Chronicle* front-page story to be about Councillor Prendeghast's groundbreaking, environmentally friendly burial, not the tank on our driveway, do you hear?"

Aldermaston opened Daniel's passenger door and slipped inside. "Drive!"

Daniel reversed in a wide arc around the courtyard. "Where to?"

"Shepherd Cottage. Let's get Diya."

Daniel chewed his cheek as he turned onto the stone track. "So," he began, "it seems an MBT is a Main Battle Tank. I should have—"

"Not your fault." Aldermaston grabbed the armrest as they dodged the potholes. "BANG, or rather, Basildon probably planted that leaflet." He sighed. "It's completely blocking the main entrance, so it is working."

Daniel swerved to avoid another dip. "Felicity's radio interview didn't quite go to plan either."

"BANG has been playing us like fools." He leaned against the passenger door as Daniel turned a corner. "Ring that number on the security leaflet and get them to collect the tank."

"Already tried." Daniel gripped the steering wheel tighter. "The number's unobtainable."

Aldermaston tutted. "Where did Basildon go after we left Shepherd Cottage?"

"Said he was going back to his apartment now that Diya was using the cottage."

Diya's face appeared at the window as Daniel pulled alongside the front door. She stepped out, locked the door, threw her handbag over her shoulder, but missed. She retrieved it before slipping into Daniel's rear passenger seat.

"While we're here," Aldermaston pointed to the stone barn, "we'd better check my half-brother hasn't made off with Millie again."

Daniel turned sharp right onto the track and pulled alongside the stone barn's wide opening.

Millie was still there. At least something was going right today.

All three got out of the car and wandered towards the puppet.

Diya stroked the effigy's hand. "I've never seen her this close before."

Daniel peered around her. "How does she work?"

Aldermaston picked up Millie's hand. "See this carbon fibre rod connected just underneath her wrist? It's a collapsible, spring-loaded pole. Press the red release catch near the wrist."

They did so together, and the poles snapped into their rigid six-foot length. Aldermaston manipulated it, so Millie waved to Diya. She giggled. It was the first time he'd seen her relaxed.

Aldermaston clambered onto the straw bales where Millie sat. "If we jump up here, there's a similar pole attached to the back of her shoulder. Release that in the same way."

Another pole unfurled, stretching to ten feet long.

"Done it?" Aldermaston leaned forward, looking around Millie's barrel chest.

"Yep," Daniel confirmed.

"If we push up with these shoulder poles, Millie will stand. After three?"

Daniel nodded.

"One, two, three——"

Together, both men pushed the poles upwards, and Millie's shoulders rose. The straw creaked as her weight rose from the bales, and her head lifted as she slipped towards an upright position.

Aldermaston struggled to push the pole higher.

"How many people operate this?" Daniel asked through gritted teeth.

"Stop!" Aldermaston called.

They returned Millie to her seated position, and the straw bales took the strain once more.

Aldermaston scratched his forehead. "Two people normally manage this." Had her joints seized in last night's frost? He felt like his had. The joys of middle age. "Let's try again."

Aldermaston called another countdown, and together they pushed the poles upwards. Millie creaked and strained the harder they pushed.

"Keep going!" Aldermaston screamed as both men put everything into pushing Millie upright.

Slowly, the fifteen-foot effigy rose to its feet, its head lifting upright as it stood tall.

Aldermaston let out a huge gasp. "You can relax now," he puffed. "Counterbalance weights keep her in this position."

Daniel stood back and admired the effigy. "She's amazing."

A series of squeaks, creaks, and groans echoed around the vast stone barn.

"Something's not right," Aldermaston muttered. "If Basildon has damaged her, I'll kill him."

An earsplitting crack ricocheted around the barn. Millie shuddered violently as Aldermaston and Daniel grappled to keep Millie upright. There was a loud crack. Her wooden chest flew open, pushing apart her multicoloured cardigan, and something huge fell to the straw-covered floor with a whomp.

Diya screamed, then fainted.

It was as if Millie had just given birth. But this was no baby.

There on the floor, with his arms and legs splayed at an unnatural angle, was Gerald Lockmount.

Dead.

CHAPTER ELEVEN

Aldermaston squinted. Was that someone in the passenger seat?

There was nobody in the approaching small hatchback driver's seat because there was no driving seat. PC Norten's long legs forced him to use the back seat. But as the passing tree branch reflections swept up the police car's windscreen, Aldermaston thought there was a passenger.

The vehicle pulled up alongside the stone barn. Sirens blared briefly as PC Norten extricated himself from the car's rear. He chuckled. "I always knock that switch with my knee."

A short, blonde-haired woman in her mid-twenties stepped out of the passenger door, slipped on her police hat, and strode up to Aldermaston. "PCSO Ceri Marker. Who might you be?" She took her notebook and pen from her chest pocket.

"Lord Mortiforde." He offered his hand.

"Lord Mortiforde," she repeated slowly, then saw his offered hand. She continued writing. "He wants me to shake hands while both of mine are busy. Question intelligence level."

PC Norten sidestepped over to Aldermaston. "When

Daniel called about another body, I thought, *What's Cartwright been throwing away now?*" He laughed. "I've only just finished all those forms from Sir Hugo's accident yesterday, Your Lordship."

Ceri peered into the barn briefly, then wandered around. "Where is this Daniel?"

"He called from the main house," Aldermaston explained. "Poor mobile signal here."

Ceri scribbled again. "And where is this dead body?"

Aldermaston led them into the stone barn and to Gerald's lifeless body.

PC Norten sniggered and pointed to Mortiforde Millie. "This is the only time of year when there's a taller muppet in town."

Ceri pulled a pair of blue nitrile gloves from her pocket. "Is this how you found him, Mr Mortiforde?"

"It's *Lord* Mortiforde," PC Norten corrected.

Ceri twanged her glove cuffs against her wrists. "He's my chief suspect at the moment." She placed two fingers against the side of Gerald's neck. "He's definitely dead."

Aldermaston pointed to Millie. "Daniel and I tried moving Mortiforde Millie. Once she was upright, Gerald fell out of her onto the floor."

PC Norten whistled. "Falling onto his head from that height would be enough to kill anyone." He tutted. "Such a tragic accident."

Ceri thrust her notebook and pen into PC Norten's hands. "Take these, you moron."

She pulled a reel of red and white police inner cordon tape from her jacket pocket and marched across to the barn's opening. Tying one end around a metal door hinge, she circled around Aldermaston and PC Norten, and ducked under her tape before tying it off on the opposite rusting hinge hook.

Ceri trudged back to PC Norten, grabbed her notebook

and pen, and then pointed to Gerald's neck with her pen. "The deceased has purple marks around his neck, suggesting some sort of ligature. He didn't break his neck falling from a height. He was already dead when he fell. This man was murdered."

"No way!" PC Norten jumped up and down, clapping his hands and breaking the police cordon tape. "A murder, Lord Mortiforde! Proper policing." He nodded towards Ceri, now wandering around the stone barn, staring at the floor. "It's amazing what they teach them at PCSO school these days. I wouldn't know what those purple bruises were."

Aldermaston pointed at Millie. "Will it be okay to move her? We need to prepare her for tomorrow's Bonfire Night parade."

Ceri scribbled in her notebook. "Chief suspect wants to move the puppet the deceased victim fell from before the police have had a proper chance to investigate the scene. Could be an attempt to destroy evidence."

Aldermaston backed away, holding up both hands. "The Borderers Guild will obviously abide by any police regulations. Do you know how long you'll be?"

"Aha!" Ceri slipped her pen through something lying on the floor. "What have we here?"

Suspended from her blue biro was a ring. A signet ring.

Basildon's.

Kitty Catchpole's green rubber boots squelched determinedly across Mortiforde Meadows towards her red-overalled son, Otis, operating their mini-digger. A pile of freshly dug earth lingered to one side as the digger's metal bucket grated against some rock. Kitty covered her ears.

The rattling diesel engine died as Otis jumped down from the open cab. He ruffled his mop of tangled brown hair.

"Problem?" Kitty peered into the trench.

"There's only a couple of feet of topsoil." Otis dropped into the muddy hole. "Could be an enormous boulder or a layer of rock."

Kitty looked around. A low November mist hung in the air as its wispy tendrils entwined themselves between the weeping willows, alder, and birch lining the riverbank. Narrow dog-walker paths criss-crossed the damp grass.

Kitty pointed to higher ground. "What about up there?"

Otis nodded and slipped back into the mini-digger. A cloud of noxious fumes spewed from the exhaust as he manoeuvred it into place.

Kitty watched her fourteen-year-old son skilfully operate the two lever controls and cut another trench, seven feet long by three feet wide. He quickly removed the topsoil, piling it to the left like the previous trench. Within minutes, the metal bucket juddered as it hit more rock.

Otis killed the engine and jumped out. "Has anyone checked whether the meadows are a suitable burial ground? They might sit on one giant slab of rock."

Kitty's eyes widened. "Don't say that! The whole town knows we're burying Councillor Prendeghast here in five and a half hours."

Otis rubbed the back of his head. "I'd better just keep digging then."

Abigail knocked on Diya's office door and waited. Why was she waiting? She was the Chief Exec. This was her building!

She barged in to find Norris, wearing a green eyeshade, sitting at Diya's desk, bashing away at a desktop adding machine. It spewed reams of numbers on a paper roll. His number-crunching fingers stopped, but the adding machine continued churning out printed paper for several seconds.

Abigail smiled. "Got everything you need, Mr Offermans?"

"If you want me gone sooner, then my only need is to work uninterrupted."

She nodded. "Happy with what you've found so far?"

Norris sighed. "I'm never happy until I've seen the complete picture."

Abigail forced a smile. "I'll leave you to it." She closed the door behind her. Norris wasn't being co-operative. Perhaps another tack was required. Her shoes struck an authoritative beat along the corridor to the Democracy Support Unit. She barged straight in and found Lisa at her desk.

"Just the person." Abigail perched on the corner of Lisa's desk. "Everything falling into place for tomorrow evening's Neighbourhood Area Forum?"

Lisa accessed a file on her computer. "I think so. There's a public notice going in today's *Mortiforde Chronicle*. I've sent Councillor Taplinski copies of the background paperwork and. . ." She handed Abigail a Post-it note stuck to the edge of her monitor. "Can you call him? He has some NAF questions."

Abigail slipped the note into a pocket.

"I've issued all the invitations," Lisa continued. "Rupert Rinde's secretary has confirmed his attendance." She clicked her fingers as a thought occurred to her and grabbed a pen. "Should I invite Rosemary? I wasn't sure of the protocol. If she's suspended from duties, then perhaps not, but does her Westminster candidacy change things?"

"Issue the invite," Abigail instructed. "Technically, she's on gardening leave. And seeing that the National Audit Office is currently sitting in Diya's office, going through the numbers, I'd like her there when they declare the project fully funded."

"That *will* happen, will it?"

Abigail stared at Lisa. "Do you know something I don't?"

Lisa shook her head.

Abigail leaned closer. "Why were you looking for Diya yesterday?"

Lisa's face flushed briefly. "To invite her to the NAF. Do you not want her there?"

Abigail folded her arms. "So you weren't making inquiries on behalf of Lord Mortiforde?"

Another slight flush accompanied Lisa's frown. "Why would he be looking for Diya?"

"Why indeed?" Abigail's mobile phone rang. It was Stoyle. She smiled at Lisa. "Need to take this. Keep up the good work."

Abigail answered the call as she stepped out of the office. "Colin, please tell me Diya's still in the country."

"No."

Abigail's shoulders dropped. "Blast!" She stormed back towards her office.

"Abigail, I can only deal with facts, and I'm calling with a fact. Nobody with the name Ms Diya Parmer has departed Birmingham International for Mumbai."

She stopped in her tracks. "So she *is* still in the country."

"Not necessarily." Stoyle clarified. "My staff only checked flights from Birmingham International with stopovers or connections to Mumbai. She could have gone directly from Heathrow."

Abigail grinned. "Thank you, Colin. You have been most helpful."

Gut instinct told her Diya was still in Mortiforde. And, judging by Lisa's flushed face, Lord Mortiforde thought that, too.

So, was Diya hiding somewhere? And why?

❀

180

"Give me strength." Aldermaston collapsed into his captain's chair. Daniel locked the office door. "PCSO Marker has declared the stone barn a crime scene. We can't move anything."

Daniel sat down beside Diya. "What? Not even Mortiforde Millie?"

"She's effectively impounded Millie." Aldermaston shrugged wearily. "At least that PCSO has a couple more brain cells than PC Norten."

Daniel laughed. "Statistically, the chances were considerable."

Aldermaston picked up his fountain pen and scribbled some notes. "She spotted ligature marks around Gerald's neck."

Diya stopped typing. "He was murdered?"

Aldermaston nodded.

Daniel twisted in his chair. "If this is about the meadows, there's some logic to killing Sir Hugo. But Gerald? He's an estate agent."

Aldermaston flicked through his notes. Daniel was right. Gerald wasn't involved in the waste incinerator project or the outcome of Mortiforde Meadows. He came across his Historic Borders Agency notes from his meeting with Stella. Had Gerald been involved when his father sold the meadows to Sir Hugo?

Daniel's computer pinged. Diya checked the screen. "We've another bid on one of the first editions. Twenty-seven thousand pounds!"

"How much?" Aldermaston sat upright. "What? For all five books?"

Diya shook her head. "That's for *one*." She tapped at the keyboard. "The other four are all at various amounts, but they're all over twenty thousand pounds."

Daniel punched the air. "That's over a hundred grand already."

Diya beamed. "That's a fifth of the shortfall, and the auctions still have another thirty hours to run."

"When do the auctions end?"

"Five o'clock tomorrow," Diya clarified.

Aldermaston leaned on his desk. "Diya, when did Basildon leave Shepherd Cottage last night?"

"About ten minutes after everyone else."

"So he packed his things and left around midnight?"

She nodded. "Didn't take him long. He only had a small rucksack."

Daniel pointed upwards. "I checked Basildon's apartment when we got back this morning. He hasn't slept in his bed."

Aldermaston pondered. Where was he now? How had Basildon lost his signet ring? Had their discovery of Mortiforde Millie blown his cover?

Kitty returned to the meadows an hour later and peered into the latest grave.

"I've hit rock again," Otis explained, "but this trench is six feet deep." He slipped his phone from his overall pocket and showed her the screen. "I checked. Six-feet-under is a phrase, not a legal requirement. Legally, the coffin should have one metre of earth on top of it." He pointed at the trench. "That's deep enough."

She peered into the hole. "Is that water?"

A few crumbs of soil plummeted into a puddle. "Wet summer. Water table might be high," Otis suggested.

Kitty watched the ever-growing puddle. "How high?"

Otis shrugged. "We could always use the pump from the farm."

She looked around the meadows. They looked like a First World War battlefield. "How many trenches have you dug in total?"

"Twenty-six!"

She waved her arm around the devastation. "Fill them in! We don't want people breaking their necks, falling into one during Councillor Prendeghast's funeral."

Then again, Kitty considered, the Ladies' Legion was keen to get as many dead bodies into the ground as possible.

Rosemary sat at her kitchen table, completing the UK General Election Nomination Form that Jessica Wallows had dropped through her letterbox. An accompanying note asked her to complete it and return it, along with her passport, before next Monday.

She reviewed the form to ensure she'd missed nothing before slotting it into the large brown envelope provided. Now, where was her passport?

She rummaged unsuccessfully through the adjacent sideboard drawers, sifting through utility bills and other legal documents. In the bottom cupboard was a leather-bound box, a treasure trove of memories. Opening it up, she saw a small, faded envelope resting on top. Her fingers hovered briefly, then put it to one side, and continued searching the contents. There were programmes from *The Mousetrap* and the English National Ballet's performance of *Swan Lake* at the Royal Albert Hall, both evenings out with Rupert over three decades ago.

Next was a Polaroid photo of a young-looking Rupert, arm in arm with her in a yellow bikini, wandering along a beach in the Seychelles. Another life. One where Rupert dictated everything.

She continued rummaging. A plastic badge slipped

between her fingers. Setting it free from the weight of memories, Rosemary stared at the European Commission identity badge with her young head and shoulders beaming back at her.

It had been a hard fight persuading her prospective employers that Rupert had hacked into her email account and sent the message turning down the job offer. Thankfully, they accepted her signed employment contract. It had been a life-changing moment. Rupert had shown his true colours. She realised then that he treated her like one of his business assets. Someone to have on his arm. Someone to make him look even more charming. But she had dreams too.

The European Commission job had empowered her. Not only had it shown her who Rupert really was, it had also shown she could stand up to him. But he was excellent at business and had impeccable contacts. So she'd decided to play the slow game. She got involved in some joint ventures with him. Business contracts formalised her relationship with Rupert. Later, she'd floated the idea of running for Parliament. He loved it. Of course he would. He'd see her as his direct link to the national government. It wasn't *her* he supported, but what he could get out of it that interested him. This time, she knew that.

Rosemary dropped the badge back into the box and continued rummaging. Moments later, she found the passport. It was still valid for two years. She placed it on the kitchen tabletop, then returned everything else into the box. Her hand hesitated above the faded envelope.

She slipped her fingers inside, but stopped. It would only upset her. Her one regret. The genuine mistake she'd made with Rupert. The past was in the past. If ever Rupert found out—

She forced the envelope back into the box. He must never find out. There was too much at stake now.

~

Peredur had thirty minutes before he and the lads stormed this morning's target at eleven-thirty. Better see if his guest had eaten breakfast.

He tucked his laptop under his arm and climbed his terraced home's creaking staircase. He barged into the back bedroom. The bare floorboards creaked under his heavy-duty army boots. The room's only colour came from the bare walls where determined purple paint flakes clung heroically to the plaster.

Behind the door, perched in the middle of the metal bed frame, sat a battered and bruised Basildon, wearing only boxer shorts. Handcuffs secured his right wrist to the bedstead. A half-filled chamber pot was at the foot of the bed frame, and an empty breakfast plate sat on the floor near his feet.

"Enjoy your breakfast, Basildon?" Peredur beamed.

Basildon struggled to see through his swollen black eyes.

Peredur perched on the edge of the bed frame and brought his laptop screen close to Basildon's face. "I wasn't expecting you to betray me so soon," he sighed. The screen displayed the CCTV feed from the barn. His finger slid across the trackpad, then double-tapped it.

"*'I know the perfect place,'* you said. *'Lord Mortiforde doesn't know the barn exists,'* you claimed."

The CCTV footage showed Aldermaston and Daniel raising Mortiforde Millie to her feet, and Gerald's dead body plummeting to the floor.

Basildon's bruised face scrutinised the screen.

Peredur chuckled. "Oh, yes! Gerald's dead, by the way. We had a minor disagreement after you left."

Basildon shook his head.

"Different economic beliefs." Peredur paused the frame and then zoomed in on Gerald's dead body slumped in the hay.

"Oh? Did you think I asked you to invite Gerald to the barn just to have a little fun?"

Basildon nodded, in too much pain to make any sound.

Peredur chuckled. "Warfare's golden rule. Only tell the foot soldiers what they need to know. You wouldn't have lured Gerald to the stone barn had you known my intentions. Which is why I won't tolerate insubordination on my watch." He leaned closer to Basildon, their noses barely an inch apart. "DO YOU UNDERSTAND?"

Basildon flinched and blinked as spittle landed on his face.

Peredur grabbed the back of Basildon's neck and pushed his head towards the laptop screen. "Look at what your insubordination has cost me!"

He tapped the trackpad. The footage jumped to when PCSO Marker was cordoning off the scene. "Not only has your incompetence led to Lord Mortiforde discovering Mortiforde Millie, but it's also led to the discovery of Gerald Lockmount's body!"

Peredur stood, tucking the laptop under his arm. "I wanted to give Gerald one last trip around town." His eyes sparkled when Basildon's face illuminated his comprehension. "Yes! Gerald was supposed to burn when they set Mortiforde Millie alight tomorrow night. And nobody would have known!" He cackled at the thought. "I was looking forward to that."

Peredur lunged, grabbed Basildon by the scruff of his neck, and pulled him to his feet. "I've always known you're Lord Mortiforde's half-brother. The whole town knows who you are." He shook his head despairingly. "What made you think you could go undercover in Mortiforde?"

He seethed. "This is Mortiforde! We're all related to someone here!" He glanced up at the ceiling. "Everybody."

Basildon's head hung low.

Peredur smirked. "But the best warriors have back-up plans. Want to hear mine?"

Basildon shook his head.

"I will get Mortiforde Millie out of that barn so I can parade her through town on Friday evening." He tapped his laptop repeatedly. "Unfortunately, Gerald won't be inside her now, will he?"

Peredur's eyes narrowed as he scrutinised Basildon. "So I'll have to squeeze you in there instead."

CHAPTER TWELVE

Aldermaston reversed the Jaguar from its usual parking spot. The back end of a Chieftain tank loomed large in the rear-view mirror. How was he going to shift that?

He drove around the side of Tugford Hall towards the rear driveway, and his dashboard illuminated with an incoming call.

"Lisa, I'm driving to Isabel's."

"Abigail knows."

Aldermaston increased his speed as he whizzed through the rear entrance. "Knows what?"

"That Diya isn't in Mumbai."

"Ah." He slowed at a junction, checked it was clear, and then pulled out. "I'm sure Diya is still safe with us."

"Takes a tank on the front gates to keep Abigail out, does it?" Lisa chuckled. "I heard the Breakfast Benny show this morning."

Aldermaston sneered. "It'll take more than a tank to stop Abigail. Thanks for the warning. We'll have to be alert. Catch you later." He ended the call and continued his journey, pondering how to broach Sir Hugo's last will and testament with Isabel.

When he arrived at The Lodge, he found Isabel crouching beside an oak barrel planter outside the front door, pulling out half-dead foliage.

"Apologies for turning up unannounced." Aldermaston closed the car door.

Isabel wiped her hands down her beige gardening overalls. "I'm trying to keep busy. Have you news?"

He wrinkled his nose. "More questions, really."

She nodded. "Come in."

She led him into the main lounge, its walls lined with oak wood panelling. Thick, uneven, ancient wooden beams supported the ceiling. Half-hearted flames in the log fire removed the worst of the room's chill, but no longer emitted a comforting warmth. Isabel poked the embers back into life and then collapsed onto a wide, fawn-coloured sofa. She gestured to a similar sofa opposite.

Aldermaston undid his Radnor tweed jacket. "Rupert told me yesterday that you inherit the meadows."

Isabel shook her head. "I'm not so sure."

Aldermaston frowned. "Rupert insisted those were Sir Hugo's wishes in his last will and testament."

"They *were*." She prodded the sofa arm. "The solicitor rang earlier. Rupert and I are to see him tomorrow morning for the formal reading of the will. Apparently, Hugo added a codicil to his will a few weeks ago."

"About?"

She shrugged. "We find out tomorrow."

Aldermaston's brow furrowed further. "Rupert was adamant that you inherit the meadows."

Isabel's hands fidgeted. "That *was* Hugo's original intention when he showed us his will eighteen months ago. I get Hugo's considerable investments and the meadows, while Rupert inherits Hugo's remaining minor share of the businesses, along with Knowton Manor and some other land." Her hand waved at the ceiling. "The Lodge is already in my name, as you know."

She picked a thread at the end of the sofa arm. "The solicitor wants you at tomorrow's will reading, too."

"Me?" Aldermaston's mind raced. *What was in that codicil?*

"The reading's at ten," Isabel continued. "Hugo's solicitors are Beauchamp, Bertie, and Brazonby on Southgate Street." She picked at the thread again. "Could we travel together? I'm not sure I'm good company for Rupert."

"Of course," Aldermaston replied. "Pick you up about nine-thirty?"

She smiled. "Thank you."

Aldermaston shuffled forward on the sofa. "When you first asked me to look into Rupert, I thought this was all about the meadows and the waste incinerator. Following Sir Hugo's passing—"

"Murder," Isabel interrupted. "Someone murdered my husband."

"Murder," Aldermaston acknowledged. "I'm still not sure if this is all about the meadows, because whoever inherits, the council could simply issue a compulsory purchase order and acquire the land that way."

"CPOs cost money and time," Isabel suggested. "A *lot* of time. My son is an impatient man who will do anything to save money." She paused. "When I say anything, I mean *anything*."

Aldermaston stood. "I won't take up any more of your time."

Isabel smiled as she stood. "Rupert's not been near. I heard his helicopter last night. He's obviously away on business." She tutted. "My son can't even look like he's mourning." She looked around. "The Lodge feels so empty. Hugo was often away on business for weeks at a time, and I'm used to being here on my own. But knowing he's *never* coming back through that door has changed The Lodge's atmosphere."

Aldermaston hugged her.

"There's much I should be doing," she said. "But I'm not inclined." She grabbed his hand. "I appreciate what you're doing for me."

They headed towards the large wooden front door.

"Is it true what they're saying on the *Mortiforde Chronicle*'s website? About another body on your estate?"

Aldermaston closed his eyes briefly. "That was another shock."

"Anyone we know?"

"Gerald Lockmount."

"Gerald?" The colour drained from Isabel's face. "But I only saw him yesterday."

"He came to see you?"

She shook her head. "I was walking the grounds for some fresh air. He drove past me and waved."

"He was here to see Rupert?"

"They meet regularly." She paused. "Well, they *did*. Especially when Rupert was investing in land or property."

Aldermaston opened the door. "What are Rupert's other land interests?"

Isabel chucked. "As if he'd tell me!"

He pondered briefly on Isabel's doorstep. First, Rupert's father, and now someone had killed one of his business associates. Everything pointed to Rupert, but there was little point in questioning him. There was, though, someone else he could ask.

Felicity pushed at Tugford Hall's attic door. It held. She rattled it, twisted the handle, and pushed again. A cloud of dust fell from the top of the door frame.

"There's a knack, My Lady." Cartwright stepped forward.

He twisted the door handle right, left, right, then kicked the bottom of the doorframe three times. There was a loud crack. More dust fell from the doorframe, and the door snapped open. Cartwright flicked a light switch inside, and an eerie glow oozed into existence.

Felicity marched into the vast attic space. "I'm looking for something suitable to bury Councillor Prendeghast in. There has to be something up here."

When she and Aldermaston married and moved into a house on the estate, some of the furniture came from here. Looking around, there was enough furniture here to fill several houses and many more of the Hall's rooms. White dust sheets shrouded most of the bulkier furniture pieces.

A corridor ran the entire length of the attic, disappearing far into the darkness. Furniture and boxes were piled on either side, under the eaves.

Felicity lifted a dust sheet, peered at what was lurking underneath, then moved on to the next. There were sixteenth-century beech X-framed chairs with faded silk coverings, eighteenth-century oriental lacquered cabinets with intricate floral designs, Chippendale cabinets and sideboards, mahogany upholstered sofas, a chaise longue, and several tables inlaid with ebony and ivory.

"This is sad," she uttered.

"My Lady?" Cartwright gently replaced a dust sheet covering a stack of nineteenth-century dining chairs.

"All this," she gestured. "Unloved."

"On the contrary, My Lady. It's here because it *is* loved. These pieces are stored here, ready and waiting for a second or third life. It's often more economical to adapt an existing piece of furniture than to buy new."

Felicity warmed to the idea. "We're too quick to buy new." She peered into the darkness at the end of the attic. Not that everyone had this much attic space, though.

Cartwright clicked his fingers. "I wonder—" He strode purposefully ahead, disappearing into the darkness.

Felicity hurried after him. Did he know every piece up here? Some of this went back generations. More shrouded furniture appeared out of the gloom, but Cartwright was nowhere to be seen.

"Cartwright?"

"Here, My Lady." She spotted him deep in an alcove surrounded by tea chests and various-sized cardboard boxes. He peered under a dust sheet. "I think we may be in luck."

Her heart leaped when she saw its shape. It looked about six feet long, three feet wide, and two feet deep.

Felicity stood back to give Cartwright room as he deferentially folded back the dust sheet, revealing—

It was perfect! A padded cushion topped the willow storage basket, turning it into a seating bench.

"Technically, it's a picnic bench, My Lady. This comes off." Cartwright unbuttoned the straps holding the wool-padded cushion in place. The willow weave was so tight it was impossible to see through the sturdy and substantial sides. There were even three handles on each side.

"Cartwright, you are a star!" She grabbed a wicker handle and lifted. The willow squeaked and groaned. Nothing moved except her shoulder joint in a way it shouldn't.

"Ow!" She massaged the pain. "That's far too heavy before we put Councillor Prendeghast inside."

"One moment." Cartwright released the leather straps from their buckles and lifted the lid. Inside were four heavy metal boxes, each with a handle on top and a small key tied to it. Cartwright heaved them out.

Felicity grabbed the basket handle again and lifted. "That's better!" She pointed to the metal containers. "What are those?"

Cartwright grabbed the key dangling from the closest one

and opened the lock. The lid sprang up, revealing a stack of paperwork.

"Typical," Felicity exclaimed.

Cartwright peered at them. "You may wish to look at these, My Lady," he said, spreading out some documents on the casket.

She reached forward and picked up a map. Outlined in red were Mortiforde Meadows.

Cartwright held up a sheet of paper. "This appears to be the paperwork relating to the sale of Mortiforde Meadows to Sir Hugo by the Seventh Marquess." In his hand was a letter, in cursive script, from Sir Hugo to Aldermaston's father.

My dear Xander,

Don't trust Lockmount. The meadows are worth at least twenty per cent more than his valuation. He's valued them at that price because he knows the regional HBA office can spend that figure without having to refer the purchase to their head office, which slows a purchase by about six months. He wants a quick commission on this.

Yes, selling the land to the Historic Borders Agency to make the land inalienable is highly commendable, but there's a time and a place to be idealistic.

Based on the figures you shared with me, if your re-roofing costs rise by over five per cent, you'll be forced to sell Tugford Hall within the next two years.

Sell the meadows directly to me at their true value. You'll avoid paying Lockmount's commission. I'll enjoy certain tax advantages from the transaction. You get a new roof, financial stability, and the community keeps you and your family here. Mortiforde would be soulless without you.

I promise I'll protect the meadows. You helped me five years ago when I was in trouble. Now it's my turn to help you.

> *Yours,*
> *Hugo*

She held the letter aloft. "Did you know about this?"

"I remember it was a period of great angst for His Lordship," said Cartwright. "I believe the current Marquess was at boarding school then. And everybody expected His Lordship's older sibling to inherit the title." He glanced down at his polished brogues.

"Go on."

Cartwright shook his head. "Forgive me, My Lady. It was wrong of me to say anything."

Felicity crossed her arms. "Cartwright, it's just us here."

He remained focused on his shoes. "Even then, the Seventh Marquess knew Master Basildon did not have the—" He selected the right words. "Right personality to be an effective title holder."

Felicity covered her gaping mouth. "Was the Seventh Marquess contemplating the estate's future because he knew Basildon wasn't up to the job?"

Cartwright faced her. "I have huge respect for the Seventh Marquess, My Lady. He always considered all his options carefully. Selling Mortiforde Meadows to the Historic Borders Agency, enabling the land to become inalienable, would have meant that at least some good would have come from what the Seventh Marquess considered a financial nightmare and, potentially, the end of the estate."

Felicity perched on the willow basket and stared at the letter. This explained Sir Hugo's support for the *Verdant Endings* project. But what had Aldermaston's father done for Sir Hugo to warrant this level of financial support?

❧

Rosemary looked at the short, bald-headed gentleman in a navy suit and red tie standing on her doorstep. "I don't need double glazing, thank you." She pushed the door closed, only to find his briefcase wedged between the door and frame.

"Excuse me! Kindly remove your—"

"Norris Offermans," he interrupted. "National Audit Office." He pulled an identity badge from his jacket pocket.

"Oh! Come in." She opened the door wide. "Tea? Coffee?" She led him into the kitchen.

"No, thank you." He planted his briefcase on the kitchen table. A thick indentation scored the leather where her front door had crushed it. He sat and took a notepad from his briefcase. "I won't keep you longer than necessary."

Rosemary braced herself for news. "Have you confirmed the shortfall?"

Norris smiled. "I'm still exploring the wider financial picture."

Rosemary picked at a cuticle on her thumb. "Either the waste incinerator project is five hundred thousand short, or it isn't. What's the wider picture got to do with it?"

Norris scribbled on his notepad. "Ms Mayedew says you're currently on gardening leave."

Rosemary sat back. "I resigned because the Socially Liberal Conservative Party has selected me as their candidate in the upcoming by-election."

Norris scribbled some notes. "Yes, I've seen your resignation letter in your staff file. And I've just spoken with a. . ." He flicked back through his notebook, "Tom Burthson, whom I understand is the local party chairman."

"That's correct."

Norris's emerald eyes stared at Rosemary. "You promised to get the waste incinerator project halted within days. How?"

Rosemary threw her hands in the air. "Because the money's not there, you numbskull! As the Director of Finance—"

"Ex-Director of Finance."

"Mr Offermans, I am *still* Director of Finance. I'm on gardening leave."

Norris uncrossed and then recrossed his legs. "Ms Sedgewicke, the National Audit Office receives many complaints and tip-offs. And some twenty-seven point six four eight per cent of these come from disgruntled employees."

"Disgruntled?" Rosemary stood. "The waste incinerator project has financial challenges. That is a fact. A fact you could see for yourself if you took the time to examine Diya Parmer's excellent records, instead of wasting time hassling me!" She headed towards the kettle.

Norris raised an eyebrow. "So, how do you account for Diya Parmer's email to the Chief Executive on Tuesday morning at seven-fifty, categorically stating the waste incinerator project's funding is all in place?"

With her back to him, Rosemary filled the kettle. She couldn't let anything slip. "Diya wouldn't send that without coming to me first. I'm her immediate line manager. She didn't even copy me in to Abigail's email," she continued. "Doesn't that tell you something? I'd love to know what she said."

Norris flicked further back in his notebook. He tapped the page. "It was perfunctory. *Dear Abigail, I'm delighted to announce that, thanks to some prudent financial planning and savings secured on some of the authority's other capital projects, I've identified £500,000 of funding we can allocate to the waste incinerator project. This means we can now proceed with the fully funded project. Yours sincerely, Diya Parmer, Head of Planning Finance,*" he read.

"Whoa!" Rosemary pointed to his notepad and collapsed back into the chair. "Diya did not send that email."

"It was in her Sent Items folder in her email account," Norris confirmed. "I saw it myself."

Rosemary pointed towards her front door. "Check all her other emails in her Sent folder. I guarantee you won't find another one signed off with *Yours sincerely*. Kindest regards. *That's* how Diya signs off her emails." She jabbed the table with her finger. "Every. Single. One. That email is a fake!"

From his high vantage point in a leafless oak tree, Peredur looked down the lane towards Knowton Manor. It was eleven twenty-eight. Two minutes. Timing was everything when storming enemy territory.

He shimmied down the oak tree into a field hidden from the lane by a hedge. In the field corner stood a Bedford QLT World War Two military personnel carrier with a quarter of his troops waiting in the back. He clambered into the front passenger seat.

"Go!"

The diesel engine shot a plume of smog from the exhaust. The armoured vehicle charged through the open gateway onto the narrow lane. Peredur grabbed a walkie-talkie from the dashboard.

"BANG Two, Three, and Four, this is BANG One, go!"

Crackling and hissing noises filled the cab, followed by three acknowledgement messages in quick succession. "Message received, BANG One, over."

Peredur thumped the back of the cab wall. "Get ready, lads."

As the armoured military vehicle approached Knowton Manor's driveway, Peredur spotted the jeep with a machine gun mounted on the back, three Bedford personnel carrier vehicles, and a low-loader approaching from the opposite direction.

He checked his watch as they turned onto the drive. "Eleven-thirty. Time for Crystal's mid-morning drink." He turned to the driver. "Agent 24, I want you to message me as soon as you have Crystal contained in the kitchen."

"Yes, Commander."

The vehicles convoyed past The Lodge and up the long drive, sweeping round in a wide arc on Knowton Manor's gravel forecourt. Peredur jumped out and hurried to the vehicle's rear. He released the rear panel, and two dozen agents in combat gear jumped out. He pushed them towards the front door. "Go, go, go!"

Agent 24 kicked in the front door's glass panels, slipped in a gloved hand, and twisted the lock. The door swung wide. A scream echoed through the doorway.

Peredur released the rear panels of the other three personnel carriers. Two dozen men jumped out of each of those and stormed in through the front door.

The radio crackled. "Commander, this is Agent 24. Our guest is secure, over."

Peredur slipped the walkie-talkie into his jacket pocket and marched in through the front door. To his left was a wide wooden staircase, which swept up in a grand curve to the first floor. He surveyed the black-and-white diamond-patterned tiled floor. The footprint of his entire terraced house would fit in here. Through an open doorway on the left, he spied an opulent drawing room. To his right were closed doors to two more rooms, between which sat a vast open fireplace.

"Commander?"

Agent 24 entered the hallway from a doorway behind the stairs, his hand resting on the shoulder of a petrified blonde woman.

Peredur stepped forward. "Hello, Crystal." He took her arm. "No harm will come to you. Your boss is away on business, but is due back later this afternoon, isn't he?"

Crystal nodded.

"Good." He encouraged her towards the stairway. "I am

the Commander of BANG, Borderlandshire Against Nefarious Government. We have an issue with your boss, and we plan to resolve it to our satisfaction."

Together, they climbed the stairs. "We simply need you to collect your things from your desk, and then you are free to leave. Please don't tell Mr Rinde what is happening."

Crystal sniffed.

Peredur paused halfway up the stairs and watched several of his men bringing in kit bags and holdalls. "Bag a bedroom. Any bedroom, whichever takes your fancy, settle in, and then meet me here in the main hallway in ninety minutes, lads."

"Yes, Commander!" they chorused.

Peredur encouraged Crystal to the top of the stairs, then turned right along the landing.

"Your voice sounds familiar," Crystal whispered. "Have we met?"

His eyebrow arched. "Well remembered. I sorted that virus on yours and Mr Rinde's computers a few months ago."

Together, they entered Rupert's office. He switched on Rupert's computer.

Crystal shook her head. "I don't know it. He doesn't trust me with it. He doesn't trust anyone with his password."

"I already know it." Peredur sat in Rupert's chair. "The virus you got came from me." He wagged his finger in Crystal's face. "Never click on an attachment you're not expecting. When you do, you need someone like me to come and clean your machines. However, I didn't clean them. I added more monitoring software."

He interlocked his fingers, twisted his palms outwards, stretched his arms, and cracked his joints. His fingers danced across the keyboard.

"Twenty-nine characters is a pretty strong password," he continued, as he smacked the Enter key and watched Rupert's machine stir into life. He turned to Crystal. "I need you to show me where Rupert keeps his thumb drives."

Crystal looked perplexed.

Peredur's fingers rubbed his forehead. "What do you call them in your emails to Rupert?" He clicked his fingers. "Dongles! Where does Rupert keep his dongles?"

Crystal pulled open a desk side drawer and—

Peredur grabbed Crystal's wrist. "Sorry. Where does he keep his *special* dongle? I'm talking about the one Mr Rinde doesn't think you know about, but you do, because you plugged it into your machine once, didn't you? I spotted it on a logging report."

Crystal closed the desk drawer. "He carries it with him wherever he goes."

Peredur sighed. "Where did you find his backup copy?"

Crystal pouted, leaned forward, and stuck her hand between Peredur's legs.

He gulped.

From the chair's underside, she retrieved an inch-long USB drive. "Is this what you're looking for?"

Peredur snatched it from her and plugged it into Rupert's computer. A window opened on the screen, with a directory of its contents. He chuckled. "Oh, yes."

"They're just boring spreadsheets," Crystal dismissed.

"They're not boring if you know what you're looking at," Peredur explained. "Especially when they contain incriminating evidence. Which is why Mr Rinde keeps these particular spreadsheets on a thumb drive, and not saved on any computer that's connected to the Internet. Otherwise, people like me could look at them whenever we liked."

~

Aldermaston triggered a doorbell chime when he stepped into the Lockmount Estate Agency.

Maureen looked up from a corner desk. A half-hearted smile creased her chubby cheeks, her eyes tearfully red.

"I wasn't sure if you'd be open," he said, taking the chair opposite her.

She shrugged. "We've two purchasers collecting keys this afternoon. And I. . ." She sighed. "Didn't know what else to do." She checked the wall clock. "They'll be here in a couple of hours. I can't believe it's midday already."

She wiped her nose with a crumpled tissue. "Today's been a blur ever since PC Norten and that PCSO came by to tell me they'd found Gerald's body. I can't believe he's. . ." She burst into tears.

"It's been a shock to everyone," Aldermaston soothed.

Maureen collected herself and flicked through an A4 diary. "What was it you wanted to chat about? Is it the stone barn Gerald looked at yesterday?"

Aldermaston shuffled in his seat. "That was a hoax to lure him to. . ." Although the estate agency office was empty, he leaned closer. "I understand Gerald met with Rupert Rinde yesterday morning."

Maureen's finger traced the appointments in yesterday's diary. She looked up at him. "I shouldn't really say. Client confidentiality."

Aldermaston nodded. "All I'm trying to do," he pleaded, "is find out why someone hacked into my email account to lure Gerald to his death."

Maureen bit her bottom lip. "What's Gerald's meeting with Rupert Rinde yesterday morning got to do with his murder?"

Aldermaston sat back in his chair. "Was it connected with the waste incinerator project?"

She shook her head. "Gerald had heard from Farmer Bell and wanted to give Mr Rinde the good news."

"Good news?"

"Yes." She smiled.

"About?"

Her smile disappeared. "Er. . ."

Aldermaston patted Maureen's hand. "Client confidentiality," he acknowledged again. "Gerald's hardly going to sack you now, is he? And what you tell me might help us find out who killed him."

A tear collected at the corner of her eye. "But Rupert has a right to confidentiality."

Aldermaston tightened his squeeze on her hand. "You're doing this for Gerald. Not for Rupert."

The tear broke free and hurtled down her cheek. "Rupert has been trying to buy some land from Farmer Bell for several years. He'd always rejected Rupert's offer, saying it was derisory. And it was. But yesterday morning, Farmer Bell relented and rang Gerald to accept."

"If Rupert's offer was derisory, how come nobody else offered more?" Aldermaston enquired. "Unless Gerald wasn't marketing Farmer Bell's land to anyone else?"

Fear flashed through Maureen's eyes.

Aldermaston cocked his head to one side. "But that doesn't make sense. Estate agents take a commission on the agreed sale price. It's not in Gerald's interest to promote a derisory offer."

Maureen stood abruptly, marched to the estate agency door, turned the lock, and twisted the sign round to *Closed*.

"I've had suspicions for a while," she began, wandering back to her desk. "I think Rupert pays Gerald a bonus for helping him secure land acquisitions at his preferred price."

Aldermaston frowned. "A bonus?"

She dropped back into her seat. "I've heard Gerald used the phrase 'an insurance payout'."

His eyes narrowed. "Go on."

Maureen took a deep breath. "Rupert Rinde drives a hard

bargain." She pointed through a glass screen to Gerald's office. "I've heard Gerald state on the phone to clients that Rupert's low offer is a fair market value price when I know it's not. If the client rejects the offer, Gerald stops promoting the property, but doesn't tell the client. After several months, he contacts them, says there's been no other interest in the property, but Rupert's offer is still on the table. It's surprising how often the clients concede. Once the sale has gone through, I believe Rupert pays Gerald a bonus to cover the lost commission."

Aldermaston processed the allegation. "So the vendor sells the land at below true market value, but Rupert's bonus means Gerald ultimately gets the full market value commission."

Maureen's eyebrows rose. "I suspect Rupert gave him extra. He saves tens of thousands of pounds per transaction."

"That's illegal!"

She nodded.

"So why haven't you told anyone?"

"No proof. None of Rupert's bonus payments goes through the agency accounts. I know, because I do them. Rupert must settle directly with Gerald."

Aldermaston stood. With no evidence, it was going to be difficult to substantiate Rupert's underhanded business dealings. Another thought occurred. "Which part of Farmer Bell's land has Rupert acquired?"

Maureen stepped over to the enormous map of Borderlandshire on the estate agency wall. "It'll be common knowledge soon, I suppose. It's these two fields backing onto Castle Ridge."

Castle Ridge? That name was familiar. "Where's that?"

"Just here," she pointed.

Aldermaston shuddered. Rupert Rinde now owned two fields beside the River Morte overlooking the Mortiforde Meadows.

CHAPTER THIRTEEN

Aldermaston rapped on his office door. "It's me."

"You alone?" Daniel called through the door.

"Yes, why?"

Aldermaston barely squeezed through the gap Daniel created before he shut and bolted it again. Diya's shoulders dropped when she saw Aldermaston. "Thank goodness."

"Abigail rang," Daniel began. "She demanded to speak with Diya."

Aldermaston collapsed into his captain's chair. "Lisa said Abigail was suspicious, but I didn't think she thought Diya was *here*."

Daniel shook his head. "I reckon she was trying it on. Said I didn't know anyone called Diya, and she must have the wrong number." He shrugged. "She didn't pursue it. Just hung up."

Aldermaston pointed to his office door. "We definitely keep that locked." He turned to Diya. "How is the online auction going?"

"Just over one hundred and forty-seven thousand." A hint of a smile crossed her face.

"Really?"

She turned back to the screen. "There's a steady stream of bids for the books. I've joined some second-hand book dealer chat forums, both here and in the US, to spread news of the first editions. It's only breakfast time on the East Coast, so I'm hoping to see more interest when the rest of America wakes up." Diya's eyes sparkled.

Aldermaston flicked through his notebook. Maureen's revelations about Gerald convinced him the estate agent was part of this whole mess and—

Two words jumped off the page from yesterday's notes. *Castle Ridge*. Those plans had fallen off Rupert's desk yesterday.

Aldermaston hit the speakerphone button and called Lisa. It rang twice. "It's me," he interrupted before she launched into her official greeting.

"Mind if I talk and chew?" she replied. "My lunch break has shrunk to fifteen minutes."

"What's Abigail got you doing now?"

A dejected sigh echoed down the line. "Reviewing the Highways Drainage (Seepage and Sewerage) Improvement Planning Sub Group's minutes for the past ten years, and identifying any Mortiforde Meadows drainage-related comments. She wants all available data for tomorrow's NAF and wants my report on her desk by six o'clock tonight."

He tutted. "She wants you too busy to help the Borderers Guild ... or me."

Lisa bit into something crunchy. "Don't forget, my Borderers Guild administrative support is the council's gift. Abigail can withdraw it at any time. And I'd much rather minute the Borderers Guild meetings than the pungent cesspit of the Highways Drainage (Seepage and Sewerage) Improvement Planning Sub Group's gatherings."

"Can you send those minutes across to Daniel? He could go through them for you and draft a report for Abigail."

Daniel's face contorted in silent anguish.

Lisa stopped chewing. "Why?"

"I have a planning query. While I could interrogate the council's Planning Portal, you might find out more by chatting to someone in the planning department."

"Okay. What am I asking about?"

"Castle Ridge."

"What's that?"

"I saw some paper drawings in Rupert's office yesterday, which he was quick to hide. Waffled something about being consulted as an adjacent landowner."

"Rubbish!" Lisa interjected. "The council has emailed all planning consultation documents for years."

"Exactly. I also know Rupert has recently bought land from Farmer Bell near Castle Ridge. And that land is on the other side of the river from Mortiforde Meadows."

Lisa whistled. "Why is Rupert buying land opposite the meadows?"

"That's what I need you to find out."

Peredur double-clicked on the *LHI Initiative* file as soon as Crystal closed the office door behind her. He grinned. The last transaction date was yesterday.

November 3rd. Mortside: Farmer Bell Fields. (Value) £250,000. (Bid) £185,000. (Insurance) £25,000. Castle Ridge.

He scanned the list. The insurance payouts were always ten per cent of the valuation, but the agreed sale price was often between twenty-five and thirty per cent lower. His gaze returned to the last transaction. *Mortside.* So Rupert *had* bought Farmer Bell's fields for his Castle Ridge project.

His breathing became erratic as his fists opened and

clenched. The veins in his neck bulged. A primeval scream accompanied his arm as it swept across Rupert's desk. Paperwork scattered high in the air, then fell like confetti. The telephone ricocheted off a chair cushion, crashing to the floor, and the computer screen shattered against a wooden cabinet. Peredur pounded the green leather-topped desk with his fists. His chest heaved as his lungs captured huge gasps of air, sending spittle flying across the desk.

Here was the evidence Rupert had bought Farmer Bell's land for his luxury development after he'd helped block Farmer Bell's mobile home park development. More evidence of social cleansing. If only the townsfolk knew.

Peredur smiled. Tomorrow night, they would.

Aldermaston scoured his notebook for further clues or connections. This was such a mess. He stopped at the words *Birth of BANG* from the newspaper clipping Daniel found in Basildon's apartment. Turning to his computer, he brought up the *Powys Gazette* website and searched the archives. The top result was from November 19th, twenty-five years ago.

Staff at a household waste site in Knighton, Powys, were shocked to discover a baby wrapped in blankets and a blue woollen hat in a carrycot in the staff Portakabin on Saturday morning. Wilfred Davies Jones, 53, of Newtown Road, Knighton, found him just after midday.

"The site was extremely busy between eleven and noon. When things calmed down, I returned to the Portakabin for a drink and found a baby in a carrycot just inside the door," he confirmed. "It was warm and asleep. We searched for the mother, but after ten minutes, we realised we had to call the police. I've

seen some strange things brought to a local tip, but this is a first for me."

Police took the baby to Newtown Hospital's maternity unit, twenty miles away, where doctors gave him a clean bill of health. Doctors believe the infant is about two weeks old and is now being looked after by Powys Social Services. Police are appealing for the mother, or any potential witnesses, to call the local police at Knighton 960999.

He contemplated Basildon's note. *The Birth of BANG?* What was it Basildon had seen here? His note made no sense at all.

"Human Resources, how can I help you?"

"It's Abigail. I need Diya Parmer's home address immediately." Abigail tapped at her keyboard while sandwiching her phone between her ear and shoulder. Despite having asked her secretary for this information two hours ago, she was doing it herself. If the National Audit Office found a shortfall in the waste incinerator project, Abigail would plug some of it through the salary savings generated by sacking her secretary.

"Let me grab some paper." Abigail searched her minimalistic desk but found nothing suitable. Her hand slipped into her dress pocket and found a scrappy, sticky note. "Go ahead."

She scribbled down the address, thanked the **HR** assistant, and ended the call. Then she turned over the sticky note and saw Councillor Taplinski's mobile number scrawled in Lisa's handwriting. She'd completely forgotten about him.

Taplinski answered within a couple of rings.

"Stefan? It's Abigail. Apologies for not calling sooner. It's been one of those mornings. You have further questions about the waste incinerator project?"

"It isn't urgent. Could we meet later?"

Abigail sighed. "I'm not sure when I'll be free, Stefan. I can't see my day improving—"

"Seven-thirty tonight? I know a nice little restaurant in town."

"Oh! I see. Er—" Her fingers stroked the neckline of her dress.

"Unless you have other plans?"

"Dinner would be lovely." She paused. "When you say you know a nice little restaurant, you don't mean The Nooseman's Knot public house, do you?"

Stefan chuckled. "Abigail, a *nice little restaurant* could never describe The Nooseman's Knot. I'm talking about Norman Foundations. It only has two Michelin stars, but is more than capable of catering to your vegetarian preferences."

Her fingers now toyed with the necklace resting on her breastbone. "That would be lovely. Could you pick me up from the office?"

"Shall we say seven-fifteen?"

"Perfect."

Abigail returned the handset to the receiver with a smile, then turned over the scrap of paper and stared at Diya Parmer's home address. Time to visit 9 Clee Way.

The twenty-minute traffic jam delighted Felicity. The Ladies' Legion protests were clearly working. Car horns blared every few minutes, and raised voices infiltrated her Range Rover's comfortable cabin. Having dropped Councillor Prendeghast's wicker casket off at Earth, Wind, and Fire, she had a vegetable crate overflowing with sandwiches and fruit to deliver to her hardworking ladies. The dashboard clock clicked to one o'clock.

She slipped into a free roadside parking space and grabbed the sandwich crate, and then ambled past Watling Street's black-and-white, timber-framed properties. As she turned the corner, a sea of banners and placards, along with the dulcet tones of 'We Shall Overcome', fluttering in the breeze, bombarded her.

Kitty, Heidi, and Margaret were armed with clipboards and speaking to the drivers of the three nearest cars, garnering petition signatories, then sending them on a diversion around the narrow Curtain Wall Road. Cordelia had been true to her word. Spread across the road were three strips of anti-intruder spikes. Parked to one side was a battered red hatchback with four flat tyres.

"Let me help, Lady Mortiforde." Cordelia hurried across from their roadside trestle tables, where several more Ladies' Legion members were handing out leaflets and seeking signatures. She took the crate of sandwiches. "Careful. Those spikes are taller than they look."

Felicity nodded at the red hatchback. "Someone didn't see them."

"Idiot thought they were plastic." Cordelia sandwiched the crate between her waist and one arm, while offering another hand to help Felicity step over the spikes. "He threatened to sue, then ran off when I asked for his insurance details. PC Norten did a registration check. It's stolen." Cordelia turned to the Ladies' Legion members. "Look, everyone! Our president has arrived."

There was a tremendous cheer and a smattering of applause.

"You're doing fantastic work, ladies." Felicity pointed to the sandwiches. "I've brought lunch, and news that I found a suitable casket for Councillor Prendeghast. We're all set! In two hours' time, we shall make history in Mortiforde."

Another cheer rose into the drab November sky.

"Lady Mortiforde," Cordelia continued. "Can I introduce our newest recruit?"

Felicity turned to see a tall woman with sunflower blonde hair and grey eyes standing before her, offering an outstretched hand.

"Rosemary Sedgewicke. Pleased to meet you, Your Ladyship."

"Rosemary's the Socially Liberal Conservative Party candidate at the upcoming by-election," Cordelia clarified. "She's campaigning against the waste incinerator project. She used to work at the council and says the waste incinerator project is still half a million pounds short."

Felicity's eyes widened. "Is that true?"

Rosemary nodded. "As the soon-to-be ex-Director of Finance, I should know."

Felicity pulled Rosemary to one side. "Do you think we stand any chance of saving the meadows?"

Rosemary nodded. "I've taken action, which will force the council to admit they're wrong. My Head of Planning Finance, Diya Parmer—"

"Diya?" Felicity grabbed Rosemary's arm. "Diya's a member of the Legion. We've been trying to get hold of her. Do you know where she lives? We only have a home phone number."

"Clee Way," Rosemary replied. "About five minutes away. But if she's there, I doubt she'll open the door to me."

Felicity glanced at her watch. There were an hour and twenty minutes until the funeral. "She might open the door to me, though."

～

Outside Rupert's office, Peredur heard a growing crescendo of voices. His troops were gathering in the main hall as instructed.

He left Rupert's office, headed to the landing, and peered over the banister at his gathered troops below. He clapped his hands three times. The echo ricocheted off the walls. A hush quickly descended.

"Friends, soldiers, BANGers. You have done well this morning."

His men cheered.

"We have a couple of hours before the owner of this delightful property," he gestured around him, "returns, so make yourselves at home."

"Can we use the hot tub, jacuzzi, and indoor pool, Commander?" called a voice from below.

Peredur grinned. "It would be a shame to waste the opportunity."

His men teased themselves with playful banter and backslapping.

"The owner will return at 1530 hours," Peredur continued, "so everyone must be in their positions at 1500 hours. Is that clear?"

"Yes, Commander!"

"Agent 24, select two men to help me with our next mission. Meet me by the low-loader in ten minutes."

Agent 24 saluted, then grabbed two men standing on either side of him.

"At ease, men," Peredur instructed. A stampede of boots headed for the hot tub, jacuzzi, and swimming pool. He stepped back, leaned against the landing wall, and checked the stone barn's CCTV feed on his smartphone. Mortiforde Mille looked despondent, slumped against the back wall.

Peredur smiled. "Cheer up, Millie. We're coming to get you."

~

Aldermaston kicked the caterpillar tracks, then wandered around to the front of the Chieftain tank. A damp patch on the gravel drive underneath it caught his eye. He bent down, wiped the discoloured gravel with a finger, and then rubbed his thumb over it. Oil. The darn thing was leaking. He kicked the caterpillar tracks again. "How are we going to shift this?"

Cartwright cleared his throat. "If I may, Your Lordship?"

Aldermaston stared at his butler. "You know how to drive a tank?"

"I have been talking to Lord Rudgington's head butler in Dorset, Your Lordship," Cartwright explained. "His father was in the Royal Tank Regiment."

Hope returned to Aldermaston's eyes. "And?"

"Tanks don't have ignition keys," Cartwright began. "Just a push button—"

"What are we waiting for?" Aldermaston clambered awkwardly onto the tank, crouching low to avoid the gun barrel above his head. He lifted the driver's hatch and peered inside.

Cartwright stepped closer. "My Lord, it's not just a question of—"

"There are more buttons on my Jaguar's dashboard than in here," Aldermaston called, his voice echoing around the tank's interior. "I'm going in." He lowered himself inside and stared at the controls, buttons, dials, and switches in front of him. "Did Lord Rudgington's chap describe the ignition button?" he called.

Cartwright sighed. "Apparently, Your Lordship, starting the engine requires pushing a series of buttons in the correct order."

Aldermaston poked his head through the hatch. "Which is?"

Cartwright's blank face told him everything. Aldermaston's gaze fell back inside the cockpit. There was a speedometer, rev counter, and coolant gauge, above which sat four colour buttons: yellow, burgundy, green, and pink.

"There are only four buttons, Cartwright. How many permutations can there be?" Aldermaston began counting on his fingers.

"Twenty-four, My Lord."

He peered through the hatch again. "Is that all?"

Cartwright shuffled on his feet. "Factorials, My Lord. Don't you remember those from school?"

Aldermaston blushed. "Twenty-four, heh?" This was achievable. He slipped his notebook and pen from his shirt pocket and threw them at Cartwright. "I'll call out the order of the colours as I press them. You write them down."

"And when the engine starts, My Lord, where will you go?"

"Let's not run before we can walk, Cartwright." Aldermaston dropped inside. "Are you ready?" he yelled.

"As always, My Lord."

Aldermaston stared at the four buttons. "Let's start with the order they're in. Yellow, burgundy, green, pink," he called, pressing them in that order.

Nothing happened.

"What about backwards? Pink, green, burgundy, yellow," he called.

Nothing happened.

"You haven't forgotten you're taking Master Harry swimming tonight, have you, My Lord?" Cartwright enquired mid-scribble.

Aldermaston waved a dismissive hand. "We'll have this sorted by then. Let's try burgundy, green, pink, and yellow."

Before he could try another combination, *The Dam Busters'* theme tune echoed around the tank's interior. Aldermaston extracted his phone from his corduroy trouser pocket and recognised the number.

"Hi Cissy," he answered. "Everything going all right with the Ladies' Legion in town?"

"Yes, Your Lordship," she began. "We're collecting loads of petition signatures. But I'm calling about Mortiforde Millie. When will the police release her? The Guild needs to prepare her for tomorrow's parade."

"Have you called PCSO Marker?"

Cissy sighed. "About twenty times in the last hour. I think she's blocked my number."

Aldermaston's eyes closed. He knew what was coming next.

"Could you call her? She might answer you as you're a … you know … Marquess."

Aldermaston checked his watch. One-fifteen. "I'll see what I can do, Cissy."

"Problem, My Lord?" Cartwright enquired.

Aldermaston hoisted himself out of the tank. "We'll have to come back to this later. There's another immovable object the Guild needs me to shift first."

Peredur eased the low-loader through Tugford Hall's rear gates with barely two inches of clearance on each side. Agents 24, 58, and 83 sat in the cab beside him, watching through the side mirrors, holding their breath.

"You're clear, Commander," Agent 24 confirmed.

Peredur tickled the accelerator pedal and quickened the flatbed truck's pace. Although Tugford Hall's chimneys poked above the treeline some distance away, this operation was more dangerous in broad daylight. He swung the vehicle left and joined the track to the stone barn, pushing the accelerator harder as the distance between them and the Hall grew.

Peredur pointed to the glovebox. "Agent 24, check the live feed on my laptop. Better double-check His Lordship hasn't just arrived."

Agent 24 reviewed the hidden surveillance camera's footage. Mortiforde Millie sat forlornly on the hay bales, almost alone.

"Our timing is perfect, Commander." Agent 24 twisted the screen towards Peredur. "It appears only PC Norten and a PCSO are there."

Agent 58 giggled. "Commander, if you recruited PC Norten, we could cut our drone use by half."

Peredur pulled up alongside the stone barn and killed the engine. He and his team jumped out of the cab.

PCSO Marker marched around the rear of the low loader. "Stop where you are! This is a crime scene."

"Good afternoon, officer." Peredur offered his hand.

Ceri shook it, then took out her notebook and pen. "Who are you, and why are you here?"

Peredur saluted. "Commander Jones."

Ceri scribbled that down, then waved her pen at his three colleagues. "And their names?"

"None of your business," Peredur snapped. "Lads, show some respect. A lady is present!"

Simultaneously, all three stood to attention and saluted.

The flattery momentarily softened Ceri's facade before she waved her pen in front of Peredur's camouflage-painted face. "What's with all this?"

He sighed. "Can't men wear make-up, too?" He placed his hands on his hips. "That's discrimination, that is."

PC Norten tapped Ceri's shoulder. "He's right. I did a course recently. We have to be careful of profile stereotyping."

Ceri glanced up at him. "Profile what?"

PC Norten shrugged. "Went over my head, which is saying

something. But Stoyle is hot on equality. You don't want a discrimination complaint against you."

She slipped her notebook and pen back into her chest pocket and strolled alongside the low-loader. "And what brings you here, Commander Jones?"

Peredur pointed to Mortiforde Millie. "We're from the Borderers Guild. Lord Mortiforde asked us to pick her up for tomorrow's parade."

Ceri glowered. "We're still processing the crime scene. Forensics have nipped off for lunch. They've only just finished examining Millie, because some woman called Cissy has called me every five minutes asking for news."

Peredur put an arm around Ceri's shoulders and squeezed. "You've processed Millie? How perfect is that? Lord Mortiforde mentioned the crime scene was being handled by an expert who would process it efficiently and quickly."

Ceri blushed. "Lord Mortiforde said that?"

PC Norten bent closer to her. "Told you Lord Mortiforde is clever. He spots things that don't even register with me."

Ceri pointed to a fallen tree trunk opposite. "*That's* capable of spotting things that don't register with you."

Peredur squeezed Ceri's shoulders again. "Give us a hand, would you? With your help, we'll get her shifted in no time. If we move her now, forensics will have more space to carry on after lunch."

"It's not police business!" Ceri defended.

PC Norten clapped his hands excitedly. "Oh, please, Ceri. I've always fancied operating Mortiforde Millie."

Peredur winked. "I'm sure with your expertise in efficiency, we can have Mortiforde Millie tucked up on the low-loader before you can say *BANG! What was that?*"

Ceri's defences crumbled. "Okay." She held up a finger at PC Norten. "But don't tell anyone. I didn't join the police force to be nice."

~

"Here it is." Rosemary strode down Diya's front garden path and rang the doorbell.

Felicity examined the three-bedroom semi-detached house on the ordinary suburban road. Sometimes she yearned to live in something normal.

Rosemary rang the bell again.

Felicity examined Diya's three wheelie bins lined up neatly under the large bay window. The green one was half full of garden rubbish. There were empty plastic milk bottles and several empty tins of cat food in the purple bin. The black bin had one small kitchen bin bag, tied and knotted, languishing alone in the corner.

"She could be in Mumbai," Felicity suggested. "Not much rubbish in here."

Rosemary lifted the letter box flap. "Diya," she called. "It's Rosemary. And Lady Mortiforde." She released the letterbox and stepped back again.

Felicity cupped her hands around her face and pressed her nose against Diya's living room window. "There's a cat sleeping on the sofa."

"That cat's there?" Rosemary knocked on the door knocker. "Diya always puts Daisy in the local cattery when she goes to Mumbai." She peered around the side of the house. "Let's check the back."

Felicity checked that none of the neighbours were watching and then hurried round the side of the house to find Rosemary standing on tiptoes by a tall wooden gate. She reached over and slid back the bolt. Together they hurried around and tried the back door. It was locked.

Diya's rear garden was a simple affair, mainly laid to lawn, with a small patio area behind the rear of the house. A wooden bench sat underneath the kitchen window.

Rosemary wandered along to the far window and checked inside. "There's no sign of life here."

"Well, what were you expecting?" snapped a voice behind Felicity.

Felicity shrieked, clutched the top of her chest, spun round, and recognised Abigail Mayedew standing there.

Abigail stared at Rosemary. "Why are you snooping around an employee's private property?"

Rosemary marched towards her. "Why are *you* here? Finally realised the council's annual leave system is wrong and Diya isn't in Mumbai?"

Abigail pursed her lips, then crossed her arms. "Having got no answer from her mobile or landline numbers, I'm doing a staff welfare check."

"Staff welfare?" Rosemary wagged a finger in front of Abigail's face. "You're panicking!"

A male voice interrupted them. "'S'cuse me, ladies. Got a package with instructions to leave it by the back door."

A fluorescent-yellow jacketed delivery driver dropped a battered cardboard box on the back doorstep. He stepped back and snapped a photo of the delivery on his phone.

Felicity called out to him. "Excuse me! The box is damaged. The contents are nearly falling out."

The driver shrugged. "I just deliver 'em, love." He slipped through the gate, whistling a cheery tune.

Felicity poked her finger through the damaged corner and pulled back some of the packaging. "Cat food," she clarified.

Rosemary stared at Abigail. "See? Who travels to another continent and forgets to order enough cat food for the neighbour to use while they're away?"

"Suggests Diya left in a hurry," Felicity concluded. "Why?"

∼

A loud clatter echoed from somewhere near the rear gates as Aldermaston slipped into the utility vehicle parked near the refuse bins. Whatever it was, it sounded big and heavy. He drove towards the rear gates cautiously, in case he met whatever was coming the other way.

He paused at the junction of the gates and the stone track and spotted the roadside vegetation still dancing in a turbulent wake. Strange. Something big had recently driven through. Puzzled, Aldermaston joined the stone track and spent the next five minutes dodging the ruts and troughs he was getting to know well. His heart lifted when he spotted PCSO Marker and PC Norten clearing things into the small boot of the police car. Had they finished?

"Packing up?" He stepped out of the utility vehicle and beamed, realising he no longer needed to play the Lord-of-the-Manor card for Cissy Warbouys.

"I enjoyed that!" PC Norten walked awkwardly towards him, arms outstretched and mid-air as if being controlled by strings. "It's brilliant how they get Millie to work, Your Lordship."

PCSO Ceri Marker leaned against the police car's passenger door. "Just waiting for forensics to return from their lunch."

Aldermaston noticed Millie was no longer in the barn. He gestured inside. "Have forensics taken Millie somewhere?"

Ceri's head fell into her hands. "What is it with people here? It's bad enough dealing with him." She pointed at PC Norten. "Those chaps you sent to collect Mortiforde Millie left about five minutes ago."

Aldermaston's eyes narrowed. "What chaps?"

Ceri sighed. "The ones you sent on the off chance we'd finished processing the crime scene."

Aldermaston placed his hands on his hips. "I haven't sent anyone to collect Mortiforde Millie."

Ceri bit her fingernail. "You sure?"

"Oops!" PC Norten chuckled.

"Describe these chaps," Aldermaston asked.

PC Norten stepped closer to Aldermaston. "There were four of them, Your Lordship. Looked good in their khaki uniforms and boots. One even had make-up on his face! Took a shine to Ceri, if you ask me." He tapped his nose. "Didn't think she'd agree to help them move Millie, but they knew how to sweet-talk her."

Aldermaston's head fell into his hands. BANG had stolen Millie back.

"Come on, Norten. We need to go."

"What about waiting for forensics?"

Ceri slipped into the police car and slammed the door.

"Better go, Your Lordship." PC Norten tutted. "She don't half order me about, considering I outrank her."

Aldermaston watched the policeman fold himself into the rear of the small hatchback, slam the driver's door, and then drive off.

He contemplated his next move. He could call Stoyle and lodge a formal complaint against the officers who'd assisted with Mortiforde Millie's theft. Then again, perhaps the threat of making a formal complaint to Stoyle would be of more use to him later.

Lisa slipped into Borderlandshire District Council's Planning Department. A constant clatter of fingers pounding keyboards, mixed with the low hum of telephone chatter, filled the air. The desks were clustered together like an archipelago of tropical islands, not that anyone considered working here as paradise. She spotted Neil Vallets alone at his cluster of desks. Fresh out of university, he was only a few months into his planning assistant role. He smiled when he saw her.

Lisa grabbed an empty chair from the desk behind and sat down. "Do me a favour, please."

His cheeky, round face grinned. "How can I help?"

"My printer's broken," she began. "IT can't sort it till Monday, but I need copies of a planning application printed for a meeting with Ms Mayedew later, regarding tomorrow night's Neighbourhood Area Forum. Printed copies would work better."

He nodded and tapped at his computer. "Need the waste incinerator plans, then?"

Lisa slipped closer and whispered, "Actually, no. Abigail's asked for a planning application on some adjacent land. Castle Ridge?"

"Castle Ridge?" He sucked on his blue pen. "Not sure I've come across that one." His fingers danced across the keyboard and smacked the Enter key. Only one result appeared.

"That must be it," she said.

He clicked the link. A map highlighted the plot of land in question. "Is this right? It's not directly next to the meadows."

Neil tapped the screen with his pen at two fields between the highlighted plot and Mortiforde Meadows. "These are not part of the planning application. They're owned by someone else."

Farmer Bell's fields, Lisa surmised. "Abigail definitely said Castle Ridge. What's the application for?"

Neil clicked another link, and a series of plans opened in a new window. "A private gated community of ten luxury five-bedroom properties." He whistled. "They'll cost a pretty packet. Their ridge-top location elevates them above the river, so no flooding issues. Pretty good views of Mortiforde Castle, too."

"Not if the waste incinerator gets built," Lisa commented.

"That's probably why Abigail wants them. Who's going to buy a luxury house next to a waste incinerator?"

She paused. "Who is the planning applicant?"

"You definitely want these printed?"

She nodded.

Behind him, the printer whirred into life. "This should tell us who the applicant is." He clicked another link.

Another window popped up with the words *Castle Ridge Properties Ltd.* There was a PO Box address underneath.

Lisa groaned. "Can we search the Companies House database while we're waiting for that lot to finish printing?"

Neil brought up the Companies House website and searched for Castle Ridge Properties Ltd. "It's new. Only registered six months ago."

Lisa pointed at the people tab. "Who are the company directors?"

Neil clicked the link. Two names appeared. They both gasped at the first.

LOCKMOUNT, Gerald.

But the second name was a bigger shock.

RINDE-SEDGEWICKE, Rosemary.

CHAPTER FOURTEEN

Felicity was preening herself in the mirror when Aldermaston wandered into their private drawing room, just as the mantelpiece clock chimed twice. The incongruity between her smart black two-piece suit and his grease-blotched, faded russet corduroys was overwhelming. "You're not coming in those!"

"Coming where?"

"Councillor Prendeghast's funeral!" She stared at his reflection, then applied some lipstick. "I assume you've moved the tank."

"Not as easy as I'd hoped." He tugged at his trousers. "That's why I'm wearing these."

She dabbed the corner of her mouth. "Get changed, then!"

Aldermaston glanced at his watch. "I might stop at Stella's on the way back, so best we travel separately."

Her eyes narrowed. "Don't be late! Oh, and park on this side of Morte Bridge, then walk across. We're blockading the roads in town to encourage people to attend the funeral."

"Is that legal?" Aldermaston brushed the back of her shoulder.

"We have a right to protest, like everyone else. I hope Abigail's walking."

"Abigail's going?"

Felicity smirked. "I suggested the public would expect her to attend a local councillor's funeral."

"You've seen Abigail today? Has she been here?" His stomach gurgled.

She grabbed her handbag from the coffee table. "We bumped into each other at Diya Parmer's house."

The hairs on the back of Aldermaston's neck rose. "Diya Parmer?"

"I mentioned her yesterday when I got back from the hospital, remember? I thought it was her Morris Minor parked out the front next to your car."

Aldermaston nonchalantly scratched his head. "Vaguely."

"Rosemary Sedgewicke was there, too. She's been selected as the new Socially Liberal Conservative Party candidate and has joined our campaign against the waste incinerator. Bit of a coup for us."

Aldermaston wiped his hands down the back of his corduroys. "And this Diya wasn't at home?"

Felicity shook her head. "Nobody seems to know where she is."

"Probably on holiday." Aldermaston spotted a metal box on the coffee table. "What's this?"

Felicity took one last look in the mirror. "Cartwright and I found it up in the attic. It's paperwork relating to your father's sale of Mortiforde Meadows to Sir Hugo."

"Really?" Aldermaston leaned across the table.

Felicity turned and smacked his outstretched hand. "Not now! You haven't time. If you're not at the meadows by three, the next *Verdant Endings* burial will have your name on it!"

∿

Kitty Catchpole squelched across Mortiforde Meadows towards Otis, standing beside the grave. The diesel pump's mechanical clatter and combustion fumes shattered the meadows' traditional tranquillity. She killed the power switch. The diesel rattle died quickly, although the hose discharging water towards the River Morte continued gurgling briefly. She pointed into the watery grave.

"How much longer to shift what's in there?"

Otis checked his phone. "Fifteen minutes ago, the water was about a foot from the top."

"That much?" Kitty grabbed Otis's arm.

He nodded. "Another ten minutes should do it. Ideally, we should keep the diesel pump going."

Kitty shook her head. "Not during an environmentally friendly funeral."

Otis rubbed his neck. "I'll keep it running until people start arriving. We should backfill the earth as soon as Councillor Prendeghast is in the ground."

Kizzy stared at the puddle below. There was barely an hour until the ceremony started. "Do what you can," she said. "But turn that pump off as soon as you see any dignitaries arriving."

The low-loader had gouged two deep tracks across Knowton Manor's pristine rear lawn, ready to unload Mortiforde Millie. Peredur watched his men, many still dripping water, having finally vacated the hot tub and indoor pool, carefully manoeuvre Mortiforde Millie onto the top lawn beside Rupert's private helipad.

"That's it, lads," Peredur bellowed. "Leave her seated. It'll make it easier to prepare her for tomorrow." He turned to Agents 24, 58, and 73. "You three set up the driveway checkpoint. Set it back a hundred yards from the road so Mr

Rinde's mother has free access to The Lodge. Our gripe is against Mr Rinde, not her."

"Sir!" All three saluted and dashed off.

His phone vibrated in his chest pocket. It was Agent 62.

"You calling from work, Agent 62?"

"Yes, Commander," he whispered. "We may have a problem."

"Go on." Peredur walked down the grass embankment onto the lower lawns.

"Lisa Duddon's asking questions about the Castle Ridge planning application."

"Is she now?" Peredur glanced back up at his men, now easing Mortiforde Millie into place.

"But something's not right."

"What?"

"She asked me to check out the developer on the Companies House website."

Peredur headed back towards the Manor. "What did you find?"

Neil Vallet's whisper softened. "Castle Ridge properties has two directors. Gerald Lockmount and Rosemary Rinde-Sedgewicke. I don't understand the hyphenated *Rinde-Sedgewicke*."

"It's okay. Good work, Agent 62." Peredur ended the call and clenched his free hand. He knew who was behind Castle Ridge. But if Lisa Duddon also knew, then so did Lord Mortiforde. Which meant he was closer to knowing what was *really* going on.

Felicity strolled across the stone triple-arched Morte Bridge and watched the River Morte's autumnal sludgy waters flow underneath, swollen by recent heavy rain. The Norman

Mortiforde Castle towered above her, perched on a rocky outcrop overlooking the river and its adjacent meadows. A waste incinerator here would be monstrous.

She could hear occasional car horns and people shouting above the weir's roar. When she reached the meadow entrance, she found several Ladies' Legion members standing firm, arms interlinked, their backs to her, blockading the road.

"How's it going, ladies?"

Heidi Yail peered over her shoulder. "Brilliant, Your Ladyship." She beamed. "We're sending all traffic into the meadows' car park." She pointed through the large, open double gates next to the turnstiles that dog walkers used at night when the car park gates were closed.

A line of frustrated brake lights glowed all along Curtain Wall Road. St Julian's church clock chimed the half hour. "Give it ten more minutes," Felicity instructed, "then come and join me. It seems we have a good crowd."

Heidi danced a little jig. "I can't believe we're doing this."

Felicity couldn't believe it either. Here they were, about to make Mortiforde history.

Aldermaston shuffled his Jaguar back and forth into a tight spot a few cars behind Felicity's. An incoming call interrupted him. Isabel's number appeared on the dashboard display. "Afternoon, Isabel. Everything all right?"

"Chief Constable Stoyle just called. It was murder. The coroner confirmed Hugo died from a stab wound to the back, which punctured his heart."

Aldermaston sighed. "I hope Stoyle apologised for his constabulary's shambolic handling of this case."

"He also confirmed the coroner was releasing Hugo's body."

"So soon?"

"We must inter him in the family vault, though," Isabel explained. "The body is still accessible should further examinations be necessary." She sighed. "Hugo should be back here at eleven tomorrow morning."

"Would you like me to be there?" Aldermaston offered.

Isabel paused. "I think it should just be me and Rupert. I'll sort a memorial service later."

"I understand." He caught the time. "Sorry, Isabel. I must dash. It's Councillor Prendeghast's funeral in fifteen minutes."

He slipped out of the car and crossed Morte Bridge, thinking about the two men's interments. Sir Hugo would have two witnesses. How many would witness Councillor Prendeghast's?

Felicity was aghast. Not only were there hundreds of people crowding onto the meadows, but there appeared to be several giant trenches scattered among them.

"Your Ladyship!" Kitty Catchpole squelched across the meadows, steadying herself with her shepherd's crook. "Here, use these." Kitty handed her a pair of black wellington boots.

Felicity berated herself. Why hadn't they considered this? It was a dank November afternoon. Oppressive grey clouds hovered barely feet above their heads, and hundreds of spectators were turning the meadows into a quagmire. She forced her feet into the wellingtons, holding Kitty's arm for support.

"There are so many people!" Kitty beamed.

Felicity held her black court shoes between her finger and thumb and considered her options.

"Here." Kitty pulled a carrier bag from her Barbour jacket

pocket. "We're needed over there." She pointed deep into the crowds.

Felicity followed Kitty's lead. "What are all these mounds of earth? Has the council sent in the bulldozers already?"

Kitty giggled nervously. "Otis struggled to dig somewhere deep enough to bury Councillor Prendeghast. Seems the meadows sit on a giant slab of rock. Took him twenty-six attempts to dig one deep enough to meet regulations."

Unease swirled through Felicity as they weaved between frustrated gathered onlookers, keen to continue their journey as soon as the Ladies' Legion cleared their roadblocks. There were lessons to learn here, once Councillor Prendeghast was in the ground.

"Here we all are." Kitty extended an arm towards a large hole in the ground, around which stood Abigail Mayedew, the Reverend Makepiece, Otis Catchpole, Arabella Bebbington, Cissy Warbouys, Rosemary Sedgewicke, and Margaret Hillbrow.

Kitty pointed to a flatbed trailer and tractor beside the grave Otis had set up with a microphone and a couple of speakers. "Otis thought this would make it easier for everyone to see and hear the vicar conduct the service, followed by your short piece."

Felicity nodded. Otis had put thought into this, which was more than Abigail had. Her now-ruined House of Bruar bottle-green velvet shoes were choking in mud.

"Thank you for coming." She extended her black-gloved hand to Abigail. "I know you have other plans for the meadows, but it's kind of you to be here for Councillor Prendeghast."

Abigail sneered as she accepted the handshake. "This might be a first for Mortiforde, but if I get my way, it'll be the last, too."

"LOOK OUT!" someone in the crowd called.

Felicity turned to see Aldermaston hurtling towards them, on his back, with his arms and legs flailing, as he slid uncontrollably through the mud. Heidi screamed and threw her clipboard and pen high into the air as Felicity and Kitty pulled her aside.

With nobody to stop him, Aldermaston slid straight into Councillor Prendeghast's awaiting grave. He smacked into the grave's watery bottom, splashing mud high into the air and across Abigail's face.

The crowd laughed and sniggered. Felicity fumed as a mud-caked Aldermaston struggled to stand upright. He finally managed to steady himself, then wiped the muddy water streaming down his face with one hand and flicked it to one side.

"Not late, am I?"

Felicity stared at her mud-encrusted, sodden husband, clutching the graveside grass. "I'm going to kill you for this!"

Peredur stepped in through his terraced cottage back door and spotted Basildon's box of Cadbury Milk Tray, still lying there. He ripped off the surrounding cellophane, threw it across the worktop, and lifted the lid. He popped a Hazelnut Whirl into his mouth. The creamy chocolate melted as he made his way up the stairs and then hammered on the small bedroom door. "Wake up, Agent 117."

He slipped into his bedroom first, where a double mattress rested on bare floorboards, and collected his electric shaver from the alcove shelving unit. He savoured the chocolate remnants. Time for some fun.

"Rise and shine, Agent 117." Peredur kicked open the spare bedroom door.

Basildon cowered at the end of the bed, his wrist still chained to the bed frame.

An aroma of stale urine hit Peredur's nostrils. "Agent 117, you are a mess and a disgrace to the organisation."

He grabbed Basildon's short salt-and-pepper hair and yanked his head back.

"But I'm not an unreasonable chap. I mean, how can I expect you to keep yourself looking good when I've chained your wrist to the bed frame?" He whipped out the shaver. "Time for a short, back, and sides, Agent 117. Can't have you looking scruffy when you die, can we?"

Aldermaston shivered beside the grave in his mud-soaked clothes as Lisa tiptoed across the muddy meadows towards him. "Don't ask," he hissed.

Lisa peered into the empty grave. "Should there be *that* much water in there?"

Aldermaston snuck another look. The water level seemed higher than when he had been in it.

Felicity scoured the meadows for signs of their star guest. "Where is he?"

Abigail tapped her watch. "Your Ladyship, will it be much longer? Only I have a local authority to run."

"He's here!" Kitty Catchpole hissed. "Look." She pointed her shepherd's crook towards the gates where Wilfred Winnow and a black Shetland pony, with a funereal feather plume attached to its headgear, eased the open black-clothed cart to a halt. Six pallbearers stepped in unison to the cart's end and deferentially slipped the wicker casket onto their shoulders.

Wilfred snapped at the reins, rang his handbell, and hollered, "Any old iron? Rag and bone?" as he headed back into town.

Lisa leaned towards Aldermaston. "Need to talk to you about Castle Ridge Properties Ltd. Rosemary Sedgewicke is a director."

Aldermaston's mouth dropped. Lisa nodded.

An enormous cheer and guffaws of laughter erupted from near the main gates. The first two pallbearers had slipped in the mud. The remaining four struggled with the extra weight they were shouldering, while their highly polished brogues struggled to keep a grip in the mud. Seconds later, two more pallbearers slipped onto their bottoms. The wicker casket fell from everyone's hands and hit the muddy ground with a jolt.

Councillor Prendeghast's last journey was the quickest he'd moved in his entire lifetime. The wicker casket aquaplaned along the squishy ground towards the awaiting grave.

Felicity grabbed Aldermaston's arm. "Do something. NOW!"

He stepped out in front of the environmentally friendly missile streaking down the meadows towards him, crouched down, pushed out his hands, and braced for impact.

WHUMPF!

The wicker coffin punched Aldermaston backwards into the watery grave. Coughing and spluttering, Aldermaston blundered blindly, battling to stand upright. When he slipped under the water for a third time, something hooked around his left arm, slid up to his shoulder, and then yanked him into an upright position.

"There he is!" cried Kitty Catchpole.

Aldermaston blinked the remaining muddy water from his eyes as Kitty unhooked her shepherd's crook from under his armpit. His blurry vision failed to hide Felicity's anger.

~

Peredur grasped his stomach with both hands and breathed deeply through the pain until the cramp subsided. He stood, trying to ease the discomfort as he handled the work call.

"And you've switched it back on again? Good. That should resolve your issue. If it happens again, just call us. My name? Perry, but I'm on annual leave tomorrow. I've put a note on the system so my colleagues know what we've done today. Before you go, on a scale of one to ten, how would you rate the council's IT Helpdesk service today? A nine? Thank you. Have a great day. Bye."

He tore off the headset and threw it beside his work laptop. His stomach muscles relaxed, so he sat down again and stuffed the printed message into the padded envelope, along with its contents, and then wrote *Tugford Hall* on the envelope using a thick black pen.

He sealed it with thick brown parcel tape, crimping the edges to ensure the contents couldn't escape.

Another stomach cramp bent him double. He grimaced at the gut-wrenching spasm. His intestines gurgled and whined. Panic set in. Would he make the bathroom in time?

He launched himself towards his ground-floor bathroom behind the kitchen while clenching his bottom muscles as tightly as his moving legs would allow.

He didn't make it.

Daniel stretched his arms and yawned. Having gone through five years' worth of minutes, he probably knew more about Borderlandshire's drainage system than Lisa.

Diya rummaged in her handbag. "You need some sugar. Here, have one of these." She pulled a toy mouse from her handbag. "Whoops! That's for Daisy when I get back home.

These are what I was looking for." She offered an open bag of peppermints.

"Thanks." He took one and unwrapped it, then waved it at the screen. "This is all pretty monotonous stuff." He popped the sweet into his mouth.

Diya peered at Daniel's screen and then tapped the monitor just below a list of meeting attendees. "Why is Gerald Lockmount's name there?"

Daniel scrolled. "Occasionally, the committee invites external experts for some agenda topics, but it's usually people from neighbouring local authorities or statutory bodies like the local water company."

He scrolled several pages until he found Gerald's name recorded in the notes. Agenda item seventeen. *Mortside Park Homes*.

"The Planning Department sought this committee's views," Daniel read, "on the above development proposal on agricultural land near Mortiforde Meadows. The applicant, Farmer Bell, wishes to site forty-five park home units across the two fields. This would be Borderlandshire's first park home site, so the committee approached local estate agent Gerald Lockmount to provide background information about such sites."

Daniel turned to Diya. "That's a conflict of interest. As the only estate agent, Gerald would market the properties and take sales fees, wouldn't he?"

Diya shrugged. "Mortiforde is a small community. People trusted him. He was a Borderers Guild member for years."

Daniel continued reading. "The Mobile Homes Act 1983 classifies park homes as caravans, despite appearing as small detached bungalows. While residents own the property, they lease their pitch from the landowner to cover the land use and services, such as electricity, water, and sewerage."

Diya returned to her chair. "That would give Farmer Bell a

guaranteed income stream. Better than the financial risk of growing crops there."

Daniel read more. "Mr Lockmount considered the density of park homes on this application to be considerable and could lead to excess surface water draining onto Birrington Road, and then overwhelming the cottages near Morte Bridge." He turned to Diya. "How could Gerald Lockmount have known that? He was an estate agent, not a drainage expert."

A small map showed Farmer Bell's two fields highlighted in red, sandwiched between Mortiforde Meadows and Birrington Road.

"Committee member Rhys Cherbury," Daniel read out, "confirmed the drainage system along Birrington Road already cannot manage rainfall running off from the adjacent Mortiforde Forest. He considered that this development would exacerbate the issue, and the weight of construction traffic using Birrington Lane during the development would further damage the existing drainage system. Based on this information, the committee recommended rejecting Farmer Bell's proposal unless the applicant rebuilt Birrington Lane's drainage infrastructure."

Diya whistled. "Rebuilding Birrington Lane's drainage system would cost hundreds of thousands. Farmer Bell won't have that sort of money."

Daniel bit his lip. "But Gerald could have made some agency fees selling those park homes."

"Park homes are low-cost housing," Diya explained. "Gerald would make more money selling higher-priced properties."

Daniel attacked the computer keyboard.

"What are you doing?"

"Planning Portal. Those committee minutes are just over three years old. The Mortside Park Homes application should still be on the council's system."

~

The afternoon mizzle graduated to a steady light rain. Aldermaston shivered at the graveside, despite Kitty throwing her Barbour jacket over his shoulders. Felicity stood on Otis's tractor-trailer, alongside the Reverend Makepiece, who, Bible in hand, seemed to think he'd catch something nasty if he got too close to the microphone and speakers Otis had hooked up to a twelve-volt battery. The repetitive doof-doofing of a low-flying helicopter passing somewhere overhead in the murky November clouds obliterated most of what the Reverend said about Councillor Prendeghast.

Abigail nudged Aldermaston's arm while they watched the mud-splattered pallbearers suspend Councillor Prendeghast's wicker coffin above the grave.

"How's Diya?"

"Who?" Aldermaston hoped his mud-smeared face hid any blushing.

Abigail sneered. "I know you're lying."

The microphone crackled, and the volume level on the speakers doubled as the Reverend Makepiece uttered the final proceedings.

"We therefore commit this body to the ground, earth to earth, ashes to ashes, dust to dust; in sure and certain hope of the Resurrection to eternal life."

Carefully, and with dignity, the pallbearers lowered the wicker coffin. It came to rest about two feet below the surface. The pallbearers retrieved the lowering straps and deferentially squelched away from the graveside.

"Isn't he supposed to be deeper than that?" Lisa nodded at the grave.

A loud boom echoed around the meadows when the Reverend Makepiece clouted the microphone with his Bible as he moved aside for Felicity.

The dried mud on Aldermaston's cheeks cracked as he offered her an encouraging smile. The speech in her black-gloved hands rustled in the breeze.

"Ladies and gentlemen. Fellow mourners." She looked up from her notes, tried smiling, then returned to her speech. "Too often, death appears to be the end. The end of a life, the end of a family line, as in Councillor Prendeghast's case, or the end of a way of doing things. But it can also be a fresh start."

Aldermaston heard the smack of heavier rain splattering her speech notes. Across the meadows, mourners raised umbrellas. Some attempted to leave, not that the slippery grass made that easy. At his feet, bigger rivulets of water weaved around the thick tufts of grass on their steadfast journey to the nearby river. Many poured into Prendeghast's grave.

"This is a historic day for Mortiforde," Felicity continued. "It's our first environmentally friendly burial. We've not embalmed Councillor Prendeghast with chemicals. He travelled here by horse and cart, not a fossil-fuelled vehicle. We're laying him to rest in a coffin constructed of natural materials that will decompose without contaminating the surrounding land."

Lisa slipped an umbrella from her shoulder bag. "Here, shelter under this."

Aldermaston stepped closer. The rain was streaking the mud on his cheeks.

"Is the coffin getting closer to the surface?" she whispered.

It was barely six inches below ground level. Aldermaston tried to catch Felicity's gaze.

"In due course," she continued, "we shall plant a tree to mark this spot where Councillor Prendeghast lies. Not only will this tree help fight global warming, but, as it thrives, Councillor Prendeghast's decomposing body will nourish it. This marks the true circle of life."

Fleetingly, Felicity's eyes latched onto Aldermaston's. He

nodded at the grave, then saw her glance downwards. She struggled to hide the horror of what was happening. He motioned with his finger to speed up.

Felicity turned a page and spoke quicker.

"We give thanks for the kind generosity of the late Sir Hugo Rinde, owner of these meadows, who granted *Verdant Endings* permission to use these meadows for our environmentally friendly burial project."

A constant waterfall of muddy rain plunged into the grave. The top of the coffin was almost level with the grass.

"I must also thank," Felicity continued, "every member of the Ladies' Legion, who has worked tirelessly to bring today's event to fruition at such short notice in order to meet Sir Hugo's condition of burying someone here before his interment—"

A piercing scream from the crowd shattered the occasion's solemnity.

"The Councillor has risen!" proclaimed another.

The eyes of the entire congregation fixated on the wicker coffin, now floating above the grave, as the crowd took a collective gasp.

This communal shock woke the Reverend Makepiece from his upright slumber. He stumbled momentarily, then saw Prendeghast's coffin floating above the ground.

"It's a miracle!" He clasped his hands together, looked heavenward, and prayed.

At that moment, the grave's water level matched that of the surrounding grass. The coffin slowly rotated on the vast body of water beneath it until one end pointed downhill. The thronging crowds parted in unison, creating a clear, direct route across the meadows.

Prendeghast's coffin began a new journey. Not to the afterlife, but towards the River Morte. It gained momentum. No sedgy tussock could slow him down or divert his course. In the distance, a solitary dog walker strolling along the riverside path suddenly noticed the coffin-shaped missile hurtling towards him. He froze momentarily, then thawed in time to pull his dachshund and himself out of the way as the coffin shot past.

In the distance, Aldermaston spied one of Otis's earlier grave-digging attempts, with its excavated earth abandoned to one side. Could this rain-pounded mound of mud bring the wicker coffin to a halt? No. There was a second collective gasp as the wicker coffin hit the slippery earth embankment and launched itself into the air. For a few seconds, Prendeghast's airborne flight was almost angelic.

The smack of willow against the River Morte's fast-flowing waters echoed around the meadows as a skirt of white spray shot up from the swollen watercourse. When the exploding froth settled, a clearer vision of the coffin appeared, floating peacefully downstream in the middle of the river.

"Didn't the Vikings float their leaders down rivers and out to sea?" Aldermaston enquired.

"They used to set fire to them first," Lisa clarified.

Felicity stood horrified beside the microphone.

Abigail grabbed Aldermaston's arm as she slipped off her shoes. She grimaced as the mud oozed between her toes. "Your Lordship, please thank Her Ladyship for inviting me to this complete and utter fiasco."

She turned to Lisa. "You've obviously finished going through those minutes I tasked you with if you're here to witness this debacle."

"I've just got to write up my report," Lisa replied, catching Aldermaston's eye.

"Good," snapped Abigail, now grabbing Lisa's arm to steady herself. "You can help me with the next phase of the waste incinerator project, then."

Aldermaston blocked her path. "And what would that be?"

A huge grin spread across her face. "You heard your wife, Your Lordship. To meet the legalities of this agreement, the Ladies' Legion had to bury a body in the ground before Sir Hugo's interment." She waved her hand around the meadows. "Do you see a dead body in the ground anywhere?"

He shook his head.

"Exactly. I'm off to organise some bulldozers."

CHAPTER FIFTEEN

Peredur marched through Knowton Manor's front doors wearing a clean pair of khaki camouflage trousers and fresh underwear. Agent 24 saluted. Peredur handed him the Cadbury Milk Tray box. "Share these with the lads. It seems chocolate doesn't agree with me."

"Yes, Commander," Agency 24 snapped. "Mr Rinde's ETA is two minutes."

"Excellent! Lead on."

Agent 24 led Peredur through the hall and across the Billiard Room, its table littered with mid-game-abandoned balls and cues on the baize, then out into the orangery, lined with citrus trees, ferns, cacti, and small palms. They stepped onto the flagstone patio as the dulcet drone of approaching helicopter blades scared the local birds from the surrounding hedges.

Agent 24 raised his voice. "I've armed some lads, just in case."

They crossed the manicured grass, then cut around a stand of Scots pines, to another vast lawn with a helipad in the centre. Peredur's uniformed men surrounded its perimeter.

"It will definitely land?" Peredur shouted.

"Agent 88 is the pilot." Agent 24 winked.

The nearby Scots pines swayed majestically as the helicopter swooped overhead. Pine needles vortexed into the air, and Peredur's eardrums battled with the reverberating air pressure.

The helicopter centred itself over the helipad and descended. Rupert Rinde scowled through the window.

The men's khaki caps blew off as they leaned into the turbulent maelstrom. Rupert's helicopter bounced briefly on its skids before the pilot cut the engine. The passenger door popped open before the engine's dying whine dissipated. Rupert Rinde climbed out, clasping his briefcase, and ducked under the slowly rotating blades.

"What's the meaning of this?" he snapped. "Get off my land immediately!" He made to hurry past them, but Agent 24 blocked his path.

"Out of my way, moron!"

Agent 24 snatched the briefcase from Rupert, passed it to Peredur, then pulled Rupert's hands behind his back and frogmarched him towards the Manor.

"Let me go!" Rupert wriggled.

Peredur noticed Rupert's small birthmark above his left eyebrow, just where Sir Hugo's was.

"It's *you*, isn't it?" Rupert hissed. "Not wearing your Guido Fawkes face mask today, then?"

Peredur opened the orangery door for Agent 24 and his captive.

"What's the meaning of this?" Rupert spat.

Together, they marched through the Billiard Room and into the hallway.

Rupert sneered. "Don't think you can blackmail me!"

At the front door, Peredur faced Rupert. "Blackmail

involves money. This isn't about money." He opened the front door and gestured. "After you."

Agent 24 pushed Rupert out of Knowton Manor and across the driveway to the awaiting jeep. He shoved Rupert into the front seat, then pulled the businessman's hands behind the seat to restrain him.

Peredur jumped into the driver's seat. "You're forgetting something, Mr Rinde." He started the engine. "Blackmailers never win. That's why you instructed me to kill Gerald Lockmount, isn't it?"

"What the blazes were you playing at?" Felicity threw her funeral coat onto their bed and stepped across to their en suite. Steam escaped from the shower unit. Aldermaston's mud-caked clothes littered the bathroom floor.

She pulled at each gloved fingertip and yelled above the power shower drone. "You turned the whole thing into a farce!"

The power shower died. Felicity sighed. "This wasn't supposed to happen." She collapsed onto the dressing table stool and sobbed. "I wanted a decent, uplifting burial."

"It was definitely uplifting." Aldermaston stood in the en-suite doorway with a towel wrapped around his waist.

Felicity threw her hairbrush at him. "I'm the laughing stock of the town, because of you!"

Aldermaston dodged the brush as it ricocheted off the bedroom wall. "I think you'll find it was I who fell into a muddy grave."

She was about to berate him again when her mobile phone rang. "Kitty, can this wait?"

"Good news, Your Ladyship."

Felicity stared at her reflection in the dressing-table mirror. "Tell me the last hour and a half didn't happen."

There was a brief pause. "We've found Councillor Prendeghast."

Felicity pictured the councillor's body washed up on the riverbank somewhere, with the willow coffin smashed to smithereens.

"The coffin got stuck in the horseshoe weir," Kitty continued. "Wedged itself right in the centre. Wilfred Winnow spotted it as he was coming over Forde Bridge with his horse and cart. He and a few others waded in and retrieved it. Coffin and body are soggy, but probably drier than if we'd kept him in the ground. So, we can go again."

Felicity frowned. "Go again?"

"Yes!" Kitty sounded a little exasperated. "Councillor Prendeghast is safely tucked up in the wicker coffin. We can still bury him. This afternoon wasn't a failure. Think of it as a dry run."

Felicity wiped her face. This afternoon had been anything but dry. However, Kitty was right. Ultimately, they were no worse off now than they had been two hours ago. She took a deep breath and stood. "Let's take some time to gather our thoughts and decide how best to proceed. Can you gather the troops here at Tugford Hall for, say … six o'clock tonight? We need a new plan of action."

"I'm onto it! Bye."

Felicity perched on the edge of the dressing table. Aldermaston was back in his red corduroy trousers and checked shirt. She forced a smile. "We've located Councillor Prendeghast, so we can have another go at burying him. This time, you're going to help."

"Me?" Aldermaston's hand clutched his chest. "But I'm still trying to find Mortiforde Millie, locate Basildon, track down Sir Hugo's murderer and—"

Felicity wagged a finger at him. "If you don't help us, you'll wish you'd stayed in Councillor Prendeghast's grave! We have to bury Councillor Prendeghast before Isabel inters Sir Hugo in the family vault, whenever that might be—"

Aldermaston began backing away. "There's something I haven't told you."

Felicity's eyes narrowed.

"Isabell called just before I arrived at the meadows."

"And?"

"The coroner has released Sir Hugo's body. His interment is at eleven o'clock tomorrow morning."

Felicity's hands clenched as she bit her bottom lip. "So the Ladies' Legion needs to sort something tonight, then, don't we?" She scowled. "And you're going to help us!"

The jeep skidded to a halt on the driveway beside the blockade Peredur's men had created earlier.

Rupert howled as Agent 24 kicked him out of the jeep. He slipped awkwardly on the stone driveway. Agent 24 marched him to the barrier blockade.

"Think of this as an eviction, Mr Rinde," Peredur began. "The proletariat is reclaiming this property. It's obscene that one man lives in a property big enough to house several families."

Rupert roared. "You can't evict a property's legal owner."

"I think," Peredur suggested, "you'll find Rinde Industries owns Knowton Manor."

Rupert sighed. "And who owns Rinde Industries, you moron?"

Peredur signalled to an agent to lift the barrier. "Doesn't matter. We're taking possession of Knowton Manor."

The red and white striped barrier rose high enough for Rupert to pass underneath. Agent 24 planted a foot against Rupert's bottom and propelled him off the property. Arms flailing, brogues blundering, Rupert's face collided with the driveway.

Peredur crossed his arms. "Guards, do not let this man pass. Is that clear?"

"Yes, sir!" they declared in unison, then trained their guns on him.

"This is preposterous!" Rupert brushed off the dirt from his bespoke three-piece dark brown cashmere suit.

"STAND BACK!" ordered the guards, releasing their safety catches.

Rupert retreated several steps with his hands in the air. Isabel poked her head around Knowton Lodge's front door.

Rupert wagged his finger at Peredur. "You won't win." He pulled his phone from his jacket pocket. "I'm calling my lawyer and the police."

Peredur glanced up at the leaden sky. "As if PC Norten will do anything." He waved to Isabel. "Don't mind us," he called. "Just a minor legal dispute."

Rupert scrolled through his phone, searching for his lawyer's contact details. "You won't get away with this. I'll make your life hell!"

Peredur's grin broadened. "Tell your lawyer he'll need an interim possession order. Probably take him a couple of weeks. Don't let him hang about. After twelve years, we can claim squatter's rights."

Rupert turned to Isabel. "Mother, I need to stay with you for the next day or so."

"I don't think so," Isabel snorted. "You threw your father and me out of *our* home once. Remember?" She slammed the door shut.

"Mother!" Rupert bellowed.

Peredur's snigger was louder than he intended it to be.

"Stop laughing, you pugnacious little cretin!" Spittle flew from Rupert's lips as he held his phone high, searching for a signal. "This is a war you'll regret starting!"

Peredur joined Agent 24 in the jeep. "I didn't start this war. It began twenty-five years ago."

Peredur floored the accelerator, sending a battery of loose stone missiles firing at a defenceless Rupert.

Aldermaston pulled in his stomach as he squeezed past the door into his office. "The sooner I can walk into my office unhindered, the better," he muttered, making his way to his desk.

"Things are getting complicated." Lisa bolted the door behind him. "But we're getting the bigger picture." She retrieved a folder from her executive bag.

"Before you begin, how's the online auction going, Diya?"

"It's nearly lunchtime on America's East Coast," Diya explained, "so the first edition book bids have really exploded. Currently, bids on all five books, the three pieces of silverware, and the rug total three hundred and forty-one thousand, seven hundred and forty-nine pounds."

Daniel vocalised everyone's thoughts. "Flipping heck!"

Diya beamed. "We still have over twenty-four hours until tomorrow's five o'clock deadline."

Lisa placed the folder on Aldermaston's desk. "Can bidders back out?"

Diya nodded. "Potentially, but there's so much excitement in the books, the next highest bidder is bound to step in." She turned to Aldermaston. "I know there's still a long way to go, but we're over halfway. Without your support and your protection, none of this would have been possible." Her eyes glistened. "Hopefully, Nani Nagma will know nothing of what I've been through over the past few days."

Aldermaston smiled.

Daniel and Lisa pulled chairs alongside Aldermaston's desk. Lisa opened the paper file.

"I spoke with Neil Vallets in Planning earlier about Castle Ridge." She spread documents out across Aldermaston's desk. "Castle Ridge is a proposed gated community development of ten luxury properties in these fields here." She pointed at the location map.

Aldermaston tapped the drawing. "This is what I saw in Rupert's office." He then drew a circle with his finger around two fields near Mortiforde Meadows. "These are the two fields Farmer Bell has just sold to Rupert Rinde at a knock-down price. So, Rupert owns all this thanks to a little agreement Gerald and Rupert had." Aldermaston shared Maureen's suspicions with them.

"That's fraud and probably tax evasion!" Daniel declared. He looked at the location map. "Why does Rupert need Farmer Bell's fields?"

"There's no direct access from these Castle Ridge fields to the Birrington Road," Aldermaston clarified. "But Farmer Bell's fields border both the Castle Ridge development *and* Birrington Road. With this land, the Castle Ridge development gains access to the public highway. And," Aldermaston wagged a finger at Daniel, "it can't be a coincidence that Farmer Bell agreed to sell to Rupert on the day the council announced the waste incinerator project is going ahead. He probably thought Rupert's offer was the best price he would ever get after that."

Diya tapped Daniel's shoulder. "Tell him about *Mortside Park Homes*."

"What's that?" Aldermaston enquired.

Daniel explained Farmer Bell's original plans to create a small development of park homes on his fields. Then he spread the Highways Drainage (Seepage and Sewerage) Improvement Planning Sub Group minutes across Aldermaston's desk.

Lisa scrutinised them. "This was before I was in post."

"Yeah," Daniel continued. "This was three years ago. These minutes show how Gerald's testimony to the subcommittee led them to recommend that the Planning Department should reject the park home application. The information is still on the Planning Portal. I also found these public comments from the public consultation process."

He placed two sheets of paper before Aldermaston and Lisa. "Gerald Lockmount objected to the development, claiming it would have a 'detrimental visual impact on the local amenity'."

"Harsh!" Lisa exclaimed. "He's effectively claiming they'd be an eyesore."

Daniel tapped another sheet of paper. "Rupert Rinde also objected because he felt it was an inappropriate development on the edge of the town in a scenically outstanding area. He claimed the local infrastructure wouldn't cope with the increased traffic forty-five new residences would bring."

Aldermaston pieced together the pieces. "And I bet Gerald's commission from selling ten properties in a gated community would far exceed anything he could get for selling forty-five mobile homes."

Lisa selected the Companies House printout. "There's one problem. The directors of Castle Ridge Properties Ltd are *Gerald Lockmount* and *Rosemary Rinde-Sedgewick*. Rupert's not connected with the company."

"Rinde-Sedgewick?" Daniel queried. "Are Rupert and Rosemary married?"

Lisa shrugged. "No. But it's a clever move if Rosemary is involved."

Aldermaston frowned. "How do you mean?"

"The Planning Department's artificial intelligence system

checks all applications for potential conflicts of interest with any council staff. If it investigated Castle Ridge Properties' directors, it would think Rosemary Rinde-Sedgewicke was a different person from Rosemary Sedgewicke."

Aldermaston whistled. "So the waste incinerator project is a smokescreen. That's why Rosemary is campaigning against it. She knows it won't go ahead. It was never going to go ahead." He prodded the architectural drawings. "This has all been about acquiring Farmer Bell's fields."

Abigail marched determinedly along the corridor towards Diya's office with her phone clamped against her ear. Her passage forced council staff aside in her wake. Some slipped into the nearest cupboard to avoid her, and others bowed or curtsied as she swept past.

"Richard, send in the bulldozers. Yes. Mortiforde Meadows. NOW!" Her face scowled as she listened to some waffle about procedures and protocols.

"I'm not asking you to flatten the site. I know we haven't issued a compulsory purchase order yet, but it would be prudent to secure the site as soon as possible."

Approaching some double fire doors, she pushed her palm out flat and barged through, sending both doors flying. A young male admin assistant screamed in pain as one collided with his nose.

"Richard, all I want is a couple of bulldozers blocking the meadows' main gates. People can still access them through the pedestrian gate turnstile. I want to send a clear signal that this authority is prepared to take action."

She entered the stairwell and descended to the ground floor. "What's the problem? It's only ten to five." Puzzled, she continued, "Finished for the day? Call them back in! Because you're the Director of Highways, that's why!"

She paused outside Diya's closed office door, pacing up and down. "Richard, pick two staff to come back in, and if they won't, then tell them to come to my office first thing tomorrow morning, and I'll sack them on the spot. Is that clear?"

She cut the call, closed her eyes, and then pounded the floor with her feet. "Why am I surrounded by halfwits?" She drew in a deep, calming breath, released it in one long, controlled exhale, then stepped into Diya's office.

Norris Offermans was slipping his arms through his navy blue jacket as Diya's computer powered down.

Abigail planted her hands on her hips. "I see someone else thinks it's a half-day, too! Or are you leaving early because you've found the waste incinerator project is fully funded?"

Norris slipped some paperwork into his briefcase. "Ms Mayedew, my investigations are still in progress. Sometimes there's only so much one can do on a computer. I've already carried out one enlightening face-to-face interview today."

He paused, then looked at Abigail. "Did you know Diya Parmer always signs off her emails with the phrase *Kindest regards*?"

Abigail shrugged. "And?"

"The email she purportedly sent Tuesday ends with *Yours sincerely*." Norris then peered at her, frowned, and pointed at her left cheek. "You have a speck of mud, Ms Mayedew."

Abigail slipped a tissue from her dress pocket, dabbed it with her tongue, then wiped her cheek.

Norris smiled. "That's it."

"Thank you." She checked the tissue and saw the faintest of mud smears. "Did I get it all?"

"Oh, yes," said Norris. "It was the tiniest of flecks, but I spotted it." He stepped around Diya's desk. "At the National

Audit Office, we look for the smallest details. Of the one hundred and forty-seven emails Diya sent to you in your first six weeks here, she signed them all off with *Kindest regards*, except for Tuesday's *Yours sincerely*. A small detail, but telling, don't you think?"

"You're here to add up the numbers, Mr Offermans, not check email sign-offs."

He stepped around Abigail and opened Diya's office door. "Which is why I'm off to the accounts department. There's an interesting discrepancy on the General Miscellaneous Irreconcilable Sundry Credit account."

Abigail frowned. "What sort of discrepancy?"

Norris wrinkled his nose. "A few pence. Might be nothing."

Abigail's mouth opened, but Norris held a single finger in the air, then used it to tap the side of his nose. "We have a saying at the National Audit Office, Ms Mayedew. The tiniest of details tell the biggest stories."

Aldermaston stared at the proposed building designs. Gated communities were popular with privacy-seeking celebrities, multi-millionaires, and bankers, but that wasn't Mortiforde. Everything his father had done as the Seventh Marquess was to bring people together, hence the food festival and the upcoming Bonfire Night celebrations. Gated communities created barriers. That's why his father never closed Tugford Hall's gates—

The tank! He still hadn't moved it. Aldermaston mentally moved another to-do item further up his list of priorities.

"These properties are obscene." Lisa rotated some designs to take a better look. "This one's got nine bedrooms! We don't have nine bedrooms at our bed-and-breakfast." She pointed to a drawing. "Look at the south elevation. All the ground-floor and first-floor rooms have enormous windows overlooking the meadows and the castle. The way the River Morte flows around the castle here has to be one of the best views in England. That's a prime site now that it has access to the Birrington Road."

Aldermaston picked another drawing. "If we're saying the waste incinerator is a hoax, why did someone murder Sir Hugo?"

Diya raised her hand. "If this is all a hoax, am I wasting my time with these auctions?"

Aldermaston shook his head. "Our hoax theory could be wrong." He turned to Daniel. "Has my half-brother turned up yet?"

Daniel stood. "Want me to check his apartment again?"

"No, not yet." Aldermaston shuffled paperwork on his desk. "Where's that *Powys Gazette* printout?"

"This one?" Diya pulled at a large sheet hanging over the back of Aldermaston's desk and passed it to him.

What had Basildon seen? He reread the article looking for clues, but nothing jumped out. What made Basildon think this story was the birth of BANG? Aldermaston pulled a magnifying glass from the back of his desk drawer and scrutinised the photo.

All looked normal until … Then he saw it. It was blurry, but suddenly everything fell into place. If Basildon's conclusions were correct, then this mess had just got even more complicated.

CHAPTER SIXTEEN

Rosemary opened her solid-wood front door. Rupert stormed past with such force that he pushed her to the ground.

"Excuse me!" she hollered, struggling to get to her feet. There was a small envelope on the wicker doormat that now bore Rupert's size ten shoe print. Someone was being presumptuous and addressed it to *Rosemary Sedgewicke, MP*. She shoved it into her trouser pocket and stomped into the kitchen to find Rupert filling the kettle. "Next time I let you into my home, don't knock me to the ground!"

Rupert grabbed two mugs from the mug tree and banged them heavily on the worktop.

She pushed past him and grabbed the mugs. "What's happened?"

Rupert slumped into a kitchen-table chair. "I've been evicted from Knowton Manor. I'll have to stay here with you."

"Evicted?" Rosemary dropped a teabag in each mug. "Isabel can't throw you out of your home."

"She might as well have done," Rupert snarled. "Wouldn't even put me up for the night at The Lodge."

Rosemary gasped. "The will! Has your father left the manor to Isabel?" She frowned. "That can't be right. Knowton Manor is a business asset. You own a majority stake."

He slammed a flat palm onto the wooden tabletop. "It's bloody BANG!"

Rosemary flinched. "BANG? What do they have to do with all this?" She grabbed the milk from the fridge.

"I've just got back from France to find an army of men squatting in my house. They frogmarched me off the premises. Said they were confiscating Knowton Manor for the masses."

Rosemary grabbed her landline phone and offered it to Rupert. "Call the police."

Rupert laughed. "PC Noodlebrain?" He shook his head. "One policeman against a hundred? They told me I needed an interim possession order. They've done their homework."

Rosemary waved the phone handset in the air. "Call your lawyers, then."

"Already have. It'll take the weekend to get it sorted. But BANG knew that." Rupert pulled his mobile phone from his suit jacket pocket.

Rosemary returned the phone to its cradle and placed a mug of tea in front of him. "Have you tried Chief Constable Stoyle?"

His mobile phone rang, and he brought a finger to his lips. His eyebrows arched when he saw the number and answered. "What are you playing at, you little sod?"

Rosemary sipped tea as she struggled to hear who he was talking to.

Rupert turned his back. "Meet me tonight. Eleven o'clock. Usual spot." He jumped to his feet, knocking the table and spilling tea everywhere. "Look, you wretched little miscreant. I told you right at the start of all this that you'd regret any attempt to blackmail me. Scum like you don't have the right to mess with people like me. So, eleven o'clock at the usual spot.

This is not a negotiation. Goodbye!" Rupert slammed the phone down so hard that more tea spilled across the table.

Rosemary pouted. "Problem?"

He slurped the remains of his tea, then brushed the spilled tea onto the floor with his free hand. "It's that idiot who called me last night while we were having dinner."

"The one dealing with the 'back office stuff', as you called it."

Rupert sneered. "There always comes a point when those cretins think they know more than you do."

"*Are* they blackmailing you?"

Rupert chuckled. "I'll soon put them straight."

She pointed to his phone on the table. "Please tell me you're not using BANG to deal with your dirty work?"

"*Our* dirty work," Rupert snapped. "This is as much about you getting elected to Westminster as it is about getting Castle Ridge off the ground."

Rosemary's eyes widened. "Ours?" she screamed. "I told you at the start I wasn't comfortable being listed as a director of Castle Ridge Properties Ltd. I understood the need to shield you from the development because everyone would soon realise the waste incinerator project was just a ruse—" She took a deep breath. "When you said you knew someone who could take care of the messy side of things, I assumed you vetted them properly. You did, didn't you?"

Rupert stared straight into her soul. "I'll sort it. We haven't come this far to be thrown off course by a devious delinquent."

Felicity banged the table in Tugford Hall's main drawing room just as the mantelpiece lock chimed six. The background hubbub of gathered women quickly subdued.

"Ladies of the Legion," she began. "It has been a

momentous day. We were and still are under an extremely tight deadline. We have seventeen hours to get Councillor Prendeghast in the ground."

A combined gasp echoed around the main drawing room.

Margaret Hillbrow raised a hand. "What happens at eleven o'clock tomorrow morning?"

Felicity glanced at the floor. "Isabel will inter Sir Hugo in the family vault."

"Can't we ask Isabel to delay?" Cordelia enquired.

Felicity perched herself on the table's edge. "The poor woman is grieving. What right do we have to impinge on that?"

The gathered women nodded.

"Where is Councillor Prendeghast?" Felicity asked.

Nancy Winnow raised her hand. "At ours. Wilf brought him back on the cart, but we can't keep him overnight. We're licensed to store scrap metal, not dead bodies."

"We must act tonight. Let's meet at the meadows at eleven o'clock. Can everyone bring a bucket?"

"Why?" Kitty called.

"To empty the water from the grave," Felicity explained.

"Otis could bring the diesel pump. That'd be quicker, My Lady."

"I don't want to draw attention to ourselves. Let's use the cover of darkness to our advantage. I want this to be a fait accompli when Abigail first hears of this at tomorrow night's NAF." She hugged her clipboard as she gazed at her assembled group. "If we achieve this tonight, we'll have shown the town that not only are we a force to be reckoned with, but when we say we're going to do something, we do it!"

A tremendous cheer and applause erupted from the group. Felicity crossed her fingers. Hopefully, once they got Councillor Prendeghast in the ground tonight, he'd stay there this time.

∼

Aldermaston tapped the photo in the newspaper article. "We need to find out what happened to this baby."

"How?" Lisa scrutinised the printout. "I can't walk into the Social Services offices on the third floor and ask them to hand over everything on him. They have a duty of confidentiality." She nodded at the clock on the office wall. "And they all went home an hour ago, anyway."

Aldermaston shrugged. "Doesn't matter. Borderlandshire's Social Services know nothing about this baby." He pointed at the top of the article. "*Powys Gazette*. This happened in Wales, not England. Powys Social Services dealt with him, not Borderlandshire's."

"We don't even know his name," said Daniel.

Aldermaston smiled. "We do. Basildon put the first clue here." He pointed to Basildon's scrawl. *The Birth of BANG?* "When Basildon fired the cannonball at the demonstrators yesterday, one protester was on the phone to someone called Peredur. Powys Social Services are bound to have given the baby a Welsh name. Peredur is Welsh, and BANG organised that protest."

"Peredur?" Daniel clicked his fingers. "I've seen that name somewhere."

"Planning Portal?" Diya suggested.

"Yes!" Daniel browsed through the Planning Portal's comments. "Here it is!" he snapped. "A Peredur Geraint Jones commented on the Mortside Park Homes application that 'this development would bring much-needed affordable housing to Mortiforde, particularly for locals with strong work and family connections.'" He looked over his shoulder at Aldermaston and Lisa. "Wait for this next bit." His finger traced the words on the screen. "'Rejecting such an application would show this authority, along with developers and those whose businesses rely upon the local housing market, has no interest in providing local homes for local people on low wages. Rejecting this application would be a blatant bias towards socio-economic cleansing of the lower classes.'"

Aldermaston flicked through his notebook and reread the note BANG hand-delivered three days ago. *You should be the ones to burn, you landed-gentry squatters.* "This is about housing."

"All of it?" Lisa enquired.

Aldermaston leaned forward. "What if BANG also believes the waste incinerator project is a hoax and a cover for the Castle Ridge development? Building a gated community on the site where much-needed low-cost affordable housing was planned would anger many people."

Lisa scribbled down the name. "There can't be many Peredur Geraint Joneses about. What makes you think Basildon's assumption about this baby being the leader of BANG is right?"

Aldermaston bit his bottom lip as his mind wandered. "I need to talk to someone first. Got to be careful about throwing accusations around. But see what you can find online. Check social media accounts and see if any previous BANG news stories in the press reveal anything."

Daniel turned to Lisa. "I've emailed a summary report of the Highways Drainage (Seepage and Sewerage) Improvement Planning Sub Group minutes to your work address. How you minute those meetings, I'll never know."

"Thanks." Lisa grabbed her bag and chuckled. "Abigail will be angry when she realises her time-wasting job actually proved useful to us." She turned to Aldermaston. "So, what's the plan of action?"

Aldermaston pointed to the metal box from the attic on Daniel's desk. "Have you looked at that yet?"

Daniel shook his head. "I was prioritising Lisa's work."

He nodded. "That's fine. There's a lot going on. Take Diya

back to Shepherd Cottage, then go home and grab something to eat. I need you back here later this evening."

"Why?"

"We've a trip to the meadows. The Ladies' Legion is determined to bury Councillor Prendeghast tonight."

~

Stefan Taplinski pulled back the green velour dining chair. Abigail took her place at the secluded dining table tucked into the bay window overlooking the River Morte. Although dark, the Norman Foundation's external lighting cast a soft glow across the restaurant's cottage garden and passing river.

In a corner, a pianist played Debussy's 'Clair de Lune', which was accompanied by the occasional crack from the ageing log fire. Cutlery clinked and wine glasses chimed between diners' giggles and hushed words in the Michelin-starred restaurant.

Stefan, in a pale blue suit and white shirt, took his seat opposite as the server handed Abigail a menu.

"My treat," Stefan offered.

Abigail peered over the menu. "If I find a Norman Foundations receipt on your expenses this month, I shall have no qualms in bringing it to the Scrutiny Commission's attention."

Stefan clutched his hand to his chest. "As if I would dare do such a thing!"

Abigail returned her attention to the menu. "According to HR's records, you did, three years ago when this restaurant first opened."

Stefan picked up a glass of water and took several gulps. "A misunderstanding," he choked. His face reddened awkwardly as he perused his menu.

"Everyone is entitled to an occasional misunderstanding," she offered.

"Quite." He continued staring at his menu. "Was the Earl of Dartbury a misunderstanding?"

Abigail placed her menu down. "Jilting me at the altar was an act of cowardice, not a misunderstanding."

Stefan lowered his menu. "Forgive me. I did not mean to pry."

The sommelier arrived with a bottle of Château Clerc-Milon Cabernet Sauvignon and poured a taster into a glass and offered it to Stefan.

"Please let my guest decide." He gestured to Abigail.

Abigail savoured the aroma, then took a sip. She nodded. "Lovely."

The sommelier topped up Abigail's glass, then filled Stefan's, before leaving the bottle on the table.

"I don't blame you for prying, Stefan," Abigail continued. "Foolish are the ones who don't do their homework." She took another sip. "This is rather good." She continued browsing the menu. "The Earl of Dartbury was a charming man and knew how to play a woman's heartstrings. I allowed him to cloud my better judgement. I've learned that lesson."

Stefan shuffled in his seat. "I hope you've not written off the male species completely."

"No," Abigail replied. "But I would ensure my heart and head had a robust conversation before making any commitment like that again."

"Is that why you moved to Borderlandshire?"

"I'm not running away."

"We all need a fresh start sometimes."

Abigail's shoulders relaxed. "It's been a hectic two months. New job, new home, new life."

"Sounds like you've not had a chance to stop and draw

breath. Makes me even more pleased that you accepted my dinner invitation."

"What was it about the waste incinerator you wanted to talk about tonight?"

Stefan crimsoned. "Ah. Would you think poorly of me if I told you it was merely a ruse to spend some time with you?"

She was about to say yes, but as she appreciated the restaurant's decadent interior and soothing ambience, she realised this was the first time she'd had a decent, adult, civilised conversation since moving here. She shook her head. "This really is delightful, Stefan."

A server stepped from the shadows. "Are you ready to order?"

Abigail pointed to the menu. "The seaweed cracker with lovage emulsion, oyster leaf, and fresh apple sounds delightful."

"The seaweed custard, beef broth, and bone marrow, for me, please," Stefan requested.

The server collected their menus and disappeared into the shadows again.

Abigail selected her wine glass again. "Who should I be more worried about? Rupert Rinde or Lord Mortiforde?"

He stared into her eyes as he let out a deep sigh. "His Lordship is popular with the townsfolk. He's still riding the sympathy wave following his parents' tragic road accident eighteen months ago. His father, the Seventh Marquess, was hugely popular. It's no secret that the town panicked when they thought His Lordship's older brother, Basildon, was the rightful heir. His eccentricity has always put him at odds with the town. But when the town learned Basildon was not the Seventh Marquess's firstborn, the sixteenth-century town walls relaxed with relief. The Eighth Marquess is truly his father's son, for which many in the town are immensely grateful. The way he stood up for the town during this year's Borders in Blossom competition endeared him further to the townspeople."

Abigail wrinkled her nose. "You like him, then?"

Stefan choked. "Can't stand the bloke! Wants the entire world to be happy and to get along nicely." He shook his head. "Life's not like that."

"And Rupert?"

"A player." Stefan's eyes narrowed as he continued to stare at her. "Bit like you. Prefers to get on with things."

Abigail allowed herself a wry smile.

"He's often too focused, though," Stefan continued. "Once he's set his sights on something, he doesn't care who gets caught in the crossfire." Stefan checked over his shoulder, then leaned across the table and whispered. "There's a rumour he kicked Sir Hugo and Isabel out of Knowton Manor when he took over at Rinde Industries."

"Harsh. Although sometimes tough decisions have to be made for the greater good. Any companions?" Abigail sipped some more wine.

Stefan draped his napkin across his lap. "There was a time. . ." He glanced up at the ceiling. "Must be nearly thirty years, come to think of it. He and Rosemary Sedgewicke were an item."

"Rosemary?" Abigail almost choked.

"They were extremely close for a long time, then suddenly she got a job in the European Commission and practically disappeared overnight. When she came back a few years ago, both of them had moved on. They seem friendly now. Although. . ." Puzzlement fell across his face. "Sometimes, two people who should be together just can't live with each other."

Abigail stared at her wine glass. Had she underestimated Rosemary? Her stomach knotted. Everyone told her Diya Parmer was a respected, diligent, and hard-working council employee. She had no reason to suspect Diya's Tuesday morning email was anything but truthful. But it would suit Rosemary if the waste incinerator project were half a million pounds short. If the townsfolk saw her as the meadows' saviour, she'd win a by-election with a landslide. Could Rosemary be behind Diya's disappearance?

"Abigail?"

"Sorry," she brushed some imaginary dust off her dress-covered thigh. "There's so much to sort for tomorrow night's NAF. I keep thinking of things I've forgotten."

Stefan raised a glass. "Here's to tomorrow night's NAF."

Their glasses kissed. Abigail forced a grin and added another item to tomorrow's to-do list. She wanted words with Rosemary first thing tomorrow morning.

Peredur sniggered as he squeezed between the Chieftain tank and Tugford Hall's gates, briefly catching his rucksack on the gate hinge. If only Lord Mortiforde knew his plans for this tank tomorrow night.

A few of Tugford Hall's East Wing interior lights glowed. The rest of the building was in darkness, save for a couple of lights illuminating the porticoed main entrance's curved stone steps. Thick cloud blocked any moonlight, but Peredur was prepared and in full camouflage gear and face paint.

His boots barely crunched the gravel as he stalked panther-like along the driveway. Only the occasional tawny owl hoot accompanied his clandestine approach. He paused when he reached the ornate balustrade separating the driveway from the basement windows below. Basildon had been slow to offer help on how not to trigger the security lighting, but as Peredur glanced up the curved stone staircase, gut instinct told him to disregard Basildon's advice.

Basildon had said to keep left up the stairs. But the steps' curved design as they negotiated a ninety-degree turn meant the tread depth was narrowest on the right. Left was safer. Left was where most people would naturally climb. Peredur tutted. He slipped ten feet to the right, where the steps were barely deep enough for a toehold, and took the first step. Darkness. Good. He took the next. Darkness still. His breathing became shallower as he continued his slow climb to the main porch.

Once at the main entrance level, Peredur slid between the stone columns and surveyed the underside of the portico roof. The security cameras were where Basildon said they would be. Nestled in the far ceiling corners, they pointed down to the front door. These stone pillars were a blind spot.

Carefully, he slipped the rucksack off his back, reached inside, and pulled out the padded envelope. He clutched it tightly to his chest while re-securing the rucksack's straps so the other contents didn't fall out.

Returning the rucksack to his back, he slipped behind the second column, gripped the package with one hand, and swung his arm back and forth. He needed just enough momentum to plant the package where needed. When it felt right, he released his grip. The package flew towards the front door.

Motion detectors alerted the spotlights above Peredur's head. Two broad beams of light dazzled the front door and half the porticoed entrance, leaving the columns still in darkness. His package landed by the front door with a thud.

According to Basildon, the triggered security lights would notify Cartwright. Peredur continued hugging the stone column and edged around it, hiding from the front door. His boot toes perched precariously on the narrow plinth as his gloved fingers clamped the stone pillar. He waited.

Someone pulled back the door's metal bolts. The hinges creaked as it slipped ajar. Cartwright's balding head peered around the door frame, glanced confusedly around, then spotted the package a few feet from the door.

Peredur watched from behind the pillar with one eye.

Cartwright checked the stone steps and portico for visitors, then bent over to collect the package. "Is there anyone there?" With no response, he slipped back inside and bolted the door.

Peredur edged around the pillar again and exhaled deeply when the lights died and a tsunami of darkness engulfed him.

One down, two more jobs to go. He pulled back his sleeve to check the time. Seven-thirty. Next stop, the council basement.

❧

Aldermaston kicked off his shoes and reclined against his bed's supportive pillows. Cartwright was serving dinner at eight, which gave him a moment to look through the metal box Felicity had found in the attic.

The bedroom door flew open, and Harry charged in, fully clothed, with an inflatable armband above each elbow. "Can we go swimming now, Daddy?" He jumped onto Aldermaston.

"Steady on!" His stomach knotted. Pain from having a seven-year-old land there, or guilt at what he was about to say? "Daddy's busy, and dinner won't be long. We don't have time this evening."

"But, Dad!" Harry whined.

"Perhaps Mummy can take you sometime."

"I wanna go swimming with you!" Harry jumped to the floor and ripped off his armbands. "You're always busy."

Aldermaston swung his legs off the bed and grabbed his son, hugging him tightly. "I know, and it's not fair. We will go."

"When?"

"When I've sorted out a few things."

"Tomorrow?" Harry's eyebrows rose hopefully, then dropped when he didn't get an immediate answer. "Fine," he sighed. "I'll put these away." He stomped out of his parents' bedroom.

Aldermaston remembered having similar conversations with his father at Harry's age. Only now did he appreciate what his father had to contend with.

He unfurled several sheets of paper from the box and spread them out along Felicity's side of the bed. That the meadows had once been part of the Tugford estate still surprised him. Yet the map was clear, as were the words *Dispose for roof* scrawled across the document's top left in his father's handwriting.

Next, he plumped for the thickest document bundle, secured with a pink ribbon. The Historic Borders Agency logo sat in the middle, underneath which sat a document: *Land Purchase Agreement between the Historic Borders Agency and the Tugford Hall Estate: Mortiforde Meadows.*

He thumbed through the papers. Stella's claim about his father agreeing to sell them the meadows was right. So why had his father changed his mind? Selling to the HBA was the *right* thing to do.

The next document was Sir Hugo's letter. A wealth of emotions stirred within him as he read it. At ten years old, he'd known nothing of the financial situation his father had faced then. His parents often commented on the financial drain these large country estates were, but he'd never thought they could lose their home. He looked around their bedroom. Were they only here now because his father had sold Mortiforde Meadows to Sir Hugo?

He reread Sir Hugo's final paragraph.

I promise I'll protect the meadows. You helped me five years ago when I was in trouble. Now it's my turn to help you.

What favour for Sir Hugo? He checked the letter's date. *27th November*, twenty-five years ago. What had his father done five years before this to help Sir Hugo? How could he find out? His father's journals!

Aldermaston flew out of the bedroom and practically slid down the banister, skidding in his socked feet along the tiled hallway to the secret door leading from their private apartment into the main hall. He slid the bolt, released the catch, and the solid door, which to anyone standing on the other side looked like a bookcase, swung open.

"Perfect timing, Your Lordship!" Cartwright stepped across Tugford Hall's main entrance hall towards him. "Someone just delivered a package. No name. Addressed to Tugford Hall. Are you expecting anything, My Lord?"

Aldermaston waved it away. "Not now, Cartwright. Give it to Felicity. She's in our private drawing room."

Cartwright nodded and headed towards the servants' stairs.

Aldermaston dashed across the main entrance hall towards the imposing wooden staircase. Taking two stairs at a time, he forked left where the stairs split and hurried to the library. He flicked a switch, and the ambient glow warmed the room's dark wood panelling. Oil paintings hung on the walls above the top of the bookcases lining all four walls. Two enormous sofas, each bearing an army of cushions, filled the centre of the room, next to an unlit open fireplace.

Aldermaston scurried across to an imposing bookcase housing thick, brown, leather-bound tomes. His fingers ran along the bottom shelf and pressed a catch in the corner. The false bookcase facade sprang open, revealing another series of shelves behind it. Shelves containing his father's private annual journals.

He ran a finger along the spines, honed in on the one from thirty years ago, and pulled it from the shelf. Then he switched on a table lamp adjacent to the sofa and sat down.

Aldermaston flicked through the pages looking for the

twenty-seventh of November, then allowed his finger to trace his father's handwritten scrawl as he searched for clues. Frustration fell across his face. It seemed the highlight of his father's day had been a Borderers Guild meeting congratulating themselves on a successful Christmas Lights Switch-On event.

Aldermaston checked back through the journal, skimming the text, looking for any reference to Sir Hugo. His hope diminished with each page turn until he spotted an asterisk at the bottom of the ninth November's entry. *Sir Hugo called. Back cover.*

He flipped to the diary's rear and inside the back cover found a folded sheet of paper taped to the flyleaf, its glue yellowed with the years. Carefully, he unfurled the page.

Hugo stopped by today. He looked drained. The bags under his eyes appeared larger than usual. He was clearly distressed, which became ever more apparent with his first question. He needed fifty thousand pounds to hire a private detective. Not only that, but he wanted me to pay the detective agency directly. He didn't want the transaction to go through his personal or business accounts.

I must have been open-mouthed, for he stared at me for several seconds, then blurted, "We have a family crisis. Whatever happens, Rupert must never know."

I knew he was desperate when he dropped to his knees. Sometimes, being a friend means not asking too many questions.

Aldermaston felt his temples pulsate. Why did Sir Hugo need to hire a private detective agency? Fifty thousand pounds was a lot of money to help a friend over three decades ago. It would be a lot of money today.

He clutched the journal to his chest. His parents had never

spoken of this. And now Sir Hugo was dead. Did Isabel know? Or did Hugo keep this from her?

A blood-curdling scream shattered the library's serenity. Aldermaston flinched, dropping the journal. He retrieved it and hurried to the library door, where he came face to face with Cartwright.

"Come quickly, My Lord," he blustered, gesturing along the corridor. "It's the package, My Lord. Her Ladyship has opened it."

CHAPTER SEVENTEEN

Peredur entered Borderlandshire District Council's offices and swiped his security pass at reception. Alfred, the authority's octogenarian security guard, sat in Shirley's receptionist chair, snoring. His bottom jaw hung low. Peredur leaned across the desk and lifted it to silence the snoring. He continued along the corridor towards the council chamber, holding his head low to avoid the security cameras. It wasn't uncommon for IT staff to enter the building for urgent, out-of-hours computer issues, but those who did weren't covered in camouflage paint.

Peredur slipped through the council chamber double wooden doors and flicked on the lights. Preparations for tomorrow evening's NAF were well underway. Staff had laid out rows of chairs theatre-style to accommodate a couple of hundred people, and a panel of desks stood on the dais. Abigail expected a significant turnout.

From his rucksack, he retrieved a large coil of blue, slow-burning fuse wire. To one end, he attached a tubular metal weight, then stepped onto the dais and threw it high above him. It flew over a strip light suspended from the ceiling, and then he caught it as it fell. He repeated this over the next three lighting units until he reached the basement door, hidden behind the curtain. He pulled the remaining fuse wire towards him, so only about a foot at the other end hung below the first lighting unit. Striding back, he counted twenty paces across the dais and stretched up. His fingers were about six inches too short to touch it. Perfect.

He returned across the chamber and noted the fuse wire hanging from the strip-light was barely noticeable. Beside the curtained door ran a ceiling-to-floor cable duct. Peredur prised off the access cover above the door frame and dropped in the fuse-wire's weighted end. It clattered down the ducting, into the basement below, dragging the fuse wire behind it.

He grabbed his rucksack and slipped through the door, pulling the curtain closed behind him. His heavy boots drummed against the staircase down to the basement entrance, where he swiped his security pass, and then slipped it into his back trouser pocket.

The basement was a mess. Several filing cabinets were out of line with the others in their row, as if they'd been hurriedly rearranged. He checked his watch. It was nearly nine. Dewi would be here soon. He had about ninety minutes to set up, leaving him thirty minutes to get to the meadows.

He grabbed an abandoned chair and dragged it to the door. This gave him the height needed to open the access hatch in the cable ducting. Nestled among the multicoloured wiring was his blue fuse wire. He grabbed it and pulled out the metal weight and excess wire.

His phone pinged. *I'm here.*

Peredur grinned, slipped across to the basement's loading bay doors, and pulled them ajar.

Dewi gave him a two-finger salute. "Gunpowder delivery for a Mr PG Jones." He thumbed over his shoulder. "Got you eight twenty-five-kilo fibreboard drums. Won't take us two ticks to unload."

Peredur slipped out to the rear of Dewi's flatbed truck. Dewi jumped up and rolled one drum along the back of the truck onto Peredur's awaiting back and shoulders. Carefully, Peredur carried the drum into the basement, placing it gently on the ground beside the filing cabinets. Seven similar trips completed the job.

"Need you to sign 'ere, mate." Dewi stepped into the basement, holding out a clipboard. He shivered. "Good job it's nippy in here." He nodded to the gunpowder drums. "They should be stored below twenty degrees centigrade to reduce the risk of accidental detonation."

Peredur scribbled a florid, indecipherable scrawl on the clipboard, then handed it back. "Thanks, mate." Peredur slapped Dewi on the back. "For everything."

Dewi grinned. "Good luck with Mortiforde Millie's parade tomorrow. That lot will make an impression!"

Peredur waved his mate off, then closed the loading bay doors. One by one, he dragged the fibreboard drums and lined them up behind the filing cabinets, out of sight. He grabbed the blue fuse wire, draped it behind abandoned office furniture around the basement, to reach the drums. He scored a hole in one drum and forced the fuse wire inside.

From his rucksack, he extracted a selection of fireworks and placed them in the empty filing cabinet top drawer. He abandoned the remaining fuse wire in the same drawer.

With everything in place, he headed towards the loading bay doors. Forcing them apart barely enough this time to slip through, he threw out his empty rucksack, then squeezed his body between the narrow gap. Something caught in his back trouser pocket. He wriggled hard. It snapped, and then he fell through the gap. Hurriedly, he closed the doors, swung the rucksack onto his back, and dashed up the ramp to the rear car park.

After running non-stop for ten minutes, Peredur eased his

pace and let his hand sweep round to his back trouser pocket. His fingers felt the tear in his camouflage trousers. His security pass! He checked his other pockets, but it wasn't there. For a split second, he contemplated turning back. No. Few people went into the council basement. And with what he'd got planned for tomorrow, he wouldn't need his security pass again.

~

Aldermaston skidded into their private drawing room to find Felicity holding a small package in one hand and a sheet of paper in the other.

He took the package from her and ran his fingers through the short salt and pepper fibres. "What is this?"

"Basildon's hair," she whispered.

"Eeuurrgghh!" Aldermaston dropped the package and wiped his hands down his trousers. Something heavy clattered across the rug to his feet when the package hit the floor. It was an old Nokia mobile handset. Aldermaston picked it up.

Felicity handed him the note. "Basildon's in trouble. So are we."

Remember, remember, the fifth of November,
Gunpowder, treason, and plot.
Your double-agent brother is now in some trouble.
His death tomorrow won't be forgot.
For Mortiforde Millie, she won't be that chilly,
with your half-brother tucked up in her tum.
But at six o'clock sharp, we shall set her to burn,
something Basildon won't overcome.
At exactly the same time, I, too, will have fun,
as the gun on the tank will rotate.
There'll be a loud blast, Tugford Hall will fall fast,

and the working class will celebrate
BANG!

Ready to do battle, Lord Mortiforde? Call me. The number's
programmed in. Just press the green button.

Aldermaston stared at the handset. The screen displayed the words *BANG Hotline*. His thumb pressed the green button. There were four rings before someone answered.

"Well, if it isn't Lord Mortiforde," a voice chuckled. "You've got my note, then. Oh, and Basildon's hair."

Aldermaston perched on the coffee table. "Peredur?" It was barely audible, but for a brief second, he caught BANG's leader off guard.

"You heard my accomplice mention my name the other day, didn't you? What else do you know?"

Aldermaston was still piecing it all together. "I think, Peredur, you and I have a lot in common."

The guffaw was so loud, Aldermaston pulled the phone away from his ears a couple of inches.

"Funny, but I'm not the one living in a stately home on a three-thousand-acre estate. What could we possibly have in common?"

Aldermaston softened his voice. "We're both where we are today because of our parents' actions. I'm not living the life I grew up expecting, and your life. . ." He considered his words. "Your life could have been so different had your parents not abandoned you at a household waste site when you were days old."

"Oh, poor you," Peredur mock-wailed, "having to live in a stately home. Life can be so cruel."

Aldermaston winced. He needed a different tack. "My start in life was vastly different from yours. But for my first forty years, I expected to live a quiet family life. Then my life turned upside down when we discovered I was my father's firstborn, not Basildon. My life changed from that moment."

Peredur tutted. "You expected a quiet, privileged family life in an estate three-bedroom cottage, but now you have a public, privileged life in a thirty-bedroom mansion. My heart bleeds."

Aldermaston closed his eyes. Softly, softly, wasn't working. "Peredur, life isn't what you are born into. It's what you *do* with it. You can either let life happen to you or you can take control of it and shape it into what you want. I can't imagine what it must have been like to discover where your mother left you. But don't let that define you."

A cackling laugh echoed down the earpiece. "You sound just like my social worker before she kicked me out of the children's home on my eighteenth birthday. Yes, life is what you make of it. And that's what I've been doing with BANG. Don't worry about tomorrow's Mortiforde Millie parade. BANG has that all sorted. Tomorrow, I shall take control at six o'clock, when two things will happen simultaneously. We will burn Mortiforde Millie at the stake outside the castle and kill your half-brother, trussed up inside her. And the gun barrel on the tank blocking your drive will rotate one hundred and eighty degrees and start firing. It'll do a lot more damage to Tugford Hall than one of your cannonballs did to my protest group the other day. So, there's a little dilemma for you. Which is more important? Saving your half-brother's life or protecting the ancestral home and all it stands for? Good luck."

The line went dead. Aldermaston stared at the handset.

Felicity sat on the sofa opposite. "What's going on?"

"That's one mucked-up kid," Aldermaston muttered. He redialled the number and brought the phone to his ear. There was a series of clicks and beeps, followed by an automated message. "This number is no longer in service."

He discarded the phone onto the coffee table. "That note is right." He pointed at the sheet of paper lying on the table.

"Tomorrow at six o'clock, they will burn Basildon at the stake inside Mortiforde Millie, and the tank out there will open fire on Tugford Hall."

"How many times have I told you to move that tank?" Felicity snapped.

"Don't you think I'd have done it by now if it were that easy?" He smacked the sofa's arm.

She squeezed his arm. "Okay, getting cross with each other won't solve our problems."

Aldermaston stood. "Cartwright can take Harry somewhere safe tomorrow after school. I don't want either of them here."

"Is Tugford Hall really in danger?"

He clasped his head in deep thought. "It's a building. It's the people in it who are important."

A knock at the drawing-room door interrupted them. Cartwright stepped in, pulling a red Henry vacuum behind him. "Excuse me, My Lord, My Lady."

With a deft kick of the foot-switch, Henry wheezed into life as Cartwright ran the floor hose back and forth across the rug, sucking up Basildon's hair.

Aldermaston stared at the rug, mesmerised by the motion. If only a Henry vacuum cleaner could clean up all of Basildon's escapades.

Norris poured the hot water into his mug on the bedside table, then dunked the already-twice-used teabag from the hospitality tray into it. Castle View B&B's teabags were impressive. Most accommodation establishments' teabags made only one decent mug of tea, but these ... He scrutinised an unopened teabag. *Welsh Brew Tea—a traditional African and Indian blend.* He licked his pencil tip and scribbled in his notebook. Did his local Waitrose store in Godalming stock them?

Turning back a page, he reread his notes. The discrepancy in the General Miscellaneous Irreconcilable Sundry Credit account was not one, but two payments. Both were from the same source: an online auction site.

He loosened the red tie around his neck and woke his laptop. Once he'd found the relevant auction site, he searched for *Borderlandshire District Council*. If his deductions were correct, he was expecting to find a listing or two.

He was wrong. There were nine listings: five first-edition books, three items of silverware, and a rug. Totting up the current auction bids for all eight objects, he arrived at a figure just shy of three hundred and eighty-five thousand pounds.

He retrieved the teabag from his mug and returned it to the hospitality tray. Would it make a satisfactory fourth mug of tea? He added a dash of UHT milk, stirred it, and took the first sip, all the while keeping his eyes fixed on the screen.

The auctions were due to finish at five o'clock tomorrow afternoon. Two hours before the Neighbourhood Area Forum.

"Diya Parmer," he muttered, "you are a shrewd and clever woman."

"Flipping heck, you made me jump!" Lisa grabbed her laptop before it slid off her lap.

Mark stood in the snug doorway, in his chef's whites, clutching a tray in both hands. "Norris Offermans. Which room?"

"Four."

"Thanks." He turned and let the door swing closed behind him.

"Remember to get him to sign for that meal," she bellowed.

The door closed with a resounding click.

Lisa resumed her online search. Peredur Geraint Jones had no social media profiles under his own name. BANG had a couple, but had posted nothing in the last six months. She'd returned her attention to the *Powys Gazette*, looking for follow-up stories to the original cutting. It took many search-term combinations to find any potential stories from twenty-five years ago. There were two. The first one was on the twenty-ninth of November.

Baby Found At Household Recycling Centre Leaves Hospital

A newborn baby discovered at the Knighton Household Waste Centre ten days ago has left hospital. Staff say the baby boy, whom they named Peredur, was doing well, and Powys Social Services staff hoped to find a loving family for him.

Police are still appealing for the mother to come forward. If anyone has any information, they should contact Knighton Police Station on Knighton 496015.

It confirmed Peredur's name. She copied the link to forward it to Aldermaston later. She nearly dismissed the second story, dated the following January.

Social Worker Dismissed For Misconduct

An employment tribunal dismissed social worker Gwyneth Cadwaladur, 49, of Llanpoole, Powys, yesterday for misconduct. It followed claims she'd accepted money in return for information relating to the abandoned baby found at Knighton Household Waste Centre in November last year.

Cadwaladur pleaded guilty to accepting £100 from a private detective for information on where Powys Social Services had placed the abandoned baby, whom nurses named Peredur. The tribunal believed her explanation that, although she reviewed the child's records, she did not find the child's location and, therefore, did not pass any information to the private detective. Had she done so, Cadwaladur confirmed the private detective had agreed to pay her an additional £900.

While the tribunal accepted Cadwaladur's apology and appreciated how her personal difficult financial situation had influenced her temptation, the tribunal dismissed her on the grounds of misconduct with immediate effect.

Lisa selected Aldermaston's number on her mobile phone and set it to hands-free mode on the settee's arm, then continued searching. She was trying to discover how a foundling like Peredur would find information about themselves.

The ringing tone died. "What have you found?" Aldermaston enquired.

Lisa shuffled on the sofa and leaned closer to the phone. She scanned her screen's search results. *The Abandoned Children's Register* looked promising. "Two newspaper reports. I'll send you the links. One confirms Powys Social Services took him into care; the other one ... Well, something's not right."

"Go on."

"A private detective tried paying a Powys social worker to find out where they had placed Peredur."

There was a brief pause. "Okay."

"You don't sound surprised."

"It fits with something I've discovered." A pen scratched on some paper. "I'll tell you later. I'm just off to bury a councillor for the second time today." The line went silent.

Lisa picked up her phone. "You okay?"

"Basildon. We received a parcel containing his hair earlier."

"His hair?" Lisa sat upright. "What, like a ransom demand?"

"BANG has him. I don't know where, so I can't do anything to save him until they parade Millie through town tomorrow."

"They're running the parade now, are they?"

"It would seem so. It would help if we knew more about Peredur. Basildon was right. That angry baby grew up to form BANG. His parents have a lot to answer for."

Lisa ruffled her hair, her eyes still fixed on her laptop screen. "Could Basildon be the baby's father?"

"No."

"You're sure?"

"Yes. But I don't know who his mother is. How does an abandoned baby find out who their parents were?"

"The Abandoned Children's Register," Lisa explained. "I'm on the site now. It's part of the General Records Office." She scrolled down the screen. "I saw it somewhere. Here we are. Once a police report confirms that the search for a baby's birth mother has ended, they add the baby to the Abandoned Children's Register. The birth certificate only shows the date and location of the baby's discovery. They leave the parental details blank."

Aldermaston sighed. "How do you process having a birth certificate with no parental details on it?"

Lisa chewed her lip. "Is your father listed as Basildon's father on his birth certificate?"

"Yes, because he always believed Basildon was his own. If we ever find out who Basildon's biological father is, the authorities can only annotate the certificate."

"Gosh, so his mother's infidelity is clear for all to see, forever."

Aldermaston gasped.

"Sorry!" Lisa whispered. "I didn't mean to upset you—"

"No," Aldermaston interrupted. "You're right. That's the point! That's what Peredur wants."

"What?"

"To put his parentage on public record, for all to see."

"Where are you going?" Rosemary glanced at the mantelpiece clock. "The ten o'clock news will be on soon."

Rupert fastened his suit jacket. "I'm meeting that delinquent at the meadows at eleven, remember?"

She scrutinised him. "You're more worried about him than you're letting on, aren't you?"

He tugged at the ends of his jacket sleeves, avoiding her gaze.

She stood. "This associate knows an awful lot of what's really going on here, doesn't he?" Her eyes narrowed. "Rupert," she whispered. "What have you done?"

He turned and headed for the living room door. "You worry too much. The conniving little knucklehead will regret attempting to blackmail me. Don't wait up."

He slammed the living room door behind him. Moments later, the front door slammed, too.

A sense of dread overwhelmed her. She slipped into the kitchen, grabbed a bottle of vodka from a cupboard, and poured herself a glass. One hand slipped into her trouser pocket as the other brought the vodka to her lips. She downed the contents in one, just as her hand found the envelope in her pocket.

To Rosemary Sedgewicke, MP. Her stomach gurgled. She'd been out campaigning earlier. Surely people realised she wasn't an MP yet? Her fingers ripped it open and retrieved a scruffy note.

Dear Rosemary,
Remember, remember, the fifth of November,
Gunpowder, treason, and plot.
The truth will soon out, of your treason, no doubt,
And the truth should ne'er be forgot.

Bile rose in her throat. Her knees buckled, and she dropped to the floor.

Treason? Treason was one of the worst crimes a person could ever commit. The waste incinerator project scam was treason. What else could it be?

Then she realised. Her throat stung as she swallowed the bile, along with the memory of the ultimate treachery she'd committed all those years ago.

CHAPTER EIGHTEEN

Aldermaston parked his Jaguar under one of Curtain Wall Road's few working street lamps and killed the engine. He spotted Felicity's Range Rover parked among a row of other vehicles. Mortiforde Meadows had never been so busy at this late hour.

"What's the plan?" Daniel slipped on his green wellington boots in the front passenger seat.

"Felicity wants Councillor Prendeghast in the grave and the topsoil replaced immediately." He thumbed over his shoulder. "There's some gear in the boot. I need to change my shoes."

They jumped out as the tailgate rose, revealing spades, torches, and Aldermaston's Hunter Balmoral wellington boots. He changed out of his brogues to the sound of clip-clopping horse's hooves echoing in the night air. Councillor Prendeghast slipped past on the back of the rag-and-bone cart. Wilfred acknowledged them from his bench driving seat.

Aldermaston locked the car. They wandered along the narrow pavement, each with a torch in one hand and a spade in the other, then turned the corner to be confronted by a group of angry women standing beside two huge bulldozers blocking the meadows' main gates and entrance.

"What the hell is the council playing at?" seethed Cissy Warbouys.

"This is outrageous!" cried Kitty.

Felicity spotted Aldermaston approaching and pointed to the bulldozers while her head-torch blinded him. "Look what that woman has done! She's blockaded the gates!"

Aldermaston shielded his eyes. In front of the gates, two large dark shadows with curved pushing blades faced each other. Both bore the slogan *Borderlandshire District Council: pushing through new developments*.

"What about the dog walker gates?" Aldermaston stepped around the bulldozers and immediately realised the turnstile wasn't an option. Barely wide enough for a single person and a dog to pass through, the coffin was too big for the small gap above the turnstile. The high perimeter fencing made it impossible for anyone to carry anything above their heads as they passed through. Designed to prevent cyclists and mopeds from entering the meadows when the gates were closed at dusk, this anti-social behaviour deterrent was also an anti-late-night burial deterrent.

"What about over the fence?" Daniel suggested. "If we park the cart alongside, can we throw the coffin over?"

"Throw it over?" squealed the Reverend Makepiece in a not-so-angelic tone from somewhere deep within the group of women. "It's sacrilegious to throw the deceased!"

Felicity nudged Aldermaston. "Now what?"

He angled her head-torch's light away from his eyes. "Is Councillor Prendeghast wrapped in a shroud? We could take him out of the coffin and push him through the turnstile in an upright position. A shroud-only burial would still be environmentally friendly."

The Reverend Makepiece cleared his throat. "Interfering

with a body prior to committal is completely unethical and possibly illegal, and I will have no part in this if you do."

Aldermaston whispered in Felicity's ear. "Smooth things over with the Reverend. I'll see what I can sort out." He motioned to Daniel. "Undo the coffin's leather straps and peek inside, will you?"

Daniel recoiled. "Me?"

Kitty Catchpole pushed him aside. "Out of my way, you great wuss!" She clambered onto the cart and knelt beside the wicker casket. "It's a dead body," she continued, undoing the three leather straps. "It won't bite you. Shine your torch this way, will you?"

Daniel directed the torch beam as Kitty flipped back the wicker lid. He gagged, burying his face in the crook of his elbow.

"Is he shrouded?" Aldermaston asked.

Kitty shook her head, then smiled at the coffin's contents. "Bless. His false teeth aren't in properly. Probably got dislodged while zipping across the meadows earlier." She leaned in and made the adjustments.

Daniel heaved.

She closed the lid and tightened the leather straps. Aldermaston helped her down from the cart.

Daniel was staring over the fence across the meadows. "There are two people by the viewpoint bench near the old oak tree," he hissed. "Who meets at the meadows at this time of night?"

The chimes of St Julian's rang out eleven times.

"Aldermaston!" Felicity strode past the bulldozers. "The Reverend insists I take him home now. He's saying that clandestine burials are unethical, and now insists that all burials should take place in daylight." She rested her head on his chest and sighed. "It's over, isn't it? We'll never get past these bulldozers before Sir Hugo's interment tomorrow."

He cupped her face in his hands and wiped away her tears with his thumbs.

She sniffled. "I've failed the Legion. I've failed Councillor Prendeghast. I've failed—"

"Stop it!" Aldermaston squeezed her cheeks so hard her lips pouted. "What you have achieved in the past few days has been amazing. And it's not over until Isabel inters Sir Hugo at eleven tomorrow." He kissed the top of her forehead, stalling for thinking time. "I'm meeting Isabel tomorrow at ten. Perhaps I can persuade her to postpone the interment."

"I'm sorry, My Lady," Wilfred Winnow interrupted. "I need to head back. Early start tomorrow morning. One of you lot will have to take him."

"What?" Felicity's gaze flipped between the cart and Aldermaston.

Wilfred pointed at Aldermaston. "You'd get a coffin in the back of your Jag, My Lord. Might need to put the back seats down, mind."

Felicity turned and clicked her fingers. "Cordelia, Cissy, Kitty, Heidi. We need your help. The six of us," her hand gesture included Aldermaston and Wilfred, "need to put Councillor Prendeghast in the back of my husband's car, got that?"

The ladies all nodded.

"Whoa!" Aldermaston held up his hands. "Then what? Put him in the recycling bin, like Sir Hugo, overnight?"

Felicity shuddered. "We have to do something."

Daniel jumped down from the cart. "I reckon that's Rupert Rinde out there. Who's he meeting here at this time of night? Something's not right."

Aldermaston grabbed his arm. "Be careful!"

Daniel headed for the turnstile. The metal gateway cranked awkwardly as he pushed his way through.

Kitty rubbed her gloved hands together. "We need to put

Councillor Prendeghast somewhere cold, where nobody goes, and somewhere we can access at this time of night."

Aldermaston pondered briefly. Then he had an idea. "I know just the place."

Daniel embraced the shadows at the meadows' edge as he crept towards his unsuspecting targets. The soft grass dampened his footsteps. He spent ten minutes covertly creeping from bush to shrub, getting ever closer to the viewpoint bench. With fewer than a hundred yards to go, he paused, working out his next move. A snatch of harsh words occasionally wafted past him, but not enough to discern what they were saying. One voice sounded like Rupert's.

Daniel spied a clump of gorse bushes a short distance to his right, and another rhododendron bush, which was behind the bench and within touching distance of it, a few feet from that. Coming from behind meant there was less chance they'd see him, but he had to be careful.

He was about to make a dash when one of them twisted round, as if checking their surroundings. He froze, fearing they'd spotted him. Moments later, they continued their conversation. Daniel released his trapped breath. It was now or never.

He scurried across the gap silently. His shin collided with a fallen tree trunk, sending him crashing to the ground head first. He landed awkwardly, but momentum rolled him closer to the gorse bush. On his back, eyes wide, staring up at the clouds, he covered his mouth.

His heart rate slowed when he heard the muffled tones of a continuing conversation, unaware of his presence. The rhododendron bush was three strides away. Gathering himself together, he peered around the gorse bush. They were still there.

Silently, he crept across to the rhododendron bush, then flattened himself against the ground. He pulled out his phone, checked it was still on silent mode, and selected the voice notes app. He pressed record, then stretched his arm, forcing his phone through the bush, getting it as close to the conversation as possible.

"… and what's this bloody stunt evicting me from my house and office, you cretin? I told you months ago that if you gave me any crap, I would destroy you."

Daniel's eyes widened. It was Rupert!

Rupert's companion chuckled. "It's a distraction. You look like a victim—"

"I *am* a bloody victim, you jumped-up little—"

The sound of gloved hands struggling to fight off attacking arms filled the air for several seconds, then halted. Daniel's ears strained. He wriggled deeper into the rhododendron bush.

Rupert's acquaintance laughed. "I have the upper hand because I've done all your dirty work. Your father's startled look when he died was hilarious. He was motionless for several seconds after I stabbed him in the back. It gave me a chance to look him in the eyes as his life ebbed away. Your eyes look just like his did then. Even your birthmark seems shocked, like his."

Daniel's heart hammered the ground so much that he feared Rupert and his conspirator could feel the vibrations. Rupert's acquaintance murdered Sir Hugo!

"Oh, and I know about your little scheme with Gerald," Rupert's visitor continued. "He wanted more, though, didn't he? That's why you asked me to bump him off. Greed. It ruins everything in the end." Leather gloves creaked as they softened their grip. "So, will you behave if I let you go? … You sure? … Good."

The wooden bench creaked as its occupants relaxed.

"Take off that stupid mask," Rupert sneered.

There was tutting. "You don't know your history, do you?

This is a Guido Fawkes mask. The man who tried blowing up the Houses of Parliament."

Rupert snorted. "And they hung, drew, and quartered him for treason, as will you be when I'm done with you."

"And there was I, hoping you might offer me a room in your large house. I'm being evicted. Got to be out by midday tomorrow."

Rupert guffawed. "So this *is* blackmail. Twenty grand, not enough for you?"

"You haven't paid me anything yet! Anyway, I've just asked you for a room, not money. It's a no-fault eviction. I don't owe any rent."

The bench creaked again. Awkwardness hung in the night air for a few long seconds.

"No, you can't have a bloody room!" Rupert snapped. "If you don't vacate my premises by tomorrow night, I'll have you and the rest of your mercenary morons evicted first thing Monday morning. Then you'll be the Mortiforde muttonhead that got himself evicted twice in three days."

From his ground-hugging vantage point, Daniel watched Rupert stand and step away from his sitting compatriot.

"This is business," Rupert spat, jabbing a finger at his seated companion. "You'll get your twenty grand when this is all taken care of. Then you can sod off out of my life!"

Rupert turned and stormed off, cutting straight across the meadows towards the bulldozer-blockaded gates.

His compatriot removed his Guido Fawkes mask. Daniel squinted hard, but it was too dark to see anything. Whoever it was, they watched Rupert intently as he walked away.

"You'll regret dismissing me, Mr Rinde." With that, Rupert's accomplice pulled up his hood and strode off in the opposite direction.

Daniel stopped the recording and inhaled a deep breath.

Who was Rupert's accomplice? There was only one way to find out.

~

"Welcome home, Councillor." Aldermaston stared at the head-end of the wicker coffin resting on the folded front passenger seat. The rest stretched across his Jaguar's folded rear seats and into the boot. In the rear-view mirror, Felicity's Range Rover pulled up behind, followed by Kitty Catchpole's battered four-wheel-drive Subaru. Aldermaston jumped out and opened the tailgate.

"The council offices?" Felicity looked at the council basement's rear entrance. "Will this be cold enough?"

Heidi, Cordelia, Cissy, and Margaret Hillbrow clambered out of Felicity's Range Rover.

Kitty cackled. "Bound to be freezing in there. We know the Chief Exec is a cold-hearted—"

"Yes," Aldermaston interrupted, heading towards the basement's rear doors illuminated by his Jaguar's headlights. "More importantly, we don't need a key."

He grabbed the sliding door handle, dug his feet into the ground, and pulled. The clanking door shuddered open a few feet. He flicked the light switch by the door, and the basement's strip-lights flickered into life. Something shiny reflected on the ground, just inside the door. Aldermaston stooped and picked it up. A security pass.

A face he'd never seen before stared back at him. Wrong. The owner's job title was interesting. *Peredur Geraint Jones. IT Support Operative.* He scrutinised the photo. So much fell into place.

"What's that?" Felicity peered over his shoulder.

"Someone's security pass. I'll give it to Lisa tomorrow." He slipped it into his jacket pocket and led them into the basement.

Cordelia shuddered. "It's warmer outside than in here."

Aldermaston sought a suitable hiding place. Even though people rarely came down here, he wanted to conceal the councillor's body as best he could. Near the wall was a rolled-up dust sheet lying beside a large wooden chest. It looked big enough to conceal the entire coffin. He lifted the lid with both hands. Blast. It was stuffed with trophies, a silver platter, a rug, and some books. Ah! The penny dropped. This was where Lisa was hiding Diya's online auction items.

"Any good?" Felicity appeared beside him.

He picked up the dust sheet. "We could lay the coffin beside this chest and cover it with this. It won't look so obvious."

"It's nearly midnight. It's the best we can do." She yawned.

They returned to the cars and extracted Councillor Prendeghast's coffin from the rear of Aldermaston's Jaguar. Carefully, they shuffled the coffin into the basement and placed it next to the wooden chest. Aldermaston covered it with the dust sheet.

The ladies returned to their cars and drove off, leaving Aldermaston to heave the sliding basement door shut with a clank and a shudder. His phone pinged as he slipped into his driver's seat. It was a message from Daniel. An audio clip.

> Listen to this. Rupert IS involved with Sir Hugo and Gerald's murders. Currently following his accomplice.

Aldermaston hurriedly typed a response.

> Be careful! Text me when you're home.

He pressed play and listened to the conversation as he drove home. Isabel's suspicions were right all along.

~

Daniel hurried after Rupert's accomplice, keeping close to the trees and bushes again. He stumbled several times, still fearful of using his torch, and then darted past a cutting in the shrubs on his right. Should he have gone that way? He retraced his steps. Was that—? Yes, there was a single turnstile gate between two properties bordering the meadows.

His wellington boots splattered through muddy puddles to reach the turnstile, which gave access to a suburban street. He eased his way through, flinching with every squeak and clank the turnstile emitted. An eerie glow emanated from the well-spaced street lamps. He checked one way down the residential street. Nothing. In the other direction, he spotted someone heading down the road. Daniel stalked the nighttime wanderer by hugging the line of parked cars.

He ducked low, stopping frequently to check his quarry was still ahead. Without warning, they stepped out into the road. Daniel hid between an estate and a hatchback. He peered through the car's windows and watched his target cross the road. He saw the Guido Fawkes mask. It was him!

Suddenly, the road was plunged into darkness. His heart pounded. Then he remembered. Midnight. The council switched off all street lighting at midnight to save money.

With this dark protective shroud, Daniel hurried after Guido. Opposite his crossing point was a narrow cut-through between terraced properties, barely wide enough for one person. He followed, then paused where it crossed an alleyway, checking both ways. He continued, emerging moments later onto another road. There was movement off to his right. Someone had just turned the corner.

Running on tiptoes wasn't easy in wellingtons. He slowed as he approached the corner and peered around a privet hedge. A dark shadow crossed the road and took another alleyway. Daniel sprinted as quickly as his boots allowed to see Guido turn left at the next road. When Daniel reached the road, he hid between two more parked cars. Guido was ahead, but not far.

Still new to Mortiforde himself, Daniel knew nothing of the streets and alleyways he'd come through. But this road seemed familiar.

Guido reached the next junction. Daniel watched him turn left, sprinted after him, then noticed him take a right, and … Daniel knew where he was. This road ran parallel to Brominster Way. His ears pounded to his frenetic heartbeat. Guido slipped through another alley on his left.

He followed at a safe distance. The alleyway was clear. Puzzled, not just about where Guido was going, but because he'd never noticed these alleyways before, Daniel approached Brominster Way cautiously. He peered around a brick wall and checked the direction Guido had taken. He felt sick. Any moment now, Guido would pass Daniel's house. Except he didn't.

He stopped outside Daniel's gate and looked up at the bedroom window. Daniel held his breath. Did he know Daniel was following him? Seconds later, Guido turned into the neighbouring front gate, inserted a key into the door, and let himself in. A light appeared in the upstairs front bedroom window.

Fighting for breath, Daniel hurried along the road and slipped into his own front garden. It took both hands to guide the key into the lock and open the door. He closed it as silently as possible, locked it, and shot the bolts at the top and bottom. He collapsed to the floor, gasping for breath, then grabbed his phone and sent Aldermaston a text.

Home okay. Followed Rupert's acquaintance. I live next door to a double murderer!

CHAPTER NINETEEN

In their private kitchen, Aldermaston turned down the radio's volume. Breakfast Benny's excitement was frenzied as he announced Abigail's blockading bulldozers on the eight o'clock news. He dialled the number, hoping he wasn't disturbing his caller too early.

Isabelle answered on the fifth ring. "Morning, Aldermaston."

"Can we chat before we see the solicitor at ten?"

"It's Rupert, isn't it?"

Aldermaston stared at the floor. "I'm afraid so."

She groaned. "Come round when you're ready."

He ended the call just as Harry stormed into the kitchen, his school tie crooked and his white shirt hanging over his school trousers.

"Daddy, can we go swimming tonight, please?"

Aldermaston crouched to straighten Harry's tie. "But it's Bonfire Night tonight."

"Oh yeah! Mortiforde Millie. The Parade. Fireworks!"

Aldermaston twisted his son round, tucked in his shirt, then turned him round again and rested his hands on his son's shoulders. "When Cartwright picks you up from school, he'll take you to the cinema, and then you can have a hamburger afterwards, because it's going to be very busy with lots of people here before the parade."

"Will he take me to see the parade and the fireworks?"

"Only if you behave." He ruffled Harry's hair.

Felicity entered the kitchen with her phone clamped to her ear. "That's right, Cordelia. I need everyone here at ten-thirty. Thank you." She placed her phone on the kitchen worktop, grabbed a mug, and poured some coffee from the percolator.

"Harry," she began, "when Cartwright picks you up from school tonight—"

"I've told him," Aldermaston interrupted. "Must dash. I'm off to see Isabel. Then I need a plan to save Basildon."

She grabbed his arm. "Ask Isabel to delay Sir Hugo's internment, will you? Cordelia's gathering the troops here at ten-thirty. We need an alternative plan of action, but—"

"Daddy, will Cartwright have some rotten fruit?" Harry picked up a banana from the fruit bowl and scrutinised it.

"Sorry?"

"Rotten fruit." He held up the banana. "For the parade."

A firework of explosions erupted in Aldermaston's head. He turned, strode back to Harry, and kissed the top of his blonde head. "You are a star! Yes, of course, Cartwright will have some rotten fruit with him."

Harry beamed.

Aldermaston turned to Felicity. "He's given me an idea. Who in the Ladies' Legion is good at burning rock cakes?"

Felicity looked at him quizzically. "What are you going on about?"

Aldermaston tapped the side of his nose. "Just had a plan to save Basildon."

～

Abigail cursed the uneven pavement on Weir Street as she headed towards Rosemary Sedgewicke's house. Her phone rang. *Unknown Caller* flashed on the screen. She chewed her bottom lip. Perhaps it was the media seeking a quote about tonight's NAF. "Abigail Mayedew, how can I help?"

"Good morning, Chief Executive, and what a fine morning it is, too," sang a cheery voice.

"Who is this?"

The voice chuckled. "Oh, you don't know me, but you will later tonight."

"If this is a crank call—"

The voice dropped to a sinister whisper. "BANG doesn't make crank calls, Abigail. This is your formal warning. We're storming your NAF meeting tonight. See you later!" The line went dead.

Abigail stared at her screen, horrified. BANG storming her NAF? Not on her watch. Defence. That's what she needed. Something to stop BANG from getting into the building, like the bulldozers blockading the meadows' gates. She called Highways.

"Richard, this is urgent, so listen carefully," she blustered. "I've received a credible threat from BANG. They're planning to storm tonight's NAF. We need to protect the council offices. I want them surrounded by heavy vehicles. No, not to keep the public out. It's a public meeting, for heaven's sake! If we surround the perimeter with heavy plant equipment, we can then filter everyone through the main entrance and control who comes in and out. Got that?"

"I could move the bulldozers from the meadows' gates, I suppose," Richard Turrpyn muttered.

"No! Find some other vehicles. We need a protective barrier surrounding the council offices."

"We don't have sufficient vehicles for—"

"Well, liaise with other departments! It's not rocket science, for heaven's sake!" She cut the call. Frustratingly, it seemed BANG had more oomph than any of her staff.

Abigail turned to Rosemary's blue front door and rapped the silver door knocker hard. The rat-a-tat-tat echo bounced off the surrounding three-storey Georgian building walls.

Rosemary's door swung open with a clatter. "What do you want, Abigail?" The soon-to-be ex-Director of Finance crossed her arms, blocking her doorway.

Abigail briefly admired Rosemary's black-flecked grey trouser suit. Perfect for swaying the public voters today.

"Diya in there?" she snapped.

Rosemary frowned. "No!"

"Poppycock!" Abigail shoved Rosemary aside and stormed in.

"What the——?"

Abigail grabbed a door handle on the right and twisted. "Diya?" She scanned the living room's two large sofas and a coffee table with the last three issues of *Borderlandshire Life* magazine resting on it.

"She's not here!" hissed Rosemary behind her.

Abigail spun around and faced her director. "Come off it," she sneered. "The council employee who declared the waste incinerator project fully funded has disappeared. You're claiming the project is still half a million pounds short, and you need that to be true if you want to be seen as the saviour of the meadows. Why else would anyone in this town vote for you in the upcoming by-election? It's in your interest to keep Diya hidden."

Abigail pushed the kitchen doorknob so forcefully that she practically fell in.

Rupert looked up from his laptop at the kitchen table.

"Rupert!" Abigail clutched her chest. "I'm sorry," she blustered, checking over her shoulder and canvassing the kitchen. "I was expecting to find Diya."

He frowned. "Diya?"

Rosemary pushed past, her shoulder clashing with Abigail's. "Diya sent Abigail the email confirming the council's funding was in place for the waste incinerator."

Abigail felt briefly wrong-footed. Here was the man the council was going into partnership with to deliver an innovative public-private sector waste incinerator project, and she was accusing his—what? She studied Rupert's face. Stefan's conversation from last night replayed in her head. Was there any truth in the rumour?

"Lost your tongue, Abigail?" Rupert poked his deep into his right cheek.

She snapped out of her thoughts. "No, Rupert. Merely reappraising the situation before me."

"And what do you see?"

Abigail placed her hands on her hips. "That the rumours are true."

Rosemary stepped closer to Rupert. "What rumours?"

Abigail smirked.

Rupert closed his laptop. "It seems rather ironic you've forced your way into the home of someone you've banned from your council building."

"There's a rumour Diya's email may not be genuine," Abigail blurted.

Rupert frowned. "You mean the council's funding isn't in place, despite you publicly declaring it is?"

"No!" Her finger jabbed the air. "I'm suggesting that Diya's mysterious disappearance suits Ms Sedgewicke's cause immensely."

Rosemary sighed. "Diya's not here. But if you think she is, then. . ." Her hand gestured into the hallway. "Search away."

Abigail stared at Rupert. "If I find you're playing games with this waste incinerator project, I can assure you this council will scrutinise every planning application of yours in so much detail we'll know what colour underwear you were wearing when the idea first came to you, is that clear?"

Rupert's birthmark rose with its neighbouring brow. "Who says I have my best ideas when wearing underwear?"

Seconds later, his grey eyes became steelier and his brow furrowed deeply. "What you need to remember, Abigail, is that the waste incinerator project existed long before you arrived." He shrugged. "Rinde Industries has been waiting years for the council to fulfil its financial obligations. A few days ago, you claimed it had, and now, here you are suggesting that may not be true. I suggest you put your own house in order before you barge into other people's."

Abigail turned, then marched along the hallway and out through the front door, slamming it behind her. A flock of pigeons clattered into the air. Chest heaving, heart pounding, nostrils flaring, Abigail knew where to look next for Diya.

Tugford Hall.

Aldermaston's Jaguar zipped along the narrow lanes, splashing through the overnight puddles. His dashboard ice indicator shivered, encouraging him to slow down. He turned onto Knowton Manor's driveway and saw the makeshift barrier as three guards pointed their rifles at him, but then stood down when he pulled in beside The Lodge.

Isabel opened the door and waved at the guards. They waved back.

"Who are they?" Aldermaston nodded in their direction.

"BANG. They've kicked Rupert out of his house." Isabel let Aldermaston in. "Nice lads, actually. I make them drinks now and then." She closed the door behind him. "Tell you the truth," she said, leading him into the kitchen, "it's been nice having them around. I couldn't get the toilet to flush yesterday afternoon, and. . ." She filled the kettle. "Don't get me wrong. Hugo wouldn't have sorted something like that. He couldn't fix a leaky tap. But the loneliness hit me, not knowing what to do next." She switched on the kettle. "Two of them sorted it for me."

"Where's Rupert?"

Isabel shrugged, then stared at Aldermaston. "Well, he didn't care when he threw us out of the Manor." She gestured to the lounge. "I've lit the fire. Still can't get warm, though. Probably won't until after the interment later."

A wall of heat hit them as they entered. The log fire roared, spat, and crackled. Aldermaston settled onto the couch opposite Isabel. He slipped his hand inside his Radnor green Harris tweed jacket pocket and pulled out his phone.

"This isn't comfortable listening." He placed the phone on the coffee table and played Daniel's recorded voice note from last night.

Isabel stared into the fireplace as she listened to the conversation. She propped an elbow on the sofa's arm and cradled her head in her hand. Tears collected in her eyes when Rupert's accomplice commented on how he'd murdered Sir Hugo.

"I'm so sorry." Aldermaston returned his phone to his jacket pocket.

She pointed to his jacket pocket. "What have you done with that recording?"

"Nothing at the moment. I wanted you to hear it first."

She nodded. "I knew. Deep down." She sniffed, then stood. "That kettle must have boiled."

While alone, Aldermaston retrieved a folded sheet of paper from his inside jacket pocket. How should he broach this?

Isabel returned, carrying a tea tray, and placed it on the coffee table. "Who was my son talking to?" She collapsed onto the sofa.

Aldermaston unpacked the tea tray. "I have an idea." He passed the sheet of paper across to her.

The colour drained from her face. "No!" Her hand clasped her mouth momentarily. "The past always catches up." She looked straight at him. "As your mother discovered."

Aldermaston poured their tea. "Basildon spotted it."

"Basildon?"

He handed her a cup. "The note in the margin? *The birth of BANG?* I think he's right. I believe that abandoned baby grew up and established BANG. And I think that's who Rupert was talking to last night."

"What a mess." She dropped the paper into her lap and shook.

Aldermaston slipped across to the cushion beside her and grabbed her hand. "Is that your grandson?"

She fumbled for her handkerchief to wipe her wet cheeks, but the emotion was too much. "How did you—?" She broke into uncontrollable sobs.

Aldermaston put an arm around her, and she fell into his embrace. "Basildon spotted the clue in that photo. It took me a while to notice."

Shock convulsed through her. "So, my son and grandson murdered Hugo. I—" Another wave of sobs overwhelmed her, and she hid her face in the tear-soaked tissue.

Aldermaston squeezed her hand. "Rupert doesn't know, does he?"

She mopped her tears.

He patted his jacket pocket. "In the recording, Rupert asks them to remove their mask. Your grandson is hiding his identity."

Isabel stared at the tea tray. "Hugo *was* right. It was *just* a business disagreement."

Aldermaston squeezed her hand again. "What was?"

"I always feared that's why Rupert threw us out of the

Manor … because he'd found out we'd hidden his son from him. Hugo denied it. Always said Rupert knew nothing of the truth."

"What is the truth?"

Isabel fidgeted with her handkerchief. "That abandoned baby in the newspaper is our grandson. We didn't know then. But when we found out, we tried tracking him down. Some poor woman lost her job over it. We never intended for that to happen." She squeezed his hand. "What sort of mother hides that from her son? But Rupert is vindictive. He's no role model for a child. I hoped our grandson would have a better life if a loving family adopted him." She nodded to Aldermaston's pocket. "Seems that didn't happen. Perhaps it's in the genes. Like father, like son."

Aldermaston patted her hand. "Sir Hugo was a good man. Not everything is down to genetics."

The clock on the mantelpiece chimed the half hour.

Isabel stood. "We'd better make a move. The will reading is at ten."

Aldermaston looked up at her guilt-ridden face. "Don't tell me if you don't want to."

"The mother?"

Aldermaston nodded.

"I'll tell you in the car."

Daniel stifled a yawn as his Toyota's wheels battled against the rough track to Shepherd Cottage. Discovering his neighbour was a double murderer had not induced a good night's sleep. When he pulled alongside Shepherd Cottage, Diya slipped out the front door, threw her handbag over her shoulder, missed, retrieved it, then locked the door and jumped into Daniel's passenger seat.

"Morning!" She beamed. "I think today will be a great day."

Daniel forced a grin. Now wasn't the time to share last night's events.

"Did the Ladies' Legion bury Councillor Prendeghast last night?" Diya pulled down the visor and used the vanity mirror to apply some lipstick.

"Things didn't quite go according to plan," he began, as he turned the car round and headed back to Tugford Hall. "Abigail has blocked the meadows' gates with some bulldozers. We couldn't get the Councillor's coffin through the turnstile."

The car caught a pothole, twisting the entire chassis momentarily. Diya drew a lipstick line across her cheek and behind her right ear. She grabbed a tissue, dabbed it against her tongue, and wiped it off. "But isn't Sir Hugo being interred at eleven?"

Daniel nodded. "The bulldozers are still there. There's no way of getting the councillor onto the meadows. The Ladies' Legion is gathering at the Hall at ten-thirty, so we need you in Aldermaston's office before they arrive. We can't have you being found before the NAF meeting."

Daniel turned into Tugford Hall's rear courtyard and hit the brakes. Diya flew forward, banged her head against the windscreen, and then rebounded into the seat.

"What are you playing at?" Then she saw.

Standing in front of Daniel's bonnet was Abigail Mayedew.

She pointed through the windscreen. "Diya Parmer, I want a word with you, NOW!"

Aldermaston pulled out of Knowton Manor's gates and headed towards town. Isabel stared out of the passenger window.

"At one time, we thought Rupert would propose to Rosemary," she reminisced. "They seemed close back then. She handled herself well at business functions. That's what Rupert liked about her."

"Nobody knows what goes on behind closed doors." Aldermaston eased off the accelerator as they approached a slow-moving tractor ahead.

"That's why your mother confided in me." Isabel's stare remained fixed on the world outside. "She knew our family secret, thanks to your father's support back then. She understood the need to confide in someone you trust. You'd go mad if you didn't. But every secret comes out in the end. The challenge is keeping it hidden for as long as possible."

Aldermaston pulled up behind the tractor at some temporary traffic lights. "When did you know about the baby?"

She turned to him. "We had no idea Rosemary was pregnant. She and Rupert had had a big falling out, and she moved to Brussels."

"Brussels?"

Isabel nodded. "She got a job at the European Commission. Rupert didn't want her to go. Bad for business, he thought. So he emailed from *her* account, turning down the job offer."

"He did what?"

"That's Rupert. Everything is about his business."

"But they honoured the job offer?"

"Yes. She disappeared quickly after that. So her sudden appearance on our doorstep several months later shocked us. She looked ill. She *was* ill. Hugo assumed she wanted to see Rupert, but he was abroad on business. But she knew that."

"Did she have your grandson with her?"

Isabel looked out of the passenger window. "She'd already left him at Knighton's Household Waste Site a couple of weeks previously. Why she didn't come to us sooner, I—" She sighed.

"Rosemary was only a few weeks into her European Commission job when she felt unwell. Initially, she thought it was stress … new job, moving to a new country, and all that. Discovering she was pregnant was a shock. Originally, she planned on having the baby in Brussels, getting a nanny, and raising him there."

"Was she going to tell Rupert?"

Isabel turned to Aldermaston. "No. And Hugo and I understood. We really did."

"So your grandson was born in Brussels." The lights changed. Aldermaston moved forward.

"Which is why there are no birth records here. He was only two weeks old when Rosemary first returned to the UK." Isabel picked at a hangnail. "If only she'd come to us *then*. She was in a terrible place. She imagined walking into Rupert's office, dropping the baby into his arms, and then walking out and returning to Brussels. But she couldn't do it. Not to her son."

"But to leave her son like that—"

"Takes courage." Isabel wagged a finger at him. "A woman never leaves their child without a damned good reason. When Rosemary turned up on our doorstep, she'd just checked out of a private clinic. Despite her mind being in a complete mess, her decision to leave her son in Knighton was a shrewd one."

Aldermaston understood. "Knighton is over the border in Wales, so the Welsh authorities processed him. Less chance of Rupert accidentally coming across him."

"Exactly."

Aldermaston put his foot down to pass the tractor. "Was it my father's financial support that Sir Hugo used to hire the private detective agency? You were trying to find your grandson, weren't you?"

Isabel blew her nose. "I'm not sure what we were thinking. We couldn't have brought him up." She paused. "If only we could have kept tabs on him, somehow. You know, make sure he was being properly looked after. Hugo wanted to provide for him if he could."

She scrunched up the handkerchief and returned it to her handbag. "We hoped he'd make contact when he was eighteen, but … it can't have been easy for him. Well, it's not easy for anyone."

Aldermaston frowned. "How would he have made contact? Foundlings have no family history to work with. Rosemary left nothing with him; otherwise, the police would have traced her."

"Some time ago, Hugo took a DNA test and uploaded his results to those ancestral databases. That way, if our grandson did the same, he could make contact. We hoped he would contact us first so we could manage our grandson's expectations. We received notification of a match about seven years ago. But they didn't make contact."

Aldermaston drove up Southgate Street and pulled into an on-street parking bay right outside Beauchamp, Bertie, and Brazonby's offices. He offered Isabel a smile. "Ready?"

She nodded.

Aldermaston spotted Rupert swaggering down from the town centre. He pointed at the solicitor's office. "Rupert's not about to get a revelation from this will-reading, is he? Hugo's not left everything to his long-lost grandson, has he?"

Horror filled Isabel's eyes. "He wouldn't. Not without telling me. All I'm aware of is the codicil that involves you."

Aldermaston opened his door. It was time to find out how.

In Aldermaston's office, Daniel cringed as Abigail became further frustrated with Diya.

"What am I looking at?" Abigail scrutinised the computer screen.

Diya's shaking hand struggled to scroll through the screen's contents. "Well, because of … as I've tried explaining … er—"

"Spit it out, woman!" Abigail stamped her feet.

Daniel placed a coffee mug beside Abigail and forced another into Diya's hands. He tapped the screen. "This is how Diya is trying to fill the waste incinerator project shortfall."

Abigail stared at the back of Diya's head. "But Diya emailed to say all the funding is in place."

"No, *she* didn't!" Daniel perched on the edge of Aldermaston's desk. "Someone *else* sent that email."

Diya twisted in her chair. "Every time I tried calling you, the IT Helpdesk intercepted it. They changed my security pass clearance, so I couldn't get to your office. They even changed the annual leave chart to show I was in India. You have to believe me!" She burst into tears.

Abigail folded her arms. "How do you sign off your emails?"

"Kindest regards." Diya wiped a cheek. "Why?"

Abigail shook her head. "Doesn't matter." She pointed to the screen. "So, what are you selling?"

"Some first edition books and some old trophies we found in the council basement," she explained.

"What?" Abigail screamed. "Are you serious?" She shook her head. Then she laughed. The laughter shape-shifted into hysteria as she headed towards Aldermaston's office door and banged her head against it several times. "What planet are you on?"

Diya trembled.

Daniel slammed his mug of coffee onto Aldermaston's table, slopping its contents everywhere. "How dare you!" He stood between Abigail and Diya. "What about a little respect for Diya, who has been working non-stop over the past few days, trying to raise the shortfall so *you* don't look stupid at tonight's faffing NAF?"

Abigail guffawed, shook her head, and then stepped so close to Daniel her shoes were practically standing on his.

Daniel almost wet himself, but the crick in his neck blocked any bladder-releasing signals travelling down his spine.

"Respect?" She prodded his forehead. "This is the woman who thinks selling off a couple of old trophies and some second-hand books is going to raise half a million pounds."

Fists clenched, Daniel spun around to look at the computer screen. Abigail's nasal exhalations blasted the hairs on the crown of his head. "Diya, what are this morning's total bids so far?"

Diya scrolled to the bottom of the screen. "Er—"

Abigail waved her hands dismissively and headed towards the office door. "Diya, it'll take more than a few jumble sale items to get me out of this bloody mess!" She opened the door wide.

"Four hundred and forty-nine thousand, two hundred and five pounds," Diya said in one breath.

Daniel's eyes almost popped out of his head. "How much?"

Abigail closed the door and stepped back into Aldermaston's office. "But that means we're only short by—"

"Fifty thousand, seven hundred and ninety-five pounds," Diya calculated.

Daniel tapped his watch. "The auction still has seven hours to run. Chances are, that figure will shrink."

Abigail paced the room. "Okay. This is good. Rosemary thinks the project is half a million short, yet we're currently only fifty grand adrift. Even if those online sales figures don't go any higher, fifty grand is nothing in the grand scheme of things. I could just sack a couple of staff. The salary savings would cover that."

She strode across the office and grabbed Diya's shoulders.

"Diya, you are a star! I knew you wouldn't let me down." She headed for the door. "Tonight's NAF is going to be so much fun. Poor Rosemary won't know what's hit her!" She stormed out of the office and slammed the door shut behind her.

They both flinched.

"Now what do we do?" asked Diya.

Daniel picked up the phone. "Now we let Aldermaston know that the cat's out of the bag."

CHAPTER TWENTY

"What's *he* doing here?" Rupert hurled an accusatory finger as Aldermaston entered Beauchamp, Bertie, and Brazonby's wood-panelled waiting room. Oil paintings of the solicitors' ancestors in drab grey suits with expressionless poses hung from a picture rail.

Isabel undid her black jacket. "Bartholomew Brazonby invited him."

Rupert turned his back. "Waste of time. We know what's in the will."

A beige-suited man in his eighties opened Mr Brazonby's office door and invited them in. "Good morning, everyone. Please come through."

Aldermaston helped Isabel to her feet, then went to follow her, but Rupert pushed in front of him.

Bartholomew Brazonby motioned to the three green leather club chairs before his desk. Isabel diplomatically selected the middle chair.

"Mrs Rinde," Bartholomew began, "our condolences again for your loss. My partners wish to be remembered to you."

Rupert sneered. "We'll remember them when you issue your bill."

Isabel nodded. "Thank you, Bartholomew."

He turned to Aldermaston. "And thank you, Lord Mortiforde, for coming at such short notice. I know you are a busy man."

"He's not the only one," Rupert drummed his fingers on the briefcase resting on his lap. "I have a business to run, and some squatters to evict."

Bartholomew opened a paper file in front of him. "I'm aware Sir Hugo shared his will's contents with close family members some eighteen months ago. Essentially, that document still stands. Sir Hugo leaves his business and land assets, with a value of six point five million pounds, to his son Rupert. His personal wealth of approximately two point seven million, in a mixture of bank accounts, shares, and government bonds, he leaves to his wife, Isabel."

Rupert crossed his legs, raising his briefcase on the highest knee. "So what's chucklehead at the end doing here, then?"

The solicitor turned several pages and picked up a single sheet. "About three weeks ago, Sir Hugo added a codicil."

Rupert smacked his briefcase. "If my father has left something to that imbecile," he snapped, pointing in Aldermaston's direction, "that was originally intended for me, I shall contest the will. Do you understand?"

Mr Brazonby smiled. "Mr Rinde, I can confirm that your father's bequest to you has not changed since he first drew up this will."

Rupert stood. "In that case, I might as well leave." He marched out of the office.

The room's atmosphere lightened.

Isabel spoke. "It's the meadows, isn't it?"

The solicitor nodded. He read aloud directly from the codicil. "I wish to leave the Mortiforde Meadows to the Eighth

Marquess of Mortiforde, and trust he will use them for the town's benefit, now and in the future, as his father originally planned."

Mr Brazonby dropped the sheet of paper onto his desk. "Congratulations, Your Lordship. You are the new owner of Mortiforde Meadows."

Cordelia's hand rose above the collected heads gathered in Tugford Hall's main drawing room. "Have we given up on *Verdant Endings*? Councillor Prendeghast is still in the council's basement, and in. . ." she glanced at the seventeenth-century grandfather clock lurking in the corner, ". . .thirty minutes, Sir Hugo's body will be interred in the family vault."

Standing in front of the room's grand fireplace, Felicity took in the sea of disappointment before her. She checked her phone, willing for a message from Aldermaston.

"His Lordship is currently with Isabel Rinde. I'm hoping he'll persuade her to delay Sir Hugo's interment."

"How much will that help?" Heidi's hand rose. "Abigail's blockaded the meadows. We still can't get Councillor Prendeghast in there, even if Isabel is kind enough to postpone."

Felicity perched on the corner of the table. "We'll have a clearer idea of what might happen to the meadows after tonight's NAF meeting. We can still do this if Isabel postpones the interment for a few days."

Their dejected faces suggested they didn't expect tonight's NAF would change the meadows' outcome. Felicity clapped her hands, trying to change the mood. "There's another matter His Lordship hopes the Ladies' Legion might help with. He's after some rock cakes."

"Rock cakes?" Kitty repeated. "We've failed to give

Mortiforde its first environmentally friendly burial. The meadows are about to be desecrated by a whacking great incinerator, and the Marquess wants a tea party? I don't think so, Your Ladyship!"

Disgruntled head shaking and petulant mutterings filled the room.

"Not a tea party." Felicity raised her voice above the hubbub. "My husband wants some over-baked rock cakes, so I'm looking for some help in the Hall's main kitchen, afterwards."

"What for?" Arabella asked. "To save the meadows?"

Felicity bit her bottom lip. "To save Basildon."

"BASILDON?" chorused the Ladies' Legion.

"That idiot?" Arabella threw her hands in the air. "Sorry, My Lady, but we have more important things worth saving." She picked her coat up from the back of her chair. "I'm sure the other ladies feel the same."

A chorus of head-nodding and belonging-gathering rustled through the room.

Felicity's phone pinged. "Wait! New from my husband." She swiped the screen.

Arabella headed towards the door. "I don't care. He can stick his tea party where the sun doesn't shine."

Felicity's gasp was so loud, it stopped Arabella in her tracks.

"Has Isabel agreed to postpone Sir Hugo's interment?" Kitty crossed her fingers on both hands.

Felicity shook her head. She beamed. "Sir Hugo has bequeathed Mortiforde Meadows to my husband."

"The Marquess now owns Mortiforde Meadows?" Kitty sought to clarify everyone's thoughts.

Felicity nodded.

Kitty's eyes widened. "But that means—"

"Exactly," beamed Felicity. She read aloud Aldermaston's message in full. "Sir Hugo bequeathed Mortiforde Meadows to me. I think they're perfect for Mortiforde's first environmentally friendly burial site."

An enormous cheer erupted from the ladies.

Arabella dashed towards the door. "I'm off—"

Felicity hurried across to her. "Didn't you hear? The Marquess supports our *Verdant Endings* project."

"I know," Arabella slipped off her coat and smiled. "I'm going down to your kitchens to make over-baked rock cakes, if that's what His Lordship wants." She turned to the other ladies. "Anyone else coming?"

It was more of a stampede than a dignified exit. Felicity only wished she knew what Aldermaston was up to.

Aldermaston marvelled at the ease with which he entered his office. Now that Abigail knew where Diya was, there was little point in keeping the door locked.

"Are you okay?" he asked Diya.

Diya nodded. "Be glad when the auctions close."

He brought them up to date with news about Sir Hugo's bequest, then pondered his next dilemma. "Right, Basildon's breakout. How are we going to do this?"

"I've been thinking." Daniel wheeled himself across the office on his chair to the other side of Aldermaston's desk. "BANG could be hiding Millie anywhere, so our only option is to do something during the parade."

Aldermaston nodded. "Exactly. Whatever we do, it'll be last minute, which is why I've asked the Ladies' Legion to help with some baking, just in case." He tapped the tip of his nose. "Millie's nose. It's a button. That's how we normally open her chest to stuff it with fireworks just before the parade. I hope Gerald didn't break the mechanism when he fell out of her chest yesterday."

Daniel leaned back in his chair. "So how do we press Mortiforde Millie's nose as she parades through town, when it's some fifteen feet off the ground and she's surrounded by armed men?"

Aldermaston stepped across to the large map of Mortiforde hanging on the wall. He tapped Forde Bridge. "Traditionally, Millie's route starts at Forde Bridge. However, she can't go up Southgate Street because the medieval South Gate's maximum height clearance is only eight feet six inches."

His finger retraced its way back down to Forde Bridge and then swept along Watling Street. "So instead, she has to come along Watling Street to Castle Street. From there, the parade route passes around the Buttermarket, past the top of Southgate Street, and then into the Market Square and the castle apron, where she's tied to the stake and burned."

"Where do we rescue Basildon, then?" Daniel scratched the back of his head.

"The Buttermarket," he pointed. "It's the narrowest point on the entire route. The property opposite juts out across the road."

"Juts out?" Daniel frowned.

Diya twisted in her chair. "It's a common Tudor design with timber-framed buildings. The upper floors overhang the previous floor, giving the property more floor space on the upper storeys than on the ground floor. The timber-framed property on the corner of Castle Street and Southgate Street has two overhanging floors."

Aldermaston winked. "Millie has to slow down here to negotiate the narrow gap between that and the Buttermarket, so as not to get caught in the overhangs. That gives us some precious time."

"Time for what?" asked Daniel.

"Time to lean out of the Buttermarket's first-floor window and press Millie's nose," Aldermaston explained.

Daniel's eyes narrowed. "That's a long way to lean out of a window to reach Millie's nose."

Aldermaston rocked back and forth on his feet. "For us, yes. But not for Mortiforde's long arm of the law."

Peredur leaned across the metal bed frame and cut the rope binding Basildon's hands. Then he pulled the back-to-front black woollen balaclava off his captive's head.

Basildon blinked and rubbed his eyes.

"Stand!" Peredur grabbed Basildon's wrist and dragged the near-naked hostage to his feet.

Basildon hitched up his bedraggled underwear with one hand.

Peredur chuckled. "I believe a condemned man should choose his last supper." He stepped closer to Basildon. "What's it to be?"

Basildon tutted. "This is Mortiforde, old bean. I'll have a Nooseman's Knot's Last Supper and a pint of their Hangman's Anaesthetic, thank you."

Peredur nodded. "Move!" He shoved Basildon hard in the back towards the bedroom door.

Basildon stumbled. His hands grabbed the doorframe to steady himself and catch his breath. He glanced over his shoulder at his kidnapper. A wry smile appeared. Then he launched himself through the bedroom door, along the landing, and down the stairs.

Peredur tutted and shook his head. When he reached the top of the stairs, he saw Basildon being restrained at the bottom by Agents 24 and 58.

"Wrap him up," Peredur instructed.

Agent 24 threw a hessian sack over Basildon's head and wrapped it tightly around him, while Agent 58 pulled the one-hundred-and-twenty-gallon barrel that had served as Peredur's television stand to the foot of the stairs. Ten seconds later, with a scream and a yelp, Basildon was inside.

"Consider it practice for tonight," Peredur snarled. "Get used to being confined in a tight wooden space." He nodded to his men.

Together, they lifted the barrel and its occupant.

"Back of the jeep, lads. Quickly and as quietly as you can. We don't want to attract any unnecessary attention."

"Yes, Commander." They shuffled towards the front door and headed up the garden path to the awaiting jeep.

Peredur wandered into his living room. With the television abandoned on the floor, the sparsely furnished room seemed even emptier. He lowered the open leaf of his drop-leaf table and slid the leg through its carpet groove back to its folded position. From the mantelpiece, he collected a sealed envelope bearing the handwritten words *To The Landlord* and placed it on the table. He pulled the front door key from his camouflage trouser pocket and slipped it into the envelope. Through the window, he watched his men slide the barrel onto the back of the jeep.

Peredur surveyed the room, replaying a series of memories. Finally, he stepped outside and pulled the front door closed behind him. The latch clicked softly. He pushed back against it to check it was secure, then walked up his garden path for one last time.

Aldermaston pulled up beside Mortiforde's Police Station, which was nothing more than a towable trailer unit. It was parked in a lay-by next to the town's railway station, and propped up on some bricks after some enterprising locals had, ironically, stolen the trailer's wheels.

He knocked on the trailer's door.

Ceri peered around the door, munching on a sandwich. "Can't you read?" She tapped on a laminated notice pinned to the door. *Closed for lunch between midday and one o'clock.*

Aldermaston pulled a memory card from his jacket pocket. "So you're not interested in any evidence proving the same people who killed Gerald Lockmount also killed Sir Hugo?"

Ceri briefly disappeared inside. "Norten, put your pizza back in the box." She opened the door wide. "You'd better come in, then."

Aldermaston clambered into the Portakabin and took a cushioned bench just inside the door. Ceri sat opposite him, lifting the lid on a laptop resting on a small circular table between them.

"Lord Mortiforde!" bellowed PC Norten as he joined them. Despite bending at the waist, his head still rubbed along the ceiling. "Want some pizza? Got my favourite toppings. Peas and chocolate."

Ceri patted the bench beside her. "Lunch can wait. This is important."

PC Norten swivelled his posterior into position.

"Lord Mortiforde claims to have evidence proving Sir Hugo's death was murder," Ceri explained, "and it was the same person who murdered Gerald Lockmount."

PC Norten shook his head. "Sir Hugo's death was a tragic accident."

Ceri held out her hand. "The evidence, please, Lord Mortiforde."

Aldermaston dropped the memory card into her hand.

"What's on here?" Ceri scrutinised it between her finger and thumb.

"My assistant, Daniel, overheard a conversation between two people last night on Mortiforde Meadows. He recorded it on his phone." He pointed to the memory card. "That's a copy of the conversation."

Ceri scribbled down some notes. "What time last night?"

"About midnight."

Ceri's eyebrows rose. "You've held onto this information for over twelve hours before bringing it to the police. Why the delay, Lord Mortiforde?"

Aldermaston shuffled on the bench. The unit rocked from side to side. "This is the first opportunity I've had. I didn't know about this until I met with my assistant a couple of hours ago and—"

Ceri scribbled in her notebook. "Witness failed to hand over evidence at the earliest opportunity, possibly to assist criminals in their escape."

Aldermaston opened his mouth to offer a rebuttal, but decided against it.

The **PCSO** slipped the memory card into the laptop and double-clicked the file. There was a lot of background noise, but Rupert's voice was clear.

"That's Rupert Rinde!" PC Norten waved a finger at the screen. He cocked his head to one side and frowned. "Don't recognise the other chap."

Ceri made notes as the conversation played out, often stopping and skipping back to listen again to crucial comments. At the end of the conversation, she leaned back on the bench. "So, you're claiming this conversation between Mr Rupert Rinde and this associate is evidence that Mr Rinde arranged his father's murder and that of his business associate, Gerald Lockmount?"

Aldermaston gestured to the laptop. "I think the evidence is clear, don't you?"

"Where is Rupert Rinde now?" Ceri asked.

Aldermaston shrugged. "Not sure. BANG has kicked him out of Knowton Manor, and he's not staying with his mother at The Lodge. Perhaps he's taken a room at the King James Hotel."

Ceri closed the laptop. "We'd better check the King James Hotel."

"Actually," Aldermaston began, "I think you should hold off until tonight's NAF."

Ceri crossed her arms. "You now want us to pause a murder investigation?" Her eyes narrowed. "Are you helping Rupert Rinde?" She scribbled further notes. "I shall have to chat to Chief Constable Stoyle about this. Just because you're a Lord doesn't give you the right to tell me how to do my job."

Aldermaston raised both hands. "Arrest Rupert Rinde now, if you can find him. But he'll definitely be at tonight's Neighbourhood Area Forum, where I think we'll learn the truth. Which would you rather do? Arrest him now, and risk not getting enough evidence to convict him. Or be there tonight, gathering all the evidence you need to prove beyond all doubt Rupert is behind these murders?"

PC Norten nudged Ceri. "It's what we did during the *Borders in Blossom* competition. If Lord Mortiforde hadn't helped me back then, Kizzy Whiffle would still be murdering her gardening television show co-presenters and supplying drugs across the country."

Ceri pondered. "This goes against everything we're taught during training."

"And how many murderers have you caught?" PC Norten enquired.

"I've only been a PCSO for three months. Give me a chance!" She grabbed her notebook. "I need to run this past the Chief Constable."

Inwardly, Aldermaston cursed. Involving Stoyle now would mess up everything. "Of course, do what you think best. When you've finished explaining everything to him, you can pass the phone over to me. I need to make an official complaint about you."

Ceri froze. "Me? What have I done wrong?"

"You assisted a criminal gang in stealing Mortiforde Millie from my land. By doing that, you've given them everything they need to murder my half-brother, which I fear will happen later tonight."

Ceri crimsoned.

PC Norten tapped the table. "You don't want a complaint on your record this early in your career."

She threw her pen and notebook onto the table and sighed. "Okay. What do you want us to do?"

"What do you mean, we have no heavy plant machinery left?" Abigail bellowed at the Director of Highways standing in front of her desk.

Richard Turrpyn's hands fidgeted behind his back. "Well, having placed what's left of our highways equipment around the council office perimeter, there's not enough to go right round. At least half of the perimeter remains exposed. We could remove the bulldozers from the meadows, but—"

"Leave them there!" Her scowl deepened. "I'm not risking the meadows now."

Richard shuffled on his feet. "My team's responsibility is to maintain the local road network, not to defend the council offices from disgruntled local taxpayers coalescing to storm the building. Although our failure to repair the potholes along Watling Street may slow them down considerably."

Abigail wandered around her desk. Richard backed away. "Can we not access any other heavy vehicles temporarily?"

Richard glanced at the ceiling. "There is one other

department with access to large vehicles, but we don't own the vehicles."

Abigail stopped walking. "Why don't we own the vehicles?"

"Privatisation," he explained. "We use outside contractors now."

"Spit it out! Which service are you thinking of?"

"Waste management."

A cluster of ideas pinged in Abigail's head. Why hadn't she thought of this before? "Dustcarts!" she screamed. "It's perfect! Barricading the council offices with dustcarts provides a visual representation of why we need the waste incinerator!"

She grabbed her phone and dialled her secretary. "Pamela, get me the Head of Waste Management immediately."

She slammed the phone down, clapped her hands, and danced an excited jig on the spot. "Let the battle commence!"

CHAPTER TWENTY-ONE

———————————

Aldermaston led PCSO Marker and PC Norten into the Buttermarket Community Meeting Room. He pointed through the corner window. "We'll see Mortiforde Millie approaching as BANG parades her through Castle Street. It's narrow between the coffee shop and the charity shop, so they'll have to slow down there, and then. . ." He pointed to the thoroughfare below them. "Where the street widens by the bank here, they'll have to manoeuvre themselves at right angles to negotiate the narrow gap at the corner just here."

He opened the nearest sash window. Cold November air rushed into the room. He turned to PC Norten. "Can you lean out the window and see how far you can reach?"

PC Norten shoved his head and shoulders through the window, then stretched out his right arm.

Aldermaston and Ceri looked out from the next window along.

PC Norten waved.

"Stretch further," Ceri bellowed. "You're not close enough."

He wriggled further through the window and wagged his fingers.

Aldermaston shook his head. "Still not enough."

The policeman elongated every part of his body to gain as much reach as possible. Suddenly, his feet slipped. His body lunged further forward, and his arms flailed like windmill sails. "Help!"

Aldermaston caught PC Norten's legs, just as the policeman's feet lost their grip on the floor. "I've got you!" He hugged the lanky officer's legs and braced his own feet against the wall beneath the window.

"That's it!" screamed Ceri. "His fingers are more than halfway to the other side." Then she hurried across to Aldermaston and helped pull PC Norten back inside.

PC Norten dusted himself down and grinned. "That was fun! So, when do we need to be here tonight?"

"About five-thirty," Aldermaston suggested. "After Millie parades past here, she'll go through the Market Square to the Castle, where they'll burn her at the stake at six o'clock. Hopefully, without Basildon inside her."

Ceri pondered. "PC Norten and I could just stop the puppet during the parade and demand Basildon's release."

"BANG's men will surround Millie and stop anyone from getting anywhere near her. They'll simply push you out of the way," Aldermaston explained.

Saying it out loud emphasised how important it was to get this right. If PC Norten failed, it would be down to Felicity and the Ladies' Legion to save the day. He slipped his phone out of his pocket and sent her a text.

Ceri stuck her head through the open sash window, looked down, then slipped back inside. "So, let me get this straight," she began. "When Mortiforde Millie approaches along Castle Street, PC Norten hangs out of the window, presses Millie's nose to release the chest cavity catch, and then your half-brother, whom you think is inside, falls twelve feet to the ground?"

Aldermaston nodded.

"What if they've bound his hands and feet?" Ceri enquired.

Aldermaston peered through the window. She was right. Getting Basildon out of Mortiforde Millie was one thing. Breaking his fall was another.

~

"Coming through!" Cordelia yelled, holding aloft the latest batch of blackened rock cakes. She negotiated between the twenty other Ladies' Legion members, busy measuring ingredients, mixing, and patting new rock cakes into shape, before slipping them onto the waiting trestle table by the far wall.

Felicity's fingers barely touched them as she encouraged the charcoal chunks into a neater pile. "How many's that now?"

"About a hundred," Cordelia suggested. "I think there's another couple of dozen to go. Better to have too many than not enough." She headed back towards the ovens.

Felicity's phone pinged. She wiped her fingers down her apron, then swiped the screen to read her husband's message.

> Practise throwing the rock cakes. Find a target
> about five inches in diameter, fifteen feet high
> off the ground, and about twelve feet away.

She selected a rock cake from the first batch, which was barely warm now. It had weight to it, so it could do some damage. She couldn't risk practising indoors. She headed out of the Tradesman's Entrance and stepped into the rear courtyard, where she considered potential targets. The recycling bins were too low, as were the shed and the other outbuildings. Behind her, the Hall's first-floor windows were at risk, if her ladies were any good at reaching fifteen feet in height. Then again, if they were poor throwers, the ground-floor windows were at just as much risk. What they needed was something that could withstand an attack from a range of artillery. What they needed was—

Felicity dashed back inside, through the main hall, and out through the main entrance. From the porticoed entrance, she could see the tank still blocking the driveway. She hurried along the gravel drive and squeezed between the tank's caterpillar tracks and the brick gateposts out onto the road. About fifteen feet above her was the gun barrel. Perfect.

Rosemary smiled as the occupant of the flat above the Lockmount Estate Agency opened the ground-floor door.

"Wot?" The unshaven chap, in his faded green-and-white striped pyjamas, tightened the drawstring around his waist. "I work nights. This had better be good."

She offered her electioneering hand. "Hi, I'm Rosemary Sedgewicke, the Socially Liberal Conservative Party prospective candidate, and I hope you'll vote for me in the upcoming by-election."

Her hand hung mid-air, hoping to press some flesh, as politicians called it, but when the flat's occupant scratched his groin first, she hastily withdrew the offer.

"I'm campaigning to save the meadows from this dreadful waste incinerator project, and at tonight's Neighbourhood Area Forum I'll reveal how this authority is lying to you—"

"Bugger off!"

She flinched as the door slammed in her face. Dejected, she took the adjacent door and entered the Lockmount Estate Agency, waving to Maureen in the back office. Rosemary admired the large map of Mortiforde on the wall and realised the entire area could soon be her constituency. Then, as a Member of Parliament, she'd have some real power. More than Abigail Mayedew.

"Sorry to keep you, Ms Sedgewicke." Maureen stepped through the glass door. "What can I do for you?"

"Has my tenant dropped off the keys? Gerald said they had until midday, and that was nearly two hours ago."

"Not that I'm aware of." Maureen checked her old desk. "But it's been non-stop all day and. . ." She pulled a small key from a desk drawer and unlocked the key cabinet on the wall behind her desk. Her finger journeyed along the rows of hooks. "No. There's nothing here. Who was your tenant?" She dropped onto her chair and interrogated her computer.

"No idea," said Rosemary. "Gerald dealt with all that."

Maureen tapped at her computer. "Mr Jones. Ideal tenant, it seems. No complaints by him or about him from the neighbours. Always paid his rent on time." She looked up at Rosemary. "Sometimes tenants post the keys through our letter box last thing, holding onto them in case they forget anything in the rush to get out. I wouldn't worry just yet."

Rosemary rummaged in her handbag. "I have a spare set. Perhaps I'll go round and check."

Maureen stood. "As the tenancy expired at midday, you don't need any permission to enter your property."

Rosemary smiled. "If my tenant is still there, I might persuade him to vote for me!"

Lisa knocked on Diya's office door, then stepped in to see Norris Offermans at Diya's desk, typing with two fingers. "Sorry to bother you, Mr Offermans." She closed the door behind her. "You've not confirmed your attendance at tonight's Neighbourhood Area Forum."

His bald head stared at her, while his two index fingers continued prodding letters.

Lisa shuffled awkwardly on her feet. "If you are attending, will you be doing a presentation?"

Norris stopped typing and raised his head. "Presentation? Ms Duddon, I'm not here to be used as a pawn by Borderlandshire District Council to bulldoze its controversial infrastructure projects through a community consultation. I'm here to ensure probity for the local and national taxpayer."

He glanced at Diya's computer monitor momentarily.

She leaned forward enough and saw Norris was browsing Diya's online auction site listings! "I'm sure the people of Borderlandshire will be extremely interested in what you have to say."

Norris sat back in his chair and twiddled his thumbs. "Here's some advice, Ms Duddon. Never forget, you are a public servant. We must be accountable for our actions. So, to answer your question, as the public will be there, it is only right that I also attend. And for the sake of clarity, I will only have three presentation slides. I find the longer a presentation, the more the presenter is attempting to justify their salary."

Aldermaston cradled the phone between his ear and shoulder so he could continue painting. "He was definitely looking at Diya's listings on the auction site?"

"I recognised the silver platter and the two trophies," Lisa confirmed.

Aldermaston glanced across his office at Diya, who'd turned at the mention of her name. "Diya, what are the bids up to now?"

"Four hundred and seventy-four thousand, four hundred and ninety-nine pounds," she whispered.

"We've less than three hours to raise about twenty-five grand," he calculated. "Thanks for letting us know. I'm putting together a brief presentation now that I've worked out what's going on. What's the best way to get it to you?"

"Email. I'll combine it with the evidence I'm putting together. Better go." Lisa ended the call.

Aldermaston threw his phone onto the desk and finished painting the enormous final letter T in red paint on the large dust sheet they'd spread out on the office floor.

"Daniel, grab the other top corner, will you?"

They both stood, holding aloft the large dust sheet, practically shielding half of Aldermaston's office. Scrawled across it in bright red paint were the words *Waste Not, Incinerator Not.*

"How does this help Basildon?" Daniel pulled the sheet taut to read it properly.

"It's a diversion," Aldermaston explained. "We don't want BANG to think this is a rescue attempt. It'll take four of us. One at each corner. When PC Norten stretches out of the window to press Millie's nose, releasing the chest cavity, we can use this to break Basildon's fall."

Daniel sniggered. "It'll be like landing on a trampoline. I hope he doesn't bounce off."

Aldermaston's office door swung open. Felicity hovered in the doorway and read the banner. "Is that for tonight's meeting?"

"Something like that," Aldermaston offered.

She motioned over her shoulder. "We're about to practise throwing these rock cakes, so it's time you explained this grand plan of yours. Their motivation to hit the target might improve if they understood why they're hurling rock cakes fifteen feet into the air."

Aldermaston nodded and dropped the dust sheet banner to the ground.

Felicity's jaw dropped. "Is that Diya?"

Diya spun round, then stood. "Your Ladyship. How lovely to see you!"

Felicity stepped over the dust sheet. "Everyone's been looking for you for days. We thought you were in India."

Aldermaston's stomach gurgled.

Felicity stared at the computer monitor. "Are you selling things online?" She peered closer to the screen. "Blimey! You've raised nearly half a—"

Aldermaston began backing away.

"ALDERMASTON!" She spun round and flung an angry finger in his direction. "You have some explaining to do!"

Rosemary stood outside 42 Brominster Way and surveyed her property. It lacked kerb appeal. Paint was peeling off the windowsills, the front lawn needed mowing, and some roof-tiles had slipped.

She knocked on the front door, then cupped her hands around her face as she peered through the front bay window. The net curtain was mouldy, and there appeared to be little furniture in the room.

It took a forceful wiggle of the key and a sharp push to get the front door open. "Hello? Anyone home?"

She peered up the bare wooden stairs and called again. Silence. She turned to the kitchen. The worktop was bare, and the only movement came from the dripping tap. The back door was locked.

Mr Jones had vacated. She entered the living room and gasped at the threadbare carpet, the barren walls, and the abandoned, poor-quality furniture. Her fingers stroked the drop-leaf tabletop. It wobbled. This all needed dumping at the household recycling centre.

She found the envelope addressed to her. There was weight to it. The key. Inside was a folded note.

Remember, remember, the fifth of November, gunpowder, treason, and plot.

Her knees buckled as she read the second line.

If blood is thicker than water, then I am your heart-stopping clot.

Felicity stormed into the Hall's main kitchen. Aldermaston followed. Entering Cartwright's domain shocked him. Flour, dough scraps, and butter covered every worktop surface. Some rock cakes were still cooling on wire racks. Stacked against the wall were several large wooden vegetable crates crammed with burned rock cakes.

"You've been raising money for the waste incinerator, haven't you?" Felicity wagged a finger under his nose.

Aldermaston held up his hands. "It's not how this looks."

"Good!" She slammed the kitchen worktop, and a rock cake fell off a wire cooling rack. "So start explaining!"

"Diya asked for help. She was being blackmailed."

"Blackmailed?"

"It was an email from Diya that led Abigail to declare the waste incinerator project was ready to roll. But Diya *didn't* send that email."

Felicity's face softened. "Who did?"

Aldermaston leaned against the kitchen doorway. "The same person who killed Sir Hugo and Gerald. They threatened Diya with family shame if she told anyone the email message was fake."

"Family shame?" Felicity chuckled. "She knew how to pull your strings!"

"What?"

"Oh, come on!" Felicity threw her hands in the air. "Family shame? That's why you throw yourself into all the work the Borderers Guild does."

"No, I don't!"

Felicity stared at him. "How many times has Harry asked you to take him swimming? Have you taken him? No, because you're always working, and it's usually the bloody Borderers Guild!" She turned and ran her fingers through her hair.

"I'm the Marquess of Mortiforde. The title carries responsibilities. You know that!"

She spun back around. "You are not responsible for your mother's infidelity. *She* brought shame on the family, not you."

"I have a duty to the town. It's what my father did, and my grandfather, and—"

"And you have a son!" Felicity snapped. "You have a duty to him, too. One day, he'll be the Ninth Marquess, and you'd better bloody hope that he doesn't resent it because of how much time the title took his father away from him!"

Tears pricked Aldermaston's eyes. "I just want what's best for everyone." He slid down the doorframe and let his head fall onto his bent knees.

Felicity slipped beside him. "I know." She kissed the top of his head. "Neither of us signed up for this. And neither did Harry. You mustn't forget that."

Aldermaston wiped his cheeks with the back of his hand. "Families, heh?"

Felicity rested her head on his shoulder. "We're not as bad as the Rindes, are we?" She paused. "Sir Hugo and Rupert are so different. Without their identical birthmarks, you wouldn't believe they were related."

Aldermaston sighed. "Did becoming a father change me?"

Felicity squeezed his hand. "When the midwife placed Harry into your arms, I watched your heart swell." She prodded his chest. "Which is why I get so angry when you put Mortiforde before your son. I know the love is in there. Your father made you the man you are today, but so too did your son the day he was born."

Aldermaston stared at the floor. "Perhaps Rupert would have been different had he known he had a son."

Felicity grabbed Aldermaston's arm. "Rupert has a son?"

He nodded. "And tonight, he's going public with that news."

Basildon squinted as someone whipped the black hood off his head. He checked his surroundings, but struggled. His hands were bound behind his back, and his feet tied to the chair legs. Citrus trees, ferns, cacti, and small palm trees lined the orangery. He was sitting at the end of a long trestle table bearing a selection of small plates.

Outside, Mortiforde Millie was lying on her back on the lawn. A BANG soldier pressed her nose. It dropped an inch, and her chest shuddered. The soldier undid her multicoloured cardigan and heaved open two hinged doors in her chest.

"Special delivery for Agent 117," called a voice, blustering in the Billiard Room.

Two BANG soldiers strode along the orangery carrying cardboard boxes and placed them on the trestle table. One wore camouflage face paint; the other wore a Guido Fakes mask. Guido pointed to Basildon.

"Untie his hands."

Basildon recognised the Commander's voice as the other cut the binding around his wrists. His hands throbbed with the sudden rush of blood.

The Commander opened the boxes, and the tempting aroma of a Nooseman's Knot's Last Supper drifted towards Basildon. His mouth salivated as the fried bacon, sausages, Boor Pie, and triple-cooked chunky chips filled the orangery. His stomach gurgled.

From one box, Guido pulled a large paper cup sealed with a plastic lid. He removed the lid and lifted his mask enough to take a sip. Immediately, he wheezed, coughed, and spluttered as he spat a fine spray across the orangery floor. "Flipping heck!" he gasped, his hoarse voice barely audible.

Basildon chuckled. "Never had a Hangman's Anaesthetic, old bean? Nooseman's Knot speciality, that is. A condemned man's last drink. Numbs all senses from the neck down." He held out his hand.

Guido handed him the paper cup, his voice struggling to recover. "The alcoholic vapours will only add to the fireworks later." He turned to the soldier beside him. "Unload all this onto the table and let the lads know the buffet has arrived."

Agent 24 unpacked the large trays of sausages, bacon, eggs, black pudding, toast, a selection of cold meats and cheeses, baby salad leaves, mixed peppers, raw onion, and cucumber, and a large crusty Boor Pie, mushy peas, with a huge serving of triple-cooked chunky chips.

Basildon swallowed a mouthful of Hangman's Anaesthetic, with no side effects. "I say! Is that my last meal?"

Guido chuckled. "My chaps need sustenance for tonight. You can have what's left."

Agent 24 picked up a box of Cadbury Milk Tray. "I forgot to hand these around, Commander. I'll put them at the end." Then he leaned across the trestle table, banged on the orangery window, and waved his comrades inside.

Basildon downed the rest of his Hangman's Anaesthetic, in fear of it being taken from him.

"Before you get stuck in," Guido said to his men as they

entered to satiate their appetites, "the explosives need to accompany the victim into Millie's chest." He gestured towards Basildon.

Basildon shook his head. "No! Not yet—"

An agent forced a rag into his mouth, bound his hands again, and then thrust a black hood over his head.

Moments later, an army of hands lifted him from the chair and carried him out of the orangery. A sudden force swept him into a cold, hard wooden container. Many hands tucked his knees under his chin and forced his hands behind his back. They wedged other objects between his back and Millie's cavity wall and every other tiny gap. All went dark with a resonating click.

Basildon shivered. "Oh, Aldermaston. I think I'm in a bit of a bind," he whispered.

Outside Tugford Hall's main entrance, Arabella waved a blackened block of dough in Aldermaston's face. "This isn't some trick, is it, Your Lordship? You'll definitely let the Ladies' Legion use your Mortiforde Meadows for our environmentally friendly burial site? Because if this is all some wheeze just to get us to save your half-witted half-brother, then I'm leaving now."

A smattering of nods and agreeing murmurs behind her caught Aldermaston's attention.

"I am fully supportive of your endeavour, and grant you permission to use my meadows as a green burial site."

"But that will only happen if they cancel the waste incinerator project, won't it, Your Lordship?" Cissy Warbouys concluded.

He took her hand in his. "I'm confident that at tonight's public meeting, the whole waste incinerator project will collapse. But we also need to save Basildon. Not only is he my brother, but his observation helped me work out what's going on. BANG has threatened to burn Basildon at the stake inside Millie. We need to set him free by hitting Millie's nose button that releases her chest doors."

Arabella and the rest of the Ladies' Legion turned to Felicity. "You're best placed to tell us whether he's lying, Your Ladyship."

Aldermaston felt his wife's gaze scrutinise his face.

"His left eyebrow is stationary," Felicity declared. "It's the truth."

Arabella swung a pointed finger in Aldermaston's face. "There are over two dozen witnesses, Your Lordship, so heaven help you if you go back on your word."

With that, she spun round, pulled back her arm, and hurled the rock cake towards the tank, releasing a simultaneous primeval scream. Seconds later, a metallic clunk echoed around them as the rock cake shattered against the tank's armoured plating. Dejected, she returned to the group.

One by one, each Legion member stepped up beside Aldermaston and Felicity, stared at the tank's gun barrel some twelve feet away, before throwing a rock cake towards it. For the next fifteen minutes, a series of heavy metal thuds or disintegrating fragments rained down on them, accompanied by despondent moans from the group.

Heidi Yail stepped up to the mark, drew back her cake-clenching hand, and motioned it back and forth several times. She paused, took two steps to the right, then repeated the process. With what seemed the most delicate of throws, over two dozen pairs of eyes widened as the spinning rock cake flew in an almost perfect trajectory. Almost. It ricocheted off the end of the gun barrel to a collective "Ooh".

"Forgive me, Your Lordship," Heidi began, "but why are we practising on a stationary target? Millie's moving when she parades through town." She grabbed another rock cake from the sackful at Aldermaston's feet.

"I have PC Norten in place," Aldermaston began, "at one spot in town when she'll be moving slowly, but if he fails—"

"He's PC Norten," Kitty interrupted. "He does nothing but fail!"

"Which is why I need you as my backup," Aldermaston explained. "The only other place we might save Basildon is when they tie Millie to the stake, ready for burning. She'll be stationary then."

"And because townsfolk traditionally throw rotten fruit at her," Felicity explained, bending down to pick up a rock cake, "nobody will suspect what we're doing until it's too late." She held the cake aloft.

Aldermaston nodded. "It'll be too late once they light the fire."

An air of solemnity pervaded the group.

Heidi nodded, took another half-step to the right, and drew back her arm. Her hand wavered back and forth several times as she gauged the required effort and trajectory. She threw. The rock cake hurtled through the air towards the gun barrel's opening. There was a collective gasp as the group witnessed the charcoal cake enter the five-inch diameter barrel opening and clatter its way down the long barrel. A tremendous cheer erupted as the ladies jumped up and down, celebrating.

Heidi slapped her thigh. "And that's why I'm captain of The Nooseman's Knot's Ladies Darts Team."

Cordelia, Kitty, Cissy, and Arabella rushed forward and threw Heidi onto their shoulders in jubilation.

Aldermaston crossed his fingers behind his back. Hopefully, Heidi wouldn't need to repeat that accuracy later this evening.

CHAPTER TWENTY-TWO

Back in his office, Aldermaston called Lisa. "Everything set for tonight?"

"I've summarised everything we've found and put it on the projector laptop. We can access it when we need to."

Aldermaston ticked this off in his notebook. "What's the order of play?"

Lisa sighed. "Depends on when the public kicks off. Councillor Taplinski has an unorthodox crowd control method."

"Oh?"

"He turns off the lights." Lisa sniggered. "It silences a room pretty quickly. When Taplinski starts talking, that's the signal to switch them on again."

Aldermaston tutted. "Tonight's NAF is about shining a light on the corruption that's been taking place here for years."

"How's the online auction going?"

He twisted around in his chair. "Diya, what's the auction total at the moment?"

Diya refreshed her screen. "Just shy of four hundred and eighty-two thousand, with ninety minutes to go. Hopefuls are now bidding odd pence figures, hoping to outbid those bidding round numbers."

Aldermaston brought the phone back to his mouth. "Did you hear that?"

Lisa whistled. "Who'd have thought we'd get anywhere near that figure when we found Diya in the basement two days ago?"

Two days? It felt like a lifetime to Aldermaston. "Right, I must dash. I'm about to make a woman very happy. But don't tell Felicity."

Rosemary stormed into her house, flung open the kitchen door, and exhaled with relief when she saw Rupert wasn't there. Wedged under a vase on the kitchen table was a note.

Got eviction business to sort at solicitors. See you at tonight's meeting. We'll soon have these Mortiforde morons in the palms of our hands. R.

She yanked open the sideboard cupboard door, retrieved the memory box, and upended it on the kitchen table. Her hands rummaged frenziedly, searching for two things. Photos, mementoes, postcards, and programmes slipped far and wide across the tabletop as she hunted. She found the latest note first. Unfurling it, she flattened it against the tabletop with the palms of her hands.

Dear Rosemary,
Remember, remember, the fifth of November,
Gunpowder, treason, and plot.
The truth will soon out, of your treason, no doubt
And the truth should ne'er be forgot.

Treason. Originally, she'd assumed this was about the waste

incinerator project. It wasn't. The treason was what she'd done a quarter of a century ago.

From her coat pocket, she pulled her tenant's note.

Remember, remember, the fifth of November, gunpowder, treason, and plot.
If blood is thicker than water, then I am your heart-stopping clot.

Her hand rubbed the top of her chest, her stomach groaned, and she belched. She dashed across to the kitchen sink and threw up. Gasping for air, Rosemary wiped her mouth, then returned to rummaging through the memory-box contents, sending several discarded documents onto the floor.

Her hands froze momentarily when she located the small brown envelope. Then she snatched at it, slipped her fingers inside, and retrieved the contents. Three documents. The first was a newspaper cutting from the *Powys Gazette* about a baby abandoned at Knighton's Household Waste Site. The second was a Belgian birth certificate for Thomas Sedgewicke, born on November fifth. Today was her son's twenty-sixth birthday.

The third was a letter from Powys Social Services dated eight years ago.

Dear Ms Sedgewicke,

We are writing regarding your request to establish contact with your son. After careful consideration and discussions with your son, he has expressed his decision NOT to pursue communication or contact.

We understand that this may be difficult news, and we want to assure you that this decision has been made with the utmost respect for your son's wishes and well-being. As part of our role, we prioritise the feelings and preferences of the child while ensuring their welfare remains paramount.

If you have questions or require support, please do not hesitate to contact us.

Thank you for your understanding.

She knew making contact after his eighteenth birthday was risky, but this was the response she dreaded. His anger was understandable. He had every right to those emotions. This was why she'd never told Rupert. Their son clearly wanted nothing to do with his parents.

She collapsed into a dining chair. It was over. Everything. Her head fell into her hands, and she sobbed.

Eventually, she wiped her cheeks with the back of her hand, pulled out her phone, and scrolled for Rupert's number. It was time to do what she should have done twenty-six years ago.

Her thumb hovered over the green call button. What would she say? How would she explain keeping this a secret all these years? How would he react? She shuddered at the thought. Part of this was Rupert's fault. If he hadn't tried sabotaging her European Parliament job, then—

She dropped the phone back onto the table and reviewed the notes again. *The truth will soon out.* Public shame. That's what their son wanted. She nodded. He deserved it. If this was all she could do to help her son, then so be it. She'd say nothing to Rupert and attend the NAF as the prospective parliamentary candidate for Mortiforde. That way, her son … their son … could have his moment of truth.

～

Aldermaston stared at the office clock and counted down the seconds. "Five … four … three … two … one … Go!"

Diya inhaled deeply, exhaled, then refreshed the online auction page. She covered her eyes. "I can't look!"

Daniel whistled. "Oh. My. God."

"Tell me." Diya refused to part her fingers.

"How fastidious is the National Audit Office?"

Diya's fingers ran down her face. "We're short, aren't we?"

Daniel nodded. "Yeah."

"Stop faffing around, you two!" Aldermaston snapped. "How much?"

Daniel turned and grinned. "After accounting for the online auction site's listing fees and commission, the total raised is … four hundred and ninety-nine thousand, nine hundred and ninety-nine pounds and eighty-five pence!"

Aldermaston's jaw practically hit the top of his desk.

Diya stared at the screen. "Short by fifteen pence."

Aldermaston practically choked. "A fifteen-pence shortfall is nothing compared with half a million three days ago!"

Tears streaked Diya's cheeks. "It's a shortfall. The National Audit Office will declare the waste incinerator project as not fully funded. Abigail will sack me. What will Nani Nagma think?"

Aldermaston squeezed her shoulder. "Abigail's not *that* sadistic. She can transfer fifteen pence from her stationery budget if she's that desperate."

Diya shook her head. "That's a revenue budget, and the waste incinerator is a capital project. Completely different for accounting purposes. When the NAF begins in two hours, technically, the waste incinerator has a shortfall. And the National Audit Office will have to declare that publicly. Abigail won't like that one bit."

∾

Norris sat back in Diya's office chair. His right eyebrow arched in surprise.

He added a row to his spreadsheet, labelled it as *Online Auction Income*, and entered the balancing figure. He pressed the Return key and watched the balancing figure change from a sea of bold, red negative numbers to three zeros with a decimal point between the first and second.

He smiled. Diya Parmer was a remarkable woman. Thanks to her efforts, he could go on stage at tonight's NAF and declare the waste incinerator project was fully funded. Right down to the last penny.

~

"Take it steady, lads," Peredur watched a dozen of his men ease Mortiforde Millie onto her feet. "Remember, she's carrying extra weight, so she may handle differently."

On Knowton Manor's lower rear lawns, two operatives working each of the main driving rods struggled to keep her steady as other men helped push Mortiforde Millie into an upright position. A muffled scream emanated from her chest.

Agent 24 turned to Peredur. "Might the crowd hear him?"

Peredur shook his head. "There'll be too much cheering and yelling." He pointed to the Orangery. "Let me show you the route."

They entered the Orangery, where someone had draped a Mortiforde town centre map over the trestle table. Peredur moved the empty Cadbury Milk Tray box off the map.

"It'll take you twenty minutes to get here." Peredur pointed to Forde Bridge. He checked the time. "You've half an hour, so you're okay."

Agent 24 pointed along Watling Street. "I take it we go up here, as we can't get through Southgate Street."

"Correct. At the top of the hill, turn left onto Castle Street. It narrows by the Buttermarket, and then you need to—"

"Watch out!" someone outside bellowed.

They glanced up to see a soldier clutching his buttocks and careering towards them. The shadowy outline of Mortiforde Millie wavered uncontrollably, arms flailing and upper body swaying, as the remaining men struggled to regain control of her.

The buttock-clenching soldier stormed into the Orangery. "Toilet?" he screamed.

Agent 24 pointed towards the Billiard Room. "Through there, on the right."

"Sir!"

Peredur glanced at the empty box of Cadbury Milk Tray. It seemed he wasn't the only one chocolate disagreed with.

"As I was saying," Peredur continued, "take care when manoeuvring Millie between the Buttermarket and the building opposite. The upper floors jut out. Turn right, follow through to the Market Square, and tie her to the awaiting stake. Then set her alight."

Agent 24 nodded. "And we all need to wear ponchos from the start?"

"Yes." Peredur grinned. "To protect yourselves from the rotten fruit and veg the crowds will throw at Millie. Most of them miss."

The Orangery door flew open, and another bottom-clenching soldier in camouflage gear dashed past them. Peredur pointed at the empty chocolate box. "How many men had those?"

Agent 24 shrugged. "At least half."

Peredur banished his fears and saluted Agent 24. "Good luck. Remember to march the lads to the council offices at 1830 hours. Make it look like we're storming the building. But

I'll formally dismiss you there. Remind the lads that the first two rounds of drinks at The Nooseman's Knot are on me."

Agent 24 returned the salute. "Thank you, sir!"

Peredur watched Agent 24 return to his men and Millie. Now, though, it was time for him to blow Tugford Hall to smithereens.

Aldermaston wandered back into his office, having checked that he, Daniel, and Diya were the last ones in the building. He grabbed his car keys and tucked the *Waste Not, Incinerator Not* banner under his arm. "You two head to Shepherd Cottage, collect the rest of Diya's things, and wait there until after six o'clock. I don't want you anywhere near this place, in case BANG's threat to demolish Tugford Hall is genuine."

Daniel slipped his arm through his navy overcoat. "Is there nothing we can do to save Tugford Hall?"

Aldermaston glanced around the room. "It's bricks and mortar. We can always rebuild. But if we don't save Basildon before they burn Millie at the stake, then. . ." He stared at his shoes. "Basildon can be a ruddy nightmare at times, but he's still family."

Diya extended a hand. "Thank you, Lord Mortiforde, for your support. I may have failed to raise the full half a million, but I couldn't have done what I have without you."

He shook her hand. "Nani Nagma will be proud of what you have achieved."

She smiled. "Ultimately, everything is about family, isn't it?"

Felicity stood on tiptoes at the top of Southgate Street, near the Buttermarket, and searched for her Ladies' Legion members.

The street lamps illuminated the townsfolk jostling their way uphill with glowing wristbands and necklaces, heading for the Market Square. The crowds were thinner at the bottom of the hill, once they'd passed through the medieval south gate, where the three-storey Georgian facades hid a mixture of private dwellings and small business offices. She scanned the faces of those approaching the Buttermarket, where the crowds were thicker as they negotiated the narrowing road between the town's older timber-framed Tudor buildings with leaded windows and supporting pillars for the overhanging first-floor storeys.

"Here, Your Ladyship!" Kitty waved her shepherd's crook in the air, then led the gathered ladies through the townsfolk to join her. Moments later, Cordelia, Arabella, and Heidi joined them, followed by Cissy and Margaret.

"Kitty, Cordelia, and Arabella, wait here for my husband. He'll need your help to create a distraction. Everyone else," Felicity continued, "follow me."

She marched her women's army into the Market Square, where the crowd was dense. The market stalls had been cleared away, creating a vast space for the crowds to gather. Double-lamped Victorian street lamps cast an orange glow across the ornate and imposing three- and four-storey properties lining the perimeter of the square. All the independent retailers had closed, but several cafes remained open, as did the greengrocer, with pre-bagged rotten fruit and veg for sale. A wide path, lined with crowd barriers, weaved through the centre, to Mortiforde Castle's gated main entrance where, next to the castle's imposing cannon, stood a large telegraph pole on a raised wooden platform, surrounded by pallets and wooden offcuts.

Heidi Yail fell in step alongside her. "Ideally, My Lady, we need to be by the barriers. The closer to Millie's stake, the better."

Felicity panicked. The crowds were twelve deep already. In

front of her was a man with a young boy sitting on his shoulders. "Excuse me, please. We need to get through."

He turned and looked her up and down. "Sod off, love. We were here first. Not my fault you're late." He turned his back on them.

"Over here, Your Ladyship." Heidi pulled her away from the crowds. "There's space at the barriers here."

"But this is far too far away," she began. "You'll never throw the rock cakes from here." She pointed up at the sky. "And you'll never hit her nose from here at this angle as she goes past. We must be thirty feet away from the stake here."

Heidi grabbed a barrier and pulled one end up. "They interlock. See? Once Millie has passed, we can unhook this and dash after her."

Felicity glanced around. The Market Square was filling quickly. "It's our only hope," she concluded. She turned to Margaret and Cissy, who were pulling their rock cake supply in Margaret's wheeled folding shopping trolley. "We'll do what Heidi says, but I'll go with her and take the shopping trolley." Then she pointed to the barriers and turned to Margaret. "Once we're through, lock these together again and stop anyone else following us."

Margaret nodded.

Felicity stamped her feet. A clear night sky sucked away the remains of the day's little warmth. There was just enough time to find out where Cartwright and Harry were. She pulled out her phone.

~

Daniel's mind raced as he and Diya headed towards the Tradesman's Entrance. "This feels wrong."

"What does?"

"Abandoning Tugford Hall." He gestured to the

surrounding building. "Aldermaston has been good to me. My first job after university was working for Kizzy Whiffle."

Diya stopped mid-step. "The mass-murdering gardening television presenter?"

"Exactly. If Aldermaston hadn't discovered what she was up to, I could have been her next victim."

Diya's hand covered her mouth.

"I lost my job and living accommodation when they arrested her. Aldermaston took me in, gave me this job, and then helped me find my little terraced place in town to rent. Without him, I don't know where I would be now."

Diya smiled. "You're right. If the auction has taught us anything, it's that you won't achieve something unless you try."

Daniel grabbed Diya's arm. "Come on. We need to go this way."

"What are we doing?"

"Stopping a tank."

Cartwright clamped his phone tight to his ear, blocking out the surrounding crowd's chatter. "Yes, My Lady. Forde Bridge. Master Harry and I have a good spot. Millie's just coming over the bridge now."

"Here she comes!" Harry jumped excitedly on the spot. "Where are the tomatoes?"

Cartwright ended the call and opened the carrier bag he'd brought with him. Waves of cheers and squeals washed towards them as the huge puppet, escorted by an army of men in green plastic ponchos, turned onto Watling Street, lined with quaint two-up, two-down cottages. There followed a barrage of thuds and splats as rotten fruit and veg smacked against Millie's torso and head, and some of Peredur's men.

Harry reached into the bag and grabbed a tomato.

"Careful, Master Harry. They're extremely squishy."

Harry cradled one between his fingers in his upturned hand. He leaned against the crowd barrier and hooked his arm over the top. "She's getting closer," he sang.

The giant puppet walked gracefully along Watling Street, despite the constant battering of fruit and veg. Leeks, potatoes, and bananas ricocheted off her in various directions. Softer substances exploded into a gooey mess as they collided with her head and body. Four BANG members took turns in pairs to control Millie, allowing the other pair a chance to clean the food debris off their ponchos.

As Millie drew closer, one BANG member suddenly grabbed his backside. "Toilet!" He shot off towards Southgate Street and the nearest public toilets.

Harry giggled, then drew back his arm, and hurled his tomato towards Millie. His line of sight was perfect until a BANG member stepped in the way. SPLAT! Right in his face. Harry grabbed another tomato. Millie was now level with him. He spun round, using momentum to boost his throw, and hurled the tomato into the air. It flew high over Peredur's men and hit Millie square on the cheek, exploding into a gooey mess.

"Yes!" Harry punched the air.

"Well done, Master Harry," Cartwright congratulated. "You nearly hit her nose then."

Aldermaston abandoned his car near Morte Bridge, crossed over, and followed the single-lane Curtain Wall Road past the meadows. The bulldozers were still blockading the main gates. Then he cut up an alleyway, past the town's almshouses, to St Julian's church. A wall of noise hit him when he emerged behind the Buttermarket and joined the thronging crowds.

Pushing against a tide of excited visitors, he broke through into the relative calm of the Buttermarket's open ground-floor space. He spotted PC Norten's head and shoulders towering above Kitty, Cordelia, Arabella, and PCSO Marker nearby.

PC Norten rubbed his hands together. "Your Lordship! You made it."

"Seems busy," he suggested.

"I think many will head to the NAF after this." Kitty beamed.

Aldermaston pulled the banner from under his arm and handed it to her. "When Millie approaches the Buttermarket, I need you four to march towards her as if you're demonstrators."

Cordelia pointed to the crowd barrier. "How do we get the other side of that?"

"I'll instruct a marshal to let us through," said PCSO Marker.

Aldermaston continued. "You need to stop them just as Millie's head draws close to that window up there." He pointed to the first-floor window above them. "When PC Norten hangs out of the window, everyone will look at him. That's your cue to move. Grab a corner each and hold the banner taut horizontally, ready to catch Basildon. Got that?"

"Yes, Your Lordship," they chanted.

A tremendous cheer funnelled along Castle Street. Aldermaston grabbed PC Norten's arm. "Time we got into our positions."

Daniel dropped in through the tank hatch first, backing into a corner so Diya could enter. Her feet dangled just above the driver's seat.

"Keep coming," Daniel encouraged.

Slowly, she lowered her feet onto the seat beneath her, then poked her head through the hatch to see where to put her feet next. She threw her handbag to the floor, then stepped down into the cramped compartment. Diya pointed to some pedals. "They look like an accelerator and a brake." She paused. "Where's the steering wheel?"

Daniel gestured to two levers. "Probably those. Turning will require stopping one of the caterpillar tracks, which will pivot the vehicle."

"Aren't you a clever one, Einstein?" snapped a voice above them. A pair of combat boots followed by some camouflage-trousered legs dropped in through the hatch.

"Who are you?" Daniel stared at the camouflage-painted face before him. Two eyes blinked. The pieces fell into place. "You're Peredur!"

Peredur slow hand-clapped his new acquaintance, then turned to Diya. "Well, if it isn't Diya Parmer." He slipped into his working voice. "IT Helpdesk, how can I help you?" His voice dropped an octave. "Tut tut, Diya. Fancy finding you here when I changed the annual leave system to show you were in India."

Diya stepped back, but tripped over her handbag and fell against the side. "You!" She lunged, waving her hands, smacking Peredur about the head and chest.

He giggled.

Daniel pulled her away. "He's not worth it."

Peredur pointed to Daniel. "You should listen to him." He placed his face within inches of hers and whispered, "There's nothing you can do to stop me. You're just a sniffling little woman working for the establishment. Out of my way!" He pushed her aside and jumped into the driving seat.

Daniel stopped her from falling, then prodded Peredur's back. "What are you doing?"

Peredur chuckled. "I'm going to raze Tugford Hall to the

ground. Need to start the engine first, so I can rotate the gun barrel one hundred and eighty degrees."

Peredur pressed four colour-coded buttons: green, yellow, pink, and burgundy. The entire tank shuddered briefly, then shook violently, as the two-stroke engine erupted into life. "Woo hoo! Houston, we have lift-off!" Peredur yelled.

Diya rummaged in her handbag.

"What are you looking for?" Daniel yelled above the diesel engine noise.

"I've got a rape alarm in here, somewhere," she replied.

Peredur spun around and wagged a finger at them. "Stay there, children, and don't touch anything!" Seconds later, he jumped out through the hatch.

Aldermaston stared through the Buttermarket's first-floor community meeting room window and watched Millie approaching. Was Basildon conscious of what was happening?

"The ladies have the banner out, Your Lordship." PC Norten sat on the window ledge and leaned back in.

Aldermaston watched the puppet draw closer. Millie's head wavered slightly as she slowed to a crawl. Below, he could hear the puppeteers' shouts above the cheering crowd. "This way. Back a bit. Mind that gutter!"

It was now or never. Aldermaston shoved PC Norten's shoulders. "Now!" He bellowed.

PC Norten leaned out the window and stretched his arm towards Millie's face. Aldermaston grabbed the officer's legs, braced his feet against the wall, and hugged PC Norten's legs so tight he practically cut off the circulation to the officer's feet.

Through the window, he watched the long arm of the law wave wildly in the air, waiting for Millie's nose to come closer.

"Any moment now!" Aldermaston yelled.

PC Norten's index finger stretched towards the nose, but missed, caressing an ear instead.

"Try again," Aldermaston hollered, gripping the policeman's legs even tighter.

Millie's head swayed back slightly before leaning forward again. PC Norten elongated his finger to its maximum length. "Here we go, Your Lordship! Any … second … now—"

Aldermaston's eyes widened as the policeman's finger touched Millie's nose. He was about to push hard against it when the puppet's head dropped unexpectedly. The crowd below shrieked. PC Norten's torso dropped below the windowsill.

"What's happening?" Aldermaston yelled.

The sound of ripping material filled the meeting room. A rip appeared in the officer's trousers near his belt. If he didn't act fast, PC Norten could plummet to the ground below in his underwear. Aldermaston lunged, grabbed the officer's belt, and heaved the policeman back through the window. They both fell backwards onto the table behind them.

Aldermaston sat up in time to see Millie's head rise into view again, now well past the window. The crowd cheered. "Why did Millie lurch like that?"

PC Norten giggled. "A puppeteer dropped the pole supporting Millie's left shoulder, grabbed his bottom, and dashed towards St Julian's church. I think he needed a toilet!"

Aldermaston grabbed his phone to text Felicity.

We've failed. Basildon's life is in your hands.

CHAPTER TWENTY-THREE

Peredur opened the tank's gun chamber and checked the gun barrel. Something was already in there. Dewi must have preloaded a shell. Excellent! He closed the hatch, then placed his finger on the red electrical-ignition button. Through the gunsight, he looked at Tugford Hall's porticoed entrance and finger-waved. "Bye-bye."

He pushed the button.

The entire tank jolted. There was a muffled boom, and a blast of white powder backfired into the chamber.

"What the—?" Peredur brushed the dust off his camouflage jacket. Upon opening the gun barrel chamber, a charred sultana fell out. Sultana? He poked his head through the turret to see Tugford Hall still standing. Perhaps Dewi had preloaded a blank. He checked for the shells Dewi said he'd left, but couldn't see them. They must be in the driver's cabin.

Peredur hauled himself out through the turret hatch and jumped down onto the tank's front glacis plate. He dangled his legs through the driver's hatch, then dropped inside.

"What have you done?" yelled Daniel.

Peredur waved a dismissive hand. "Test shot," he said,

searching the driver's cab. "There they are!" He spotted two shells in a cardboard box under the driver's seat. "These will do the real damage."

As he bent down to pick them up, Diya whipped out her rape alarm and pressed the button. "Take that, you thug!"

There was a momentary pause, as Diya realised it wasn't her rape alarm she'd pulled out, but Daisy's new toy mouse.

Peredur's eyes widened. His entire body convulsed. "GET IT AWAY!" He backed into a corner, his eyes fixated on Diya's handbag horror. As she stepped closer, Peredur released a primeval scream.

~

Felicity returned her phone to her pocket as Mortiforde Millie entered the Market Square. "It's down to us, ladies," she said, nodding towards the approaching puppet.

Margaret offered Felicity the shopping trolley. "Did you really expect the men to do it?" She winked.

A series of whumpfs, clonks, and splats echoed around them as the gathered crowd threw rotten missiles at Millie. A slime of seeds, slush, and fruit skins covered the green-ponchoed soldiers.

Felicity looked up at Millie's nose as she drew alongside them. "Seems bigger from this angle," she said to Heidi.

Heidi pointed to Millie's chest. "Is His Lordship's brother in there?"

"He'd better be after the effort we're putting in," Felicity replied.

Millie creaked and groaned with each step towards her final destination. When the remaining BANG soldiers passed by, Heidi held up her hand. "Let's wait until they're just putting Millie in place, then make a dash for it."

"We're here!" chorused Arabella, Cordelia, Kitty, and

PCSO Marker, pushing their way through the crowds with the banner.

Felicity held her breath as Millie's head bobbed above the crowds towards the castle entrance. When the puppet reached the stage, it turned to face the crowd.

"Now!" Heidi squealed.

Felicity and Heidi dashed through the barrier gap. Margaret's shopping trolley wheels bounced awkwardly across the cobbled paving stones. Thankfully, the heavy rock cakes prevented it from toppling over. Behind them followed Arabella, Cordelia, Kitty, and Ceri.

At Millie's burning site beside Mortiforde Castle's entrance, Heidi dashed ahead to find the right spot. Felicity looked at the spectacular sight before them. Millie stood on a wooden platform two feet above the ground. Behind her was a twenty-foot telegraph pole, to which the puppet was currently being secured. Underneath and surrounding the wooden platform was a collection of pallets and wooden offcuts. Behind them, the crowd's excitement grew as they chanted the puppet's name.

Felicity pulled up alongside Heidi, unzipped the shopping trolley, and handed her two rock cakes. Heidi grabbed them and assessed her throw.

"Come on, ladies!" Felicity encouraged the banner women into position. "Get as close to the platform as you can."

The four women grabbed a banner corner and fanned out, pulling it horizontally taut.

"Throw something, Heidi," Felicity yelled. "It's game over once they light the bonfire."

Heidi retracted her arm, then hurled the first rock cake. It bounced off Millie's chin.

"Step closer," Felicity bellowed.

Heidi edged forward a half-step and dropped the second

rock cake into her throwing hand. Her eyes remained fixed on Millie's nose.

Felicity crossed her fingers and muttered under her breath. "Please let this one work."

Heidi screamed as she hurled the second rock cake into the air. It scudded towards Millie's face, smacking her right on the nose. All six women cheered, the nose half-depressed, Millie's chest groaned, and—nothing happened.

"Again!" screamed Felicity. She pulled another rock cake from the shopping trolley and threw it towards Heidi. A man with a burning torch wandered around the back of the bonfire. Smoke billowed behind the stake. Flickering flames appeared at the bonfire's rear.

"Now, Heidi. Now!" Felicity screamed.

Heidi's arm pulled back. She took a deep breath and closed her eyes.

"Forget the visualisation!" Felicity shrieked. "Just throw the damn rock cake!"

Heidi's guttural scream propelled the rock cake through the air. Time slowed as the blackened bakery block cartwheeled towards the giant puppet. A streak of yellow flame flashed skywards as an oily pallet ignited under the platform. The rock cake disappeared briefly, consumed by fiery gases, reappearing moments later when the air cleared.

Felicity held her breath as the rotating rock cake smashed into Millie's nose, depressing it further, before exploding into a thousand charcoal fragments. Millie shuddered, her barrel chest relaxed, dropped half an inch, then sprang open with a loud creak, ripping apart her multicoloured cardigan. Her chest doors swung wide, revealing a white-clothed bundle bound in rope. It teetered momentarily.

The crowd gulped.

"Catch him!" Felicity pointed at Basildon.

Her four catchers moved back and forth haphazardly,

struggling to keep the banner taut, while anticipating where Basildon would fall.

Millie shuddered violently, her chest dropped forward, spewing its contents. The trussed-up parcel plunged, just as a flame caught the fuse wire leading to Millie's head. The two passed each other at the puppet's waist. Bundled Basildon fell into the centre of the *Waste Not, Incinerator Not* banner seconds later, dragging its corner women closer together.

Seconds later, the sparking fuse reached Millie's head and fizzled out. A sonic boom pulsed through everyone's stomachs within a three-hundred-metre radius, pre-empting the largest firework explosion Mortiforde had ever seen. Colourful rockets shot high above the castle from the back of Millie's head, exploding in spherical, multicoloured, beautiful bursts. Mesmerising Catherine wheels spun from her eyes, and golden fountains showered sparks from each ear.

Burnt gunpowder and firework aromas filled the air. The crowd oohed and aahed, then applauded and cheered, while PCSO Marker used a penknife to cut the rope. When the last strands snapped, the white cloth unfurled, revealing Basildon, bald, half-naked, and bound further at the feet and ankles.

Felicity placed a finger on his neck and held her breath. Seconds later, she released it.

"He's alive."

Diya stared at the toy mouse she'd taken delivery of a few days ago and held it by the tip of its six-inch tail. She swung the mouse closer to Peredur. "*This* scares you?"

"Musophobia!" he screamed, cowering in the corner. "Fear of mice. Ever since—take it away!" His voice rose two octaves.

She swung the toy mouse in a circular motion and stepped closer to him.

Peredur squealed. "No! Please! I beg you!"

Courage coursed through her. The man who'd threatened her on Wednesday morning was cowering at her feet. She bent forward, teasing the toy mouse closer to his sniffling face.

Peredur shrieked and convulsed.

"Now you know how I felt on Wednesday morning, when you threatened me. You had no right to terrify me like that!" She stamped her foot.

Peredur's wide eyes fixed on the mouse, swinging inches from his face.

"But you don't scare me now." Diya stood upright. "When I was little, Nani Nagma always said, *Satyameva Jayate*. It's Sanskrit for *truth alone triumphs*. The email you sent in my name was a lie, but tonight, truth will triumph." She wagged a finger at him. "You can't bully me anymore."

She winked at Daniel. "If you don't leave this tank and the Tugford Estate in the next five seconds, I'm going to shove this mouse down your trousers so fast—"

Peredur's fear propelled him out of the tank so quickly he barely touched it.

Daniel jumped onto the driver's seat and watched Peredur flee. "Flipping heck! He's shot off down the lane towards town." He peered down at Diya. "You did it, Diya. You scared him off." He checked behind him. "And Tugford Hall is still standing."

Abigail's white Audi coupe approached the council offices slowly. She'd nipped home to change into her most authoritative-looking, two-piece royal blue trouser suit, and as she drove around the perimeter road, her smile extended to a grin. The Director of Highways had surpassed himself. Spotlighted by the streetlights and parked nose-to-tail tight against the perimeter fence and hedges, were diggers, drain-unblocking trucks, and dozens of dustcarts.

But something wasn't right. Crowds were gathering around the council's main entrance. They were yelling and punching angry fists in the air. Abigail pulled over into a space on the other side of the road.

"There she is!" bellowed one woman. "Calls a public meeting, then stops the public from entering!" Jeers and catcalls travelled through the evening's darkness.

Abigail avoided them and strutted towards the perimeter, looking for the gates, but as she drew closer, a streetlight illuminated the problem. Two dustcarts, parked cabin-to-cabin, blocked the main gates. Suddenly, an arm from near a dustcart rear grabbed her and pulled her into the semi-darkness.

"Thank goodness you're here."

"Richard?" She dazzled him with her phone's torchlight. "Why are there two dustcarts blocking the council entrance?"

Richard sighed. "I was categorical, Abigail, you must believe me. 'Do not block the council gates', I instructed. I couldn't have made it any clearer."

Abigail lowered her phone. "The autopsy can come later. Get these two dustcarts moved! We can't have a public meeting if the public can't get in! This'll be a disaster."

"I can't," Richard hissed. "The drivers have gone home with the keys. They made it quite clear they weren't hanging around unless they were getting paid overtime, and you mentioned nothing about relaxing budgetary rules to cover overtime expenditure. By the time I got here, the drivers had disappeared."

Abigail seethed. "Call them, and point out that I'm more than happy to sack those who won't come back."

"I tried that. They're not answering their phones." He paused. "Well, not to me, anyway."

The crowd was burgeoning now that Mortiforde Millie's

fireworks were over, further fuelling the agitation and anger. Their chanting echoed around. "Let us in! Let us in!"

Abigail ran one hand through her tousled hair while the other selected Lisa's office number. "Please still be in the office." She crossed the fingers still entangled in her hair. Moments later, Lisa answered. "Thank heavens," she blurted before Lisa could speak.

"I thought you'd be in the council chamber by now."

"So did I," Abigail muttered. "Nobody can get in. I need you to find someone in Highways who can access the Highways Drivers' WhatsApp group."

"Okay. What message are we sending?" A retractable pen clicked in preparation.

Abigail rubbed her forehead. Threatening mass sackings now wouldn't work. The drivers had the upper hand, and time was of the essence. "Offer a two-hundred-pound Christmas bonus in this month's wages to the first two drivers who can get here within the next ten minutes. Got that?"

"I'll text you when it's done. Bye."

Abigail waved her phone at Richard. "Those bonus payments are coming off your salary."

Aldermaston pushed against the Market Square's oncoming crowd, now heading towards the NAF, as he made his way towards Mortiforde Millie's smouldering remains. He reached the crowd barriers to find Felicity and her Ladies' Legion members surrounding a near-naked bald man being assessed by two volunteer St John Ambulance medics.

"He's badly shaken," Felicity began. "The medics are checking him over."

Basildon looked up. "Hello, Old Bean. It seems I was nearly toast."

Aldermaston jumped the barriers and hugged his half-brother. Basildon screamed. Aldermaston released his grip.

A medic twisted Basildon around and spotted some bruising on his back. "Broken ribs, probably. You need a hospital." He grabbed his radio and put in the ambulance request.

"We could have got you out earlier if that flipping puppeteer hadn't dropped the rod and dashed off clutching his bottom earlier," Aldermaston explained. "Millie veered off just as we tried pressing her nose."

Basildon chewed his lip. "So it *was* my box of Milk Tray on the table then."

Aldermaston nodded to Felicity. "Did he hit his head when he fell?"

"Subversive distraction, Old Bean." Basildon tapped the side of his nose. "Spy tactic. Spike something with a potent dose of laxatives, and you never know when it might buy you some extra time." He winked. "I took the Commander a box of spiked chocolates a couple of days ago. He must have shared them with the troops."

Aldermaston shook his head. Only Basildon could inadvertently interfere with his own rescue. "You were right, by the way."

Basildon shivered. "About?"

The medic draped a red blanket over his shoulders.

"The Birth of BANG."

"Ah." Basildon nodded. "Been working on this for a while now."

Aldermaston thumbed behind him. "I'm sure all will become clear at tonight's NAF."

Felicity placed a hand on Aldermaston's forearm. "We ought to make a move."

Aldermaston's phone rang. "It's Daniel." He turned his back on them all as he answered it. "What's the damage?"

"There isn't any!" Daniel squealed. "Diya was brilliant! She frightened Peredur off with a toy mouse before he could do anything."

Aldermaston put a finger in his other ear. "Toy what?"

Daniel laughed. "We'll tell you later."

"What's that throbbing noise in the background?"

"Tank engine. Peredur started it. Needed it running to rotate the gun barrel."

"You're still at Tugford Hall? You need to get here quickly. The NAF starts soon."

Daniel tapped Diya on the shoulder. "Come on, we need to go."

Diya stared at the tank's controls. "How do we switch off the engine? We can't leave it running, can we?"

Daniel randomly pushed buttons. "Nothing's happening!"

"We'll have to drive it." Diya jumped into the driver's seat.

"What?"

"We'll go to the council offices in this. It can't be that difficult to drive."

Before he could say anything else, Diya released the brake lever and pushed the accelerator with her foot. The engine clattered noisily. She nodded up at the hatch. "You'll have to direct," she yelled above the revving engine. "I can't see much through that." She pointed to a small peephole ahead.

Daniel poked his head through the top hatch. "Head straight. We need to clear the gates first." He watched Diya push both track levers in unison.

The tank lurched forward violently. Daniel braced himself as he peered into the darkness. He checked back inside, banging his head several times as the tank kangarooed forward. "Headlamps," he shouted. "We need light." He scanned the interior and spotted a panel of switches. "Try those to your right."

Diya worked across the panel, flicking each switch up, pausing briefly to assess the action, then flicking it back down again. She hit the jackpot on the second row.

"That's it!" Daniel screamed. Then he saw a tree only metres away. "Right! Turn right!" he bellowed through the hatch.

Diya retracted the right lever so quickly that the tank rotated two complete circles.

"Stop! Now straight," he ordered, still half dizzy.

The left caterpillar track swung into action again, and the tank lurched forward along the narrow lane.

"Why's everyone outside?" Kitty commented as the Ladies' Legion, Felicity, and Aldermaston hurried along Watling Street towards the council offices.

Aldermaston was in awe. Had the whole town turned up for Abigail's NAF? Chants of "Let us in! Let us in!" wafted towards them.

Aldermaston spotted Abigail lurking in the shadows beside two dustcarts further round the council's perimeter fence. "Back in a moment," he whispered to Felicity.

He took a circuitous route away from the crowds, then double-backed, using the dustcarts' shadows to conceal him. Abigail's exasperated tone penetrated the darkness.

"Having their tea? Didn't you mention the bonus?" Pause. "Oh, for f—"

"Everything all right?" Aldermaston hoped he didn't sound too flippant.

Abigail continued, "Lisa, up the bonus to three hundred pounds, then call me as soon as anyone responds." She finished the call and forced a smile. "Lord Mortiforde. So pleased you could make it."

He gestured to the expanding crowd. "As did most of the town, it seems." He pointed towards the gates. "Shall we go in?"

Abigail retreated into the shadows. "BANG threatened to storm the NAF, so I ordered a ring of steel around the council offices. Two dustcart drivers had insufficient brain cells to comprehend that blocking the main gates would mean nobody could access the building for tonight's meeting. They're now having their tea and—" She peered over Aldermaston's shoulder. "Oh, heck!"

The clomping of rhythmic marching boots pounding the tarmac crescendoed, overpowering the gathered crowd's hysteria. "Left—left—left, right, left!"

A company of camouflage-uniformed soldiers wearing green balaclavas trooped towards them. The crowd parted, slowly at first, then quicker when they realised the soldiers weren't stopping for anyone.

"Well, if we can't get in, neither can they!" Abigail stormed towards the approaching army.

Aldermaston hurried after her.

"Stop!" Abigail waved her hands in the air.

"Present arms!" yelled the leading soldier.

In unison, the platoon dropped their shoulder-resting machine guns into battle-ready positions.

The leading soldier flung his free arm forward and yelled, "CHARGE!"

One hundred pairs of army boots pounded the tarmac as the men rushed towards the blockading dustcarts.

Abigail screamed and spun round, colliding with Aldermaston. "Run! They're storming the building!"

∼

"Diya, slow down!" Daniel braced his arms against the tank's open hatch as they ploughed their way along Watling Street. The road narrowed near the brow of the hill, so the three-storey Georgian buildings lining both sides drew closer, further emphasising their speed. Ahead, the residents' parked cars tightened the road gap further.

"The brake pedal doesn't work!" Diya screamed.

Daniel dropped through the hatch to see Diya's foot flat on the floor. "Pump it!"

Outside, a horn blared. Daniel jumped up to see a single-decker bus coming straight at them, headlamps flashing. "Left! Left!" he screamed to Diya.

The tank lurched left, hit a streetlamp, knocking it fifty degrees, causing it to flicker, and then continued along the pavement, sending pedestrians fleeing.

The bus careered past, horn still blaring.

"Right! Right!" Daniel yelled, encouraging Diya back onto the road. The tank's front corner clipped a parked moped, knocking it under the caterpillar tracks, crushing it.

"I'm pumping, but nothing's happening!" shrieked Diya as she pummelled the foot pedal while pulling the caterpillar track levers, sending the tank into a zigzagging course.

"Keep pumping," Daniel bellowed. He glanced up to check the road was clear. As they approached the brow of the hill, he realised that the gap between the parked cars lining both sides wasn't big enough. "Oh, bugger!"

Pedestrians looked on in horror. Car owners jumped into the road and waved their arms frantically, then panicked, and dashed for cover in doorways or down alleyways.

The tank veered right, then left, then right. It took seconds for the first small hatchback to crumple under the tank's weight. Daniel braced himself as the front of the tank rose a couple of feet, then crashed back down when the hatchback's roof collapsed. A driver hurled obscenities at them until ear-splitting screeches drowned them as the tank gouged a six-inch-wide channel along the length of his parked Audi SUV.

Daniel's teeth ached as metallic screeches pierced the evening air, and glass windscreens exploded as the unstoppable tank crushed each subsequent parked car. He grabbed his phone from his pocket. He needed to warn Aldermaston.

~

As Aldermaston and Abigail dashed away from the council offices, Aldermaston heard other noises. Metallic screeching noises. Suddenly, several cars came speeding towards them down Watling Street, horns blaring and headlamps flashing. Some veered to the roadside in panic, while others took any side road they could. People screamed. A new sense of panic found a toehold and spread rapidly among the fleeing crowd. The tarmac vibrated. A distant rumbling grew louder.

Abigail and Aldermaston snuck into a side alleyway.

"This isn't good," Abigail muttered.

The Dam Busters' theme tune rang out from Aldermaston's jacket pocket. The rumbling grew louder; the screams more penetrating. He grabbed his phone and answered it.

Daniel bellowed, "TELL THEM TO MOVE!"

"Why? What's go—"

"We're in the tank. Diya's driving, and the brakes don't work!" The line cut.

Tank? Brake failure? The rumbling grew louder. The ground shook. He remembered the oil patch on his driveway. Oh, heck. Aldermaston ran out into the road, waving his arms and shouting, "GET OUT OF THE WAY!"

The frightened crowd was momentarily dumbstruck, unsure of which way to run. Echoing screams pierced the night air.

Aldermaston glanced back at the dustcart barrier. A couple

of BANG's soldiers were on top of the vehicles, offering a helping hand to those still on the ground. Those waiting to climb up were now looking nervously over their shoulders at the approaching commotion. Those at the back panicked first, breaking ranks, scattering in all directions, leaping across parked car bonnets, over fences, and up street lamps.

Two large headlamps crested the hill as the recognisable outline of a tank careered towards them. With the gun barrel pointing behind it, it looked like it was reversing. Aldermaston squinted and saw Daniel standing up through the driver's hatch, waving his arms frenetically, encouraging everyone to move.

"Is this how BANG storms buildings?" Abigail grabbed Aldermaston's upper arm.

"Actually," he began, "this is your Head of Planning Finance arriving."

Abigail's eyes widened. "Diya?"

Aldermaston looked at the blockading dustcarts. The few soldiers standing on top now appreciated the predicament they were in. "I think Diya's about to earn a three-hundred-pound Christmas bonus."

Abigail's grip on Aldermaston's arm tightened as the tank hurtled past them at top speed. They watched Daniel drop back inside the tank, just as the remaining BANG soldiers abandoned their attack and hurled themselves off the dustcarts. The tank engine's scream caused Aldermaston to cover his ears.

Abigail thrust her face into Aldermaston's shoulder. "I can't look!"

BOOM!

Aldermaston's internal organs shuddered, and his legs wobbled as the ground shook. Two dustcarts danced, gyrating on the spot as the tank ploughed through them. Their rear ends collided with the tank's rear, flipping them onto their sides with another ground-shaking shudder and metal-scraping screeching. The tank's left track mounted the single security bollard centred in the council's entrance, forcing it up at an angle. Once it reached the point of no return, the tank toppled onto its side. Sparks pirouetted through the air as the tarmac driveway struggled to stop the tank's momentum, but eventually brought it to a halt outside the main entrance's revolving doors.

The crowds, who'd first run away from the council offices, now turned and made their way back. The few remaining BANG soldiers shot off towards The Nooseman's Knot.

Aldermaston and Abigail hurried towards the tank. Daniel crawled out of the driver's hatch first. Then he pulled out Diya. She stumbled to the ground, dropping her handbag. Daniel helped her to her feet, where she collected her handbag and threw it over her shoulder, successfully catching it for the first time.

CHAPTER TWENTY-FOUR

"Order! Order!" Abigail banged the tabletop.

Aldermaston switched off his phone and passed it to Daniel, sitting in the front row. Since his assistant had confirmed Tugford Hall was still standing, he'd messaged Cartwright to take Harry home.

"Order! Order!" Abigail yelled again, her gavel banging failed to silence the twice-than-legally permitted capacity crowd of nearly three hundred local citizens in the council chamber, all chanting "Waste Not, Incinerator Not." The air rocked with anger now that they'd finally made it inside the building.

Rosemary fidgeted in her seat beside Aldermaston, seemingly oblivious to the crowd's chants. Also at the top table were Abigail, Rupert Rinde, and Councillor Taplinski, who was shuffling through his agenda papers. Behind them were three chairs, where Norris Offermans and Diya sat, leaving one empty. Councillor Taplinski nodded to Lisa, standing by the curtained basement door. She winked at Aldermaston and then flicked the light switch.

The sudden darkness instantly killed the chanting, leaving a hushed murmur of panic.

"Thank you, Lisa," said Stefan. "Good evening, ladies and gentlemen," he continued, as the lights flickered on. "Welcome to tonight's Neighbourhood Area Forum meeting to discuss the proposed waste incinerator project on the Mortiforde Meadows."

The crowd, now dazzled by the returning lights, mumbled incoherently.

"I would like to thank the council's chief executive, Abigail Mayedew, for allowing the town to have this adult conversation."

"Conversation?" bawled someone from the back. "Diktat more like!"

"Hear, hear!" chanted another group. The crowd erupted into a raucous cacophony of jeers, boos, and hisses.

Stefan nodded to Lisa.

Darkness engulfed them again, subduing them long enough for Stefan's voice to penetrate the background hubbub.

"Ladies and gentlemen, you will have your opportunity to speak."

Lisa switched on the lights, then snuck into the empty chair behind Aldermaston and next to Diya.

Stefan continued. "I call upon Rupert Rinde, of Rinde Industries, to share the benefits a waste incinerator could produce for Mortiforde."

"It won't produce as much hot air as the council currently produces," yelled a woman near the front. A cheer echoed around the chamber.

Rupert grabbed the presentation clicker from Abigail and walked across to the laptop perched on a lectern at the end of the dais. The projector suspended from the ceiling woke, and an image of the waste incinerator appeared on the large screen on the wall behind them. The crowd booed and hissed.

"At present," Rupert began, "all non-recyclable household waste collected by this authority goes into landfill. That's a desecration of the local environment. It also produces atmospheric-warming greenhouse gases as it decays."

He clicked to the next slide, showing rubbish-burgeoning barges floating down the River Thames.

"Not only that, but many London authorities send their landfill abroad at enormous expense. We could burn it for them at a fraction of the cost they pay to send it abroad. Not only will the Mortiforde Incinerator burn all waste at such high temperatures, ensuring there are no greenhouse gases, but the incinerator will also produce electricity, providing cheap power for Mortiforde and the surrounding villages."

Rupert's next slide displayed two huge downward arrows pointing to bags of money. "This will lower electricity bills and local taxes. Everybody wins."

Stefan gestured to Rupert's seat. "Thank you, Mr Rinde, for that enlightening presentation. I have to be honest, I don't understand why anyone would be against lower electricity prices and lower tax bills."

"Not at the cost of the meadows!" one man bellowed.

Stefan jumped in quickly. "We'll now hear from Ms Sedgewick, the prospective parliamentary candidate for the Socially Liberal Conservative Party." He leaned forward and offered an encouraging smile.

Rosemary continued fidgeting with her fingers and thumbs.

Aldermaston elbowed her. "You're on!"

Startled, Rosemary looked at Stefan, who nodded again. She stood. "Er ... er. . ."

"Come on, love!" jeered an audience member. "You said you could quash this project. Now's your chance."

She sniffled.

Aldermaston noticed her teary eyes. "Are you okay?"

"For heaven's sake!" Abigail stood. "Ms Sedgewicke wants

you all to vote for her in the by-election because she claims she can save the Mortiforde Meadows. According to her, the council's funding is half a million pounds short. Well, let's sort this out once and for all, shall we? I call Mr Offermans from the National Audit Office to the stage." Abigail gestured to Norris.

He wandered over to the laptop.

"Mr Offermans," Stefan began, "please introduce yourself."

Norris faced the crowd. "I am Norris Offermans, an experienced auditor of thirty-two years, seven months, and six days, from the National Audit Office. I was called in to confirm the waste incinerator project's funding status."

"Who called you in?" Stefan asked.

"The National Audit Office operates an anonymous hotline. We respect that anonymity." He displayed his first presentation slide, a spreadsheet. "As of Wednesday night, these figures suggest a shortfall of half a million pounds in the proposed waste incinerator project."

The audience cheered.

Norris held up a finger. "However, further scrutiny of the council's financial system alerted me to the efforts being made by Diya Parmer, Head of Planning Finance, to raise funds via an online auction site."

"Online auctions?" Stefan twisted to look at Diya. "Surely that's against local authority regulations."

"On the contrary," Norris continued. "The National Audit Office commends the use of innovative fundraising methods. Online auctions allow market forces to determine the true value of local authority assets. Ms Parmer's council asset listings have raised a significant sum. I can reveal that, after deducting all necessary charges and fees collected by the online auction site, Ms Parmer raised the grand sum of. . ."

Norris pressed the clicker, and Diya's fundraising figure

appeared on the screen. The crowd's gasp sucked the presentation screen forward two inches.

"Four hundred and ninety-nine thousand, nine hundred and ninety-nine pounds and eighty-five pence," Norris enunciated.

Kitty called out from the front row. "Look, there's still a fifteen-pence shortfall!"

On the screen, the fifteen-pence discrepancy loomed large.

Stefan turned to Abigail. "Seems Diya Parmer has failed to balance this project's books."

Lisa squeezed Diya's hand.

Norris held up his finger again. "It was the fifteen-pence discrepancy that led me to Ms Parmer's innovative fundraising efforts."

His next slide displayed a long list of financial transactions. "I want to bring the audience's attention to these two figures here." Using the presentation clicker's red laser light, he highlighted two transactions.

Diya's hands clasped the top of her head.

"This is Democracy Support's General Miscellaneous Irreconcilable Sundry Credit account. These two transactions are from the online auction site. It's a verification check," Norris continued. "The online auction site pays two micro-payments into the bank account , which only the legitimate account holder can confirm." He turned to face the protesting congregation. "As you can see, one payment is for nine pence, and the second is for six pence. A total of fifteen pence. I consider these payments to be legitimate income for the waste incinerator project."

Norris clicked to the next slide. "Once added to all the other funds generated by the auction, you'll see that as of five o'clock this evening, I, Norris Offermans of the National Audit Office, hereby declare the waste incinerator project fully funded ... to the penny."

The roar of three hundred angry citizens caused the council chamber roof to shudder.

~

Leaning against the wall outside the council chamber's doors, Peredur stifled a giggle as he listened to the events unfolding inside. The chamber doors shuddered at the crowd's reaction to Norris Offerman's funding announcement. Peredur dropped his Guido Fawkes mask over his camouflage-painted face, pulled a starting pistol from a holster under his camouflage jacket, and held it aloft.

"Time to make an entrance," he whispered, barging in through the double doors.

~

Aldermaston stared in disbelief at the unfolding riot. Arms flailed, feet kicked, teeth bit, and fingers pinched, while placards and posters hurtled through the air.

"You lied!" one angry man bellowed, pointing at Rosemary. "You said you'd stop this!" The crowd turned on her, chanting, "Liar! Liar!"

An ear-splitting crack of gunfire sent everyone dropping to their knees and hiding behind chairs.

"Well, well, well, what have we here?" The interloper strode towards the dais in camouflage gear, army boots, and a Guido Fawkes face mask. "If it isn't the Establishment in all its glory."

Aldermaston peered above the tabletop and watched the armed intruder wave a pistol above his head. Rosemary gasped, her eyes locked onto the man strutting towards them. Peredur was here. Aldermaston glanced at Rosemary. She seemed to realise who he was.

"Security! Escort this man off the premises immediately!" Abigail flung her arm in his direction, desperately scanning the crowds for any security personnel.

PCSO Marker pushed through the crowds. "Stand still! Put your hands up!"

Peredur chuckled. "Or what?"

Ceri held a small CS spray canister at arm's length. Peredur whipped out a taser from his trouser-knee pocket. "This outranks yours."

"Whoa!" Aldermaston darted between them, holding up placatory hands. "Let's calm down." He turned to Ceri. "Put the CS spray down."

Her eyes remained fixed on Peredur's taser as she returned the canister to her holster.

Aldermaston turned to Peredur. "Your turn now, Peredur."

Peredur sneered. "I'll keep it close, thanks. After twenty-six years of being shafted by the State, one learns not to believe a word the Establishment says."

Aldermaston directed the crowd's attention to Peredur. "Ladies and gentlemen, this is Peredur Geraint Jones, leader of BANG, Borderlandshire Against Nefarious Government. He's why we're all here tonight. Isn't that right, Peredur?"

Tears cascaded down Rosemary's face.

Peredur whipped off his Guido Fawkes mask and clapped mockingly. "You've done your homework, Aldermaston."

Aldermaston picked up the presentation clicker from the top table, nodded to Lisa, and then turned to the crowd. "All this," he gestured, "has never been about the waste incinerator project. Because *there is no* waste incinerator project."

"Poppycock!" Abigail snorted. "Since I arrived at the Authority six weeks ago, this project has been the closest it's been to getting off the ground. And as Mr Offermans has confirmed, it is a fully funded project."

Lisa woke the laptop, and the overhead projector splashed a new image of a park home site onto the screen.

"Some might say," Aldermaston continued, "this waste incinerator story began five years ago, when the council rejected Farmer Bell's planning application for Mortside Park Homes."

Peredur crossed his arms. "You *have* been busy, Aldermaston." He turned to the crowd. "He's not as thick as his older half-brother. How is he, by the way? Had a lucky escape, it seems." He paced to the opposite end of the dais. Ceri backed away. Peredur turned to the projector screen. "Show us what you have, then."

Aldermaston clicked on a map showing the Mortiforde Meadows, the River Morte, and some fields opposite, outlined in red. He highlighted them using the laser light.

"Farmer Bell owned these fields, and five years ago he submitted a planning application to site forty-five park homes here," Aldermaston began. "This would have been Borderlandshire's first park home site. For someone like Peredur here, a twenty-one-year-old young man desperate to buy his own home in his local town, this was a potential step onto the housing ladder. But the council rejected Farmer Bell's planning application."

"All because of that man there!" Peredur stormed across to Rupert and dragged him to his feet. He pulled back a fist.

Rupert braced himself. "What? This has nothing to do with me!"

Peredur released his grip, dropping Rupert to the floor, and laughed. "You and I both know that's not true."

Aldermaston moved onto the next slide, showing the minutes from the Highways Drainage (Seepage and Sewerage) Improvement Planning Sub Group.

"Our local estate agent, Gerald Lockmount," he continued, "gave evidence at this committee, claiming forty-five park homes would put excessive pressure on Birrington Road's drainage system. Based on that information, the committee recommended rejecting the application unless Farmer Bell could meet the extortionate, several-hundred-thousand-pound cost of upgrading Birrington Road's drainage system. Unsurprisingly, he couldn't."

Aldermaston paced the dais, getting into his stride. "Without the service-fee income these park homes could have generated, Farmer Bell opted to sell these fields." He turned to the crowd. "Which agency do you think he approached?"

"Lockmounts!" they chorused.

"Exactly. Mortiforde's one-and-only estate agency is involved in *every* property transaction." Aldermaston moved on to the next slide. A spreadsheet appeared on the screen.

"Since Gerald's murder," he continued, "it's come to light that he and another party have been abusing this monopoly. Picture the scene. Farmer Bell instructs Gerald Lockmount to sell those fields. Along comes Rupert Rinde—"

A series of boos and hisses rang out from the crowd.

"—who offers Farmer Bell one hundred and twenty thousand pounds *less* than the asking price."

A deeper series of boos rumbled round the council chamber.

"It's business," Rupert jeered. "He didn't have to accept that price."

"Didn't he, Mr Rinde?" Aldermaston stared at him. "Even five years ago, there were rumours of the meadows being a potential site for a proposed waste incinerator project. Who'd want to buy fields next to a potential waste incinerator site? What farmer would want to grow food on fields next to a waste incinerator, chucking out toxic fumes into the air?"

"Objection!" Abigail stood. "The incinerator burns the material at such high temperatures that there are no fumes."

Aldermaston turned to the crowd. "Do we believe that?"

"NO!" they chorused.

"But this is where Gerald Lockmount and Rupert Rinde's little wheeze comes into play. You see, when anyone else made an offer for the fields, Gerald Lockmount failed to pass it on to Farmer Bell. Instead, he told the prospective buyer that their offer had been rejected. Unaware of this, Farmer Bell assumed nobody was interested in his land."

Rupert pointed at Aldermaston. "That's slander! Say any more and I'll see you in court."

"But on Wednesday morning," Aldermaston continued, "comes the announcement that the council's funding is in place, making the likelihood of an incinerator on the meadows seem even greater. Farmer Bell felt he had little choice but to accept Rupert's derisory below-value offer."

Aldermaston directed the laser pointer at a line in the spreadsheet on the screen. "And this line here shows Farmer Bell's land was valued at a quarter of a million, but he agreed to sell for one hundred and thirty thousand. To recompense Gerald for his lost commission, Rupert paid Gerald an additional twenty-five thousand on top of his standard estate agency commission on the price, directly into one of Gerald's personal accounts."

Another collective boo echoed around the chamber.

"So Rupert bought the Mortside fields at a bargain price, and Gerald earned more than he would have had the land been sold at true market value."

Rupert waved a dismissive hand. "A bloody spreadsheet proves nothing."

"Gerald's secretary found this spreadsheet on his laptop," Aldermaston clarified. "She's confirmed that the figures in the sales column match the figures you paid for all these land purchases."

Peredur pulled a thumb drive from his camouflage pocket and waved it at Rupert. "That spreadsheet looks remarkably similar to the one I found in your office, labelled LHI Initiative."

Rupert stood so quickly his chair flew backwards. "I'm not stopping here to be insulted by morons who—"

"Hold it right there, buster!" Ceri hurtled across the stage, clutching her CS spray. "I'm arresting you for conspiracy to defraud, bribery, and corruption—"

"Naff off, you nincompoop!" Rupert sneered.

Ceri lunged, and a burst of CS spray flew towards Rupert's face.

He screamed, shielding his face with his hands, and crumpled to the ground.

Abigail grabbed a water bottle from the table and poured some into his eyes.

"She's blinded me!" Rupert screamed. "I'll sue the constabulary."

Peredur smirked, then paced the stage. "But, Aldermaston, do you know why Mr Rinde wanted Farmer Bell's land?"

Ceri clicked her fingers with her free hand and pointed at Peredur. "It's Lord Mortiforde to you."

Peredur sneered. "Titles are designed to keep the little people in their place. He's no better than me."

Aldermaston clicked on the next presentation slide. "If we go back to the map, you'll see these two fields next to Farmer Bell's land have no access to Birrington Road. Strange then, that Rupert's newly acquired fields are part of a planning application submitted by Castle Ridge Properties Limited, to build a gated community of ten luxury properties."

Abigail stared at the screen, perplexed.

Aldermaston clicked through a selection of architect's drawings, illustrating these substantial properties overlooking Mortiforde Meadows and the castle. "These properties would have the best views in Borderlandshire."

"That's ridiculous!" Abigail scoffed. "Nobody would buy a luxury house overlooking a waste incinerator."

Peredur clasped his forehead dramatically and threw his head back. "Do you want to tell her, Aldermaston, or shall I?"

Abigail stared at Aldermaston. "Tell me what?"

Aldermaston wandered towards Rupert. "Mr Rinde has no intention of building a waste incinerator on the meadows. Ironically, like everyone here, he, too, doesn't want to see the meadows built on. It'll ruin the view of his prestigious gated community development."

He pointed the laser at the screen behind them. "Without Farmer Bell's fields, his luxury gated community has no road access. The Castle Ridge development is pointless without access to Birrington Road. This project cannot proceed without Farmer Bell's fields. So what better way to get them at a knockdown price than to propose building a waste incinerator right next door?"

A red-eyed Rupert thumped the tabletop. "This is preposterous! I know nothing about this Castle Ridge development. Who are the developers?"

"Castle Ridge Properties Limited." Aldermaston pointed to Lisa. "Let's check the Companies House website, shall we?"

Lisa brought up the website and found the entry for Castle Ridge Properties Limited.

"Under the *People* heading," Aldermaston continued, "we can see who its directors are."

Rosemary shuffled to the end of the dais, her eyes focused on her feet.

Peredur blocked her exit. "We're just getting to the best bit. Back in your seat now!"

She trembled, turned without looking up, and returned to her seat.

"First, there's this name—" Aldermaston waited for Lisa to

scroll down the screen. The crowd gasped when they saw Gerald Lockmount's name appear.

Peredur put his hands on his hips. "Mr Lockmount is what one would call a sleeping partner. We all know who was calling the shots, don't we, Mr Rinde?"

"You've got no evidence of that!"

Lisa continued scrolling, and the crowd's gasp doubled in volume when the name *Rosemary Rinde-Sedgewicke* appeared.

Abigail smacked the table. "What's the meaning of this?" She turned to Rosemary. "You cannot be a company director without council approval. And," she pointed to the screen, "hyphenating your name to avoid the authority's checks and balances implies criminality!"

Peredur faced the agitated crowd, arms outstretched. "Do you get it now?" he bellowed. "This is what BANG has been campaigning against for years! This is how the nefarious Establishment works against us little people all the time. These people," he pointed to the top table, "have ridden roughshod over us for years. They've concocted a lie about a waste incinerator being built on the meadows. They tricked Farmer Bell into selling his land for less than its true market value by convincing the planning department to reject his plan for affordable homes."

He paced the dais' edge. "This town doesn't need a gated community! It needs affordable housing for local people."

"Hear, hear!" cheered the crowd.

"And the woman who has been campaigning for your votes," Peredur bellowed, "telling you she'll save the meadows from the waste incinerator that we now know *was never going to happen*, is behind one of the biggest luxury developments this county has ever seen."

Peredur stamped his feet in rage. "Not only is she colluding with that man over there to hoodwink you all into believing the meadows were at stake, but she was also using the opportunity to secure a role as your local Member of Parliament. She wants you to give her even more power!" Peredur prodded his chest with his finger. "And people think I'm deluded!"

Abigail strode across the stage and grabbed Peredur's arm. "I've had enough of your false accusations—"

"Accusations?" Peredur pulled his arm from her grip. "You've not been in this town for two minutes, and yet you're happy to destroy it. You think we're country bumpkins who don't understand the world. But it's *you*," Peredur prodded her shoulder, "who has no idea who you're dealing with." He pointed to Rupert. "You thought he was a respectable businessman!"

Abigail glanced at Rupert. "Mr Rinde knows business."

Peredur threw his head back and laughed. "That man over there," he pointed to Rupert, "paid me to kill Sir Hugo."

A wave of shock exploded through the gathered crowd.

Peredur continued pacing. "Yes! Kill his own father! Sir Hugo wanted to stand as the town's MP, but Rupert wanted to make sure the Socially Liberal Conservative Party selected Rosemary as their candidate. So he got me to bump off Sir Hugo."

"What?" Rosemary suddenly awoke from her stupor. She clasped her mouth, mumbled about feeling sick, then bent over and threw up in a nearby wastepaper bin.

Ceri pointed at Rupert. "I'm arresting you for conspiracy to murder," then turned to Peredur and said, "and you for the murder of Sir—"

Aldermaston grabbed her arm. "Not yet," he whispered. "There's more to come."

Peredur continued. "As Director of Finance, Rosemary knew the council didn't have enough money for the waste incinerator project. So, their plan was simple. Bump off Sir Hugo, make out the waste incinerator project was ready to go ahead. . ." He turned to Abigail. "That was me, by the way. I sent the email from Diya's email account saying the money was all there." He pointed to Rupert but looked at the crowd. "Something else he asked me to do. He needed the threat to look genuine. How else would Farmer Bell finally sell out to him?"

Abigail shot a horrified look in Rupert's direction.

Peredur waved at Abigail. "Sorry, I haven't introduced myself, have I? I'm Peredur Jones, IT Helpdesk support. I also put Diya on annual leave for two weeks."

He turned to Felicity, cleared his throat, and in a falsetto voice, two octaves higher than his usual voice, said, "I heard Sir Hugo at the Ladies' Legion meeting when he granted them use of the meadows for their environmental burial scheme. I'd already helped myself to a dagger from your armoury. The man didn't know what hit him."

He coughed, and his voice returned to normal. "Throwing his body in the recycling waste bin has a certain irony, don't you think?"

"So it wasn't an accident?" PC Norten scratched the back of his head.

Peredur turned towards the crowd again. "So who killed Gerald Lockmount?" He pointed to himself, then to Rupert. "He told me to. Gerald threatened to go to the police, exposing all of this, unless Rupert paid him more money. But Gerald had served his purpose by now, so Mr Rinde paid me to move him up the housing ladder to that grand estate in the sky."

The NAF audience shifted uncomfortably in their seats as they comprehended what was happening.

Aldermaston spotted Lisa recording the confession on her phone. PCSO Ceri Marker handed the CS spray to PC Norten, then slipped the handcuffs from her belt. "Rupert Rinde, I'm arresting you for—"

It was now or never. Aldermaston grabbed Peredur's shoulder with one hand while pulling a handkerchief from his jacket breast pocket with his other. "I said earlier that this goes back five years to Farmer Bell's original park home site proposal. But it doesn't, does it, Peredur? This story really goes back twenty-five, sorry, twenty-six years."

Before Peredur could answer, Aldermaston dabbed the handkerchief with his tongue, grabbed Peredur's chin, and wiped the camouflage paint from above his left eye. He pointed to it. "That birthmark above your left eyebrow is why we're *really* here."

Peredur grinned.

Aldermaston clicked to the presentation's next slide, and the *Powys Gazette* newspaper cutting filled the screen. "Twenty-six years ago, someone abandoned a baby at a household waste site in Knighton." He pointed the laser at the screen and circled it near the baby's head. "If you look closely, there's a small red birthmark above the left eyebrow. Just like yours. Happy birthday, by the way."

Rupert scrambled to his feet, his hands in cuffs, and stared at the screen. "I don't understand."

A baffled murmur swept through the gathered crowd.

Aldermaston addressed the crowd. "This is the story of an angry little boy."

"No!" Peredur snapped. "It's about them." He pointed at the top table. "They're socially cleansing Mortiforde!" He pulled out his eviction notice from his jacket pocket and waved it in the air. "Today, my landlord evicted me from my home. A place I've lived for over five years, since I left the so-called care of social services. *My* home. A no-fault eviction!" He waved his eviction notice at the crowd. "And why am I being evicted?" He spun around and pointed at Rosemary. "Because my landlord is standing for Parliament and needs the money. Isn't that right … MUMMY!"

An audible gasp echoed around the council chamber.

"I didn't know you were my tenant!" Rosemary collapsed

to the floor, wailing, as her outstretched hands begged contact with her long-lost son.

~

Rupert strutted awkwardly towards Rosemary. "Is this true?"

"My baby!" Rosemary screamed.

"Back off!" snapped Peredur.

Rosemary cowered against the floor. "I didn't know what to do," she blubbered.

Peredur's face flushed through its camouflage paint. "As soon as you saw this," he pointed to his birthmark, "nothing could hide the fact that Rupert Rinde is my father."

Rupert edged closer along the dais, his cuffed hands outstretched. "You knew I was your father, yet said nothing?" He stared at Peredur's birthmark. "That's why you wore the Guido Fawkes mask every time we met!"

Rosemary snivelled. "I was in an awful place after your birth. I didn't know what to do. That birthmark meant I couldn't leave you anywhere in Borderlandshire. The authorities would have traced your identity within hours." She pointed an accusatory finger at Rupert. "He would have ruined your life. He doesn't know how to love."

"No! You *both* ruined my life." Peredur backed away from her. "All this," he waved his arms around the council chamber, "is because you don't care about people. You're as bad as each other. Power and deals are what you love." He pointed to Rupert. "You want to build extravagant houses only the rich can afford, pushing out the lower classes, and you," he directed his finger at Rosemary, "want to be a politician for the power it gives you."

Abigail stormed around the table. "This is clearly a family matter that needs resolving in private."

"Private?" Peredur growled. "You don't get it, do you? You

all created this mess by working secretly. My father and Gerald Lockmount worked privately to rig the housing market in Mortiforde. My mother and father worked privately to get her elected to Parliament. Everyone in a position of power ends up abusing that power."

Abigail placed her hands on her hips. "You're the one hijacking a public meeting!"

Peredur guffawed. "Who blockaded the meadows before this so-called public consultation?" He waved his finger in a circular motion, high above his head. "Who put a ring of steel around this building? This NAF is naff! This isn't a consultation exercise. It's a sham. You'd already decided the scheme would proceed, because it makes you lots of money."

"I make no personal gain from this project," Abigail yelled. "But it could bring in a substantial income for the council."

"Yeah, and once the money's rolling in," Peredur sneered, "who'll be asking for a substantial pay rise?"

"There's nothing wrong with performance-related pay!" Abigail snapped.

Peredur stepped closer. "There is if a bully rides roughshod over the local townsfolk to force a project through in the first place!" He stuck two fingers up at her, then faced the crowd, arms outstretched.

"Ladies and gentlemen," he bellowed. "It's Bonfire Night. Back in 1605, Guy Fawkes tried blowing up the Establishment when it ignored the will of its people."

Peredur pulled a box of matches from his chest pocket, selected one, and struck it. His eyes widened as the flame exploded into life. Then he wandered across the dais, holding aloft the burning match. "Guy Fawkes placed thirty-six barrels of gunpowder under the Houses of Parliament, hoping to blow it sky high, killing the politicians and the attending royal family. He only failed because the authorities caught him before he had time to light the match."

He held the flame just below the fuse wire dangling above him. Within seconds, it flashed into life, spitting sparks across the dais. Peredur beamed at the crowd. "Where Guy Fawkes failed, Peredur succeeds."

Aldermaston hurled across the council chamber and smashed the nearest fire alarm.

Peredur erupted into a fit of manic laughter. "You have five minutes to escape before this reaches the gunpowder I put in the basement."

Outside the council offices, Aldermaston checked his watch. "If his five-minute threat is accurate, the building is going to go up any minute now."

Felicity peered over his shoulder. "Are we safe here?"

Shielded by Abigail's encircling dustcart barrier, they watched as the final straggling members of the public, assisted by council officials, crossed the council car park and escaped past the tank. Once off the premises, most of the crowd hung around, intrigued about what might happen next.

"That Peredur was angry, wasn't he?" Cordelia commented.

"What do you expect?" said Kitty. "Rupert Rinde was his father. Temperament is genetic. I euthanise any bad-tempered animal on my farm. They're not safe to have around."

Daniel herded the remaining stragglers to safety. "I think that's everyone." He looked back over his shoulder.

Fire engine sirens approached from Watling Street. Abigail stepped closer to Aldermaston and Lisa. "Anyone seen Rupert? Or his son?"

Rosemary gasped. "They're still inside!"

Aldermaston stood on tiptoes to peer above the crowd, but it was difficult to—

BANG!

The ground shuddered. Dustcarts rocked violently. Screams pierced the air as the shockwave blasted everyone to the ground.

A huge mushroom-shaped fireball billowed into the night sky above the council offices, illuminating the entire town.

Rosemary dropped to her knees. "My son is in there!" A guttural scream escaped from deep within her.

A loud screech pierced the air as a rocket shot high into the sky, then exploded into a ball of golden glitter.

"Ooooh," went the crowd, followed by light applause.

Seconds later, another rocket screeched high above them, detonating into a sphere of blinking blue brilliance. The crowd crooned with an "Ahhhhh."

Abigail clasped her hands to her head as she took in the wreckage and devastation. "The council offices have been annihilated."

Kneeling on the tarmac, Rosemary released another gruff scream. Her outstretched hands grabbed at charred ashes and debris raining down on them.

Aldermaston's eyebrows arched as he turned to Abigail. "I don't think she'll get many votes in the by-election. She might want her old job back."

Abigail grabbed Diya's arm. "Diya Parmer, I hereby promote you to Acting Director of Finance for Borderlandshire District Council. Your steadfast determination to resolve the funding issue throughout this entire debacle shows your unwavering loyalty to this organisation. There'll have to be a proper interview, but the job's yours, anyway. What do you say?"

"Thank you, Ms Mayedew!" Diya beamed. She turned to Aldermaston and hugged him. "Thank you, Your Lordship. I couldn't have done any of this without your support."

"I'm sure Nani Nagma will be delighted when you give her the good news."

Abigail stared at the burning flames now licking the upper troposphere. "Not sure how far that half a million pounds will stretch to rebuild these offices."

Aldermaston's stomach twisted. "Yeah, about that. You're watching it go up in smoke."

Abigail did a double-take. "What?"

He pointed to the burning council offices. "All the items Diya listed on the auction site were in the basement. With no items, the auctions are null and void."

A scattergun of cracks and squeals echoed through the air as a further series of fireworks exploded.

"Oh, for heaven's sake!" Abigail howled. "Why does everything go wrong around here?"

Aldermaston and Felicity suddenly turned to one another. "Councillor Prendeghast!"

"What about him?" Abigail enquired.

Aldermaston winced. "He's in the basement, too. We put him there last night until we could rebury him in the meadows."

Lisa giggled. "He always said he wanted his ashes interred in the building he'd spent most of his life in."

Aldermaston stroked his chin. "If you're looking for a positive, there is something you could do, Abigail."

"Anything," Abigail insisted. "Some good has to come out of this awful mess."

Aldermaston pointed to the dustcarts. "You could always empty the dustcarts' contents onto the burning council offices. It would save it from going to landfill. It's not quite the incinerator you had planned. But here in Mortiforde, Abigail, we do things differently."

CHAPTER TWENTY-FIVE

Aldermaston smiled at Stella Osgathorpe sitting across the table in Tugford Hall's armoury. Two days had passed since the Bonfire Night events, and the Borderers Guild had joined with Isabel Rinde and the Ladies' Legion to witness this historic moment for the town. Abigail sat huddled in a corner, arms crossed, checking her watch every ten seconds. Her expression competed with that of the dour woman in the Gainsborough painting that Cartwright had finally returned to its rightful place on the wall.

"And you're happy for the Ladies' Legion to continue using the Mortiforde Meadows as an environmentally friendly burial site?" Aldermaston asked.

Stella beamed. "Of course." She looked along the table at Felicity and the other ladies. "Such deferential respect will only enhance the natural beauty of the meadows and the surrounding castle landscape. And Lord Mortiforde's signing over of the meadows to the Historic Borders Agency allows us to decree them inalienable, thus protecting them for the townsfolk forever. You're righting a wrong, Your Lordship."

"It's the right thing to do *now*," he clarified. He nodded to Bartholomew Brazonby.

The solicitor slid two copies of the document across to Aldermaston and handed him a pen. "To transfer ownership of the meadows from yourself to the Historic Borders Agency, I just need you to sign here, here, and here, on both copies."

Aldermaston signed with a flourish.

Brazonby slid another document and a pen to Stella. "And Ms Osgathorpe, if you could sign where the tag indicates on this document, this will formalise the agreement between the Historic Borders Agency and the Ladies' Legion, allowing them to use the site as an environmentally friendly burial ground in perpetuity."

He passed another document to Felicity. "And if I could ask Your Ladyship to sign this copy of the document on behalf of *Verdant Endings* and the Ladies' Legion."

Daniel slipped to the end of the table and held aloft his smartphone. "I think this historic moment calls for a photo. Smile!"

Everyone affixed ceremonious grins on their faces. Applause followed the click of the captured image as Aldermaston, Felicity, and Stella passed the signed documents back to Mr Brazonby. Aldermaston slipped a copy to Lisa, sitting behind him.

"Congratulations, Your Ladyship," Barnaby began. "Mortiforde now has its first official green burial ground." He turned to Stella. "And once we've completed the paperwork, the Mortiforde Meadows will be inalienable."

Further applause echoed around the room.

Aldermaston turned to Isabel, sitting at the other end of the table. "I hope Sir Hugo would approve."

She smiled. "I'm sure that's why he left the meadows to you." She sighed. "I wish he were here to help me sort Rupert's legacy. You never imagine having to sort out your son's funeral, let alone your grandson's, too. Had Peredur not perished with Rupert in the explosion, he'd have had a legitimate claim on Knowton Manor. Rather ironic for someone who struggled to find somewhere in this town to live." She sighed. "They both broke the law, and they paid the ultimate price."

"What will you do with Knowton Manor?" Aldermaston enquired.

She wrinkled her nose. "I might convert it into small one- and two-bedroomed apartments, suitable for local people, charging at an affordable rent based on the local wages. It could become Peredur's legacy. I didn't agree with his motives, but ultimately, his heart was in the right place."

Aldermaston nodded. "I may do something similar with the stone barn."

Abigail raised a hand. "Mrs Rinde, I wonder if I might have a word, please?"

Isabel stood and slipped on her coat. "How can I help?"

Abigail chewed her lip. "The council is desperate for some temporary accommodation while the insurance company sorts out rebuilding the offices. The staff are working from home. Who knows how many are watching daytime television when they should be working? Anyway," she continued, avoiding Aldermaston's gaze, "Knowton Manor has sufficient space for the council's core officers temporarily, if you'd consider renting it to us on a short-term lease." She gestured to Barnaby Brazonby. "I'm sure your solicitor could draw up a rental agreement that we both found agreeable."

Aldermaston stood and winked at Isabel. "Why not offer the building to the council as temporary accommodation on condition that they supported a planning application to turn it into affordable housing once they left?"

Abigail's smile turned sneer-like. "I'm sure we can come to some arrangement that supports an appropriate planning application to meet the needs of those who feel disenfranchised by Mortiforde's current housing stock."

"Excellent," Isabel beamed. "I'll leave you to discuss this with Mr Brazonby, then." She wandered over to Aldermaston and grabbed his hands. "That keeps everyone happy, doesn't it? You're good at doing that. Your father would be proud. As would your mother. Why don't you and Felicity come back to The Lodge for dinner?"

He sensed Felicity's stare intensifying, even though she was standing behind him. "Thank you, Isabel, but I'm taking Harry swimming."

She gripped his hands tighter. "Good for you. Savour these precious moments. Children grow up so fast. Be grateful you have them in your life."

Isabel pulled to leave. "What about ... You know? Basildon's biological father," Aldermaston whispered.

Her smile softened. "I made a promise," she began. "And I intend to keep it." She paused. "If there's one thing this whole episode has taught us, is that it is better to be the person we are now, rather than become the person we think our past wants us to be." She pecked him on the cheek. "And I'm not just talking about Basildon. You're doing a sterling job as Marquess. Copy your father's wonderful traits, but remember you're your own man, too. One day, Harry will inherit. How you do the job will influence his stewardship of the title. Be the Marquess you want *him* to become."

She patted his hand. "How is Basildon?"

"Recuperating in his apartment. The hospital discharged him yesterday."

She buttoned up her coat. "Good. Well, if you'll excuse me, it's time I headed back home."

Felicity slipped an arm through Aldermaston's. "We must go too. The swimming pool beckons."

Lisa tapped him on the shoulder. "Do you want to take

these with you?" She slipped a few sheets of paper into his hand.

"What are they?"

"It's next week's Borderers Guild meeting agenda regarding the Christmas Lights Switch-On next month."

"Christmas Lights Switch-On?" Felicity queried. "What's to plan? Surely, someone just needs to flick a switch?"

Aldermaston's shoulders dropped. "No, dear," he sighed. "This is Mortiforde."

AUTHOR'S NOTE

I can't remember when I first heard of Guy Fawkes and the Gunpowder Plot of 1605, but I'm sure, as Daniel points out to Lisa in Chapter 2, it's a British historical event every child learns of during their first years at school. But it wasn't until I was researching something else for an article that I stumbled across a loose Welsh Border connection.

Although the attempt to blow up England's Parliament occurred on 5th November 1605, its origins lie over seventy years earlier, in the reign of Henry VIII, when he broke away from the Roman Catholic Church. Catholics felt marginalised and, later, persecuted, as England adopted a more Protestant theology.

Queen Mary I's reign (1553 – 1558) saw England reconcile with Rome and Catholicism revive, but Queen Elizabeth I, upon her coronation in 1558, reintroduced Protestant practices. Indeed, in 1559, the authorities passed a law forcing those who refused to attend Protestant church services to pay a fine. In 1581, a further law substantially increased that fine, and authorities declared anyone attempting to persuade another to convert to Catholicism guilty of treason, punishable by death.

In the late 16th century, there were several plots to oust Elizabeth I and replace her with the Roman Catholic Mary, Queen of Scots. They failed, which ultimately led to Mary's execution in 1587.

When Elizabeth I died in 1603, James I, the son of Mary Queen of Scots, succeeded her. As the son of a Catholic, Roman Catholics hoped for better tolerance and understanding of their religious beliefs. Indeed, when James' wife, Anne of Denmark, converted to Catholicism, they hoped it signalled a new era of understanding. It didn't. James found himself pressured by the anti-Catholic House of Commons to be less sympathetic to the Catholic cause.

So in 1604, a group of Catholics in the English Midlands, led by Robert Catesby, plotted to blow up King James I during the State Opening of Parliament. Other conspirators included Thomas and Robert Wintour*, Thomas Percy, John and Christopher Wright, Francis Tresham, Robert Keyes, John Grant, Thomas Bates, Ambrose Rookwood, Sir Everard Digby, and Guy Fawkes.

The plotters initially began tunnelling from a rented property next to the Houses of Parliament, but later rented a basement under the House of Lords. This is where Guy Fawkes, as the gunpowder expert, stored the gunpowder and covered it with wood.

Security staff searched the basements on 4th November as part of the State Opening of Parliament security procedures and discovered Guy Fawkes beside his woodpile. Somehow, the security staff deemed his excuse plausible, and he thought he was safe.

However, Lord Monteagle received a tip-off a few days prior to the State Opening of Parliament, encouraging him to stay away from the event. He passed this on to the authorities, who undertook another search of the building. This time, when they approached Guy Fawkes, they discovered thirty-six barrels of gunpowder under the wood. Oops! Funnily enough, they arrested Guy Fawkes.

King James gave permission for Fawkes to be tortured. However, Fawkes held out under interrogation for several days, giving the other plotters time to escape. Most conspirators fled back to the English Midlands, heading for Holbeche House in Staffordshire, barely fifty miles from the English/Welsh border.

Holbeche House was owned by Stephen Littleton*, a sympathiser, and the conspirators prepared the house for a long siege. Those unprepared to fight were told to leave. Stephen Littleton and Thomas Wintour headed for a property called Pepper Hill, near Boningale, Shropshire, owned by John Talbot, whom they thought would help their cause. However, Talbot refused to help, forcing both Littleton and Wintour to go on the run. For the next two months, they survived by wandering the countryside, hiding in barns and houses, stealing or catching their food.

The authorities captured them on 9th January 1606, at Hagley Park, eight miles from Kidderminster, on the Worcestershire/Shropshire border.

All the main conspirators were executed, as well as some of their sympathisers, including Littleton.

While the exact locations of where Littleton and Wintour spent their two months roaming the countryside are unknown, the fact that they came within fifty miles of the Welsh border and were in Shropshire (which is where my fictional Borderlandshire is based) soon set my creative juices flowing. What better way to add a quirky twist to the famous 1605 Gunpowder Plot than writing a book about a young man who sought revenge on a local authority, which concluded with the successful blowing up of the local council building?

So while Mortiforde Millie is fictitious, the idea that some of the Gunpowder Plot conspirators were roaming the Shropshire countryside, here in the Welsh Borders, is potentially feasible.

Perhaps one reason Bonfire Night remains in the British calendar of traditions is down to a chap called Edward Montagu. On 23rd January 1606, just two weeks after Littleton and Wintour were captured, and days before they were executed, Montagu introduced the Observance of 5th November Act 1605, requiring churches to hold thanksgiving services every 5th November to commemorate the plot's failure. The Act remained on the statute books until 1859.

* The spellings of Wintour and Littleton vary throughout history, with some sources using Winter and Lyttleton instead.

ACKNOWLEDGMENTS

Thank you to all those writer friends who kept enquiring how the third novel was coming along. Only good writing friends know how to turn a nagging "when are you going to pull your finger out and get that third novel finished?" into a helpful "how's it going, what are you stuck on?" offer of assistance.

I'd also like to thank my agent, Kate Nash, for her continuing support, and the ongoing encouragement from the Tuesday Zoom Club (which now meets on a Monday).

This book wouldn't be what it is today without the proofreading skills of Helen Baggott and the eagle-eyed beta-readers, Mandy Bailey and Francesca Riccomini, who helped identify those moments in the book where what I'd imagined in my head isn't quite what appeared on the page.

And thank you again, Catherine Clarke Design, for another wonderful cover.

ABOUT THE AUTHOR

Simon Whaley is the author of the Marquess of Mortiforde Mysteries and many other humorous non-fiction books (including the bestselling One Hundred Ways For A Dog To Train Its Human). His articles have also appeared in publications such as BBC Countryfile, Country Walking, The People's Friend, and The Countryman.

He lives in Shropshire, a county on the Welsh Borders that many UK residents struggle to locate on a map, and can often be found pounding the hills as he dreams up new ideas for more books.

You can find out more about Simon and his work via his website: www.simonwhaley.co.uk (and don't forget to sign up to his newsletter at www.simonwhaley.co.uk/newsletter/).

If you'd like to be the first to know of new Marquess of Mortiforde mysteries as they're released then sign up to my free, occasional newsletter, *Writing from the Welsh Borders* at: http://www.simonwhaley.co.uk/newsletter/

Alternatively, follow me on social media via:

Website: www.mortifordemysteries.com
Facebook: facebook.com/SimonWhaleyAuthor
X: x.com/simonwhaley

ENJOYED FLAMING MURDER?

I hope you enjoyed reading *Flaming Murder*. Please consider leaving an honest review (which can be as short or as long as you like) on the store from where you purchased it.

Thank you.

SIMON WHALEY'S NON-FICTION BOOKS

Books for Dog Lovers

One Hundred Ways For A Dog To Train Its Human

One Hundred Muddy Paws For Thought

Puppytalk: 50 Ways To Make Friends With Your Puppy

The Bluffer's Guide to Dogs

Books for Walkers

The Bluffer's Guide to Hiking

Best Walks in the Welsh Borders

Books for Community Project Fundraisers

Fundraising For A Community Project

Books for Writers

The Positively Productive Writer

Photography for Writers

The Complete Article Writer

The Business of Writing - Volume 1

The Business of Writing - Volume 2

The Business of Writing - Volume 3

The Business of Writing - Volume 4

The Business of Writing - Volume 5

www.ingramcontent.com/pod-product-compliance
Lightning Source LLC
Chambersburg PA
CBHW050957210726
48287CB00004B/1268